Could You But Find It

Could You But Find It

a novel
by
Robert Cilley

This is a work of fiction. Any resemblance of a character to some actual person, living or dead, whether as to name or personality or anything else, is not intentional.

Some of the characters

Abdullah, son of Hamid. One of the Sufis at Wadi Qadr.

Ahmed, son of Abdullah. Another Sufi. He came to the wake.

Arnold Devore. Owner/operator/counterman of the Diner.

Bivens. Army "technician" in Bragg's unit.

Bud. Owner of Bud's Tire & Auto. He built the Jeep.

Calvin Zorn. Retired banker.

Andrew **Compton**. Army general. Boss of Menendez and Bragg.

Demir Shahin. Nisa's big brother. Business major at Emory.

Emily Phillips. Wade's sister, Bart's paternal grandmother.

Enver Ziya. History professor, former diplomat. Dilara's father.

Fareed Ziya. Mehmed's younger son, Murad's brother.

Hamid, son of Issa. A Sufi of about Wade's age.

Thomas L. **Harper**. Major. Head of Project Clevis's science team.

Hickson. S.C. Law Enforcement Division (SLED) agent.

Dr. **Hodge**. Medical doctor at Clemson.

Jason. Roland Bathori's assistant.

Lorraine Phillips. Bart's mother.

Margaret Adams. Wade's housekeeper.

Mehmed Ziya Enver's brother, Dee's uncle. Father of Murad and
        Fareed. Calls himself the Imam Muhammad

Elizabeth **Menendez**. Army colonel.

Murad Ziya. Mehmed's older son, Fareed's brother, Enver's nephew.

Nathan **(Nate)** Huntsinger. Traxell International's New York CEO.

Nelson. Head of Traxell's IT department.

Nisa Shahin. Demir's sister. Attends college at Greensboro.

Jim **Perkins**. Chief of the Larson fire department.

Ron Sheridan. Jamaal's father. Retired army sergeant.

Randall D. **Salinger**. Colonel, head of Project Clevis.

Sidney. Army man, but his exact title and duties are need-to-know.

Tanvir **Singh**. One of Nelson's IT people at Traxell.

Lester **Thurmond**. A researcher at RPI.

Raymond **Travis**. Army "technician" in Bragg's unit.

Henrik **Verhoeven**. Chairman of Traxell International.

A hair perhaps divides the false from true;
yes, and a single alif were the clue—
could you but find it...

Omar

Prologue

No one had visited the site of the old temple for a long time; only priests and their attendants could come here, and there was seldom any reason to do that. The temple had stood on a ledge overlooking the harbor, almost at the peak of the mountain. There were, of course, temples in the city below, quite a number of them, but the one on the mountain was different. The city temples were long and narrow, with side walls and shallow porches. This one had been square, and surprisingly small: crossing from one side to the other took five paces, at most. It must have had a roof at one time, but the Earthshaker had long ago brought that down, along with the columns that would have supported it. All that remained were the stone floor, and the altar at its center. Probably it had been an altar; no one really knew. All anyone did know was that the place was very old and very sacred, the most sacred spot on the island.

The attendants were still fussing with the bronze gong that one of the donkeys had carried up the long, winding path from the city. Ordinarily the gong had a place of honor in the city's largest temple, ready to ring but never rung; no living person had heard it. Its use was part of a ritual the priests had learned, but had never needed to perform. Until now.

The four of them stood looking down at the harbor, dressed in the old-fashioned robes that tradition required. From where they stood, the city looked cheerful and alive. White walls, red tile roofs, green gardens, all testified to a vibrant, prosperous community. The testimony was a lie; the harbor showed that. The fishing fleet was gone, along with the trading vessels that should have lined the wharfs. The city was still beautiful, but it was a beautiful corpse. Its life, its people, had fled.

"Knirra, are you sure?" the taller of the priests asked. "You can read the omens as well as I can: the Earthshaker has awakened. If we hurry, we can still find a boat, and join our daughters on the mainland."

Knirra, the senior priest, looked sadly down at the city, her city. "Of course we can join them, but what would we tell them? That they should build new temples for us? So that we can worship the goddess who could have helped us, but whom we are afraid to approach?"

The tall priest sighed resignedly. "I suppose you are right, but the goddess can be fickle. If she refuses us, we will have done this for nothing."

"We will have done what we could. That is all anyone can ask."

"And, if what we can do is not enough?"

Knirra shrugged. "Then we will have died trying. Everyone dies, eventually." She glanced at the attendants, and saw that the gong was ready. The four of them formed a circle around the altar and joined hands. She told the attendant at the gong, "Count to twelve, then strike it." The earth trembled, the third time that day. To her colleagues, she said, "My friends, it is time." They cleared their minds of everything except what the ancient ritual required, and then, together, they pulled open the door of the goddess's temple, and began the journey from which they knew they would never return.

Chapter One

Lorraine Phillips was sure she would have a daughter. Her name was going to be Victoria Elizabeth, exactly the sort of name a girl should have, to give her a head start on life. Give a girl a limp, wimpy name like Nancy or Alice, Lorraine believed, and you end up with a limp, wimpy girl. It never occurred to her that Victoria Elizabeth's little friends might call her Beth, or Libby, or worse yet, Vickie. No one had called Queen Victoria "Vickie," now had they? When she found out her daughter was going to be a son, she had stayed true to her principles and named him Victor Albert. On the first day of kindergarten, when the other mothers told their children to share, and not cry, and to wipe their noses, the only thing Lorraine told her son was, "Don't let them call you anything but Victor," and so Victor he was. Whatever may be true of little girls with strong names, little boys with priggish, stuck-up names get teased about it, a lot. Of course, there are worse names than Victor. Lorraine, was a lover of all things English, and had seriously thought about calling him Locksley.

Victor's father had died the year the boy was born. Lorraine never said what he had died of, but Victor eventually found a copy of the obituary in the library archives, where he read it had been a stroke. Between his father's life insurance and what his mother made as a paralegal, there had been enough for them to get by, but although Lorraine never said it in so many words, Victor came to understand that the money it took to feed and clothe him could, in his mother's opinion, have been put to better use. She had a wonderful collection of Toby jugs, tea pots, and supposedly limited-edition plates with pictures of English notables and their castles, but she had no place to display them to best effect. One day, Victor knew, his bedroom would become that place.

They lived in Charlotte. They had no family in Charlotte, but every Christmas for as long as Victor could remember, his uncle Wade had driven up from South Carolina. Victor called Wade his uncle, but the old man was actually his great uncle on his father's side. Wade lived about a three hour drive from Charlotte, but according to Lorraine, he didn't just live in a different state; he lived on the frontier itself. "I'm not even sure they have indoor plumbing," she would say, "and people sneak around there, hunting and who knows what." Victor asked Uncle Wade about the plumbing, and got one of the old man's rare chuckles. "We get by without a lot of the things that Charlotte has," he said, "but our plumbing is as good as any." When Victor asked about the things they did without, Uncle Wade opened that day's paper to its B section, the part devoted to local news. He pointed to one of the several stories of killings and robberies. "What few of those we have," he said, "make the front page." Lorraine always seemed to be on edge when Wade visited. "You watch out for that old man," she would say. "If he does or says anything you don't like, you yell, understand?" What Victor understood was that his mother didn't like Wade, which made him wonder why she let him visit at all. At least partly because Lorraine didn't trust Wade, Victor did, so he asked Wade about the visits. "There is an old saying," his uncle had replied. "It says that a golden key will unlock any door. I send her a check every month, and in return I get to visit at Christmas."

Despite living in the wilderness, Uncle Wade always managed to find some special Christmas presents. The first ones Victor could remember had been little hand puzzles, the kind made from twisted nails. For some reason they never came with directions, but eventually the boy would solve them. When he was fourteen, the gift had been a set of mechanic's tools, along with a disassembled bicycle. Again, there were no directions. It had taken him the better part of two weeks to get the bicycle put together without having parts left over, but he did it. The bike had led to a paper route which, in addition to basic economics, had taught him how to tell the difference between the dogs that bark and wag, and the dogs that bark and bite.

Then there were books, not only at Christmas, but apparently whenever Wade had felt like sending something. There didn't really seem to be a theme; a collection of Martin Gardner's word puzzles might be followed by a book of Charles Fort's oddities. Victor once asked his uncle how he picked the books. "They were written by people who knew how to think, and how to wonder," Wade had said. "Most people don't do either one." The boy tried to make sense of that. If most people didn't think, then who runs the world? "Ah, that is the question, isn't it," his uncle had said.

He liked Uncle Wade, and he thought Uncle Wade liked him, but it was hard to be sure; the old man tended to be solemn and reserved, even by the standards of old men. Still, when he came for a visit, he always asked Victor how he was doing in school, what he was doing with his spare time, or what he thought about this or that recent event, and he always seemed to be interested in the answers. The one question he never did ask was what the boy wanted to be when he grew up. Victor once asked his uncle why not, since other adults routinely did ask it. "Because it's a stupid question," his uncle had replied. "Anyone old enough to give it a serious answer thinks he already is grown up." But while Uncle Wade never asked what Victor wanted to be, he did ask what Victor wanted to do. The boy didn't know. Get a part-time job and go to trade school, probably. He didn't mention college, and when Wade asked why, he just shrugged and said he hadn't really thought about it. "Would you keep an open mind on that?" the old man had asked, and Victor promised he would.

Victor only saw Wade get upset one time. Coming home from school one afternoon, he was parking his bike by the front porch when he heard his uncle's voice, which was odd because it wasn't Christmas. "Lorraine," he was saying, "I need to talk to the boy about this! I made his father a promise, and I keep *my* promises!" Victor heard his mother yell something in reply, of which only, "...you and his father both in Hell..." came through the door clearly. Victor ducked around the side of the house, wanting to hear, but not wanting to be seen. There was more yelling, and then Uncle Wade stomped out the front door. Lorraine appeared behind him and threw something at his back. "Take your damned book and don't come back, ever!" she screamed, and the old man never did. Victor couldn't even guess why Wade had brought a book instead of just sending it, but he knew it had been meant for him, and he knew it was gone. He imagined how it would feel to tell his mother that he knew she had, in essence, stolen something from him, and how hurtful it was, but he didn't. For one thing, he didn't want to let her into his inner world, and for another, he didn't want to hear another of her lectures about Hell, and how a child who doesn't honor his mother would spend the rest of eternity there.

Lorraine Phillips knew all about Hell. There was, of course, no chance that she herself would go there, but all disobedient children did, and once there they stood forever in a lake of fire, along with politicians, lawyers, and the rest of the heathen. The heathen were a catch-all group that included most Protestants and all Catholics, plus Muslims, Jews, Hindus, Buddhists, and as she put it, whatever the Japanese are. Hell was obviously a very bad place, but to hear Lorraine describe Heaven, it wasn't much better, except there was no lake of fire. According to her, the very few who would be joining her in Heaven would stand forever in a sort of choir loft, doing nothing but singing praises to God. Lorraine's God was not the kind and loving God that most children sing about in Sunday school. Hers had a violent temper and a constant need for flattery which, Victor came to think, would have gotten a human put into an institution. He brought that up to the Youth Minister at their church one Sunday, and before he got home Lorraine had heard all about it. The belt-whipping that followed had lasted fifteen minutes without a pause. He had tried not to cry, but once he realized she wasn't going to stop until he did, he gave up. He missed school the next day. His mother's excuse note said he had a stomach bug.

◇◇◇◇◇◇◇◇◇◇◇◇◇◇◇●◇◇◇◇◇◇◇◇◇◇◇◇◇◇◇

There were a few other kids in Victor's neighborhood, but no playmates. Between soccer practice and softball, swimming and dance, the other kids' parents made sure they had no free time to waste on casual fun. So for the most part, Victor's free time came down to a choice between hanging out at home, or hanging out at the library. Librarians don't generally like being used as free day care, but Victor was a quiet, polite little boy, and librarians are, after all, trained to do more than return books to the shelves, so an understanding was reached. They wouldn't create any problems for Victor, and he would let them suggest what he should read. At the end of each week, they would gather around him and ask him what he had found interesting and what had seemed dull, after which they would confer and make the next week's suggestions. He once said something to his mother about talking to a group of librarians, but she told him to stop lying, and he never mentioned it again.

Despite being well read, Victor was not a memorable student. In class, he said very little and never asked questions; his teachers typically forgot him a year or two after they had had him. True, whenever they called on him he knew the answer, and he did score well on tests, but to most of his teachers that meant he needed less attention, not more. He hadn't planned to take the SAT, since college was not going to be an option, but in the end he did take it because, like every teenage boy, he could be bribed. A letter from Uncle Wade arrived at the school office on his seventeenth birthday, and its message was short and to the point. "If you take the SAT," the letter said, "I will give you a dollar for every point you make." Victor signed up for the test, and he also signed a form that came with the letter, to let Wade get a copy of his score. He hadn't mentioned it to his uncle, but he was going to need the money. Whether or not his mother intended to toss him out the day he turned eighteen—and he was pretty sure she did— that was when he intended to leave. He had looked into renting a furnished room, or maybe an apartment, but every place he looked they required an up-front payment of first-and-last months' rent plus a security deposit. Without the SAT money, he wouldn't have enough. His score ended up in the 98th percentile, which didn't surprise him. He knew he wasn't a dummy; he just didn't see any point in having other people know it. He thought that Uncle

Wade probably knew, but that was all right; Wade was family. In fact, not counting the librarians, Uncle Wade was pretty much all the family he had.

While other kids in his class worked on college applications, Victor read the course guide from the local community college. He knew what the job market was for unskilled labor, and he figured trade school was his best chance not to end up seedy and toothless behind the register at some all-night beer store. He needed a copy of his transcript to go with the application, which meant he had to talk to the guidance counselor, Mrs. Fleming. He had met with her once before, when the SAT scores came back, and she had asked him then what colleges he was looking at. He wasn't looking at any. "Is it money?" she asked, which led to a discussion of scholarships. It was a short discussion. For most scholarships, in addition to good grades he would have to have played some sport, and he hadn't. For a need-based scholarship, his mother would have to fill out a financial affidavit, and that, he knew, was not going to happen. The one time he had asked her about it, he got the answer he had expected: "My money is none of anybody's business, young man, and that includes you." No matter how he looked at it, he kept coming back to trade school and a part-time job. So, when his homeroom teacher gave him a note to go see the guidance counselor during his fifth period study hall, his first thought was that another hour of his life was about to be wasted talking about college. He was half right.

"When did you settle on Clemson?" Mrs. Fleming asked as soon as he sat down.

Having no answer, but having to say something, he fell back on every teenager's utility reply: "Huh?"

"Clemson. I just found out." She pointed to a letter on her desk. "It's not a scholarship I had ever heard of, but it's a full ride, and it's not contingent on anything. Congratulations."

That made no sense at all. "I think somebody typed in the name wrong. I haven't applied for any scholarship, plus I haven't applied to go to Clemson."

She would have told anyone else not to make stupid jokes,

but a little time spent going through Victor's records had told her, as it would have told his teachers, that he was anything but stupid. She looked again at the paper in front of her. "You're Victor Albert Phillips?"

"Yes."

"Your mother's name is Lorraine?"

"Yes."

"Well, I have a letter here from a lawyer named Emmett Schroder, who says that the board of trustees of the Green Cove Trust has awarded you a full four-year scholarship to Clemson University, including room and board, everything." She looked at him over the tops of her glasses. "And you don't know anything about it?" He assured her he didn't. "Well then," she went on, "do you know anything about this? It was in the envelope with the letter." She handed him a cashier's check.

Victor had never heard of a Green Cove Trust, but the amount on the check was the same as his SAT score. "Huh," he said again, "I kind of do," and he told her about the bribe.

The story of the bribe led to a discussion about Uncle Wade and, after some casual-seeming questions, about his mother. That took a while, and when he was through, Mrs. Fleming nodded, almost imperceptibly. "I see. Be here again tomorrow, same time." She said that in the tone a surgeon uses when he holds out his hand and says, "Scalpel."

Guidance counselors see students come and go, year after year. Some counselors come to think of themselves as mere rocks in the stream, diverting the flow of the student's life a little, briefly, but not really making any lasting difference. They give out forms, they answer questions, perhaps they run off a copy of a blandly generic letter of recommendation, then they mark one more day off the number they need for retirement. Genella Fleming had colleagues who saw their jobs that way, and some days she did too. But every now and again she would see the chance to make a difference, and she did not let those chances go by. She thought about Lorraine Phillips, and her lips drew back from her teeth. Athletes and soldiers sometimes see that look on the face of a confident opponent, and it isn't really a smile. "Guess what, honey," she said to herself, "your boy has somebody on his side now, and she's better at being a bitch than you are." From her desk drawer she pulled a little book, full of names and numbers and cryptic notations, information she didn't want on the school computer. Yes, there it was. Five rings later a voice answered hello. "David?" she said sweetly, "Ginny Fleming. Have you got a minute?"

◇◇◇◇◇◇◇◇◇◇◇◇◇◇◇◇●◇◇◇◇◇◇◇◇◇◇◇◇◇◇◇◇

Fifth period the next day found Victor back in the chair in Mrs. Fleming's office. On her desk was a stack of paper, and a pen. "Victor, I need you to sign down here," were the first words out of her mouth.

"Don't I need to read it?"

"No, just sign it. It's an application to Clemson, and it needs to go out in today's mail." That wasn't actually a lie, because if she was going to mail it, it really would need to go out today. That it wasn't going in the mail, that she was going to drive down to Clemson with it that afternoon, didn't alter the case at all.

"Uh, if I'm not eighteen, won't it need my mother's signature somewhere?" He didn't want to cause problems, but if he was right, there already was a problem.

"Oh, that," she said casually. "I've taken care of that." She flipped the form over, and sure enough, there was Lorraine Phillips' signature, big as life. And again, she hadn't exactly lied; she really had taken care of it. Parents sign a lot of school forms over the years; they are all stored on pdf files in the system's computer, where the guidance counselors have access to them. Lorraine's signature was one of those illegible collections of loops and squiggles that is, ironically, every forger's dream. With a readable signature, someone can say, 'Hey, this r doesn't look like that r,' whereas one illegible squiggle looks pretty much like another. And with only a little practice, one can look exactly like the other.

"When..." Victor paused. Did he really need to know when...or if...his mother had signed that form? "Um, sorry; I forgot what I was going to ask. Sign here?"

"Yes, and initial here."

He did. "Mrs. Fleming?"

"Yes, Victor?"

"Thank you." He hoped she didn't notice the quiver in his voice when he said it.

His mother answered the phone. She always answered the phone. He thought it was her way of saying that it was not the house phone, it was her phone. She listened for a moment, mumbled something, then looked at Victor. "When did you become Mr. Phillips?" she wanted to know. He bit back several clever answers, and went with the safest, a shrug. "Well, Mr. Phillips, you have a call." She handed him the phone, but sat down nearby, not even pretending not to listen. It was, after all, her phone.

"Mr. Phillips?" asked a man's voice, after Victor had said hello.

"Uh, yeah, this is Victor Phillips," he managed, feeling off balance.

"My name is David Garrison. I am assistant dean of admissions at Clemson University. I believe you sent us an application recently?"

I suppose you could say recently, he thought; it was yesterday. "Yes, that's right," he said out loud. His mother pursed her lips, probably wishing he had said something more informative. He wasn't planning to.

"I wonder if there might be a time that we could meet and discuss it." It didn't really sound like a question, and anyway there was no pause for an answer. "I'm going to be in Charlotte this Saturday. Would that work for you? Eleven o'clock, say, at the Myers Park library?"

"That would be fine," Victor said. Lorraine raised an eyebrow. He was going to ask how he would recognize this Mr. Garrison, but decided he could figure it out. Later that night, it occurred to him to wonder how someone from Clemson knew that he lived in the Myers Park section of Charlotte, let alone that there was a branch library there.

"Excellent. I'll see you then." Victor hung up the phone, and his mother gave him a hard look. He knew she wanted to know who it had been, but if she wasn't going to ask, he wasn't going to say. He savored the silence for a moment, then went back to his room.

◇◇◇◇◇◇◇◇◇◇◇◇◇◇◇●◇◇◇◇◇◇◇◇◇◇◇◇◇◇◇

A tall man in a brown suit was standing at the top of the library steps. "Mr. Phillips?" he held out his hand, "David Garrison. Pleased to meet you." They shook hands. Victor hadn't shaken a lot of hands, so he made a mental note of how an expert did it: firm, but not tight, and not protracted. Good to know.

"I hate that you went to all this trouble," Victor said.

"We try to be flexible." Dean Garrison's voice was blandly pleasant, his face an unreadable mask. Victor knew perfectly well that university deans, even assistant deans, do not travel out of town on a Saturday to meet with nobodies who have only applied the day before. And yet the man in the brown suit acted like he did it every weekend. If David Garrison had heard Victor's thought, he would have laughed. Not out loud of course; anyone who has to attend board meetings learns not to do that. Even widening your eyes when a department head says something stupid, can be a fatal career move. Those who have survived in the academic jungle as long as he had, have learned the art of camouflage.

"I have read," Victor said, almost musingly, "that one of people's most common fantasies is that they are actually the children of royalty, or maybe of space aliens, and that their real parents will one day come back for them. If either were true in my case, that might explain how we come to be here today. Little else would."

It took a conscious effort this time for the dean to keep a straight face, but he did. Two things struck him about Victor. First, the boy was right about the fantasy, and second, his grammar was a little bookish, but it was correct. Any admissions officer knows how rare correct grammar is in the spoken English of high school seniors. Granted, the kid's SATs were good, but a lot of good SATs come from cram courses, or from a knack for standardized tests, and Dean Garrison didn't have much faith in them. "We don't get much royalty at Clemson," he said after a moment. "They seem to prefer M.I.T. for some reason." Which is probably for the best, he thought. They tend to be somewhat inbred, but between their money and their status, it is next to impossible to flunk them.

Victor nodded. "Well, that's not one of my fantasies, and anyway the royals have always struck me as maybe a little bit inbred." He thought of the faces on some of his mother's commemorative plates.

Dean Garrison smiled, in spite of himself. He decided he liked this boy, and since making that decision was his main reason for driving to Charlotte on a Saturday, his task here was nearly done. "Just out of curiosity, did you have any interest in Clemson before Professor Dawson arranged for that scholarship?"

"Well honestly no, I...did you say *Professor* Dawson?" Victor had never known what Uncle Wade did before he was Uncle Wade.

"Actually, *Dr.* Dawson would be correct, but I'm told he preferred Professor. He's long retired, of course, but Professor Dawson taught at Clemson for thirty-six years. There was once a lab building named for him, but it's been torn down to make room for a practice field." One of those stupid ideas that nobody dared question, he thought. "Perhaps you don't know a lot about Clemson, Mr. Phillips, and I'm not here recruiting, so I'll simply say this: We respect tradition, to an extent you don't commonly see. One of our traditions is legacy, and if Professor Dawson vouches for you, you are legacy." And Ginny Fleming's approval doesn't hurt, either, he thought. Ginny had steered some good students toward Clemson, but she had also, very discreetly, warned him about one particularly bad one who had almost gotten in. The coaches had wanted that kid in the worst way, and putting his veto on the application had almost gotten David Garrison fired. Then the news broke about the boy raping those girls at Kansas. He had to give coach Edmunds credit, though. The man had stood up at a board meeting and told everybody, "I was wrong about that Simmons boy, and David here was right. He has saved this school a lot of embarrassment." You don't get many moments like that, and for that one he owed Ginny. "All of which is to say, welcome to Clemson, Mr. Phillips." He paused, remembering some pretty rough things Ginny had said about Victor's mother. "Where shall I send the paperwork? Mrs. Fleming's office?"

"No, I have a mailbox." He wrote out the address. "Can I ask you something?"

"Certainly."

"The scholarship is from a Green Cove Trust. How did you know Uncle Wade had something to do with it?"

"Mrs. Fleming said you thought there might be a connection, so I called up Emmett Schroder and asked him."

Victor thought for a moment. Schroder...that was the lawyer who had sent Mrs. Fleming the letter about the scholarship. "A lawyer can tell you that?"

"Not ordinarily, but he said he was acting as a trustee, not as a lawyer. According to Mr. Schroder, if someone from Clemson called about the Green Cove scholarship, it was all right with Professor Dawson that his connection to it be known."

"Oh." There wasn't much else to say. He had never had an address for Uncle Wade, and there was no phone listing for him, but it shouldn't be too hard to find an address for Emmett Schroder, Attorney at Law.

◊◊◊◊◊◊◊◊◊◊◊◊◊◊◊●◊◊◊◊◊◊◊◊◊◊◊◊◊◊◊

As she had with the telephone, Lorraine Phillips had always made it clear whose house Victor lived in. All through his childhood, it had been things that weren't going to go on in this house, or people that he was never to bring to this house, or authority that had better be respected in this house. As his eighteenth birthday approached, "this house" came to be replaced more and more by "my house." It didn't take a genius to see where that was going.

Among the books that Uncle Wade had given him had been a collection of old sayings and proverbs. A lot of times, one proverb would contradict another, but it seemed to Victor that on the issue of his eighteenth birthday, the old sayings all agreed: Fortune favors the prepared. So, he prepared. He would turn eighteen about two weeks before graduation, and he didn't want to spend those two weeks on the street. One of Victor's friends was a boy named Reuben Lazano. Lorraine would have said he was Mexican; in point of fact, his parents were naturalized citizens, originally from Guatemala, but to Lorraine, all Hispanics are Mexicans, and all Mexicans are Catholics, which would guarantee Reuben and his parents first-class tickets to Hell. But since she never asked Victor about school, she had never heard of Reuben, and Hell-bound or not, Mr. and Mrs. Lazano were happy for Victor to stay with them, once Reuben had told them why.

For weeks before his birthday, Victor had sorted through the stuff in his dresser ("No, my dresser," his mother's imagined voice corrected him), separating his few keepsakes from the rubbish of childhood. The rubbish he threw away, a little at a time, and the keepsakes, along with the clothes that still fit him, he smuggled out of the house. All of it went to a trunk in the guest bedroom at the Lazano house. There were other details, of course. He had filed a form with the Post Office to have his mail forwarded to the box he had rented at Mr. Mailbox. He paid for the trunk and the mailbox with tips he had saved from his paper route. His actual earnings had disappeared into the household budget, but it never occurred to Lorraine that a paperboy might get tips. The cashier's check for the SAT score lay in an envelope in his mailbox, waiting for the day he turned eighteen. Mr. Mailbox didn't ask how old you were, but banks did. He didn't know which would have galled him worse, losing the money, or seeing his mother spend it on "collectible" plates of plump English aristocrats.

◇◇◇◇◇◇◇◇◇◇◇◇◇◇◇◇●◇◇◇◇◇◇◇◇◇◇◇◇◇◇◇◇

His birthday fell on a Friday. He got up at six and fixed his usual breakfast of oatmeal. He ate slowly, not because the oatmeal was any better than oatmeal ever is, but because it wasn't time yet. He had checked his birth certificate, which said he had been born at 7:12 a.m. When his mother came into the kitchen, there were still two minutes left. A quick glance was all she needed to find something to criticize. "Don't you think you need a sweater?" she said. It wasn't a question; it was never a question. It was a command: go put on a sweater, and the only correct response had always been, "Yes ma'am." He had once tried to tell her that nobody except dorks and the older teachers wore sweaters at school, but that hadn't gone well. After that, he had knuckled under, worn the sweater, and crammed it in his locker as soon as he got to school.

"No, I don't think I need one; it's going to be nice today."

She looked puzzled, then irritated. "I said, put on a sweater."

He shook his head, slowly. Ninety seconds. "No, you asked what I thought. You said, 'Don't you think you need a sweater'."

"Are you talking back? You better not be talking back, do you hear me?" Victor said nothing. "I asked you a question, mister," she said, her voice getting louder and higher. As it was with the question that wasn't a question, the only acceptable response to "Do you hear me?" had always been "Yes, ma'am." He glanced at the clock. Fifty seconds. "I said, *do you hear me!*" Now she was almost screaming, and her face had turned the color of ketchup.

Victor nodded. "Yes, mother, I hear you," he said softly, "I just don't care any more." He stood up. Breakfast was over. Childhood would be over in...about twenty seconds.

"What did you say? What did you say to me? The Bible says to honor your mother, have you forgotten that?!" In his imagination he saw the lake of fire, bubbling and chuckling as it cooked all the disobedient children.

"Forgotten?" he asked quietly. Five seconds. "No, I don't think I've forgotten anything." He took his house key out of his pocket, laid it on the table, and walked toward the front door. It was time to go.

"Don't you turn your back on me, you ungrateful little heathen." He was actually about an inch taller than she was. He opened the door, wiped his feet on the mat, and kept on going. As he got on his bicycle and pedaled away, she was screaming something about not bothering to come back because his stuff would all be in the trash. That was funny. Except for a drawer full of sweaters, the only things that weren't already at Reuben's were his bicycle and the clothes on his back. As her voice dwindled behind him, he looked around and smiled. There were flowers in the yards he passed, and the sky was a perfect Carolina blue. It was, he thought, a good day to be born.

Chapter Two

"*Hi,*" said the stick-on name tag. "*I'm* _____." He wrote *Victor*, and was about to stick the tag to his shirt when it hit him: nobody at Clemson knew him as Victor. Was he a Victor? He didn't really feel like a Victor, but what else was there? Albert? That didn't feel right either. Vic, maybe. No, that was more a noise than a name. Surely there was something better.

Al, maybe. Was he an Al? No, Al was too...short? Abrupt? Something. Anyway, it didn't fit. Bert, maybe. He tried that on his tongue a few times, and it still wasn't quite what he wanted. His mother, he decided, had been cleverer than he had realized. There wasn't a whole lot you can do with Victor Albert. He was almost ready to stay Victor when, for no particular reason, he remembered a girl he had known in high school. He hadn't exactly dated her since he couldn't afford to take her anywhere, but they had hung out a little. Her name was Margaret, but she went by Meg. He didn't have to be Vic, or Al, or Bert; if she could be Meg, he could be whatever he wanted it to be. He made a squiggle with the marker. "Uh, could I have another name tag? I've messed this one up." Sure, no problem. "*Hi,*" said the new name tag. "*I'm Bart.*"

Some people believe that, at the core, a thing is what it is, and that what you call it doesn't matter. "A rose by any other name would smell as sweet," was the way Romeo's Juliet put it. Juliet was wrong. A person's name is the clothing his ego wears, and as the old saying goes, clothes make the man. The way someone dresses tells the world who he is, where he stands, what he thinks. Of course, there is such a thing as a visual lie, like when an undercover policeman dresses up as a gang banger, but like any other lie, the more it gets told the more the teller comes to believe it. Pretty much, a person is what he thinks he is, and what he sees in the mirror has a lot of influence on what he sees in his mind. Young Mr. Phillips had found that out in his high school drama classes. No matter how well he memorized his lines, the characters he played never really came to life until dress rehearsal. Only then, wearing the character's clothes, did he feel the character's real personality, and sometimes that personality hadn't been what he expected. Maybe changing names would be like changing costumes, he thought, and he wondered if he would like this Bart person.

He could find out who Bart was later. His more immediate concern was finding out who his roommate was. He hadn't met him yet, but the guy's stuff screamed *Hi, I'm an Athlete*. On the roommate's bed were piles of gray work-out shorts, gym shirts (size XXL), a mountain of white socks, and a five-spring chest expander. Bart tried out the expander, and got maybe an inch of stretch from it. From the size of the shirts, Bart figured this guy wouldn't need weights; he could go out in the parking lot and lift cars.

He had just gotten his own clothes put away when the door opened and a middle-aged black man walked in, followed by someone whose name tag said *Hi, I'm Jamaal*. Jamaal was carrying a stack of iron barbell disks; the older man had the rod. There was a moment of silence, which Jamaal finally broke. "What in the hell are you?"

Bart didn't know yet, but that was going to be hard to explain. So, suddenly faced with somebody who could wear XXL shirts without having them hang loose on him, he said the first thing that came to mind. "Five foot nine, a hundred fifty pounds."

Apparently that wasn't the right answer. To no one in particular, Jamaal said, "No, now this is just wrong. They're not going to stick me in with some skinny-ass white mother…"

"Boy," interrupted the older man, "don't you say that word." He added the barbell rod to the stuff on the bed and held out his hand. "I'm Ron Sheridan. And this," he nodded sideways, "is my son Jamaal. Jamaal forgot to send back his dorm paperwork until real late." He gave Jamaal a look when he said that, then turned back toward Bart. "Pleased to meet you."

Bart shook the hand the way Dean Garrison had shaken his. "Bart Phillips," he said. "Mine went in late, too." Which meant, in both cases, that you take pot luck on dorms and roommates. Bart had a sudden thought, and a grin flickered across his face. It was just for an instant, but the older Sheridan saw it and lifted an eyebrow. "I was just thinking how orientation would go if my nametag said, "Hi, I'm a skinny-ass white mother.""

Jamaal shook his head. "Wouldn't be helpful," he said. "At least with a name, people find out something they don't already know." He and Bart looked at each other for a full second before they both lost it in sputtering laughs. Laughing while holding a hundred pounds of weight disks is an acquired skill, and it turned out Jamaal hadn't acquired it. Nobody's toes got broken when the disks hit the floor, but they made an awful racket, and from down the hall came a shout about keeping the noise down. Jamaal stepped out the door and scowled. The voice said "Holy shit!" and somewhere a door closed with a bang.

Mr. Sheridan looked around at the room. "I swear I think the barracks at Wood had bigger rooms than this." Not only was the room small, it was stark, almost monastic, but the two Sheridans needed less than an hour to change that. Up went a life-size poster of a Rams lineman even larger than Jamaal. Up went a picture of a pretty girl in a cheerleader's uniform. Up went the speakers for a sound system a movie theater might envy. And, solely through Ron Sheridan's efforts, up went a set of curtains on the room's single window: flowered, with a ruffle at the top. Jamaal didn't say anything, but he looked like he had just eaten a bad pickle. "Suck it up," his father said. "Your mama worked real hard on these, and I'm not going to be the one to tell her she wasted her time."

Bart fought the urge to comment, and lost. "You know, really, they're not so bad. Those are earth colors, and I'd say you're an autumn." Jamaal was naturally dark, and now he got darker. Bart couldn't tell if it was a blush or homicidal rage, but if the guy couldn't take a joke, now with a witness present was a good time to find out.

Jamaal could take a joke. In fact, more than one of his teachers had put the words "smart-ass" in his permanent record. He appreciated a nicely timed zinger when he heard one, but nicely timed or not, the skinny kid had now involved himself in the matter of the curtains, so he was going to be involved in the solution. He thought for a second, then nodded. "Suppose," he said to his father, "that Bert here..."

"Bart," said Bart.

Jamaal looked at the nametag. "Whatever. Suppose, now, that Bart had brought curtains too. That could have happened, couldn't it?"

"Uh, no it couldn't," Bart said. "I didn't bring any curtains." Or much of anything else, he might have added. Everything he had, had fit nicely in the trunk he had brought from Reuben's, and it was put away already.

"Maybe not," Jamaal said firmly, "but you could have. And if you had, I wouldn't have to have flowered curtains, would I." Bart had grown up hearing questions that weren't really questions, and he recognized one now. Jamaal went on, "And since you bringing curtains would be a good thing, that must be what happened." He nodded decisively.

"Boy," said Mr. Sheridan, "you can twist it any which way you like; I'm not going to lie to your mama."

"It wouldn't be a lie, papa, not really. It's like it says in that poem about the jug: truth is beauty and beauty is truth. It's a beautiful idea, so somehow, some way, it has to be sort of true." The other two just looked at him, saying nothing. "I mean, by the time you get back home, there are going to be different curtains up, the ones that Bart here actually did bring," he looked hard at Bart, "but has forgotten about. Right?"

Bart didn't need to have spent time on stage to know a line cue when he heard one. "Oh. Yeah," he said. "Those curtains." The reed bends with the storm and survives, said the book of old sayings, while the oak stands firm and is broken. *Hi*, said Bart's mental nametag, *I'm Reed.*

Jamaal grinned. "You tell mama how much I appreciate the curtains, but that I'd feel really bad telling Bart here that we had to use mine and not his. After all, roommates have got to get along." He gave Bart a seismic slap on the shoulder, and together they faced Ron Sheridan.

Ron had misgivings, and not just about the curtains. Roommate pairings are like blood transfusions: if you mix the wrong types together, bad things happen. This pair should not work, he thought, and yet there they stand, side by side, already co-conspirators. "So, it's like that, is it?" The boys nodded, and Ron noticed they hadn't looked at each other before they did it. Three decades in the Army had given him a feel for when a unit starts to come together, and this unit was doing it. "Huh. Well, I put them up, but I'm not taking them down. It's bad enough I have to witness a fraud; I'm damned if I'll aid and abet it. You know that when your mama comes to visit, there had better be some kind of curtains in that window." As he said it, he was not pointing at the window; he was pointing at Jamaal.

Jamaal smiled with a serenity that Buddha might envy. "Yes sir, I understand. There'll be curtains, don't you worry. Just not...flowered, you know?"

The older man sighed. "Yeah, as a matter of fact I do." The master bedroom at the Sheridan house had flowered curtains, and tiebacks, and a valance. He looked at Jamaal, then at Bart. "You two going to be all right?"

"What do you mean?" asked Jamaal.

"You know damn well what I mean. The only roommates you've ever had were at football camp, and they were...athletes." Both boys knew exactly which color of athletes he meant.

Victor would have left that alone, but Bart saw possibilities. "What makes you think I'm not an athlete?" he asked. He hadn't had any time to prepare, but his drama classes had included improvisation, when he was given a character and a situation, and had to come up with his own lines. He put on his best expression of wide-eyed-innocence. He could, after all, be a varsity golfer or something.

"Well, you're..." a skinny white kid, Ron thought. He looked to Jamaal for help, and saw how hard his son was working to keep a straight face. "Wait a minute," he said, turning back toward Bart. "Are you messing with me?"

Bart amended his look to one of injured innocence. "Sir,

how could you think that?" Behind him Bart heard Jamaal snort. "You're supposed to wait for the punch line," he said in a stage whisper.

"You ain't right," Ron pointed at Bart. "And you," he said to Jamaal, "ain't right either. Both of you, get your asses out of here; we're going to lunch."

◇◇◇◇◇◇◇◇◇◇◇◇◇◇◇◇●◇◇◇◇◇◇◇◇◇◇◇◇◇◇◇◇

Over lunch, they talked. Wood, Ron explained, was Fort Leonard Wood, where he had spent the last four of his thirty years in the Army. After he had retired, the family had moved off base to the nearby town of Devils Elbow. Ron had been a sergeant, involved with special training, but he didn't go into much detail about that.

Bart, for his part, didn't go into any detail about his family, beyond saying that his father was dead and his mother still lived in Charlotte. The two Sheridans were good with that, but as Ron found out when he got home, his wife wasn't. Any woman, Nura Sheridan told him, would have come away from that lunch with Bart's mother's name, at a minimum. What kind of work did she do? Ron didn't know. Had she helped Bart move in? Ron didn't know. The only thing Nura knew was that Bart's mother had thought of curtains, which spoke well of her. Were they handmade, she asked, or had they come from a store? Ron said he hadn't thought to ask. That was so like a man.

As it happened, the curtains came from a store. Any college town has stores that cater to students' peculiar needs, and that includes curtains. Jamaal paid for them because, the way he saw it, it was his mother's flowered ones that had caused the problem. That suited Bart. His paper route tip money was all spent, and although he had some of the SAT money left, and the scholarship included some walking around money, he didn't feel good about using it, at least until he absolutely had to. He had enough clothes to last him until summer if he took care of them.

He had taken care of his own clothes since first grade, so

he knew from experience what not to do to them. For one thing, he knew not to wash white things with colored things, and certainly not with a brand new deep red sweatshirt. Jamaal didn't learn that lesson until the second week they were there, when the boys took their laundry downstairs to the coin machines. At the end of the spin cycle, Jamaal reached into the washer and brought out an armload of pink underwear. "No!" was all he said, but he said it a lot, and with real feeling. Bart told him that wearing pink underwear to football practice would be a bold fashion statement, but Jamaal disagreed. He muttered something about being back in a minute, then he left at a dead run. Twenty minutes later he was back, with a three-quart jug of bleach. He dumped all the used-to-be whites back into the washer, fed it more quarters, set it for hot wash, and emptied the jug into the machine. "There," he said as he pushed the Start button. "That'll take care of them." Bart figured that was true, but not in a good way. He remembered the time he had bleached some gym socks. They came out white, but the elastic stuff in the fabric hadn't survived. Neither did Jamaal's, but he didn't find that out until the next day when he dressed for class, or tried to. His socks drooped limply around his ankles, and he muttered something that sounded vaguely ugly. When his briefs did the same thing, his comments were explicitly ugly and richly detailed. Bart recognized most of the words, but since he hadn't grown up around drill sergeants he hadn't known they could be strung together into long sentences.

Society has a lot of rules for getting along, but between roommates there are very few, and one stands out above all the others: You don't betray your roommate. The rule is based on practicality: you have to sleep sometime, and paybacks are hell. A roommate is fair game for ribbing, but you don't rat him out for a cheap laugh. Nobody except Bart ever knew about Jamaal's underwear problem, or how he dealt with it, except that some store clerk must have wondered why a student would need so many new socks and briefs all at once, and so early in the semester.

◊◊◊◊◊◊◊◊◊◊◊◊◊◊◊◊●◊◊◊◊◊◊◊◊◊◊◊◊◊◊◊◊

When Ron brought Jamaal home for the four-day-long Thanksgiving break, Nura expected to find out all of the things about Bart's family that Ron should have been able to tell her earlier. She didn't. Bart had never brought up life before college, and Jamaal hadn't asked. "You don't even know if he went home for Thanksgiving?" Nura wailed. "He could be sitting alone in some joint right now, having a Thanksgiving burger, and you didn't think to ask him to come home with you?" Jamaal had never really liked the old Uncle Remus stories, but right now the words, "Tar-Baby ain't sayin' nuthin" seemed like a sound policy, and he followed it. "Well I'm just going to call his mother right now and apologize. What's her name?" Jamaal didn't know that either, which set off another tirade about men in general, and her men in particular. All things considered, Thanksgiving at the Sheridan house could have gone better.

◇◇◇◇◇◇◇◇◇◇◇◇◇◇◇◇●◇◇◇◇◇◇◇◇◇◇◇◇◇◇◇◇

Bart was not, as a matter of fact, at some joint having a Thanksgiving burger. One of the local churches had a covered-dish supper for the students who weren't going home. They did it every year, and the ladies of the church always fixed their best recipes for the occasion. Southern church ladies are ordinarily the nicest people there are, but if one of them brings soggy dressing or out-of-a-tube biscuits to a church dinner, the others are going to talk about it. "Bless her heart," they'll say, "and her mother was such a good cook, too." So while Jamaal was pretending to like the oyster-and-chestnut dressing his mother made every year, Bart was covering a split-open biscuit with giblet gravy.

The girl behind him, whose name tag said Dee, took a look at what he had done and asked, "What exactly is that?" She spoke with the faintest of accents. French, maybe.

"Giblet gravy."

"And giblet is...?" No, not French. Maybe Italian. She looked kind of Italian.

"It's chopped-up liver and heart and gizzard, I think." And maybe some other stuff too, Bart wasn't sure. Best not to bring that up.

Dee didn't look reassured. "Gizzard?"

"It's, uh..." How do describe a gizzard to an Italian? "It's this sort of stomach a bird has, where it grinds stuff up." He thought pea gravel might be involved too, but decided it was best not to bring up what he'd rather not have to explain.

She hesitated, then did as she had seen Bart do. "Thank you," she said. No, not quite Italian, he thought. Spanish maybe? He had taken Spanish in high school, and had picked up a little more during his stay at Reuben's.

"De nada."

She looked amused. "Do I really sound Spanish?"

"Uh, maybe, a little." Damn, he thought, that was lame.

"No, not even close." She showed him a quick, impish grin, and went to sit with some other girls at a table that had only room for her.

When Bart and Jamaal compared how their Thanksgivings had gone, it turned out to be pretty much of a draw. Jamaal had been with family, which gave him a point, but Bart had eaten better, which brought him back even. Bart had met a cute girl who had, as Jamaal summed it up, "scraped you off her shoe like stepped-on bubble gum," which would have given Jamaal the winning edge except that his high school sweetheart, now a junior, had somehow gotten over him. "Real quick, too," he said, as he took down her picture. He had thought they were staying in touch through webcams and email, but when he got home and called her, she had mentioned other plans, and hadn't suggested he call back. He checked around, and found that the other plans involved one of Jamaal's former teammates, who was this year's football captain. "What's he got that I haven't got?" Jamaal asked Bart.

Bart thought of several answers, and settled on the safest.

"Body heat," he said. "You can't send that over a webcam."

It was a drizzly, gloomy night, and talking about lost love was only making it gloomier. They decided food might help, and their evening jog took them to a pizza place near campus. Bart had never been interested in exercise, but Jamaal had other ideas. "I don't want people saying, 'There goes Jamaal; you know, his roommate's a wimp." Bart had tried to say that walking to class would take care of that, but Jamaal had just snorted. "Walk, hell," was how he put it, and so there were pushups, and crunches, and things Bart assumed were from Army training. And every night, no matter the weather, there had been a jog, longer each time. Bart couldn't feel much difference, except that he didn't get winded as quickly as he had at first, but Jamaal seemed satisfied with the pace of progress.

Midway through a jalapeño, bacon and onion pizza, Jamaal remembered the assignment his mother had given him. "Oh yeah, mama wants your mother's phone number."

Bart weighed the idea in the balances and found it wanting. "I don't think that would be a good idea," he said softly.

Jamaal waited.

Bart stared across the restaurant. "Your mother's name is Nura, isn't it? Pretty name. Do you know my mother's name?"

"Uh, no." Jamaal's mother had wanted to know that, too.

"And do you know why you don't know my mother's name?" Jamaal didn't say anything. "It's because I never talk about her. Never; not a word." That was true, Jamaal thought. He was about to say so when Bart went on. "If you were adopted, and you found out your birth mother had given you up just because she didn't want to be bothered with you, how would you feel?"

"Pretty bad, probably."

"Yeah, pretty bad. Now suppose it was like that, but that instead of putting you out for adoption, she had just kept you around. Would you feel any different?"

"I dunno; I don't guess I would."

"Uh huh; well I don't have to guess. Do you remember your eighteenth birthday?" Jamaal did. "Okay, let me tell you about mine."

The story took a while to tell, and Jamaal didn't interrupt. When it was over, the pizza was gone and the mood was somber. "Did she at least come to your graduation?" Jamaal wanted to know.

"No," said Bart, but he smiled a little as he said it, remembering. His mother hadn't been there, but in her place there had been half a row of librarians, who had clapped and cheered like soccer moms when he crossed the stage. So yeah, he had had family there.

"I wonder," Jamaal asked, "how she would feel about you having a black roommate."

"That wouldn't bother her a bit; she's not a racist. No, what would set her off is your name."

"Huh?"

"Jamaal. It's an Arab name, right? I've been meaning to ask you about that. How come a Sheridan gets named Jamaal?"

"Because of my grandmother, mama's mama. She was all into the black power thing in the sixties. She named mama Nura because she said it wasn't a slave name. Mama named me Jamaal to make her mama happy."

"But your sister is named Katie. How'd she get a pass?"

"She didn't, that's just what she calls herself. Her real name is Kadijah, but she'd hurt me if she knew I told anybody."

"Well there you are then. Let me lead you through this: You and your sister and your mother have Arab names, so you're Muslims."

"What? No, we're Presbyterians."

"Not the way my mother sees things. You see, you have Arab names, and all Arabs are Muslim, and Muslims are heathens, and the heathen are damned. Are you with me so far? What all that means is, you're going to Hell. Maybe we can be roommates there, too."

"Well that's just...wait a minute, you're going too?"

"Oh yeah. After all, I didn't wear a sweater after I was asked what I thought." Twenty minutes earlier, Jamaal wouldn't have understood that. Now he did. "So anyway," Bart continued, "you, me, your mama, your sister, we're all going to Hell, and if your mother calls mine, that's where the conversation is going to go, real quick."

Jamaal thought about that. "OK then, so what should I tell her?"

"You could tell her I escaped from the gingerbread house, and I didn't think I should mark the path back to it."

"Huh?"

"Hansel and Gretel."

"Oh, right. Kids escape, everybody lives happily ever after."

"Something like that."

"I'm not sure that's how I need to explain it," Jamaal said, "but I'll think of something." The drizzle had turned into a light rain by the time they jogged back to the dorm, but that was all right; it fit the mood.

Chapter Three

The bell rang, marking the end of class and the start of the race for the exits. Jamaal was halfway up the center aisle when the professor's voice rang out: "Mr. Sheridan, I need to see you for just a moment." Jamaal winced. In his experience, nothing said in that tone of voice was ever good news, at least for him. Whatever it was, he hoped it wouldn't take long; he had another class in ten minutes.

"Europe Through 1500" was taught in one of those fan-shaped rooms that has curved, steeply rising tiers of seats, and a small stage at the bottom. It looked a lot like an ancient Greek theater, but whether this semester's play was a comedy or a tragedy was still unresolved. The grades from their pre-finals were supposed to have been posted that day, but Dr. Ziya had said the grading was taking a little longer than he had hoped. The way Dr. Ziya structured pre-finals was that if you passed, you passed the course. If you failed, it didn't count against your grade, but you had to take the real finals.

In any other class, Jamaal would already have been out in the hall, because in any other class, he would have been on the back row. He had been large for his age even in first grade, and had quickly found out that size matters. A teacher, scanning the classroom for someone to call on, may honestly intend to pick a student at random, but random is a hard standard to meet. Despite good intentions, a teacher is likely to pick a student who, for whatever reason, stands out. Jamaal had learned that when he sat on the back row, his size wasn't quite as obvious, and so he got picked (or, as he saw it, picked on) less often. But on the first day in Dr. Ziya's class the back row had already been colonized by other large persons, his teammates on the freshman football squad. They were, Jamaal had already decided, slackers, and he didn't want to be lumped in with them. Jamaal knew all about collective punishment; it was one of his father's favorite training tools. If a private screwed up, the whole unit paid for it. After a few doses of that, the unit persuaded the screw-up to do better.

But for that system to work, the regular guys had to outnumber the screw-ups, and in Europe Through 1500, the slackers on the back row had Jamaal outnumbered, so he sat down front.

"This will only take a minute, Mr. Sheridan," said Dr. Ziya, but he said it the way a dentist might say that something wasn't going to hurt much. He took an exam booklet out of a folder, glanced in it, and said, "Yes, here we are. I, ah, had some difficulty with your handwriting in two places, and I want to make sure I understand your answers."

"Yes sir." Handwriting? Was that all?

"Here, for example," said Dr. Ziya, looking at a page that Jamaal couldn't see. "Do you recall how you described Gaius Caesar?"

Jamaal thought about it. Gaius...wasn't he the one who...oh yeah. "I believe I said he was crazy, sir."

"Yes, yes you did. That word is quite clear. But I'm not sure I'm reading the—how do you say it?—the adjective clause correctly. Do you recall exactly how crazy you said he was?"

Oh dear God, what did I say, Jamaal thought. It had been a long test, and toward the last his answers might have gotten a little...casual. Gaius had been pretty damn crazy, but had he said that? Then he remembered: he had let Smart-Ass Jamaal answer that one. "Um, I believe I said he was as crazy as a shot cat, sir." He could see how that might be a problem. Dr. Ziya spoke very good English, but it was book English; he wasn't, as they say, from around here. Jamaal could well believe he had never heard of somebody being as crazy as a shot cat. Did they even have cats where he came from? "It means very crazy, sir. I'm sorry that I wasn't more clear."

Dr. Ziya smiled, briefly. He had asked a member of the English department about the shot cat, and even though he still wasn't sure why a dead cat was the American standard for insanity, it apparently was. In any event, 'very crazy' was a good shorthand description of the emperor who had, among other things, named his horse to the high priesthood. "Ah. Just so. I have only one other question. You said that the Holy Roman Emperor, Henry

IV, had cold feet, in reference, I assume, to his standing barefoot in the snow at Canossa. But then you added a second descriptive which is less clear, unless again I am misunderstanding your writing. Were you perhaps thinking of bezants?"

"I don't actually know what a bezant is, Dr. Ziya, so I wouldn't have meant that." This time Jamaal knew perfectly well what he had written. What he couldn't remember was why it had seemed like a good idea.

"A bezant is a golden disk. You see them on many medieval coats of arms, although not, as it happens, on the arms of Henry IV. Do you recall what you said?"

Jamaal recalled. "I, ah, said he had brass balls, sir. Cold feet, and brass balls." The phrase did have a nice ring, he thought.

"Meaning?" Dr. Ziya asked. He had meant to ask the English professor about that too, but had forgotten.

"Uh...boldness, courage, that sort of thing."

"A useful expression, to be sure; I shall have to remember it. All right, thank you Mr. Sheridan. Those were the only issues I had. I hope I haven't made you late to your next class." Jamaal took the hint, and hurried out. Alone, the professor took out his phone and tapped in a number. "Hello? This is Enver Ziya. No, I teach here at Clemson. Coach Edmunds, I am afraid we have a problem."

◊◊◊◊◊◊◊◊◊◊◊◊◊◊◊●◊◊◊◊◊◊◊◊◊◊◊◊◊◊◊

"Before we go, there's something that's come up that I need to, ah, clarify. Sheridan, up here. The rest of you, stay. You need to hear this."

Jamaal felt like he was in one of those horror stories where you've gotten on the wrong side of a Gypsy woman and your life goes all to hell. He stood up and walked to the front of the class where in his mind he saw the coach standing by a chopping block, wearing a black hood and holding an axe. There was some muffled whispering behind him.

Coach Edmunds' classroom was also his office. Up front

was his desk, his chair, and the folding chair he used for occasions like this. The folding chair gave a pained little squeak as Jamaal settled onto it, but Jamaal's chairs tended to do that. On the wall behind the coach were a lot of framed pictures from when he had played in the pros, along with a diploma and a couple of certificates. The coach was silent, as if deciding how to broach a painful subject. Finally, he spoke. "Sheridan, I had a real interesting talk this afternoon with one of your teachers. Do you think you can you guess which one?"

Jamaal thought he could. "Was it Dr. Ziya, sir?" he asked, hoping he was wrong.

"Why yes, Sheridan, yes it was." Based only on voice, someone might have thought the coach was in a jovial mood, but Jamaal noticed he was strumming the fingers of one hand on his desk while he spoke. "Dr. Ziya. Do you know, I had never heard of Dr. Ziya before today, and suddenly I find out my entire freshman squad has him for a history course. I assume the word got around that it was an easy course. I think maybe it was, last year. Hasn't turned out that way this year, has it Sheridan?"

"I really don't know, sir. Dr. Ziya hasn't finished grading the exams."

"Oh but he has, Sheridan," said the coach. "He has, yes. He finished grading them three hours ago." He looked at the ceiling for almost thirty seconds. "Do you know what happens to a player who flunks a course, Sheridan?"

"Uh, not in detail, sir. Something bad?" There was some snickering from the rest of the class.

"I suppose that would depend on what you mean by bad," Coach Edmunds said, still looking at the ceiling. "Being suspended from the team, maybe losing a scholarship, would that be bad? Tell me about that test, Sheridan, the one where you compared some Roman emperor to a dead cat." That got several giggles from the group, which the coach squelched with a look.

"It...it was just a list of people, and we had to say something short and descriptive about each one. Like, if it had said 'Vince Lombardi,' you might answer, 'Winning was a habit.' I didn't think the test was all that bad."

"Not all that bad," Coach Edmunds repeated softly, leaning back again and closing his eyes. A vein on his forehead stood out, but otherwise he seemed to have entered some sort of Zen state. "So tell me, Sheridan, how did you study for this test that wasn't all that bad?"

"Well, you see, my roommate and I play a sort of trivia game. He'll ask me some history question, and if I get it right I get to ask him a sports question. It's gotten to where we have to work real hard to trip each other up." And of course, he thought, you have to have read the material, but that was kind of obvious, wasn't it?

"You studied. By playing trivia. With your roommate." His doctor kept saying he should do something about his blood pressure. Maybe he was right.

There was a long pause. The whispering and giggling had stopped. Jamaal stood it as long as he could, but finally said, "Coach? Can I ask you something?"

"Oh by all means, ask away." Except, he thought, if it's a trivia question, I honestly think my head will explode.

"Does Dr. Ziya think I cheated? He asked me some questions today that made me wonder." The class had been wondering too. Even the ones who hadn't been there to hear Jamaal called back had heard about it.

"I asked him that same question, and he was very up front about it. He said that yes, he had considered the possibility, but he didn't think you would have remembered your answers, or been able to explain them, if somebody had just fed them to you. That, and you sat on the front row, where he could see you. He knows you didn't use a phone, that you didn't have on ear buds, and that you didn't take out any notes. So no, Sheridan, he doesn't think you cheated."

"Then...what's the problem? Did I fail? Some of my answers were a little...offhand, but I thought I did all right." The class was dead quiet.

Coach Edmunds' eyes opened, and his chair rocked

forward. "Off...hand." He said it with a grimace, as if it tasted bad. "You wrote on a university exam that somebody had brass balls! If that's your idea of offhand, Sheridan, I'd hate to see your idea of smart-assed!" He stopped, closed his eyes, took a deep breath, and continued at a more conversational pitch. "But no, you didn't fail. God knows why; I'd have flunked your ass just for that crack about the dead cat, but no, you passed. That's the good news. The bad news," he paused, knowing he had everybody's attention. "The bad news is that out of my entire freshman squad you, Sheridan, are the only one who *did* pass!" He stood up as he said that, slamming both fists down on his desk so hard that the wall shook and the pictures rattled. Chuck Edmunds was as large as Jamaal, and he knew how to intimidate. Suddenly, he wasn't facing Jamaal; he was facing the class, and his face said, 'I am the Devil, fear me.' In a voice that was neither loud nor soft, more of a low growl, he said, "Sheridan, go. I have things I need to discuss...at length...with the rest of these fine gentlemen." Jamaal didn't have to be told twice.

◇◇◇◇◇◇◇◇◇◇◇◇◇◇◇◇◇●◇◇◇◇◇◇◇◇◇◇◇◇◇◇◇◇◇

What they had done, it turned out, was to smuggle in a phone that had web access. Then the one with the phone had entered each name in a search box, and then written down the first descriptive phrase he found. Then he let the guy next to him see his answer, and from there it went down the row. It would have been less obvious if each one had paraphrased the answer, but a concise descriptive phrase cannot easily be reworded and still make sense unless you understand what it means, and if anyone on the back row had understood the subject well enough to do that, they wouldn't have had to cheat. The result, predictable in hindsight, was that nobody had changed any of the answers. When Peterson, the one with the phone, had looked up Henry IV, the phrase he had picked was, "Paris is worth a Mass," and so the whole row had written "Paris is worth a Mass," which unfortunately summed up Henry IV the French king, and not Henry IV the Holy Roman Emperor. All of their answers had been like that: some right, some wrong, but all of them word for word the same.

About twenty minutes after Jamaal left, the yelling and desk-pounding part of Coach's discussion began to taper off. Two or three of his pictures now hung crooked, but at least none had fallen off the wall. The squad was supposed to have read "Beowulf" for English class. None but Jamaal had, but the others had at least read the graphic novel, so they had a vivid mental picture of what Coach might have done if one of his pictures had come smashing down during his tirade. It would have been what Grendel had done to the Danes: arms over here, legs over there, guts and eyeballs somewhere else. But at least then it would have been over.

"Now let's be clear on one thing," Coach Edmunds said, having already made himself painfully clear on several things. "You're athletes, and I understand, cheating does go on in athletics." That got their attention. Maybe this wasn't going to be so bad after all. "Basketball players fall down on the floor when nobody's touched them. That's cheating. Soccer players do the same thing. NASCAR drivers say, 'If you're not cheating, you're not trying.' I know it goes on, and you know it goes on." He paused, knowing some fish would rise to the bait.

"Uh, Coach?"

"Yes, Peterson?"

"If cheating is okay, then how come you're yelling at us? Just cause we got caught?" There were some nods of agreement, as the coach knew there would be. He had dealt with this issue before.

"No, getting caught is not what you did wrong. Getting caught just means you were clumsy about it. And no, I did not say cheating was okay; I said cheating goes on, *in athletics*. Well, when you morons took that test, *you weren't on the god-damned football field, were you?* Peterson! Tell me where you were."

"Uh, a classroom?"

"Yes, but not just any classroom. You were in a *Clemson* classroom. You see this?" He pointed to a diploma hanging crooked on the wall. "It says I'm a Clemson graduate. That means something to me. If—and I do mean if—any of you gets one, it'll mean something to you, and it won't mean you cheated and got away with it. Now, you have two weeks before the final, the one that counts. You're going to spend that time reading, and you're going to spend that time studying. For all I care you can spend that time playing trivia with Sheridan's roommate, but whatever you have to do to pass honestly, by God you're going to do it! Now get the hell out of here!"

Chapter Four

I, Wade Hampton Dawson, being of sound and disposing mind and sound memory, do hereby make, publish, and declare this writing to be my Last Will and Testament. As Executor of my estate, I designate Emmett Schroder, Esquire, of Larson, South Carolina. I direct that my said Executor have my body cremated, and the ashes scattered. To my housekeeper, Margaret Adams, I bequeath the sum of fifty thousand dollars, together with my thanks for putting up for so long with a crotchety old man. Among my possessions will be found two bells, the larger being made of bronze, the smaller of iron. The larger bell I give to the First Baptist Church of Oak Grove, South Carolina; the smaller I give to my old friend, Hamid ibn Issa, who will know where it goes. My Jeep I give to my great-nephew (my sister Emily's grandson), Victor Albert Phillips. The cat which I feed is a free spirit, and does not belong to anyone. Nevertheless, I request that my executor arrange for him to have a dry place to sleep, and for some food to supplement the birds he eats. The rest and residue of my estate I give to the Keowee County animal shelter, to be used, sold, given away or discarded, as they may see fit. In testimony whereof I hereunto set my hand in the presence of three persons whom I ask to bear witness to the same.

"That's it?" the old man asked after he had read it. "I should be paying you by the word instead of by the minute."

"My instructions, you may recall, were to keep it short and simple," said Emmett Schroder, Esquire. "Hell, Harley would charge you another fifty dollars just to listen to you gripe about his bill. Wouldn't he?" The question was directed at Harley Bishop's three secretaries, on loan from the law office across the street. He got no answer; a good secretary knows what to hear and what to miss. "Hmph. Well, all of you come over here where you can see." They gathered around the desk. To his client, he said, "Right there, full name." Wade scrawled his signature and dated it. "Now tell the witnesses what you just signed."

"This is my last will," Wade said solemnly.

"Would you show the witnesses your driver's license." Wade got out the license, which Emmett leaned over to see. "No older than that? Hard to believe. I told Calvin you were at least a hundred and six." To the witnesses, he said, "All right, now you see this paragraph that says you know who he is, and that he said he knew this was his will, and that you saw him sign it? If you agree that those statements are so, I need for each of you to sign down below, on one of those lines where it says Witness."

The witnesses had performed this ceremony dozens of times, and they didn't really need to be told what to do, or where to sign. As for having the client say what he was signing, Harley Bishop generally just told his clients, "Sign here," and to the witnesses, "Sign there," but that was not how Emmett worked. When Emmett had passed the bar and needed to get sworn in as a lawyer, the court clerk had sent him upstairs to the main courtroom. He had expected to take the oath in chambers during a recess, but instead, old Judge Cressy had stopped court, stood up behind the bench, and read out the oath, line by line, with Emmett repeating it after him. Then he had come down off the bench and welcomed Emmett into the bar with a handshake. The ceremony took almost a quarter hour, and Emmett had apologized for using up so much court time. "Son," the judge had said, "In the forty-odd years since I took that same oath, I have learned this: if you do the little things right, somehow, someday, whatever time it costs will turn out to have been well spent." Emmett had taken that to heart, and from that day forward, every time a client signed a will, he treated it as though it was the first time for everyone concerned. Over the years, several of his wills had been challenged, but not a single one had been broken.

"Now, Evelyn, would you notarize their signatures?" Evelyn Pitman in particular didn't need to be told what to do. After almost twenty years as Emmett Schroder's secretary, she knew how wills were signed, and how they were probated, and everything else about the machinery of a law practice. When Billy Jenkins had left the firm to become the Honorable William P. Jenkins, Emmett had seriously suggested that she get a law degree, take the bar, and join the firm as his partner. "It'd make an honest woman of you," is how he put it. Evelyn told him she was at least as honest as he was, and that she liked doing what she was doing. What she didn't have to say was that, for all practical purposes, they already were a partnership. He decided what needed doing, she saw to it that it got done right, and, at the end of each month he paid her what he paid himself. The state bar wouldn't have liked that—splitting fees with a non-lawyer violates one of the thousand rules that supposedly keep the profession pure and holy—so the firm's books showed her making a flat salary, plus end-of-month bonuses. The bonuses always turned out to be whatever it took to make the monthly split come out even, but Emmett figured that how he calculated a bonus was none of the state bar's business.

Notarizing the signatures marked the end of the ceremony. Emmett thanked the witnesses and asked Evelyn to put the will in the office safe. Then he drummed his fingers on his beat-up old desk for about thirty seconds. "I've got a question," he told Wade, "and if I'm going to be your executor, I need to know the answer. Why?"

"Why. Do you mean why, or why now?"

"Let's start with just why. You could have run the Jeep through the trust, and we'd have made sure the boy got it. Why make your connection to him public?"

"The connection is easy enough to find, and I want it to look like the Jeep is all he gets."

Emmett digested that. "Okay, so where is the Jeep? You haven't driven it in a couple of years; you drive a leased car. I should know; the trust makes the lease payments, and I write the checks."

Evelyn's voice floated around the corner. "I write the checks. All you do is sign them."

"Write, sign, whatever. My point is, if I'm going to get the Jeep to the boy, I need to know where it is."

"It's in a shed, up at the cabin. I've got the keys and the title right here." He produced an envelope from an inside jacket pocket.

"Evelyn..."

"I know, I know: put it in the safe." She came in for the envelope, and gave Wade a hard look. "That's all you're going to leave him to remember you by? A Jeep that'll probably turn over and squash him?" Evelyn took Consumer Reports, which over the years has had many unkind things to say about Jeeps.

"Well there is the scholarship," Wade said, a little defensively.

"No, I mean personal to you. He can't look at a scholarship twenty years from now and remember his dear old uncle, and that Jeep will be in the junkyard long before then."

"I don't think he'll have any problem remembering me," the old man said softly. "That's what my journal is for."

Evelyn thought she knew what Wade meant. A week before, Wade had asked her to put a leather-bound volume in the office safe. It was an odd book: column after column of five-letter words that weren't words. The letters looked random, but according to people Wade had asked, a big enough computer would find that they weren't. A code-breaker, faced with a truly random text, would realize it was unbreakable and give up. That wasn't what Wade wanted. If someone got hold of that book, Wade wanted him to waste a lot of time on it; it would serve them right for snooping. He had taken his plaintext and run it through an early version of a public-key encryption program. The later versions of the program were supposedly unbreakable, but the early versions had a theoretical vulnerability if someone wanted to burn through a lot of mainframe time to find it.

The chime on the front door dingled, and Evelyn went out front to see who it was. The law office had been a house originally, a craftsman-style bungalow from the 1920s. Its living room was now Emmett's waiting room, and its yard had been paved for parking, but it still had a feature that many more modern law offices lack: a back door. There always seemed to be two or three people in the waiting room who had showed up without appointments, and who each wanted "just a few minutes," so when Emmett was due for court and didn't want to run the gauntlet, he would duck out the back. By the time Evelyn came back in to say Emmett's 3:30 appointment was there, Wade had used Emmett's door and slipped away.

"Did you remember to ask him that last question?" she asked.

"Which question?" Emmett asked innocently, knowing perfectly well which question.

"The 'why now' question. Why, after not making a will all of his adult life, did he all of a sudden want it done in a hurry?"

"I dunno," he lied. "I'll ask him at the game tomorrow night." He didn't have to tell Evelyn what game. For upwards of twenty years, every Wednesday night, five men had gotten together in Calvin Zorn's basement rec room and played poker: Wade, Emmett, Arnold Devore, Jim Perkins, and Calvin. Calvin's wife had come downstairs to watch once, and the intensity of the game had made her so nervous she had had to leave, which had suited the men perfectly; their conversation tended not to be in the diplomatic, indirect language that women prefer. Emmett had already known a little bit about Wade's health, and as of a few minutes ago, he knew quite a lot. The old man had been having a pain where he hadn't had one before, and his doctor had found an aneurysm. It was not where it could be fixed, the doctor told him, and it could rupture at any time, probably quite soon. When it did, the doctor had added, that would be that.

The doctor thought the old man would be upset to know he could, and probably would, drop dead at any moment, but he was wrong: Wade accepted the news with philosophic calm. Emmett knew why. He knew that Wade wanted his will done today because he needed it today. Emmett couldn't tell Evelyn, though. Wade was his friend, but Wade was also his client, and Emmett never, ever repeated what a client told him in confidence. Wade would not be at the game tomorrow night, because Wade would not be alive tomorrow night.

Chapter Five

Mr. Bart Phillips
Room 5, Geer Dormitory
Clemson University
Clemson, South Carolina

Dear Bart,

Emmett misplaced your letter, and has only just now passed it along to me. Apparently it got into an open file folder on his desk the day he got it, and he ran across it yesterday when he checked on something in that file. I have gotten my mail through his office for at least a decade, so I can well believe you had no luck finding an address for me. Concerning the scholarship, you are quite welcome. That is the sort of thing the trust was set up to do, and I am gratified to have lived long enough to see it begin to fulfill that part of its purpose.

Look for a letter from Emmett sometime quite soon. I trust very few people, but I trust Emmett. I even play cards with him for money, although I would advise you against that. I did not know where to send your graduation present--I knew you would not get it if I sent it to Lorraine's--so I have left it with Emmett. I think you will find it interesting, perhaps even rewarding.

Oh, and for what it's worth, "Bart" was a good choice. It fits you.

Wade

Dr. Lester K. Thurmond
Chemistry Department
Rensselaer Polytechnic Institute
Troy, NY

Dear Dr. Thurmond:

One of your former graduate assistants spent the summer with us as an intern. He brought with him a draft of your paper, "Surprising Properties of Amorphous Alloys," which quite frankly, I believe to be groundbreaking. Of particular interest to me was page 8, where you discuss properties of an iron/silver alloy. If correct, those properties

44

would make that alloy ideal for a defense application we are developing. Could you tell me where you obtained the sample you tested? We have not been able to duplicate the alloy you describe, and would very much like to work with the supplier. This is, you should know, a matter of national security.

> Sincerely,
> Steven A. Jameson, manager
> Special Projects Division
> Carlisle Macrotech, Inc.

Steven A. Jameson, manager
Special Projects, Carlisle Macrotech
Willard Industrial Park, Newton, Mass.

Dear Mr. Jameson:

Thank you for your interest in my research, and particularly for your kind words about the paper. I got the sample you referenced from a man I sat next to at a seminar some years ago. I told him I was working with silver alloys, and he said he had one I might find amusing. That was his word, not mine. I believe he made the sample himself, but I have no idea what process he used. I did not publish the paper because, lacking additional samples, I cannot be sure that my results were not unique to the batch I tested. I wish I could be of more help.

> Lester K. Thurmond, PhD

Major Thomas Harper
308 Army Pentagon
Room 3A241
Washington, DC 20310

Dear Major Harper:

We find that we cannot proceed further with the Clevis Project bidding process. We had a good-faith belief that we would be able to meet your specifications, based on some research work of Lester Thurmond at RPI, but a material critical to our design turns out to be unavailable.

Regretfully,
Steven A. Jameson, Manager
Special Projects Division
Carlisle Macrotech, Inc.

Mr. Bart Phillips
Room 5, Geer Dorm
Clemson University
Clemson, South Carolina

Dear Mr. Phillips:

I am sorry to have to inform you that your great uncle, Wade Hampton Dawson, passed away yesterday evening. The doctor tells me he thinks it was a stroke. For whatever consolation it might be, he went peacefully, sitting in his favorite chair with his cat in his lap.

As per his instructions, there will be no funeral as such, but there will be a wake, on the 21st of December, which I believe falls within the winter break at Clemson. If you can make it, I can find a place for you to stay, or you could stay at Wade's old cabin. If you cannot make it—and I understand this is short notice—I will make arrangements to get your inheritance delivered to you: a Jeep which Wade used to drive. I presented the will for probate this morning, and even though it is technically somewhat early to be distributing assets to heirs, I do not think that will be a problem.

In addition to having been one of my first clients, Wade Dawson was one of my dearest friends, and I will miss him. But he asked that when I wrote you, I include two lines from an old poem that he said summed up his situation:

"I warmed both hands before the fire of life;
It sinks, and I am ready to depart."

I look forward to hearing from you.

Sincerely,
Emmett Schroder,
Attorney at Law

◇◇◇◇◇◇◇◇◇◇◇◇◇◇◇◇●◇◇◇◇◇◇◇◇◇◇◇◇◇◇◇◇

Mrs. Nura Sheridan
31 River Street
Devils Elbow, Missouri

Dear Mrs. Sheridan,
   Thank you so much for inviting me to spend the Christmas break with Jamaal and your family. It was very kind of you to think of me, and I had looked forward to meeting you. Unfortunately, I have just been notified of the death of my great uncle Wade, and in connection with attending his wake, I will be spending the break in Larson, South Carolina, where he had his home. Again, thank you for asking me.

Bart Phillips

◇◇◇◇◇◇◇◇◇◇◇◇◇◇◇◇●◇◇◇◇◇◇◇◇◇◇◇◇◇◇◇◇

```
To:     Clevis team leaders
From:   Colonel R. D. Salinger
```

I have scheduled a Clevis Project meeting for 1500 hours today in Room 240. Bring your key people. According to Major Harper, we have a problem.

Chapter Six

"What do you think? Is Carlisle just trying to jack up the cost?" The speaker was Col. Randall Salinger, the man in overall charge of Project Clevis. Clevis, depending on who was asked, was essential to national security, or at least an interesting avenue to explore, or a complete boondoggle. One of the major defense suppliers, Traxell International, had developed a mini-drone it called a Feathercopter. Feather, as the Clevis staff called it, was small, quiet, and all but invisible to radar. Traxell said it was a triumph of innovative design, but that design had involved some tradeoffs. To minimize Feather's weight, the Traxell engineers had given it a very small motor. That gave it a low heat signature, which was good, and low power, which was not so good. The limit on payload was where the Clevis project came in. Clevis was a broad-spectrum sensor which, on paper, was light enough for Feather to lift. Clevis gave Feather a mission, and an advanced new device with a mission was all the Traxell lobbyists needed: the project, they told anyone who would listen, was absolutely essential to the nation's defense. In reality, as Col. Salinger knew perfectly well, Feather/Clevis would, at best, be only marginally better than existing equipment, but acting on knowledge like that was a policy decision, and colonels do not make policy. His job was to get Clevis off the ground, and this new problem with the sensor array was making that job difficult. He was not happy.

"Carlisle thinks they could do it if we up the payload specs by 175 grams." That was Major Thomas Harper, sitting at the Colonel's left. His team had designed Clevis around Carlisle's original numbers, and he was not happy either.

"A hundred seventy five grams. That's what, about six ounces?" The colonel mused. "Might as well say six pounds. We're up against Feather's limits already." Not good, he thought, not good at all. If Clevis went into the crapper, his future in the Army would go right along with it. In the Army, you get moved up or you get moved out, that was the rule, and nobody moves up from a failed project. If Clevis crashed, he could retire as a colonel now, or he spend a couple years behind a desk at Fort Armpit, but one way or another he would retire as a colonel. Definitely not good. "Carlisle isn't the only company that can make sensors," he said, grasping at straws.

Around the table there was a lot of paper shuffling, but nobody answered. Finally Major Harper shook his head. "We sent the specs to every maker on the approved list. A couple of them asked how firm the weight specs were, but only Carlisle sent a proposal."

"Okay," the colonel said, "let's look at the problem a different way. Carlisle can make the sensors if they can get this...this stuff. So what is it, and who makes it?"

"Apparently, nobody," Major Harper said morosely.

There was a snort from the colonel's right. "Maybe not now, but for the right money, I'll bet somebody will." Captain Bragg had little patience for the theoretical. Figure out what needs done and do it, was his motto. He was in charge of the non-technical part of the project, but no one on the Harper staff could quite give Bragg's team a name, or wanted to. Partly that was because Steve Bragg's people took care of a lot of different tasks, so no single title would be accurate, but there was also the way he and his people took care of problems. That was something the others really did not want to know about.

The colonel looked thoughtful. "Reverse engineer it, you mean? Good idea, Steve." That might be expensive, the colonel thought, but expense wasn't a problem. If you can tack the words "national security" onto a project, the money will appear. He smiled, and everybody relaxed a little.

Everybody, except Tom Harper. "I don't know."

Colonel Salinger lost his smile. "What do you mean you don't know? How hard can it be? We find out what the stuff is, we give the recipe to our lab boys, and they make some. Problem solved." Even as he said it, the colonel wished he hadn't. Major Harper was no fool, and if he thought there was a problem, there probably was a problem.

"I've had my people working on that," said the major. "We

already know what the 'stuff' is; we just don't know how to make it."

Captain Bragg grunted. "Put Traxell to work on it. They made a mini-copter out of ceramic foam, for God's sake; you know they can make a piece of metal, no matter what it's made of."

Major Harper fought the urge to call the captain an ass to his face, although behind his back he regularly called him that and worse. "I hope you're right," he said, and mentally added, but you're not. "This isn't ordinary metal. It's amorphous, what we call a metallic glass. That's not new; a couple of companies make it, but the only amorphous casting alloys on the market are based around zirconium. The stuff Carlisle had is an alloy of iron and silver, and it's really pure, electronics grade pure. We could make something that clean if we could get iron to alloy with silver, but it won't. The mixture curdles as it cools."

The colonel and the two officers sat at one end of the table; the staffers sat at the other. In front of each man was a tablet computer; except for the uniforms, it looked exactly like a corporate board meeting. One of Harper's staff looked up but said nothing. Staffers don't interrupt officers, but the major noticed the look. "Matthews, you have something?"

"Sir, they might have done it by sintering." That got a lot of blank looks. "You grind your subject materials into superfine powders, mix them, then you compress the mixture until it forms a solid."

Major Harper nodded approvingly. Matthews was one of his sharper guys. "I like it. Follow up on that." Matthews nodded.

Captain Bragg didn't change expression, but added one more item to his mental list of Tom Harper's shortcomings. To Bragg, a team was a unit, not a collection of grandstanding individuals. If one of Bragg's people had an idea, he told it to Bragg, who could bring the idea up when, and if, the time was right. As if in response to his thought, a message appeared on the screen in front of him, from the sharpest member of his own staff, Bivens: *Carlisle's supplier knows how to make it. We could ask them.* Capt. Bragg glanced down the table and gave an almost imperceptible nod. Well done, soldier, it said. He typed, *Find out who*. Captain Bragg appreciated the value of ambiguity. Instant messages are recorded somewhere, but anyone looking at those two messages would see nothing remarkable. After all, "ask" and "find out" can have many meanings, and some of them are perfectly legal.

◇◇◇◇◇◇◇◇◇◇◇◇◇◇◇◇●◇◇◇◇◇◇◇◇◇◇◇◇◇◇◇◇

Bivens came prepared. FISA, the Foreign Intelligence Surveillance Act, didn't apply to this sort of operation, but almost no one knows what FISA covers and what it doesn't. If this chemistry prof wanted to see some authority, Bivens had a FISA search warrant in his jacket pocket, ready to whip out. At least it said it was a FISA warrant. It even looked like one, which had probably been a waste of his time since, again, almost no one knows what a real FISA warrant ought to look like. That was one of the things Captain Bragg liked about Bivens: even on trivial things, Bivens sweated the details. The captain could have sent any of his three men to Rensselaer Polytechnic, but Bivens was his best, which is how Bivens came to be sitting across the desk from a balding little man named Thurmond. "So you see, it really is a matter of national security," he was saying. "We're not interested in causing any problems; we simply need to know the name of the person who gave you that alloy sample."

Dr. Thurmond hesitated. "I assume this will remain confidential, Captain Wingate?" Bivens nodded. "Some of my faculty colleagues have never really forgiven the Army for Vietnam, and if they knew I was cooperating..."

Bivens smiled reassuringly. "FISA is an interesting law, Dr. Thurmond. You can't say you got the request, and we can't say— and won't say—that we made it, or what you told us." He thought that was probably true, but true or not, it seemed to put his listener at ease. Captain Wingate certainly wasn't going to say anything; he was in Korea just now, and didn't know Bivens had assumed his identity for the day. Bivens had never met Wingate, but with a little cotton in his cheeks and a pair of glasses, they could have passed for twins. That had saved him some time, since he only had to run off a copy of Wingate's ID from the computer, instead of creating an identity from scratch.

"The man who gave me that sample was a professor at what was then Clemson College, Dr. Wade Dawson. I corresponded with him, off and on, for several years. He retired to a place called Larson, somewhere in South Carolina."

Bivens wrote *Larson, SC* down on a card and tucked it into his shirt pocket, then he thanked the man and went out to the car he had rented and started back home. He would rather have driven something sporty, but the gate guards might have been curious about that. If you drive a clean, well-maintained Crown Vic and you're younger than seventy, no one is going to doubt that you work for the government. All Bivens had had to do was to get some real-looking government tags, and the big stamping machine at the warehouse had gotten that done in a few minutes.

Captain Bragg's team worked on one project at a time, and right now that project was Clevis. Theirs was not the only operations team, but how many other teams there were and what their projects might be was on a need-to-know basis, and very few needed to know. One who did was Sidney, the person who scheduled time in the warehouse where the printing equipment was, and the stamping machine, and the other tools that made what the teams used. When a team needed something, its leader would call Sidney and tell him how much time would be required, and what materials. Sidney assigned a time, and when the team got there, everything was ready. The only person the team actually met would be Earl, the man who ran the machines. Earl used to be short and graying, but then one day he was taller and younger. His shirt still said Earl though, which was more than Earl generally said.

There was a derelict gas station just off the highway, where Bivens switched plates, cutting the fake government ones into pieces with some tin snips he had brought. He distributed the pieces among the many nearby rubbish heaps, along with the cut-up captain's bars that "Wingate" had worn. The uniform jacket, the FISA warrant and Wingate's ID he burned in a barrel, with a little help from some charcoal lighter he had brought. The fire was hot and quick, and then he was back on I-95, heading south.

Just east of Baltimore, there is a stretch of I-95 where the highway makes an almost ninety degree curve. Driving north, the curve is toward the right. A man in a Buick, just approaching that righthand curve, rolled down his window to flick out a cigarette butt. The butt blew back in and landed in his lap, where it quickly got his attention. The Buick veered left, then overcorrected right until suddenly it was sideways in the road, squarely in the path of a flatbed Peterbilt. Making a fast lane change in a loaded semi is not a good idea, but that is a mere fact, and a fact weighs nothing when balanced against an instinct. The driver of the Peterbilt instinctively jerked his wheel sharply left to avoid T-boning the Buick, and instead he T-boned the median barrier. That stopped the cab, but not the cargo, a load of steel pipes, which came across the median like so many hollow steel javelins, straight at a clean, well-maintained Crown Victoria in the inner southbound lane. It took a while for the State Police boys to get to the scene, but when they did, their report to the EMTs was short and to the point: "Two casualties, both D.R.T."

In the ambulance, the younger EMT was baffled. "I thought I knew the police codes, but that's a new one on me." This was his first wreck call.

"You won't find it in the books," his partner explained. "It means, dead-right-there."

"Yeah? Since when can a trooper pronounce somebody dead?"

"They don't say it very often, but when they do, you can rely on it. They're telling us not to take any risks getting there quick, cause this ain't nothing but a body run." The new guy didn't buy it. In his opinion, only a doctor or, as he saw himself, an almost-doctor, can say that somebody was absolutely, positively, not-ever-coming-back dead. He held that opinion for exactly as long as it took the ambulance to reach the scene. The pipes that had come through the Peterbilt's cab had cut its driver in half at the waist. The guy in the Crown Vic looked fine, except for a one-inch-diameter pipe sticking out of his chest. His eyes were still open, his face frozen in a look of almost comical surprise. "Quick and clean," said the older man, who had worked a lot of wrecks. "Take it from me, there are plenty worse ways you can go." The younger man looked like he might want to disagree, but just then the rest of his lunch came up, so the conversation pretty much died right there.

◇◇◇◇◇◇◇◇◇◇◇◇◇◇◇◇●◇◇◇◇◇◇◇◇◇◇◇◇◇◇◇◇

The soldier entered Capt. Bragg's office and then stood quietly. The captain finished initialing a form and looked up. "Yes, Travis?"

"Sir, there's been a bad wreck on I-95 east of Baltimore. The overhead shots of it on the news are showing a Crown Vic right in the middle of it."

"And you think I need to know about this, why?"

"Sir, we haven't heard anything from Bivens in a couple of hours, and 95 is what he would be using. The State Police won't release any names until next of kin are notified, but I thought the possibility of it being Bivens should be brought to your attention." That was how the captain liked it: facts first, then speculation, if asked.

"Hm," said Bragg, thinking out loud. "He does favor Crown Vics for this sort of job, which raises the odds a little, but he's a careful driver and he did take the emergency maneuver course, which lowers them back. Probably isn't him. Still, if it is...if it is, and we don't act fast...we could have a situation." He made his decision. "Yes, I agree, this was worth knowing. Find out if it's Bivens, and if it is, get McIntyre and do what you need to do."

"Yes sir." Travis left. He didn't need to be told what might need doing. The captain stared at the papers on his desk and frowned. If it was Bivens, the troopers weren't going to find any next of kin, because Bivens didn't have any. He would have his real ID, but nothing else, nothing compromising. Still, the team needed to know, not only because they took care of their own, but also to find out what he had learned from Dr. Thurmond. If they had to go back for the information, Thurmond might get curious, and curiosity was every team's worst enemy. Some information stays secret because it is well hidden, but most of the time a secret survives simply because no one thinks to look for it.

Chapter Seven

The town of Larson sits in a valley in northwestern South Carolina, an area called the upstate. Farther south, the woods consist mainly of white pines, but in the upstate, hardwoods predominate, and people drive from as far away as Atlanta to see the fall colors. There are cabins in the hills above town where the summer people can get away from the heat and humidity of the lowlands, or keep their boats between trips to Lake Keowee. The summer people don't know how to drive the area's curvy two-lane highways, but except for that they generally aren't a problem and they do spend money, so the locals make them welcome. The leaf-lookers, however, are fair game, and every fall ramshackle sheds appear along Highway 28, selling peach cider, boiled peanuts, and jellies that only a tourist would think are normal. The locals don't eat boiled peanuts or corn-cob jelly, and whatever else they might drink, it isn't going to be peach cider. Once the leaves are off the trees, the summer people and the leaf-lookers go back to wherever home is, and the locals more or less hunker in for the winter.

Driving from Clemson to Larson takes about half an hour. On a bicycle it takes longer, but it isn't a bad ride if the rider hasn't packed too much, which Bart hadn't. In his backpack were two shirts, two sets of underwear, a jacket and some books. If the cabin had running water and a sink where he could wash his clothes, he figured that was enough to get him through the three weeks of winter break. Clemson students can stay in the dorms during Thanksgiving's long weekend, but not over the winter break. The students who don't go home can travel, or stay with friends, or stay in a motel, but they can't stay in the dorms. Students who need a ride somewhere have a bulletin board they can check, but nobody was going anywhere near Larson, which had left Bart with the bicycle option. Luckily, the weather was mild, and the traffic was light.

Christmas, for all of its commercial gaiety, can be a lonely time. For some, the season is depressing because those who once made the holiday special are gone. For others, Christmas disappoints simply because it isn't like how it was when they were children. People who grew up decorating real trees will never forgive the inventors of the chillingly cold aluminum version, and those whose childhoods were brightened by beautifully gleaming aluminum trees will never be happy with the ones made of optical fibers. Bart's Christmases had been brightened by Uncle Wade's visits, but except for that the day hadn't amounted to much, so not going "home" for Christmas hadn't bothered him in the slightest. And despite what he had written to Jamaal's mother, he really hadn't wanted to spend Christmas in Devils Elbow either. Every family's Christmas has evolved into something unique to that family, and as new in-laws always discover, stirring a stranger into the recipe will usually give the dish an off flavor. The family's normal Christmas routine is disrupted and despite, or maybe because of, the efforts to make the stranger feel welcome, he or she feels like an intruder. Before Bart had gotten the letter from lawyer Schroder, it wouldn't have occurred to him to spend Christmas at Larson, but at least no one there was going to mess up their own holiday trying to fit him in.

The painted greeting on the town's water tower was starting to fade, but its message was still clear: "Welcome to Larson," it said in large letters, below which it added, "Gateway to..." something. Whatever Larson was the gateway to had been painted over, and the word "Nowhere" added in sloppy black letters. Bart suspected a high school rivalry, but in the vandal's defense Larson really didn't look like the gateway to very much. For the last couple of miles, he had passed some stubbly cornfields and a few houses, and that was all. Judging by how close the houses were to the road, sitting on the porch and watching the cars go by had once counted as entertainment. Now those houses all had satellite dishes, and their porches didn't look like they got much use. A billboard said that Bud's Tire and Auto was ready to handle all his motoring needs, and a smaller one assured him that Caroline's Diner, straight ahead on the right, had the best country breakfast around. Sure enough, just up the road on the right was a one-story building with a gravel parking lot and a sign on the right end of the roof saying *Diner*. It gave the place an off-balance look, but if the word *Caroline's* had ever been on the roof, the blank place was the only sign of it. Still, it looked like the only diner around, so maybe it didn't need a name. Anyway, it was close to lunchtime so Bart decided to give it a try. Behind the counter was an unshaven man in what had probably been a white apron earlier that morning. Bart knew he shouldn't say it, but he couldn't help himself: "You know, you don't look much like a Caroline."

He had half expected a snarl and an order to get the hell out, but instead the man nodded gravely. "I'm going to take that as a compliment," he said." I try to look a little less like a Caroline every day. What'll you have?" He gestured to a menu-board on the wall behind him. In addition to the Country Breakfast, it listed the usual burgers, dogs, and fries, and something called the Country Lunch.

"What's the Country Breakfast?" Bart wanted to know.

"Country-style steak, milk gravy, grits, a cathead biscuit, and coffee," said the cook.

"And the Country Lunch?"

"Barbecue, coleslaw, baked beans, a roll, greens, and a drink."

Bart was curious. "What kind of greens?"

The man gave him a reproving look. "Now really, would you know the difference between turnip greens and creasy greens?" Bart admitted that he wouldn't. "Well then, they're greens, and that's all you need to know." That actually made sense in a cock-eyed sort of way, so Bart ordered the Country Lunch. "What you going to drink?" the man wanted to know.

"I don't know; what goes with barbecue?"

"Beer, but you ain't old enough, so I would say iced tea."

"Kind of early in the day for beer anyway, isn't it?"

"I take it you don't fish."

"No, I never got into it. Name's Bart, by the way." Bart held out his hand.

The man wiped his hand on his apron and shook Bart's. "Arnold. Take a seat, anywhere you like." Arnold poured a big glass of tea, and started assembling a Country Lunch from bins in a steam cabinet. Bart took a stool at the counter, and when the plate was ready, Arnold brought it over, along with a bottle of what looked like mustard. Bart gave the bottle a quizzical look. "That's barbecue sauce, in case you want to juice it up."

"I thought it was mustard."

"No, that there's Carolina Gold sauce; it's how we eat it here. You must be from the other Carolina."

"Yeah, Charlotte, but not anymore."

"Charlotte. Okay, so you're used to red sauce. I've got some, if you want it, but you ought to try out the gold while you're here."

Somebody else came in just then, so Bart was left alone to ponder the subtleties of barbecue sauce. The Country Lunch was a lot better than he had thought it would be, even with the mystery greens. Arnold hadn't brought him a check, so when he was finished he went over to the cash register where Arnold was using his apron to polish a spot on the counter.

"Something else?" Arnold asked. "I've got some nice fried pies, made local."

"No, I need to be on my way. About how far is it to town?"

"Downtown? Maybe a mile." Arnold examined the place he had been polishing, and decided it needed more attention.

"Uh, I guess I need to pay you, then."

"You'd think so, wouldn't you, but Emmett told me if a Bart came in, to put it on his tab. Oh, and he said for me to send you straight on to his office when you finished here. Go to the courthouse square, take a left, then a right, then another left onto South Rutledge. Go one block, then take a right on Wagener for a block and a half and you're there. You'll see his sign."

It took Bart a few seconds to absorb that. "You know Mr. Schroder?" he asked, and immediately realized how lame that was, since the man had called him Emmett.

Arnold grinned. "Son, Larson ain't real big, and this is the only diner in town. I know just about everybody." Plus, he thought, I've played poker with the sorry rascal every week since before you were born, so yeah, you could say I know him.

    The Keowee County Courthouse is not hard to find. It sits in the center of town, where Pickens Street and Rutledge Street would intersect if it weren't for the courthouse square. A two-story, red brick building, its most prominent feature is a dome held aloft by columns. On the lawn in front of the courthouse there is a granite post, two feet by two and about six feet tall, on top of which stands a life-size marble statue of a Confederate soldier. According to the inscription on the block, the statue was placed there by the United Daughters of the Confederacy in 1908. When Bart got there, some ladies who looked like they might have been present for the unveiling were standing around, pointing and gesturing up at the statue while speaking to, or more accurately shouting at, a middle-aged man in a dark uniform. Bart couldn't hear what they were saying, but he could guess the subject: somebody had put a Santa Claus suit on the statue, and they weren't happy about it. This was too good to miss. He rested the bike against a telephone pole and walked over toward the commotion.

    According to its badge, the dark uniform belonged to the Fire Chief. The Chief was doing his best to say something, but while his voice was louder than any one of the ladies, they had the advantage of numbers. It quickly became clear that they were more than unhappy about the Santa suit; the words desecration and sacred memory got a lot of use, but none of the ladies was yielding the floor to any of the others, so the overall effect was total chaos. Finally a large-framed woman with unnaturally black hair elbowed her way to the front of the group and shouted them all down. Then she squared off with the Fire Chief. "Jimmy Perkins," she said, poking a finger at his chest, "you get that ladder truck out here right now and get that abomination off of Deo, and I don't mean maybe." Bart wasn't sure he had heard that right, but when he glanced at the statue's column he saw, right above the UDC inscription, the motto of the Confederacy: Deo Vindice.

Chief Perkins shifted a wad of tobacco from one cheek to the other, turned his head and spat, making a dark brown stain on the light brown grass. "Well Alma, I'll tell you what. You pass the hat and come up with two hundred dollars, and I'll do it, cause that's what it costs the department every time we roll out Engine Number 3, two hundred dollars." He had known Alma Waters since third grade, when she had been God, the Devil, and his teacher, all rolled up in one.

"Now you listen here Jimmy," she said, wagging the finger in his face, "This is an emergency, and I know for a fact the fire department doesn't charge for emergencies. You don't charge to get a cat out of a tree, do you?" The other ladies murmured their agreement.

"Firemen only do that in Disney movies," he snapped. "Real firemen put out fires, and no, we don't charge for that. But Santa, as you may have noticed, is not on fire." Hearing their hero disrespected got the whole gaggle stirred up again, but the Chief had said what he had to say. He shifted his chaw again, spat suspiciously close to Miss Waters' shoe, and walked briskly away. Bart went back to his bicycle, leaving the old ladies to console Private Vindice as best they could.

He remembered the directions Arnold had given him: partway around the square, a block down Rutledge, then right onto Wagener. Sure enough, in front of a nondescript one-story bungalow, there was a sign: Emmett Schroder, Attorney at Law. Across the street was a flat-roofed windowless white brick building whose sign, much larger than lawyer Schroder's, proclaimed it to be The Law Offices of Harley Bishop, LLC. In the Schroder firm's parking lot were two cars; in the lot for The Law Offices of Harley Bishop, there were six. Bart parked his bike and climbed the steps. A little bell above the front door gave out a silvery dingle when the door brushed it, and the woman at the reception desk looked up and smiled. "Oh good, right on time," she said. "More than I can say for Emmett; he got held up in court. Have a seat, he shouldn't be more than a few minutes." She went back to whatever it was she had been doing, which seemed to involve reading a long document and making occasional notes in the margin.

"Uh, ma'am?" Bart said tentatively. The woman looked up. "I don't actually have an appointment, so I'm pretty sure I'm not on time."

The woman looked at him over the top of her glasses. "Well of course you don't have an appointment. Emmett doesn't make appointments on court days. But he bet me a dollar you'd be here around twelve thirty, and I said it would be closer to one. And it is..." she looked at her watch, "twelve fifty. So you're right on time as far as I'm concerned."

"But ...if you don't know who I am, how did you know I'd be here at all, let alone when?" He didn't know which he wanted to know more.

"You are Victor Phillips, except you go by Bart, because who else would you be? We knew you were coming because you wrote Emmett you'd be here for the wake. You live in a dorm at Clemson, and everybody knows Clemson students can't stay in the dorm over winter break, so we figured you would come as soon as exams were over. We didn't know when you would start out, or whether you'd stop at the Diner, but that just made the bet more interesting. Now relax and have a seat; I've got work to finish," which was Bart's introduction to Evelyn Pitman.

Fifteen minutes later, a stocky, out-of-breath man in a rumpled suit came through the door. Evelyn didn't look up from what she was doing; she simply held out her left hand, palm up, and said, "Dollar."

The man looked at Bart. "What time did you get here?"

"Ten 'til one."

"Damn," the man said without heat, taking out his wallet. He extracted a one and laid it on Evelyn's still-open palm. "What took you so long?"

"I would've been here sooner, but I stopped to watch a—I don't know what you'd call it—on the courthouse lawn. There was this statue in a Santa Claus outfit, and a bunch of old ladies, and..." How do you describe something like that?

"Aw, hell, I forgot that was today."

Bart thought about that for a few seconds. "You, uh, knew it was going to happen?"

Emmett Schroder, Esquire—because, as Evelyn would say, who else would he be?—smiled the smile of the wrongly acquitted. "No, of course not. Not that anybody can prove, anyway. Did it get the garden club ladies riled up?"

"Is that who they were? Yeah, they were all upset, and the Fire Chief didn't calm them down any. He wouldn't bring out a ladder truck unless they came up with two hundred dollars."

"Serves them right. Last Spring those same old biddies pestered the city council to build them a rose garden out in front of the fire station, and somehow or other the cost of it came out of Jim Perkins' budget. Well you know what they say about paybacks." He started down the hall, then half-turned and said to Bart, "Come on back; we've got stuff to talk about."

◇◇◇◇◇◇◇◇◇◇◇◇◇◇◇◇●◇◇◇◇◇◇◇◇◇◇◇◇◇◇◇◇◇

Emmett's office had been the den, back when the building had been a house. A fireplace occupied half of one wall, made of bricks that had been painted so many times that they looked slightly melted. In the hearth was a banker box with "Owen appeal" written on it in heavy black letters, on top of which was a cat basket, complete with a prosperous-looking orange cat. The cat stood up, stretched, looked at Bart for a couple of seconds, then curled back up and closed its eyes. "That," Emmett said, "is your great uncle's cat, or, as he put it, it's the cat that he fed. I've gotten stuck with taking care of it. Do you like cats?" he asked hopefully.

"I don't know; I've never been around a cat."

"Neither had Wade, until this one's great grandmother showed up at the cabin."

"It just showed up?"

"Uh-huh. He told me he was sitting by the fire one cold

night when he heard a noise at the door. When he looked outside a big calico cat dashed past him into the cabin. By the time he had closed the door, the cat was curled up on the hearth like it had been there all its life."

Bart had to smile at the thought of his solemn, dignified great uncle being colonized by a stray cat. "Where do you suppose it came from?"

"I expect somebody put it out. People do that. They drive out in the country and leave a dog or a cat, figuring it'll find a home. Usually it'll starve, or freeze to death. I wouldn't have thought anybody'd take one as far as Viney Cove, but apparently somebody did."

"Viney Cove? I would have thought it was Green Cove."

"It was, until it got timbered back in the '20s. Then it grew up all sawbriers and grape vines, and people took to calling it Viney Cove. Since then the trees have grown back and the vines are pretty much gone, but the name stuck. Anyway, about the only thing in the Cove is the cabin, and the road up to the cabin is private, so probably somebody dumped the cat down at the state road and it hiked in."

"So Uncle Wade had a cat. I never knew that. Why didn't he just take it to the animal shelter?"

"Well, even though the old rascal would never say so, I think he liked that cat, and back then they mostly euthanized strays after a day or two. But he always called her Cat; he never would name her."

"He never got her spayed either, obviously," Bart said, looking at the orange cat on the banker box.

"Well you see, he never would admit that she was his cat. Same thing with Orange Cat here. He did get them their shots, though, I'll say that for him. Anyway, so much for cats. You sure you want to stay at the cabin? It gets cold up there in December, and the only heat is the fireplace."

Bart hadn't thought of that. "Is there firewood?"

"I don't know; there likely is, but it may be no-count. There is an axe, though, and since the trust owns the whole Cove,

64

and I'm a trustee, I hereby give you permission to chop and split any tree that strikes your fancy. Good exercise."

From down the hall came Evelyn's voice: "This from a man who gets winded just walking here from the courthouse."

Emmett sighed, shook his head, and rolled his eyes as if to say, you see how I suffer. Then he called down the hall, "Evelyn, would you get the...." He didn't finish the sentence before Evelyn appeared in the doorway.

"The title for the Jeep, the keys for the Jeep, and the keys for the chain and the cabin," she finished for him. "And, since I knew you'd forget it, the graduation present." She handed Bart a box wrapped in heavy brown paper and tied with string. The box was about the right size for a shirt, but when Bart shook it, it gave out a muffled rattle.

"Okay, well then we're good to go," Emmett said.

"What about food?" Evelyn asked.

"Huh?"

"Food. I'll bet you a dollar there's nothing up there but canned soup." She gave Emmett a smug look, "And you know I've got the dollar."

"I can eat soup," Bart volunteered.

Emmett ignored him. "Does canned beef stew count as soup?"

"Of course it does," Evelyn said. "Now, bet or no bet?"

Emmett thought about it. "No bet; you're probably right. We'll stop along the way and pick up something."

She shook her head. "I can just imagine. I think I'd better come along, just to make sure you get some actual food." Before either of the males could say anything, she had gone back up the hall. By the time they had reached the waiting room, a sign had appeared on the front door: "Closed for the afternoon," it said. "Next time, make an appointment."

Emmett had thought he could drop in at a convenience

store, get some hot dogs and buns, maybe a bag of chips, and that would take care of the food issue. Evelyn set him straight on that. "What if it snows? What if he's snowed in three or four days. He can't live on hot dogs and potato chips." Emmett pointed out that he had lived on hot dogs and Cheetos one entire summer when he was in law school. "Yes, and look how you turned out," she said, without elaborating. There was an area known as Oak Grove between Larson and the Cove. It amounted to little more than an intersection, a few houses, and a Baptist church, but it did have a combination grocery store and Post Office where they spent a half hour finding necessaries that Emmett was sure were already up at the cabin, but not sure enough to risk another dollar. They ended up with a buggy load of food, seasonings, toilet paper and, at Bart's request, a fruitcake.

"You actually like fruitcake?" Evelyn asked, making a face.

"I love it; always have," Bart replied. "A good slice of fruitcake and a cold glass of milk is the best snack in the world."

"Ugh," she said. "Christmas tradition?"

"No, but I would have it at school, or at friends' houses."

That it wasn't a tradition didn't surprise Emmett. Wade had told him about visiting Lorraine's house at Christmas, and how there wasn't a tree, or a wreath, or any other sign of the season. It was, he decided, time to change the subject. "Do you remember if Wade ever mentioned anybody named Hamid ibn Issa? I'm supposed to get something to him, and I don't have any idea how to contact him."

Evelyn said, "I thought you were going to ask Wade about that."

Emmett frowned. "I did. He said don't worry about it, that it would take care of itself. Well, so far it hasn't. So," he turned back toward Bart, "do you know anything about him?"

"Uncle Wade never mentioned him. He didn't talk much about himself."

"He told me a little. He was in North Africa with Operation Torch during the Second World War, but he didn't go into detail. Most of the guys I knew who came back from that war didn't talk much about it. I think maybe they had to do things civilians wouldn't understand. Anyway, he was in Algeria, or maybe Tunisia. When he was telling me what he wanted in his will, he called this Hamid his old friend, and if they met during Torch, he really would be old, assuming he's even alive."

"What are you supposed to give him?"

"A bell, one of two bells he said he was leaving. He didn't say where they were, either. That's another reason I wanted to go to the cabin, in case he left them up there."

◇◇◇◇◇◇◇◇◇◇◇◇◇◇◇◇◇●◇◇◇◇◇◇◇◇◇◇◇◇◇◇◇◇◇

A couple of miles past Oak Grove, they came to a bridge with a sign that said Green Creek. Just across the bridge, on the right, was a gravel road, blocked at the edge of the woods by a chain strung between two posts.

"Not much to discourage visitors," Bart said

"Normally you'd be right," Emmett replied, "but people around here know not to go past the chain."

"Hmph. That sure wouldn't work in Charlotte."

"It doesn't work here either, usually," Emmett replied. "But I let it be known I would take it personal if somebody broke in there, and since I've defended most of the thieves around here, they don't want to piss me off. They go in here and steal something, they know they'll either have to take the public defender, or else pay Harley Bishop. Thieves are lazy, but they're not stupid."

"Some are," Evelyn said from the back seat. "I know your client list, remember?"

"Hmm," Emmett thought about that. "Okay, let me rephrase. Most thieves are no stupider than the average, but even the dimwits know not to crap in their own mess kits."

◇◇◇◇◇◇◇◇◇◇◇◇◇◇◇◇◇●◇◇◇◇◇◇◇◇◇◇◇◇◇◇◇◇◇

The cabin had a musty smell, but a little airing out helped with that. It had power, but no telephone. Bart had a cell phone that he had bought with some of his SAT bribe money. At Clemson it worked all right, but in the cove it got no bars at all. After Emmett and Evelyn had gone, he hiked up one of the side slopes and was finally able to get one bar. He wouldn't have bothered, but he had promised Jamaal he would call when he got settled in, and so there he was, standing on a rock outcropping at dusk, trying to hear his roommate over occasional gusts of wind. "Tell me about the Jeep," Jamaal was saying. "What year? What color? Details!"

Jamaal was a car buff; Bart wasn't. He could tell a Jeep from a Volkswagen, but the fine distinctions had never interested him. "Well, it's a 1972 CJ-5, sort of a brownish yellow." That was about all he knew.

"Sweet. For a Jeep, that's a classic," Jamaal said. "What shape is it in?"

"Uh, pretty good, I guess. It doesn't look like it's been wrecked."

"No, I mean, is there play in the ball joints? Is the valve cover leaking oil?" There was no answer from Bart's end. If Jamaal had inspected the Jeep, he would have known everything from what the oil smelled like to whether the shocks were mushy. This wouldn't do at all. "Okay, let's start with the basics. What engine does it have?"

That one Bart knew: "Gasoline engine." That got a groan from Jamaal, which Bart ignored. "I don't even know if it runs. The battery's dead, and Mr. Schroder didn't have jumper cables. He's bringing a charger up tomorrow."

"So you're stranded in a cabin in the woods with no telephone. I've seen movies that start out like that, and none of them are comedies, if you catch my drift. What are you going to do when Leatherface shows up? Ask him for a head start?"

Three months earlier, Bart wouldn't have had a clue who Leatherface was, but Jamaal had enough horror movies to have his own film festival, and by now Bart had seen at least half of them. "You know, I could have gone all night without thinking about that. Thanks, friend."

"Anytime. But seriously, what are you going to do if there's a problem?"

"Well, first of all, I'll keep the door locked, and close the shutters."

"That seems like a solid plan to you, does it?"

"No, seriously, this place is built like a bank vault."

"It's a cabin, right? Leatherface has a chainsaw, remember?" Apparently, Jamaal hadn't exhausted the subject.

"Yes it's a cabin, but no, it isn't a log cabin, like I thought it would be. It was built before the Civil War, out of rocks, big rocks. Mr. Schroder said the shutters were added during the War, something to do with bushwhackers. Anyway, the windows are too narrow for somebody to slip in, and the shutters are sheet iron, kind of rusty but still in one piece. The door is oak, and it's about two inches thick. Leatherface better have a real good chainsaw, is all I've got to say. I'm just glad Uncle Wade kept the hinges oiled, cause that's one heavy door."

"Sounds good, long as the boogeyman doesn't set fire to the roof," Jamaal said, way too cheerfully.

"The roof is made of slate," Bart told him. Then, hoping to change the subject, he added, "Oh, and there's water. It comes from a spring up the hill somewhere. There's even a water heater, and a big old claw foot bathtub. And yes, I know what you're thinking: there is an indoor toilet."

"That's good. Did I ever tell you about the time I went into this outhouse...?"

"Yes, you did," Bart cut him off. There are places you particularly don't want to find a black widow spider, and there are stories you really don't need to hear twice. The gusts of wind were getting harder, and colder. Bart was starting to wish he'd brought a warmer jacket. "Hey, I've got to go. I'm freezing my tail off up here on a rock, and I've got a nice fire going down in the cabin. Talk to you later."

"Yeah man, go get warm. Let me know how the Jeep runs."

Between bicycling from Clemson to Larson, then hiking up to the outcropping and back, it had been a tiring day. Bart heated up some of the canned soup that had, in fact, been the cabin's only food supply, and then he went to bed. The next morning, after fixing himself some of the bacon and eggs that Evelyn had insisted they get, he opened Uncle Wade's graduation present. It was a jigsaw puzzle, but a really odd one. The box said Stave, a brand he didn't recognize, and a sticker on the box said "custom." The pieces were quarter-inch-thick wood, beautifully cut but very oddly shaped. Taped to the outside of the box was a note, in Wade's shaky writing: "I believe you can do it." It was only after he had worked on it all morning, only to find that the pieces could go together more than one way, that he realized how hard the puzzle really was. Maybe he would have it done before he had to go back to Clemson, but the more he worked at it, only to find that it had tricked him again, the less sure he was.

There was no telling how long the Jeep had sat there in the shed behind the cabin, but except for the dead battery, there didn't seem to be anything wrong with it. Jamaal had told Bart to sniff the gas cap to see if the gas had gone stale. "If it's gone bad, there'll be a kind of sweet smell," is how he had put it, but Bart didn't smell anything at all, and tapping on the underside of the tank confirmed that it was empty. Emmett had had it titled to Bart, and the next afternoon, along with a charger, he had brought two five-gallon cans of gasoline and a new tag. Once Bart had gotten the hood open, they cranked it until it caught, and then it ran fine. To Bart, the engine looked like an engine ought to look: there were wires and hoses, and a couple of belts. He thought Jamaal would probably want more detail than that, but details would have to wait until he got the Jeep to Clemson.

Lorraine had consented to Bart taking Driver's Training because it didn't cost her anything ("but don't think for a minute that you're going to be driving *my* car, young man"). His group had driven around Charlotte in a cheap four-door sedan with "Student Driver" warnings posted front and rear, but he had never driven a stick shift. He knew more or less how what the clutch did, and the knob on the stick showed where the gears were, but between theory and practice there is a gap, and bridging that gap generated a lot of gear-grinding noises. After a few miles he more or less had the hang of the higher gears, and when he got back to Clemson, he only stalled the Jeep at two intersections. That got him honked at, but he didn't care. He was eighteen and he had wheels. Life was good.

Chapter Eight

The Friday prayers were well attended, which was always flattering, but in truth the attendees were not nearly as important as the television cameras. The television audience was what truly mattered, and it was for their benefit that the Imam's entrance had been scripted. Imam Muhammad was not a Bedouin. The one time he had ridden a camel, it had tried to bite him, but today he swept into the mosque in the flowing robes of the desert, as though he really had been raised in a tent. His sermon was a great success. In beautiful, almost poetic Arabic he had denounced the wickedness of the House of War, the Muslim term for the non-Muslim world, and he had spoken in graphic terms of the eternal torment awaiting idolaters. He never actually said the idolaters were Roman Catholic, or Greek Orthodox, or Hindu, but at one time or another he mentioned crucifixes, and icons, and animal-headed statutes as examples of what he meant. His listeners had heard all this before, or variations of it, but today he added a new example: the veneration of the tombs of certain Sufi notables. Honoring the bodies of those persons, he said, and making pilgrimages to their shrines, could perhaps be seen as a form of idolatry. He made no special point of it, and after that one mention he had gone on to other subjects, but the program had a schedule, and the schedule said it was time to mention the Sufis. Over the next weeks, he would make other references to them, and to the issue of tolerating idolatry, and he would first suggest and later insist that the toleration of sin is itself a sin. Once that point had been firmly made, and the people had dealt with the Sufis, it would be time to compare the Sufi shrines to certain other places, places considered holy by the Shi'ites. Before very long, the entire Sunni world would be watching his sermons, either televised or recorded, and then he would tell them what God wanted them to do next.

"The problem is trivial," said the tall man in the dark suit, "and the solution is obvious: ignore it. Why are we even discussing this?" The tall man's name was Murad, and he was speaking to his brother.

"Have you read the article?"

"I skimmed it. Some American disapproves of father's sermons. Surely that is no surprise, and just as surely, it is no cause for concern. I may even point to the article as proof that father is worrying the Crusaders. You are becoming a woman, Fareed."

Not for the first time, Fareed considered whether it would take one shot or two from his little Walther pistol to take the sneer off of Murad's face. If only they were not brothers, he thought. Perhaps one day he would learn that one of them was adopted, and then there would be a settling of accounts. Until then, he must wear the mask of acceptance. "Would you be more concerned," he asked, "if the writer were not a Crusader? If he were, that is to say, a Believer?"

"I do not care what he says he is. The people see all Americans as Crusaders, and that is how they will see this scribbler."

"Then suppose that he is not American. Suppose that he is Turkish."

That got Murad's attention. "I might be interested, in that case, except that, as I recall, the person makes his living teaching at an American university. That connection should be enough to discredit any opinion he has."

"Do you think so?" Fareed had played enough poker at MIT to know when it was time to show his hole card, and he showed it now. "Then suppose that this Turkish teacher is our father's own brother. Do you think our people will discount that?"

"Uncle Enver? He wrote that rubbish?" Murad's voice had lost its tone of cool detachment.

Not so smug now, are you, Fareed thought. "Perhaps," he said softly, "it would be better next time to do more than skim what I bring you. If you missed the name, what else did you miss? Did you see the editor's note, saying that this was only the first part of a two-part article? Let me tell you what Part Two is likely to say. That father is not really an Arab, and that his name is not Muhammad, but Mehmed, and that father's sons, you and I, are arms dealers. Uncle Enver knows all that, or had you forgotten? You know how that will make the program look as well as I do." Fareed did not want to elaborate on that theme, because more and more, the program had begun to look to him like a scheme by Murad to stir up a war between the sects. Murad had been buying huge quantities of weapons from eastern Europe, more than enough to equip his father's followers. Fareed had asked his brother if he planned to equip both sides, but Murad had simply smiled and said nothing.

Murad picked up the article, which Fareed had copied from of the Middle East Journal's winter edition. "The Rats in the Walls of the House of Peace" was its title, by Enver Ziya, PhD, Clemson University. "Clemson," Murad muttered. "That is in New Jersey, is it not?"

Fareed shook his head. "No, you are thinking of Princeton. Clemson is in South Carolina." He had had to look up the location, but Murad need not know that. Murad passed himself off as being oh so educated and urbane, but to Fareed's way of thinking, his own degree from MIT was incomparably better than Murad's from Cairo University. All Murad seemed to have learned at Cairo was to speak Arabic with an Egyptian accent, although Fareed had to agree, reluctantly, that an Egyptian accent was an asset. The old United Arab Republic, that brief marriage of Egypt and Syria, had died for any number of reasons, but one symptom of its last illness had been the habit of the Egyptian film industry of giving respectable people Egyptian accents, while the villains and fools had always seemed to sound Syrian.

"When is the second part of the article supposed to come out?" Murad asked.

"The Journal publishes quarterly, so the next edition will be in the spring."

"If something were to happen to him between now and then," Murad mused, "would they still publish it? Probably they would." He stared off into space, seemingly oblivious to his brother's presence.

Fareed waited, but when Murad showed no sign of coming back into the moment, he broke the silence. "Did you seriously just think about having Uncle Enver killed? What kind of nephew are you?"

Murad looked at Fareed and said nothing for a full ten seconds. "The program is obligatory; the Mufti says so." That was true, up to a point. A Mufti's job is to give opinions on questions of Islamic law, but his opinion could often be guided by how a question was phrased. In this instance, Murad had asked the Mufti whether a Muslim who turned to idol worship was an apostate—one who has abandoned the true faith—and the answer had of course been yes. Murad's next question had been, what does the law say about apostasy, and the answer had been that an apostate must be killed. He had very carefully not asked whether the veneration of shrines actually was idol worship. "That the program will involve the deaths of many, both Believers and Infidels, is a fact to be faced," he continued, in a voice that was strangely soft and uninflected. "The writer of that article, uncle or not, is an enemy of the program, and is thus an enemy of God. If he has to be among those who perish, then he has brought it upon himself. So no, the fact that we are related does not trouble me in the slightest." And if the program requires it, he thought, the fact that you and I are related will trouble me even less.

He might as well have spoken that thought out loud, because Fareed understood it perfectly well. The day will come, dear brother, he thought, the day will come. Two shots, just to be sure. "With all respect to the Mufti, I think it is a mistake to make a martyr out of a mere critic," he said, "and that would be true even if he were not father's brother."

Murad knew Fareed was right, but he still disliked being lectured by his younger brother. That went against the natural order of things. "Perhaps father could talk to him."

Fareed shook his head "Father would have to read the article first," he pointed out. "Do you foresee any conversation going well after he has done that?"

Murad ignored the question. "Will you at least try to be helpful? Does Enver have a wife?"

"Father once mentioned that his brother had a wife. She died in childbirth, though."

"Childbirth? Did the child survive?" Murad was gazing into space again.

"Yes, brother, we have a cousin, named...Dilara? Yes, that is it: Dilara Ziya. You actually met her, last year at Oran."

"I don't recall her. Was she in any of the photos? I wonder, could Uncle Enver be...persuaded, let us say...to withdraw the rest of the article, if his daughter's wellbeing depended on it?"

"So now you plan to harm a cousin you did not even know you had?"

"You barely knew her name, and now you are deeply concerned for her? You really are turning into a woman, Fareed. Go, add up some figures or whatever it is that you do. There are people I need to call." Murad made a shooing motion with his hand.

The shooing motion finally decided Fareed. The answer was neither one bullet nor two. His little Walther held seven in the magazine and one in the chamber. Eight. That should be enough, if the moment ever came. And he was increasingly sure that it would.

Chapter Nine

Bart had wondered how long he would be at the cabin before boredom set in. He had always thought of nights as quiet times, despite the distant sounds of traffic, trains, and barking dogs. At the Cove, he came to understand what true quiet was. During the day, there were a few bird noises, and some skittering sounds that were probably squirrels, but at night, it was quiet, and it was dark. There was a blanket chest at the foot of the cabin's one bed, and in it Bart found a feather comforter. Wrapped in it, he was able to spend some time each night in a rocker on the cabin's front porch, just looking at the stars and thinking about nothing. Then he would go inside and work on the puzzle.

Saying that Stave makes devious puzzles is like saying Ferrari makes sporty cars: it is true, but so incomplete as to count as false. This particular puzzle had a picture, or at least a design, on both sides, but in color and style, the two sides didn't actually differ all that much. It also had pieces that could fit in different places, but putting one in the wrong place led to a dead end, eventually. More than once, he had had to break apart some group that had taken him an hour to assemble. It would help if there were corner pieces, but there weren't. Two pieces would come together and form a right angle, but until they did, they looked like any other pieces. Clearly, this was going to take a while, but with nothing else to do at night he thought he just might solve the puzzle before he went back to school.

The first breakthrough came when he noticed that one of the pieces had a mark on it, a short segment of ballpoint pen ink. He looked for other pieces like that, and found three, and they fit together. The marks were the outline of a bell. Now he had a starting place, and by the time the sun came up, he had enough of a group assembled that he knew he had to call Emmett. He couldn't call from the cabin, but since he was getting tired of his own cooking anyway, there was an obvious solution. A half hour later, he was parking the Jeep in front of the Diner.

"What would you have, sir?" Arnold asked, in the worst

British accent Bart had ever heard. Receiving only a surprised silence in reply, he added in his usual upstate drawl, "I'm supposed to play a Brit in the Community Theater's winter play, and I'm practicing the accent."

"What play?"

"*The Importance of Being Earnest*. I play the butler."

"Merriman? Good role. Not a lot of lines to memorize, and half of them are *Yes, Miss*."

Arnold raised an eyebrow. "Now how the hell do you know that?"

Bart grinned. "I directed *Earnest* last year for drama class. It's a good play."

"If you say so; kind of wordy if you ask me, except for my part. Anyway, what'll you have?"

"Coffee, and the Country Breakfast." He took the coffee over to a booth, and called Emmett's office. "Ms Pitman? This is Bart Phillips. Does Mr. Schroder have a few minutes open this morning?"

"Oh, let's see. He's got some people coming in at 10:30, but until then he belongs to whoever walks in the door. And just so you know, if you call me Ms Pitman again, you go on my list. My name is Evelyn. Are we clear?"

"Yes, ma'am."

"Good."

When Arnold brought the food, Bart asked him, "Do you know anything about Jeeps?"

"Not a whole lot. I know somebody who does, though." He called out toward a booth at the other end of the diner. "Bud? You got a minute? Somebody I want you to meet." A lanky older man got up and joined them. "Bart, Bud." To Bud, he said, "Bart here is friend of Emmett's. He needs to know something about Jeeps."

Bud gave Bart the once-over and apparently decided that he would do. "Jeeps in general," he asked, "or that one in particular?" he pointed out the window to where Bart had parked.

"That one," Bart said.

Bud slid into the booth where Arnold had been. "Arnold,

I'm going to need some more coffee." To Bart he said, "That's old man Dawson's Jeep, ain't it?" Bart told him it was. "Thought so. A parent knows his own child. Do you know anything about her?"

"It took me ten minutes to get the hood open," Bart admitted, "so I guess you could say I don't."

"Good," Bud grunted. "Less to unlearn. How'd you end up with it, if you don't mind me asking." Bart told him. "Well then, this'll be easier to explain, since you already know your uncle had some odd notions. You see, there's not much about that Jeep that ain't odd. She started out life as a regular, stock CJ-5. Fellow over in Easley bought her new, used her for camping. Well, he passed on, and his widow left the Jeep out in the barn for a few years, until their boy was old enough to drive. Boy was named Leroy, as I recall. Anyway, Leroy thought the Jeep was too plain, so he got a paint shop to put him some flames coming out the wheel wells. Then he decided that if it looked fast, it ought to be fast, and it wasn't. It came from the factory with an inline six, not a bad engine but not a powerhouse either. Leroy took her to some jackleg mechanic who told him the way to hot her up was to drop in a blower." That got him a blank look. "Sorry, a supercharger, an air pump that blows more air through the carb than the engine can suck in on its own."

"Did it work?"

"That would kind of depend on what you mean by work. It did give her more power, no question about that. Leroy wore out a clutch showing his friends he could bring smoke with all four wheels, but the troopers around Easley got to know him too well, and he couldn't stand any more points on his license, so he calmed down. Well, summer came, and he figured it was time to take her down to Myrtle and show her off. You know that stretch of I-20 from Columbia to Florence? No? Well, it's long, and straight, and you don't never see a trooper on it. I don't know why they even bother to put up speed limit signs. Anyway, Leroy was cruising along down there, and the redneck in him couldn't stand it any more; he just had to know what she would do." Bud chuckled.

"Let me guess: he raced somebody."

"No, but he did something almost as stupid. He took the Stanley challenge."

"Uh, the what?"

"It's one of the great car myths, except maybe it ain't a myth; nobody really knows. Supposedly, the Stanley brothers offered a big chunk of cash to anybody who would drive a Stanley Steamer at full throttle for ten seconds. And supposedly, nobody ever took them up on it. Probably Leroy never heard of it, but he took it anyway."

"Did he wreck?"

"No, not exactly, except for the motor; he wrecked hell out of that. Those old AMC sixes weren't designed for the kind of pressure you get with a blower. He had the pedal down for about eight seconds before the first rod broke, and after that it got ugly. I mean parts coming up through the hood ugly. Leroy had her towed back to Easley, and I bought her for parts. I don't know how, but Arnold heard about it," he said loud enough for Arnold to hear.

Arnold looked up from stacking plates and shrugged. "Hey, people tell me stuff."

"Uh-huh. Well anyway, Arnold here knew old man Dawson was looking for something with four-wheel drive, and that's how I came to meet your uncle. By the time we were done, that Jeep had...well, the best word for it is mutated."

Bart was almost afraid to ask. "Mutated...into what?"

"Well, let's just say she's kind of like one of them wolf-dog mixes. She'll behave just fine if you don't startle her. I gave her a stronger transmission, a better transfer case, a bigger clutch, and a whole lot better engine."

"Can you tell me about the engine? My roommate asked me what it had and I didn't know what to tell him."

"Tell him it's a short-block Chevy V8, with EFI and HEI."

"I'm sorry, what are those?"

"You weren't kidding about not knowing anything, were you. Electronic fuel injection and high-energy ignition. Don't stomp on the gas unless you mean it, cause she'll jump like a scalded dog."

"Uh, can a Jeep really handle that kind of power?"

Bud smiled knowingly. "Not usually, no, but I worked on that too. The side frame rails are full of lead shot, set in epoxy, and the suspension is tuned real nice, if I do say so. She's a little heavy for a Jeep, but she ain't gonna roll over."

Bart had to ask. "Do you know how fast she'll go?"

Bud's smile turned into a grin. "Yeah I do." Then he gathered up his coffee cup and slipped out of the booth.

Bart called after him, "Uh, how fast?"

Bud turned back toward him. "Oh, you mean in numbers. Couldn't say; the speedometer don't go past ninety."

"It'll be just a minute," Evelyn told Bart. From down the hall came a flushing sound, followed by the squeak of a door hinge. "Okay, go on back."

Emmett was just settling back in his chair when Bart got to the back office. The orange cat, which had been curled up on top of a filing cabinet, stood up and stretched, first backward, then forward, before dropping onto the floor with a thump. As soon as Bart sat down, the cat jumped in his lap and curled up. "It's a sign," Emmett said. "It tells me you're meant to have him." He didn't sound very hopeful.

Bart shook his head. "Can't have pets in the dorm," he said, absently stroking the cat. The cat gave a low-pitched purr, but otherwise it didn't move.

"So, how do you like life in the wilderness?"

"I've found stuff to do," Bart replied, "and I think I've found something else." He explained about the puzzle, and the little bell-shaped drawing. "I've been working from there outward, and I've gotten enough done to see that it's a sort of map, or at least that side of it is. I took a picture of what I've done so far." He gave Emmett his phone.

Emmett studied the picture for a full minute. "Uh-huh," he finally said. "Yeah, okay, but where...oh I see. Well I'll be damned."

"You know where it is?"

"I think so. I be surer if there were some more landmarks, but I think it's right here in Larson. You see here, there's a little oil lamp?" Bart nodded. "And right near it, a little fur hat? If the lamp is the courthouse..." he lapsed back into silence.

"Wait a minute. Why would an oil lamp mean the courthouse?"

"Because of what's up on top."

Bart tried to remember. "It's a dome."

"No, it's a dome on stilts, what architects call a lantern. Lantern, lamp. I like it. And so, if the fur hat is a Santa Claus reference, you know, the Confederate statue, that gives us the map's orientation."

"No, that can't be right. Uncle Wade was dead before the Santa suit got put on the statue, so he wouldn't have had them put it on the puzzle."

Emmett pursed his lips, as if choosing his words carefully. "It is possible," he said, "that Wade knew about the Santa suit well in advance. It is even possible that some of his friends put it on the statue. I am only speculating, you understand, but all of those things are possible. What I do know is that if the lamp is the courthouse lantern, and if the hat represents Santa, then the bell shape would be..." he went over to his desk and opened the phone book to a map of Larson. "Uh-huh, that makes sense. I should have thought of that. It's the old Hutton mill." He rummaged around in his desk drawer until he found a pair of keys on a ring with a tag. "Evelyn? Cancel my 10:30. I think I'm about to have one less thing to worry about."

◊◊◊◊◊◊◊◊◊◊◊◊◊◊◊●◊◊◊◊◊◊◊◊◊◊◊◊◊◊◊

The old mill was the only building on its block. Two stories tall and built of red brick, it had originally had windows, tall ones with shallow brick arches. Somebody had bricked them all in a long ago, but they hadn't bothered to match the new bricks to the old, and the effect was not attractive. They parked around back, at the loading dock. A sign there had once proudly proclaimed, *Hutton Steam Cotton Company*. The sign and the pride had both faded, and the sign had been joined by a newer one that said, *No Trespassing*. "You can ignore that," Emmett said as they walked around to the front of the mill. "The trust owns it; bought it a while back."

"What would the trust want with an old mill?"

"We don't want it; nobody wants it. It's stood empty for years. We're going to have the fire department do a practice burn on it one day, then we'll clear the lot and sell it." Emmett put a key into the office door's lock and tried to turn it.

"It looks like you'd lose money doing that," Bart said.

"Of course we lose money; a trust is supposed to lose money, or at least spend it. I only remember one time we didn't lose money, and that was a pure fluke. We bought a warehouse that stood about two blocks from here. We were all set to burn it when Calvin noticed something about it. Except for the outer walls, all of it—floors, columns, everything—was full-cut pre-blight chestnut. Cabinet shop over in Greenville paid us a bundle for it. This one," he looked up at the old mill, "we'll lose money on, but the town ends up with one less eyesore, and that's the sort of thing Wade wanted the trust to do." He tried the other key, which worked.

The office was empty, and dark. Emmett flipped the wall switch, and looked surprised when a light came on. "Hmph," he grunted. "Power's supposed to be off. I'll have to check on that." At the back of the office was a door that led into the main part of the building. Emmett led the way. "In here is where the big machines were." He felt by the door for another light switch, found it, and flipped it. "Nothing here now, of course," he said, then found he was wrong. Standing in front of them was a half-naked man holding a broken pool cue like a club. They stood there for almost a count of ten, until Emmett broke the silence. "Floyd, what in the hell are you doing here?"

Floyd, as it turned out, was living there. In a corner of the big room was a bedroll, a hotplate, an ice chest and a radio. It reminded Bart of several of the rooms in his dorm. "Becky caught one of her moods," Floyd explained, "and when she's like that there's no living with her." Emmett asked if Becky's mood might have included a protective order, and Floyd said yeah, it might have, but that she would drop it like she always did if he stayed out of her hair for a while. "I was sleeping under the loading platform. Well one day up by the courthouse I saw old Doc Dawson, and he asked how I was doing, and I told him, and he said I could camp in here. And I really appreciated that, cause it was real cold out. He even got the power turned on for me. All he asked was that I keep an eye on the place, and not make a mess." He gestured proudly at his corner. There were a few empty cans, but they were stacked neatly against the wall. It was, Bart thought, actually neater than a lot of dorm rooms.

"What were you supposed to keep an eye out for?" Emmett asked.

"Make sure nobody broke in and messed with his stuff," Floyd told him. "You know, like bums and stoners and all." Bart thought Floyd himself looked a lot like a bum or a stoner, but this didn't seem like a good time to bring that up.

Emmett raised an eyebrow. "The stuff he didn't want messed with, do you know where it is?" Other than what Floyd had in his corner, the room was bare.

Floyd shook his head. "Mr. Schroder, you've always done right by me, but Doc Dawson said nobody, and even though you're somebody..." He trailed off, not quite sure how to bridge the gap between nobody and somebody.

"Floyd," Emmett said, "you do know that Dr. Dawson passed away earlier this month, don't you?"

"I knew he hadn't been around in a while, but I didn't know why. Gee, that's too bad."

"Well it is, that's a fact," Emmett nodded agreement. "But I have to do his estate, and that means I have to get his belongings together, so let's start over. Where is his stuff?"

Floyd looked either thoughtful or confused, it was hard to tell, then he seemed to come to a decision. "It's upstairs," he said finally. "Freight elevator's through there." He pointed to a wide door. "Only it's locked, and I don't have a key."

Emmett took out the key that hadn't fit the office door. "I'll bet I do."

The top floor had once been the mill's warehouse. Now it mostly held broken furniture, old ledger books, and heaps of cotton that had probably been in bales before the mice got into them. The debris had been shoved to one end of the room, and in the cleared space was a lumpy shape covered by a dusty tarp. Among the things under the tarp was a church bell, strapped to a pallet, and beside it a little wood box, about ten inches on each side. The box's lid, Bart noticed, was carved with swirling curves and squiggles. That wasn't all, though. Six large crates stood in a row, all marked *Zambelli*. One of the crates had an envelope stuck to it with a thumbtack, bearing the words "For Emmett," in Wade's shaky writing. Emmett read what was in the envelope, read it again, then chuckled. "Yeah," he said softly. "Yeah, I can do that."

Chapter Ten

The man in the white shirt was used to talking to crowds, and he didn't need a microphone to do it. In his best pulpit voice he called out, "How many of you came here to hear a sermon? Raise your hands." A number of people laughed, but no hands were raised.

From the other end of the front table boomed the voice of Emmett Schroder, at the volume he usually reserved for the courtroom, "Let the record show that the motion dies for lack of a second." The laughter became more widespread.

The man in the white shirt waited for the chuckling to die down. "Much as it pains me to admit it, brother Schroder is right, so you need not worry. I am here today, not as preacher, but as a friend of the late Wade Dawson. As are you all." That drew a couple of amens from the crowd. "I knew Wade well. He was a gentleman, in the old sense of the word. He was also probably the best educated man I ever knew, but he once told me his education had chiefly taught him how little he really did know. He was a generous man, but you won't see his name on any donor list, unless you count 'Anonymous' as a name. He never wanted credit for what he did, but over the years I noticed that if I mentioned a need to Wade, 'Anonymous' usually took care of it. Jim tells me that when the fire trucks needed tires, tires the department couldn't afford, 'Anonymous' took care of that too. Wade was not, I have to admit, a religious man, not in the usual sense, but he wasn't an atheist either; he simply had his own views, and he lived by them. Friends and neighbors, Wade Dawson loved this community, and for him 'love' was a verb, something you do, not just something you say. He was a good man, and I for one will miss him." He raised his glass, which contained ginger ale. "And so, a toast: To Wade!"

"To Wade!" responded the crowd, whose glasses for the most part did not contain ginger ale. Nobody there had ever been to a wake, and they hadn't known what to expect. Emmett had never been to a wake either, but he had a notion it wasn't supposed to be sad, and since he was in charge, it wasn't going to be. What Wade's friends had found when they got to the county fairground was an old-fashioned pig picking, complete with beer kegs and a bluegrass band. Arnold had roasted the pig all day, and now as dusk came on, everybody was getting into the spirit of the thing, which was nothing at all like a funeral service. When the preacher had given his toast, Emmett gave the band a nod, their cue for one last song, a bluegrass version of "I'll Fly Away." Before it was done, the crowd was singing right along: *When I die, Hallelujah, by and by, I'll fly away.*

Emmett leaned over toward Jim Perkins. "Your boys all ready?"

"Anytime you like," the Fire Chief replied. "Just say the word. You sure this is legal?"

"Absolutely. I'll need a minute or two, then I'll give you the go-ahead." It was getting dark, and the air had a definite nip to it. It was almost time. At a signal from Emmett, two burly men came forward, and picked up a wooden beam that had lain unnoticed at the edge of the crowd. They took the beam over to a box that had been serving as a table for the beans and slaw, then lifted the box out of the way to reveal a gleaming bronze bell, easily a foot and a half tall, which they hooked to the beam before carrying it to the front table. Emmett had borrowed a gavel from the courthouse, and now he pulled it out of his coat pocket. Without further ceremony, he gave the bell a good whack with the gavel, and the resulting sound quieted the crowd better than a bailiff could have. Many bells, particularly large bells, do not ring with a pure note; they sound something like "Baw-ung." The bell that hung between the two big men gave out a pure, sweet "Bong." Emmett rang it once more, then nodded to the men, who put the bell back where they had gotten it. He had the crowd's attention. "As Executor of the estate of the late Wade Dawson," he said, "I now deliver to Preacher Rayburn the bell that Wade left to the First Baptist Church of Oak Grove. Come on back up here, Preacher," he gestured to the stunned-looking man in the white shirt. "I asked Wade about this particular gift, and here is what he told me: 'I don't always agree with the preacher, but his motives are pure and that counts for a lot more than people think'."

The preacher walked slowly back to the front table. When he got there he said, "I am seldom at a loss for words, but this is…" He paused and collected himself. "Our old bell was put in when the church was built, back in '22. Some of you may not have known it ever had one, because there hasn't been a bell at First Baptist since our fifty-year anniversary, when the boy pulling the bell rope pulled it too hard, and broke the bell. I know, because I was that boy."

He probably had more to say, but Emmett took advantage of the pause and stood up. "There is one last detail," he called out. He nodded to Jim Perkins, who said something into a radio. At the edge of the fairground, the pallets from the Hutton mill had been unpacked, and their contents arranged according to a diagram that had come with the shipment. There was a muted "whump," and the first of the big Zambelli skyrockets streaked upward, soon to be joined by others, until the night sky was full of fire and sparkles. As the grand finale reached its climax the largest rocket in the shipment took off, ending in a shower of colors that went on for almost ten seconds. In a low voice, Emmett said, "Scatter ashes: check." There was about an inch of beer left in his glass, and now he hoisted it to the sky. "Good bye, old friend," he said, and tossed it back.

It was starting to get chilly. Emmett had stayed to see that everything got cleaned up, and the operation was about finished. The men he had hired were loading the last of the empty kegs into the back of their pickup. Bart had hung back too, since there hadn't been much chance to talk during the festivities. "I just wanted to thank you for giving Uncle Wade a grand send-off," he was saying to Emmett when two men approached them out of the darkness. One was Preacher Rayburn.

"Emmett, I've got to run, but before I do there's somebody

here who wants to meet you."

The young man with the preacher was shorter than the average, and a little darker. "The imam—I am sorry, the preacher?—saw me sitting alone, and was kind enough to explain what was happening. The proceeding was not exactly what I was expecting." He gestured to his clothing, a dark business suit. "I had read about American funerals, and was expecting something altogether different."

"The deceased was altogether different, too, and this was his idea," Emmett said. "What can I do for you?"

"I had wished to speak with a member of the Dawson family, and because you seemed to be in charge, I assumed you were such a relative."

"I am not," Emmett said, "but Bart here is his great nephew."

The man turned to Bart and bowed slightly. "For myself, my father and my grandfather, let me express our sadness at the passing of Mr. Dawson. It is our sincere hope that God will find pleasure in your great uncle."

Bart tried to think of something solemn to say in reply, but Emmett spoke first. "Would either your father or your grandfather be named Hamid, by any chance?"

The young man's face brightened in a smile. "Grandfather is indeed Hamid, son of Issa. Do you know him?"

"I have never met him, but Mr. Dawson mentioned him as an old friend."

"Grandfather has often mentioned Mr. Dawson, as well. They were indeed friends, starting a long time ago. When grandfather got the telegram, it was his wish to come here himself, but he is too frail for the journey, so the honor fell upon me."

"The telegram?" Emmett asked.

"Yes. Mr. Dawson sent grandfather a telegram, inviting him to this service."

"You didn't think that was at all odd?"

"I thought it was very odd, but grandfather apparently did not. 'There are things that old men sometimes know,' he told me."

Bart found that surprising, but Emmett seemed to accept it. "Mr. Dawson gave me the duty of delivering something to your grandfather. If you could take it back with you, I would be very grateful."

"Certainly, I am honored by the task. Will it fit into the boot of the car?"

"It will," said Emmett. He walked toward his own car, and returned a minute later with the small, ornamented box from the Hutton mill, which he handed to Ahmed.

"Thank you. I will make sure that grandfather receives it. Do you know what is in the box? The persons at the airport may ask."

"I know that it's a bell," Emmett said. "And I know that I was told to give it to your grandfather. Beyond that, I can't say. Perhaps the writing on the box will help."

Ahmed was holding the box almost reverently. "The writing is highly stylized; the letters are entwined in artistic ways which make it difficult to read. I will need better light before I can even hazard a guess. May I open it?"

Emmett shrugged. "I don't see why not. If you're going to carry it on a plane, you shouldn't have to take my word for what's in it."

Ahmed eased the box open, and removed the bell, touching only the little ring at its top. He shook it lightly and let it ring, then he held it at eye level, closed his eyes, and seemed to be meditating. Finally, he opened his eyes, and placed the bell back in its box. "Sirs," he said, in a voice that was a little shakier than it had been earlier, "this is very rude, I know, but I must let my grandfather know what I am bringing him." He took out a phone, glanced at its screen, then put it back in his pocket, bringing another one out of a different pocket. "Ah good, one of them works here," he said, walking off a short way. He tapped on its screen twice, then held it to his ear. After almost a minute, he said something, then waited. Finally, he apparently reached the person he wanted, and there followed several minutes of increasingly agitated conversation. When the call was over, Ahmed rejoined

Emmett and Bart. "Grandfather reiterates his..." he groped for a word, "...his condolences. He says that the bell will hang in a special niche in the shrine at Wadi Qadr, beside its twin."

"It's twin?" Bart said.

"The shrine is devoted to the memory of the saint who founded our order. His vocation was as a worker in metals. After many years of study and meditation, he was able to cast some of the metals he used without the use of fire. He passed the secret on to his successor, along with a little bell that he had cast, the twin of this one. Since then, each successive master of the shrine has left behind a little bell to mark his own tenure. Some are cast of bronze, some of brass or silver. Only one, the first, is cast of iron. A few of the retired masters have attempted iron, but they have all failed, all but one. Two hundred years ago, more or less, the senior master was able to liquify the iron, but not for long enough for it to be cast, and he emerged from the attempt deranged. I hate to ask, but was Mr. Dawson...?"

Emmett shook his head. "To the very end, he was as sane as you and I. And he cast that bell several months before his death." I should know, he thought; I was the one who poured it into the mold.

Ahmed considered that for a moment, then asked, "Did he, perhaps, pass the secret on to anyone?"

Emmett said nothing and looked at Bart. "I didn't know anything about any of this," Bart said, "and he certainly didn't pass any secrets on to me."

Emmett shrugged. "And not to anyone else that I know of." Did 'anyone else' include himself, Emmett wondered. No, he decided, not technically.

Ahmed bowed slightly toward the other two. "I am pleased to have met two who knew him, and I shall be honored to carry the bell to my grandfather. May God be with you." And with that, he strode back to his car with the little box.

"I think," Bart told Emmett, "that was the strangest story I have ever heard. Why do I get the feeling that you already knew it?"

"I knew Wade a long time," Emmett replied. "Plus, I'm the lawyer for the trust. Did you ever wonder where the trust got the money it spends? The alloys that Wade made, some of them, were pretty exotic. The more exotic an alloy was, the more a lab would pay for it. That bell that he gave to the Baptist Church was plain old bronze: copper and tin; but the way it was cast made it special. You would be amazed what the trust could have gotten for a piece of amorphous bronze that size." Emmett had used an old courtroom trick, one that evasive witnesses often use: answer a slightly different question than the one you were asked. He really hadn't wanted to discuss what he knew about melting iron, or what could go wrong in the process.

The night had gone from chilly to cold. As Bart drove back up to the Cove, he thought about Ahmed's story. It was simply unbelievable, except that Emmett believed it, and Uncle Wade said he could trust Emmett. And there were the bells, weren't there, ringing pure and clear. He pictured Wade in a black robe, maybe with a wand, mumbling arcane words over a crucible. That was absurd. Wade had been a scientist, and science didn't work like that. Did it?

Chapter Eleven

College administrators have a lot of concerns. Faculty pay, athletic rankings, building upkeep, all these and more clamor for their attention. Providing convenient parking for students is fairly low on their priorities list. The R-2 lot, where Bart's new permit let him park, was almost a half mile from Geer Dorm. Bart could have saved himself a lot of walking just by leaving the Jeep at the cabin, but an eighteen year old with a car does not leave it parked in a shed. That is not how guys think.

Jamaal might have greeted Bart with, "How was your Christmas?" or "Did you hear that Peterson passed History?" He didn't. His first words were, "Weren't you going to send me pictures of the Jeep?" That *is* how guys think. Bart's excuse—that he had gotten sidetracked by a jigsaw puzzle—got him nowhere, even when he added that it was a really hard puzzle. Ten days of work on it had enlarged the completed patch to about six inches across, but he wanted to see it all. He put what he had finished back into the box and brought the whole thing back to the dorm, where it lay spread out on his desk. Jamaal eyed it with suspicion. Bart thought about explaining that Uncle Wade could supposedly melt metal with mind rays and that the puzzle might contain the key to the process, but that sounded crazy even to him, so he knew how it would sound to Jamaal. Best to leave that for later. He told Jamaal the puzzle had a lot of sentimental value, and that he owed it to Uncle Wade to finish it. "If somebody gave me a puzzle like that," Jamaal said, "I think I'd owe him a fat lip. Now, are you going to show me that Jeep, or do I have to hunt around in R-2 until I find it?"

Ten minutes later they were standing by the Jeep. To a casual observer, the Jeep looked like an ordinary CJ-5. Jamaal was not a casual observer. First he walked around it, then he squatted down and peered at the springs and shock absorbers. "It's had some work done on it," Bart volunteered.

"*Some* work?" Jamaal rubbed his chin. "You remember *Invasion of the Body Snatchers?* Well, somewhere there's an empty pod that this thing came out of. None of the springs are original, or the shocks either. They're painted to look like factory units, but they're not." He looked sideways at Bart. "You got any idea what's under the hood?"

"A little," Bart said, trying to sound innocent. He was enjoying this. "I mean, I talked to the man who worked on it. He said it was it was a good engine."

"Uh-huh. Well, it's time to take a look." Jamaal bent over, reached in without looking, and pulled the hood release that had taken Bart so long to find. With the hood open, Jamaal stood and stared into the engine compartment for a full minute, without saying anything. He squatted down, looked underneath again, then stood back up with the air of someone who has an opinion.

"Well?" Bart said.

Jamaal nodded slowly. "Whoever did this knew what he was doing," he finally said. "And yeah, it's a real good engine, and it's put in right, but its weight ought to make the car handle like a pig. Does it?"

One of the poets that everybody praises but nobody reads said that the child is father of the man. The poet missed an important truth, which is that between the child and the man is a transitional zone, the guy. No truth about men, or about boys, entirely applies to guys. Guys have their own truths. Guys do not, for example, say what they really want. They live in a social jungle, and a known desire is a chink in their armor, a weakness that an enemy can exploit. A guy who wants to seduce a girl can easily tell her he loves her, because it isn't true. A guy who actually does love a girl will eat glass before he tells her, because if she doesn't feel the same way, she can use what she knows to hurt him.

Jamaal really wanted to try out the Jeep, but under guy rules he couldn't say so. Bart couldn't have explained that, but deep down he understood it, so when Jamaal asked how the Jeep handled, Bart heard the real question: Can I give it a test drive? "Only one way to find out," he said, and tossed Jamaal the key. Thirty seconds later they were pulling out of R-2 onto Perimeter Road, and not long after that they were cruising up Highway 28.

On a long straightaway, Jamaal worked his way up through the gears, then glanced at the speedometer and backed off. When they got to where the highway wasn't straight, he took the Jeep into the curves, tentatively at first, then faster until, again, he looked to see what speed they were going. Finally, he pulled over at a cider stand that was closed for the winter, killed the motor, and got out.

"She rides good," he said. "Too good. You got any idea why?"

"There's some extra weight," Bart said casually. "The side rails are full of lead shot."

"Lead shot," Jamaal said, sounding as though Bart had said 'fairy dust'. Then he thought about it. "Actually, I guess that would make sense." It still bothered him that the Jeep handled well in curves; she ought to be front heavy, with that V8 under the hood. Where, he wondered, was the balancing weight in back? He looked behind the seats, but everything looked normal. It wasn't until he stood back and took it all in that he realized how Bud had done it. The tailgate had none of the usual raised sections that make thin steel more rigid. Instead, it was flat and smooth. Jamaal worked its latch and pulled the gate. It lowered, but not quickly. "What the...?" he muttered, then lay down and looked underneath. "It's sprung like an oven door," he called out.

"Why would anybody do that?" Bart asked.

Jamaal got back to his feet and rapped a knuckle on the tailgate. "Because it's real heavy," he said. "It's half-inch sheet steel. You know, all in all, I think this is the strangest car I've ever seen."

The man in the raincoat had specific instructions: take the girl, but leave the father. That made perfect sense to him; after all, somebody had to pay the ransom. Except for that, how he did the job was left up to him, so he had taken care of some personal business at the same time. The guy he had whacked, a State Law Enforcement Division agent named Phelps, wouldn't be missed until tomorrow, and by then this job would be over. Phelps had been checking up on the man in the raincoat, asking people questions about where he got the money he spent, and whether any of them had seen him on certain days, days when the man had, in fact, been practicing his trade. Well, so much for Phelps. The man parked in a visitor space and marched into the Admin Services building. "Good evening," he said to the woman at the main desk. "My name is Phelps." He showed her Phelps's SLED badge, and it had the effect he expected. When he asked her about a student, she was Little Miss Helpful.

"Dilara Ziya?" she said. "Why certainly, sir, let me look her up." She tore a copy of the campus map off of a pad and circled two buildings. "Here is where we are, and over here is her dorm. If there is anything else I can do, you just let me know." He promised he would, and told her his report would mention how helpful she had been. The RA at Dilara's dorm was less inclined to tell him anything, until he said he could charge her with obstruction. Then she said Dilara had told her she was going to join her father for dinner. She gave the man directions to Hardin Hall, where the History faculty had their offices. He hadn't planned on meeting the father, but that was all right. Maybe he'd rough the guy up a little, to show him he meant business. Or maybe he'd rough him up just for the fun of it.

◇◇◇◇◇◇◇◇◇◇◇◇◇◇◇◇●◇◇◇◇◇◇◇◇◇◇◇◇◇◇◇◇

Bart looked at his watch. Kind of late, but maybe if he hurried he could catch Dr. Ziya in his office. He was halfway up the walk leading to Hardin when he heard a man's voice yelling something, and what sounded like muffled screams, all coming from inside the building. The voices got louder, until suddenly a large man in a raincoat kicked the door open. He was carrying a girl under his arm, the way a child carries a rag doll, her own arms pinned at her sides. The man looked up just in time to see Bart, standing on the walk about ten feet in front of him.

According to experts, the best thing to do when you see a crime in progress is to call 911. Bart wasn't an expert. Instead of fumbling for his phone, he ran toward the man, yelling.

The man in the raincoat agreed with the experts. People had called 911 on him several times over the years, and by the time the police had gotten there, he had always gotten away. A crazy person running at him was not what he expected, and it gave him a problem. He had Phelps's pistol, but Phelps's holster was right-handed, which put it on the same side as the girl he was carrying. He let her go and reached for the gun, but it was only partway out of the holster when Bart reached him. By football standards, Bart's tackle wasn't very good; the man absorbed the jolt and remained standing, but the pistol got knocked to the ground. The man drew his fist back to break Bart's face when the girl gave him a shot of the pepper spray she had had in her jeans pocket. The spray only hit one of his eyes, but one was enough to take his attention off Bart. He bent over to get the pistol, but Bart got to it first. If the man had known that Bart had never actually held a gun before, even a cap pistol, he would probably have wrestled him for it. But being half blind and unarmed, he decided not to risk it, and instead took off running. He could always come back later. The girl collapsed into a heap on the lawn. When her father staggered out of Hardin, blood oozing from his scalp where the man had slugged him, he saw a stranger standing over his daughter, holding a pistol.

Enver Ziya's faculty bio mentioned his time in the Turkish diplomatic service, but it left out the firearms training he had gotten from the service's security people, or the little automatic they had issued to each of the diplomats. He kept it in the desk drawer in his office. Now he aimed it, exhaled half a breath the way they had taught him, and fired. The shot should have found his target's heart; that is where he aimed it, but it was getting dark, and he didn't see Bart turn a little at the last instant. Bart felt a sudden jolt to his left shoulder, followed by a lot of pain. He heard a girl's voice screaming something. Her words made no sense, but everything was starting to get confused, and he felt himself falling.

If he had understood Turkish, the last words he heard before the darkness closed in would have been, "Papa no, it wasn't him!"

The man who wasn't Phelps had parked around the corner from Hardin, in a Faculty Only slot. Now, as he staggered back to his car, he was just in time to see a tow truck hauling it away. Waving his arms and yelling for the truck to stop, he ran out into the street, directly in the path of the last campus bus of the evening. Campus busses don't run especially fast, but like all busses they don't stop especially fast either.

When the campus police found Agent Phelps' ID on the body, they cordoned off the area and called in the state police. The nearest agent, a man named Hickson, was thirty minutes away in Anderson, but a friend of his in the Highway Patrol gave him a ride and he was there in fifteen. By that time, EMS had already taken away a young man with a bullet in his shoulder, but the campus police had made sure the professor and his daughter remained available for questioning.

"So let me see if I've got this," Agent Hickson said to Dr. Ziya. "You're saying that one of our agents came to your office, and then pistol whipped you for no reason at all." The professor nodded. "Then he grabbed you," he pointed at Dilara, "carried you down the hall, kicked open the door, and some skinny kid, who just happened to be there, tried to tackle him. That's what you're telling me?" This time it was the girl who nodded. Hickson met her gaze for a long moment, waiting for her to look away or to start adding details the way liars tend to do. Finally he gave up and glanced back down at his notes. "I see. Then you," he looked back at Dr. Ziya, "you came to, went out, saw the kid, and shot him in the back. Now even assuming I believed the rest of your story, doesn't that sound a little odd? Maybe a little, I don't know, ungrateful?"

"He was holding a gun," began Dr. Ziya, "so I thought..."

"I can't confirm what you thought. I can confirm what you

did, and it doesn't make sense. You know why? Because it was Phelps, that's why. I knew Phelps. I went through training with him. He was a good agent. And yet you're telling me he came all the way up here from Charleston just to slug you and snatch her? You're going to have to do a lot better than that, or I'm going to have to..." His phone's buzz interrupted him. He glared at it, saw who was calling, and answered it. "Hickson. Yes sir? Yes sir, I did, but the bus dragged him at least forty feet, and his face was, you know, kind of filed off. But he had his ID, and... Oh. Yes sir, I see." He tapped the screen, and the phone went dark. "I think the picture may have clarified a little," he said, in a more subdued voice than before. "I don't know who your visitor was, but they found Phelps behind a bush in his yard in Charleston, with a bullet in the back of his head." Hickson's phone buzzed again, but this time there was no conversation. Over the last hour, other agents had been arriving to help process the scene, and one of them had just sent Hickson a picture. He studied it a while, then said simply, "Well now." He turned the phone so that the Ziyas could see it. It showed a photo of Dilara, happy and smiling.

Dr. Ziya frowned, and his lips tightened. "May I ask where you got that?"

"It was in the dead man's coat pocket," the agent said thoughtfully. "I think we're done for now. Here's my card. If you remember anything more, let me know." It was time, he thought, to talk to the skinny kid.

◊◊◊◊◊◊◊◊◊◊◊◊◊◊◊◊ ● ◊◊◊◊◊◊◊◊◊◊◊◊◊◊◊◊

Bart found himself in bed. He tried to sit up, but the attempt made him dizzy and he lay back down. A black woman in a white coat appeared from somewhere, looked him over, and said, "Little early to be doing that, I think. You ever been drunk before?"

"Huh?" He tried to sound indignant, but it came out as a croak. "No, I've never been drunk."

"Well you are now, so enjoy it while you can, because what

I used will wear off pretty quick, and when it does you're going to have what the dentists like to call a little discomfort. You feel any yet?"

He took inventory. "No, why would I?"

She held up a gloved hand, and showed him a little chunk of what looked like copper. "Let's just say that between what this did to your shoulder, and what I had to do to dig it out, you're going to spend a week or two wishing you hadn't been shot."

"I got shot?" He remembered a blow from behind, but then...nothing. "Why?"

"I couldn't begin to guess, but there's people wanting to see you, and I expect they can tell you. You want me to send them in?"

"Do I have a choice?"

Dr. Hodge—that was the name on her lab coat—gave a snort. "Let me tell you something. You're my patient, and if I say you can't have visitors, you can't have visitors. I don't have any problem at all telling that crew they have to wait."

Bart thought about it. "You know, now might be a good time. If I say anything wrong, well, I'm drunk; my doctor says so."

She gave him an approving nod. "Yes I did, didn't I." She opened the door, and four men filed in, three in suits and one in the uniform of the campus police, with captain's bars.

One of the suits spoke first. "Mr. Phillips? My name is Hickson. I am an agent with SLED. I need to get your statement about what happened tonight."

One of the other suits interrupted. "Mr. Phillips? I'm Parker Dewalt, general counsel for Clemson University." To Hickson, he said, "Don't you need to read him his Miranda rights?" Dewalt handled only civil matters, but he remembered Miranda from law school.

Agent Hickson shook his head. "He's not in custody, and he's not a suspect, so no, I don't." To Bart he said, "Let's start with why you were out in front of the Hardin Building at night. Can you tell me that?"

"I was taking something to show to Dr. Ziya. It's a picture

of some Arabic writing, and I thought he might be able to read it."

"So you know Dr. Ziya. Does he know you? On sight, I mean; would he recognize you?"

It took Bart a few seconds to sort out what agent Hickson had said. "No, wait, I don't know him. My roommate has him for a class."

Hickson wrote that down. "Okay, you don't know him, but you were on your way to see him. What happened when you got there?"

Bart thought. "I heard a fight or something, inside the office building, and then the door came open and this man came out with a girl under his arm. That didn't look right, so I ran at him."

"Didn't look right," the agent wrote. "Anything else?"

"I ran into him," Bart said. "Then he dropped the girl and drew a gun, and the girl sprayed him in the face with something, and he dropped the gun. Or maybe he dropped it earlier, I'm not sure. Then I guess I must have picked it up."

Hickson wrote furiously. "You guess?"

"It happened real fast. Anyway, he ran off and I went over to see if the girl was all right. Something hit me on the shoulder, and the next thing I know, Dr. Hodge is asking me if I've ever been drunk before."

Hickson frowned. "You'd been drinking?"

Dewalt, the attorney, leaned forward to hear Bart's answer, but it was Dr. Hodge who spoke up. "He wasn't on anything when they brought him in; I checked. Then I shot him full of painkiller." To Bart, she said, "You getting any feeling back in that shoulder?"

"A sort of a dull ache. It's not bad." But the ache was getting less dull all the time, he noticed.

She glanced at the readouts behind him, then rolled her eyes. "Boys." She had treated enough of them to know how they thought: they would die in silent agony before they would tell a woman they hurt. To Hickson she said, "I think you need to be wrapping this up."

Agent Hickson glanced over his notes. "Actually, I think we're done. Mr. Phillips, thank you for your time."

Bart held up his good arm. "Agent Hickson? Can you tell me something? Who was the man who shot me? And where was he taking that girl?"

"The guy you tackled? We've finally run his prints. He was a thug for hire out of Charleston. But it wasn't him who shot you. That would be your Dr. Ziya. He says he thought that, well..."

Bart remembered. "Oh. Yeah, I can just imagine what he thought."

Dr. Hodge decided that was enough talk, and pointed to the door. Once they were far enough outside the building that no one would overhear, they stopped. "If I might have a minute," said Agent Hickson, "I need to check on something." He stepped away from the group, spent a few minutes on the phone, and came back. "The State will not be bringing criminal charges."

Mr. Dewalt, the attorney, looked puzzled. "What would you have charged him with? He's the one who got shot."

Hickson shook his head. "Not Mr. Phillips. Dr. Ziya. It isn't assault if he thought he was protecting his daughter."

"Now just a damn minute," sputtered the campus police captain. "He could have killed that boy. Who are you to say there won't be any charges?"

Agent Hickson considered his alternatives, and decided on the one that wouldn't get him in front of a review board. "You know who I am, Captain," he said. "I think you mean, who made the decision not to prosecute. That would be the attorney general. Would you like to talk to him about it? I'll just have to hit redial, and you can tell him he's wrong, that the state should prosecute the man for trying to save his daughter. Shall I make that call, captain?" He waited. "I didn't think so."

The captain had turned white, then red. "Oh yeah? Well, let me tell you something. Your boss may say shooting a student is all right, but he had a gun on campus and I'm going to charge him with that."

The fourth man cleared his throat. Up to this point, he

had said nothing, and even now, he spoke softly; one advantage of being a university president is not having to raise your voice. "No Captain, you will not; the matter ends here. I trust we are clear on that." Without waiting for a reply, he turned and walked to his car. The meeting was over.

Chapter Twelve

"Murad? I am sorry; I thought this was Mehmed's number. I would like to speak with my brother."

Murad's voice was as smooth as silk. "Uncle Enver, it is so good to hear you. I am afraid father has retired for the evening; we are, you might recall, six, seven hours ahead of...where are you, South Carolina? But I will be happy to deliver any message you have for him."

"That may not be necessary; I think that you may be the person I should be talking to anyway. There was an attempt on my daughter this evening."

"Little Dilara? I trust she is all right." Only an attempt, he thought. So much for hiring a so-called professional. How much did Enver know?

"She is fine; thank you for your concern. My own concern is that it not happen again. Do you join me in that concern, Murad?" Enver kept his voice calm and even. This was not the time for emotion. Later, perhaps.

"Uncle, what are you saying? My cousin is very dear to me. Just as you are. I would certainly not want to do anything to endanger her." He paused. "Just as I am sure you yourself would not."

So there it was. "Let us not play games, nephew. The kidnapper had a picture of Dilara, one taken when we were in Oran. Of those who were there, I have no doubt who would do such a thing. Tell me clearly, Murad, what is it that you want?"

"What I want is unimportant, uncle. Your concern should be what your brother, Imam Muhammad wants. God has chosen him to restore the House of Peace to the dignity it had in the time of the Caliphs, and God's will is not going to be thwarted by an academic critic," he spat out the syllables, "snapping like a dog at the Imam's ankles. You have caused your brother pain with that poisonous article you wrote, and if, as the Journal said, there should be a second, more particular article, you would cause him still greater pain. Should that happen, I would feel obliged to share my father's pain with both your daughter and yourself. Is that clear enough, uncle?"

"Admirably clear," Enver said, fighting the urge to scream curses at the evil worm his nephew had become. "I would be remiss if I repaid your clarity with anything less. You have pretended to be an Arab for so long, you have forgotten what it is to be a Turk. Let me remind you. A Turk defends his child. And, if circumstances require it, a Turk avenges his child. It would be good for you to ponder that, nephew." Having said what needed to be said, Enver hung up.

Murad threw his phone across the room. No one spoke to him like that! With an effort, he calmed himself. Vengeance would come, but the program must come first; if he could not prevent the publication of the rest of the article, the program's timetable would have to be shortened. Once the people had tasted blood, it would no longer matter what some journal article said. God is great, if you believed what the people chanted, but according to them, God is also merciful and compassionate. Fortunately for God, Murad thought, He had a servant who had neither of those weaknesses. It had been a mistake to send a stranger on family business. As soon as the matters at hand allowed for it, he would correct that mistake, in person.

Chapter Thirteen

Bart opened his eyes to find Dr. Hodge looking at his readouts. "Good morning," she said. "How you feel?"

"Remember that discomfort you mentioned?" he said. "Well, it got here."

"On a scale of one to ten, ten being as bad as you can stand, how bad?"

He thought about it. "About a five, I guess."

"Uh-huh," she said. "That means at least a six. Want anything for it?"

"No. I'm good." She rolled her eyes and made a note on his chart; Bart wondered what she had written, then decided he probably didn't want to know. "So, when do I get to check out of here? I've got classes starting tomorrow."

She looked over his chart again. "Stitches come out in ten days, and I'm going to give you some antibiotics and some pills for the pain, but I think you're releasable. Putting your shirt on won't be any fun for a while, though. Speaking of which, we had to cut your shirt off of you last night, so you won't be wearing it any more."

"I called my roommate. He's bringing me one."

"Big fellow? He's out in the lobby, along with your girlfriend."

He thought about that. "Uh, last I checked, I didn't have a girlfriend. Besides you." He gave her a wink. "I mean, you have seen me naked."

"Huh. Well, I'm taken, so don't turn down any offers. Who do you want to see first?"

"Jamaal, the big guy. He can help me get dressed. I don't want to hit the dating scene in a backless dress." He pointed to the hospital gown.

She took one last look at him, shook her head, and as she was leaving, said, "Has anybody told you lately you're not quite right?"

A minute later, Jamaal came in. "You know what that

doctor told me? She said if I didn't take good care of you, she'd come looking for me. That's a mean woman."

"She'll do it, too," Bart said.

"So what happened to you? When you didn't come in last night, and I heard the bus had hit somebody, I got kind of worried."

"No, that wasn't me." So that's what happened to the thug, Bart thought. Good enough for him. "All I've got is a hurt shoulder, so I'm really glad you're here. It really hurts when I lift my arm, and I thought you could help me get my shirt on."

"Sure. I hunted for one that looked good, but all I could find was this." He held up Bart's other—as Bart thought of it—good shirt.

"There is nothing wrong with plaid flannel," Bart said, renewing a running debate they had been having since early November. With Jamaal's help he got his clothes on and felt like he was fit to be seen in public. When they got to the lobby, a girl stood up. Bart thought she looked familiar. "It's...Dee, isn't it? From the Thanksgiving dinner?" Then he realized who else she was.

She looked surprised. "Bart? I didn't recognize you last night." To Jamaal, she said, "Do you know what he did? Didn't he tell you?"

Jamaal gave Bart a disapproving look. "No, he didn't." When it happens at night and involves a cute girl, roommates are supposed to hear about it. Especially when the girl seems to be grateful.

"He saved me from being kidnapped," she said. "I can't believe he didn't tell you."

Jamaal looked at her, then at Bart, who avoided eye contact. "You did what?"

"Tell you later," Bart muttered.

"He tackled the man and got his gun. It was awesome. Then Papa shot him."

"The man? Or Bart?" Jamaal said it as a joke.

"Bart. Then the man got run over by a bus. He didn't tell

you that either?" That was simply incredible. Her roommate knew every detail about last night, including who was wearing what.

"No," Jamaal said ominously. "But he will. It sounds like he deserves a good slap on the back." He edged toward Bart, who sidled away from him.

"I know what he deserves." She stood on tiptoes and gave Bart a kiss on the cheek. He blushed the color of the red parts of his shirt. "Thank you thank you thank you!" she said, then glanced at her watch. "Ooh, I've got to run." She had gone a little distance when she turned and added, "Oh, and when you can, would you drop by Papa's office? He promised me he would not shoot." Then she was gone.

Outside, Bart found an interesting cloud formation, and was studying it when Jamaal finally broke the silence. "Did they give you breakfast?" They hadn't. "Okay then, let's take care of that, somewhere we can sit down and talk. Because you've got a hell of a lot of explaining to do."

The faculty secretary's desk sat on a platform, a two-step riser the drama department's scene shop had made for her. She needed the platform, she told them, because looking up at the people who approached her desk was giving her a stiff neck. The real reason was that, if she had to look up at them, the students got entirely the wrong impression of where they stood on the scale of importance. Meeting them at eye level while she was still seated was much better. Better yet was making them break the silence. Bart found out how that worked during the minute he stood in front of her desk without getting any sign that she knew he was there. Finally, he cleared his throat and said, "Uh, could I go in to see Dr. Ziya?"

"Faculty members' office hours are plainly posted on the board," she said, without looking up. To get to the hallway with the faculty offices, a visitor had to get past her, and her job, as she saw it, was to filter out the hoi polloi. "You students seem to think you can just sashay in whenever you want, like this was a barber shop. Now if you'll write down your name and the reason you need to see Professor Ziya, I will get back to you with an appointment time. During office hours." She shoved a pad in his direction.

Bart wrote his name on the pad, but the reason for the appointment was a problem. Saying the man's daughter had said to drop by didn't seem like it was going to be good enough. "Never mind," he said, wadding up the paper. "Sorry to have bothered you."

Now she looked up. "No bother at all," she said with a cold little smile. "You have a nice day."

Back on the walkway, Bart paused at the scene of last night's excitement. If the local TV station got wind of it, they would inevitably run a "News Special" asking, "Is your child safe at college?" What they ought to run, he thought, was an ad campaign for designer pepper sprays. He was looking at the walkway, thinking how that might work when a pair of shoes came and stood in his field of vision. He looked up to see Dee, who was holding two lidded cups of coffee.

"You look like you are thinking," she said. "What are you thinking about?" Males, whether boys or men or guys, do not do well with that question. Males tend to think in pictures, and describing a picture is like describing a dream: not always possible, but always less interesting to the listener than to the dreamer.

Suddenly back in the moment, Bart went with the last image he had had. "Pepper spray as jewelry," he said. "They could call it, 'This year's hottest fashion accessory'."

Dee had just taken a sip of coffee when she got the pun, and now her laugh sprayed coffee all over Bart's shirt. "I am so sorry," she said, "but that struck me as really funny, because...well, you know why."

"That's okay," Bart said. "You can't hurt flannel."

"Did you find Papa? He really wanted to see you."

He shook his head. "I couldn't make it past the secretary. Shouldn't she be guarding a golden treasure at the mouth of some cave?" Dee looked puzzled. "Like a dragon, I mean," he explained.

She thought for a second. "Oh, Beowulf, also Siegfried. I was raised on different legends, but I have read those. She has always reminded me of a spider, sitting in the center of a web, but yes, the dragon image is better. Come, it is time to pilfer the dragon's treasure. Would you get the door?" And so, side by side, they marched up the steps and into the cave mouth.

"Faculty members' office hours are...oh, it's you," said the dragon, finally seeing Dee. She didn't sound pleased; apparently they had met before.

"We are going in to see Papa," Dee told her as she breezed past. "Both of us."

In an office near the end of the hall, Dr. Ziya rose to meet them. Dee handed him one of the coffees. "Ah, thank you. I have been needing this." He sipped the coffee and smiled. "Amazing, this is actually drinkable. I did not think anyone here knew how to make it."

"I had to tell them how," she said. "Triple espresso with six sugars. They wanted to put a warning label on it."

"They should warn against what they usually make," he said, then he noticed Bart. "Are you going to introduce me to your friend?"

"He is the one you shot," Dee said brightly. "I found him for you."

"You are the one?" he said. "I cannot tell you how much I regret doing that."

Bart blushed as red as he had when Dee kissed him. "Sir, I know what you saw. I would have done the same thing."

Dr. Ziya noticed Bart's shirt. "That looks like the shirt you had on. Is that blood on it? "

Now it was Dee's turn to blush. "No, it's latte. I spit it on him."

The professor shook his head. "Another American custom you have picked up? It seems uncultured, somehow. Here is how a Turk thanks the man who saved his daughter." He spread both arms and before Bart could back away he found himself in a bear hug. "Papa?" Dee said in a stage whisper, "bullet wound," while pointing at Bart's left shoulder. The professor let him go and, not knowing what to say, sat back down at his desk.

"Is that really the shirt you had on?" Dee asked.

"No, they threw that one away."

"Well, it looks just like it. Why would you have two identical shirts?"

Bart was hurting too much from the bear hug to come up with a good reason. Groping for some way to change the subject, he told Dr. Ziya, "I was coming here yesterday to see if you could help me with something." He got out his phone and brought up a picture. "Can you read this? I think it might be Arabic."

The professor studied the image. "Yes, it is, but it is written in a highly ornamented version of the Maghrebi script, from northern Africa. He traced the curves with his fingers, then pursed his lips. "Yes, all right, I have it. It is a line from the poet Omar. In the Fitzgerald translation, that line reads, 'Turn down an empty glass.'"

"What does that mean?" Bart asked.

"The glass would be a wine glass," the professor said. "Omar uses a lot of wine references, but he almost never means actual wine. Sometimes he means the emotional side of religion, but at other times he means the sensual side of life. As I recall the context of that line, the poet was saying, as if on his deathbed, that he had drunk the wine of life to the bottom of the glass, or that he had completed some other task that he had set for himself. Does that make sense, given where this text came from?"

Bart thought that it did, but before he could explain they were interrupted by a polite tapping on the office door. Dee opened it to find the university's lawyer standing in the hall, looking surprised. "I'm sorry," he said. "The secretary said I wouldn't be interrupting anything important, so I assumed..." He saw Bart, and suddenly looked very unhappy. "Mr. Phillips. Oh dear, I had hoped to speak with the professor before he spoke with you." He turned toward Dr. Ziya. "Professor, my name is Parker Dewalt. I am the general counsel for the university. I would suggest that you not speak with Mr. Phillips unless I am present."

He looked like he had more to say on the subject, but the professor interrupted him. "And why is that, Mr. Dewalt?"

Bart thought he knew the answer. "He's afraid I'm going to sue you and the university. Isn't that right, Mr. Dewalt?"

The lawyer got a sour look. "The possibility cannot be overlooked."

"Sure it can," Bart said. "I'm not going to sue anybody. Clemson didn't send the bad guy, and I would have done the same thing Dr. Ziya did, except I would have missed. If you want something that says I won't sue, just write it out, and I'll sign it."

Every profession has its share of complete fools, but Parker Dewalt was not one of them. He would rather have gone back to his office, pulled down a formbook, and drafted a comprehensive three-page release, but he knew a rare opportunity when he saw one. Five minutes later, he handed Bart a single page document, neatly hand-written. "Ethically, I have to tell you that you should have another lawyer look this over before you sign it," he told Bart.

"You're probably right." Bart got out his phone and tapped in Emmett's number. "Evelyn? This is Bart. Is Mr. Schroder free for a second? Great." There was a pause, during which Mr. Dewalt wondered why a student would have a lawyer's number so handy. Then, "Mr. Schroder? I've got a paper I want to read to you, and I need you to tell me if I can sign it; is this a good time?" It was. He read the release, then gave a quick account of what had happened the night before. "Yes, I'm sure. Thanks. What do I owe you? Wow, then really thanks." He tapped the phone dark, and said "I sign here?"

"Yes, but we'll need a notary," the lawyer replied. Dr. Ziya made a call, and the dragon lady came in carrying a notary seal. In a minute, it was done, and she left to make copies.

Dee had leaned over to watch, and to read the release. Now she pointed to some words in the second line. "According to this, somebody owes him ten dollars." Sure enough, the release recited that it was given 'for ten dollars and other valuable considerations'. Mr. Dewalt was about to explain that the words were boilerplate, a mere formality, but then he thought about how much the university had just potentially saved, and pulled a ten out of his wallet. "Good," Dee said. "Papa can take care of the other considerations. Papa, I think you owe him a shirt. If you will pay for it, I will pick it out." Then she added, "And it will not be plaid flannel."

Bart gave her a suspicious look. "Did Jamaal put you up to that? He thinks I've got bad taste in clothes."

She tried to look innocent. "I do not remember exactly what we talked about. But you might look better in something else."

Before Bart could defend his sense of style, the professor asked a question. "You mentioned someone named Jamaal. Is his last name Sheridan, perhaps?" Bart nodded. "And you are roommates?"

"Yes sir," Bart said. "He's the one who said you could probably read that text I showed you. He thought you were an Arab, though."

Dr. Ziya gave a tight smile. "Some in my family pretend to be," he said, "but no, we are Turks."

The dragon lady returned with the copies, which seemed to signal the end of the meeting; Bart and Dewalt went their separate ways. Alone with his daughter, Enver gave her a hug. "That is an unusual young man," he said.

"And lucky," Dee said, thinking of where the bullet wound might have been.

"Luck is capricious," her father said. "It may be there when you need it, or it may not. No, he has something much more reliable than luck. He has brass balls."

◇◇◇◇◇◇◇◇◇◇◇◇◇◇◇◇●◇◇◇◇◇◇◇◇◇◇◇◇◇◇◇◇

"So what did he say?" Dee's roommate had hung on every word of Dee's account, and Dee had saved the best for last.

"Wait, first you have to imagine the scene. Here I am, sipping my coffee, and there," she gestured, "is my dignified doctor professor father."

"Yeah, he is a little stiff," Tori admitted. Tori Lasker had met Dee at freshman orientation, and they had hit it off immediately. Each already had a roommate, but a couple of hours of harassing the housing office, plus dropping Dr. Ziya's name every now and again, had gotten them put together. Tori was the taller of the two by several inches, with hair that was whatever color she wanted it to be. This week it was red. "C'mon, you were up to the part where everybody had gone except you and your father. What did he say? You're killing me."

"If it had not been my father, I would swear he had set me up for it. I said that Bart was lucky, and he said no, that Bart had something better than luck: brass balls."

Tori's mouth dropped open. "He didn't! I would have peed myself. You didn't tell him what it meant?"

"No. Perhaps you can do that, the next time he takes us to dinner."

Tori laughed. "Yeah, right, I'll be sure and do that. But back to your blushing ninja: what kind of shirt are you going to get him?"

Dee thought about that. "How many kinds are there? You have brothers; will you help me?"

Tori nodded. "Sure, but I'll have to get a look at him first, to get an idea what might look good on him."

Dee kept a straight face, but inside she grinned. When she met Bart at the Thanksgiving dinner, she had said to herself, you and my roommate would make a cute pair. "Of course," she told Tori. "I understand."

Chapter Fourteen

"How did you like Larson?" Captain Bragg asked.

McIntyre shook his head sadly. "Sir, I have to tell you. Larson is the most boring place on the planet, and I don't exclude the poles."

"I take it you didn't find anything." The captain didn't sound surprised. The trip had been a long shot, but he had to be sure. Going through Bivens' effects, they had found an index card. More accurately, they had found part of a card; the pipe that skewered Bivens had sheared off the rest of it. The scrap that survived had two words on it: Dawson, and Larson. There were a number of towns named Dawson, and each of them had its share of people named Larson. Checking them out had taken a while. Looking for Dawsons in places called Larson promised to be quicker, since there were only two Larsons: one in North Dakota, and one in South Carolina.

"Larson, North Dakota, isn't even a town anymore, sir; it got dissolved when the population hit fifteen. Not fifteen hundred, fifteen. I spoke with every adult there, and nobody has ever heard of anybody named Dawson. I didn't envy Travis his trip to South Carolina, but I stand corrected." McIntyre had been brought up in Philadelphia, and his impression of the South was not favorable.

The captain drummed his fingers on the table for a moment. "The Buddhists say envy is based on a delusion, the belief that the object of desire is what it seems to be. Boring or not, your assignment was better than Travis's; if only because you came back from yours alive." He said it very quietly. The captain thought of himself as tough and blunt, and he wanted others to think of him that way, too, but he cared for his people, and his people knew it. Or they had known it; with both Bivens and Travis gone, his team, his people, now consisted of McIntyre.

"How...how did he die?"

"According to the coroner in Greenville, he fell off an overpass, and then a train hit him."

"Greenville?" McIntyre asked. "What was he doing in Greenville? That's, what, thirty or forty miles from Larson."

"I don't know what he was doing there, but I do know this: he was dead before he hit the tracks. Coroner said he died of a broken neck. Our people agree, only it wasn't the kind of broken neck you get from a fall, and there was almost no bleeding. Somebody killed him, and tried to make it look like an accident."

"Random killing?"

"Maybe. But I think we have to assume that it wasn't."

"But, who knew anything about the Dawson thing, except Dr. Thurmond?"

Bragg frowned. "Nobody, and I would love to know who else Thurmond talked to. Only thing is, he's dead too. He died of a heart attack last week, and it was one of those heart attacks that nobody saw coming. I think somebody else is looking for the same thing we are, and it looks like they're ahead of us."

McIntyre thought hard. "Carlisle stood to make some money selling sensors to Traxell, so I guess they would have some motive. But Traxell..." Bragg nodded, and gestured for him to continue. "Traxell stood to make a whole lot of money selling Feather to the Army. If Traxell had the metal process, they could make the sensors in-house, and then market Feather to whoever wants it. That's a whole lot of motive. Doesn't prove anything, but..."

Bragg nodded. "But it suggests a line of inquiry. Have yourself a good dinner tonight, then get some sleep. Because first thing in the morning, we're going to South Carolina."

"We, sir?"

"We. If somebody has killed one of mine, I want to meet him, in person. Be here at six in the morning, and pack for a stay; we may be there a while."

◊◊◊◊◊◊◊◊◊◊◊◊◊◊◊●◊◊◊◊◊◊◊◊◊◊◊◊◊◊◊

"Are you sure there's nothing missing?" Evelyn asked. "That makes no sense at all. Why would somebody go to all the trouble to break in, and then not steal anything?" She and Emmett had been going through drawers and files for the last hour. Evelyn liked her desk to be arranged a certain way when she started work in the morning, and this morning, something had been moved. If Emmett worked late, he would sometimes move her stapler an inch out of position, just to see how long it took her to notice it. This morning it wasn't the stapler, it was a heavy glass ashtray where she kept paperclips. "Did you mess with my ashtray?" she asked Emmett. He denied it. "You're sure?" He was sure. "Then somebody was in here." Emmett knew better than to doubt her, and the little infrared camera that he had installed after a break-in last year confirmed it: two men in ski masks had very carefully ransacked the office. The camera recorded single-frame shots, taken every few seconds, so the men seemed to jump around, but one of the shots clearly showed one of the men opening a file cabinet drawer.

Emmett ran through the blurry photos again. "They were snooping, not stealing," he said. "There's only one file near there that a professional thief might be curious about, and that's the Dawson estate file." He chuckled. "That must have been disappointing. All they'd find in it is a copy of the will, and that's already on file at the courthouse." He knew it had been professionals because they had gotten in without doing any damage and had left no sign they had been there except for Evelyn's ashtray. He was beginning to appreciate Wade's circumspection, how he had made it hard to know who had gotten what, using only public records. The real Dawson files, for the trust and the estate, were in the vault at the bank, all but the book that Wade had specifically said to leave in Emmett's office safe.

"Should I call the police?" Evelyn asked.

"Nah, remember last time? They'd just get fingerprint powder everywhere, and still not find anything." The orange cat walked past, then turned and rubbed against his ankle. "A fine watch-cat you were," Emmett told the cat, which very pointedly ignored him. The bell on the front door dingled. "Whoever it is," Emmett said, "I don't have time for them; I'm due in court." He ducked out the back door.

At the front desk stood a pair of men in dark suits and short haircuts. The older of the two spoke to Evelyn. "Good morning," he said. "We are with the FBI." They showed her plausible looking ID cards, neither of which said Bragg or McIntyre. "We are here to see Mr. Schroder." Without waiting for her to respond, they marched down the hall toward Emmett's now-empty office. On the way over from the probate clerk's office, Bragg and McIntyre had debated what method to use. With secretaries, gentle diplomacy usually paid off. Diplomacy takes time, though, and they didn't have time. The steamroller approach they had settled on was a gamble, but when it worked, it worked fast.

Receptionists in large offices tend to be insecure. They sit at the bottom of the office pecking order, so they know their jobs are at risk if they offend someone important. Faced with someone who looks and acts important, they will usually assume he actually is important, and will let him through. Across the street at Harley Bishop's office, the steamroller routine would have worked. Evelyn was neither insecure nor afraid of what her boss might think. When Emmett was out of the office, she was the boss, and people who threw their weight around were fair game.

Before the orange cat had come to the office, Evelyn had heard the expression cat-and-mouse, but she hadn't really understood it. Then one day the cat had actually caught a mouse, and now she knew. The cat had killed the mouse, eventually, but first he had had some fun with it. Evelyn had liked the cat better after that; it thought the same way she did. When Bragg came back up the hall, she gave him her best I-wish-I-could-help-you voice: "You didn't find him? Then he must have left for court. Is it something I can help you with?" She would have bet a dollar the answer was no. Important people don't like interacting with mere mortals.

She was right. "No," Bragg said. "Our business is only with Mr. Schroder, and it's a matter of some importance." He had considered saying it involved national security, but decided to save that for later. "Would you call him please?"

Oh you pushy bastard, she thought. Out loud, she said, "Why certainly, I'll be happy to." She punched in Emmett's number, and waited a moment. "Mr. Schroder?" she said, still using her Scarlett O'Hara voice, "there are some gentlemen here from the FBI, who say they just have to see you right away. They need you to come back to the office. Oh dear, they won't like that at all, but I will tell them, I surely will." She showed Bragg a mournful face and said, "I'm afraid Mr. Schroder can't leave court just now; you know how judges are. Perhaps you'd care to wait?" In fact, Emmett was in the jury room, having coffee and swapping gossip with the other lawyers while the DA called the docket. Evelyn never called him Mr. Schroder unless she was up to something, and he was sorely tempted to come back to the office just to watch the doctor operate. But that would spoil her fun, so he told her to follow her evil inclinations, and went back to his coffee.

The older agent seemed to do a quick calculation, then said, "No. We'll go to the courthouse. I expect the judge will know to cooperate. Thank you for your time." And off they went.

Evelyn looked at the orange cat, which had curled up on one of the waiting room chairs. "What do you think?" she asked the cat. "Justice, or mercy?" The cat jumped to the floor, came over, and rubbed past her ankle. "Do what a cat would do, in other words?" she said, and nodded. "I think so too: justice." She picked up the phone and tapped in the number of the criminal court clerk. "Doris? Evelyn. Is Billy on the bench yet? Well then, could you patch me through to chambers? Thanks, hon." There was a pause, then, "Billy? Fine, thank you. I just had a visit from a pair of government types who wanted me to jerk Emmett out of your court. Yes they did. Well, they're on their way over there now, to tell you how to do your job. I just thought you should know."

"All rise! Oh yes, oh yes, oh yes. This court is now open and sitting for the dispatch of business, the Honorable William P. Jenkins presiding, you may be seated." Ever since the Norman Conquest, bailiffs have opened court by calling out oyez, the French version of hear-ye. The Norman Conquest was a long time ago. In Keowee County, the call had evolved into 'Oh yes', which made as much sense to the audience as 'Oyez' would have. Like so many other court traditions, that was simply how things were done.

Another court tradition is the rule that says a judge has whatever authority is required to maintain order in the courtroom. Someone who commits an act of contempt in a South Carolina courtroom can face up to six months in jail, and the hearing is very short. In fact, the hearing can amount to exactly this: "Gentlemen, I find as a fact that you have entered the well of the courtroom without being licensed to practice law, that you have approached the bench without leave of court, that you have interrupted court business, and that you have told the court it needs to release an attorney who has clients on the docket, which misstates the court's needs; all of which facts, as a matter of law constitute direct criminal contempt of this court, and I accordingly find you, each and both, in contempt. You are hereby sentenced to forty-eight hours in the common jail of Keowee County. Bailiff, they are in your custody."

◇◇◇◇◇◇◇◇◇◇◇◇◇◇◇◇●◇◇◇◇◇◇◇◇◇◇◇◇◇◇◇◇

Probably, Judge Jenkins had thought the FBI agents would call their office, and that their Director would call the AG, who would call him, and it would all be smoothed over. None of that happened, and the two faux agents served every hour of the forty-eight. When they got back to their car, it had gotten a parking ticket, which McIntyre took as yet more proof that Larson was a hick town. Not that he needed more proof; the last two days had been like a bad dream.

It wasn't until they were several miles out of town that McIntyre was sure they were being followed. "Sir, we have a tail." Bragg glanced in the side mirror and saw a red Ford pickup. He asked how long it had been there. "Since right after we passed that diner, sir. I've tried slowing down so they could pass, and they slowed down too."

Bragg looked again. "Well they're not going slow now." The pickup came up fast behind them, then pulled out to pass. When it got beside them, it swerved right, slamming into the side of the car. McIntyre twisted the wheel, hit the brakes, and somehow kept the car in the road. "Nicely done," Bragg said.

"Thank you, sir; lots of practice," McIntyre grunted. That special driving course was paying off after all. The pickup had dropped back after hitting them, but now it was coming again. McIntyre hit the gas, but the car, an economy rental, didn't get much faster. "I don't think I can outrun them," he said, "but if they try that again, I might have a surprise for them." He didn't have to wait long. The pickup closed the distance, and once again went left to pass. McIntyre did the same thing, staying in front of them. For a mile, they swerved back and forth, until the pickup's driver decided it was time to end this nonsense. The truck backed off, then came up fast behind them, obviously intending to ram. McIntyre gritted his teeth and muttered, "Gotcha!" The road at that point had a ditch and a high bank on the right, and a steep drop-off on the left. McIntyre waited until the truck was almost on them, then swerved left as he had done before. The truck corrected, wanting to ram, not to pass. Now McIntyre swerved a little to the right and slammed on his brakes, so that the truck hit them off center. The car spun completely around and ended up in the ditch; the truck's back end came around and went off the road to the left, then the truck disappeared down the slope. After that, there was silence.

The car was a wreck. It lay on its left side in the ditch, its roof against the bank, its front wheels pointing in different directions. Bragg struggled clear of the airbags, then heaved his door open. It was like coming out of a submarine hatch. "Mr.

McIntyre," he said, "I don't think they give a medal for combat driving, but you deserve one. That was good work."

"Thank you, sir," came McIntyre's muffled voice. After a while, he climbed out of the car, and they took inventory. They had some bruises, and had to brush off a lot of powder from the airbags, but nothing seemed to be broken. It was time to see how the pickup had fared. They drew their weapons and went to the other side of the road.

The pickup was resting against a tree partway down slope, its doors open. Bragg saw a sparkle of light from somewhere near the truck, then heard a whicka-whicka sound as bullets cut through the air beside him, followed immediately by the sound of gunfire. They jumped back. "There were two of them," Bragg said. "If they know what they're doing, that one down there is alone. He'll try to keep us interested while the other one sneaks up on us. Can you get a cell signal?"

McIntyre checked "Yes, sir. Barely." He called a number he had memorized, and was surprised to recognize the voice that answered. "Sidney? Is that you?"

"Not in this context, Mr. McIntyre," said the voice evenly, "unless you have called the emergency number to reserve warehouse time." McIntyre explained the situation. "I see," said the voice. "I can have an asset nearby in..." there was a pause, "slightly under an hour. If that is inconvenient, and I would imagine that it is, you will need to improvise. Try to keep me informed of your movements."

An hour. That was not good. Their choices were to pick a direction and hope to avoid meeting the bad guy, or split up and guarantee that one of them did meet him. Or they could hunker in behind the car and hope to win a siege. Those were not good choices. As part of their FBI disguises, they were each carrying a Glock pistol. A Glock is a fine weapon, but whatever the others were using had longer range and a higher rate of fire. McIntyre considered calling 911, and was on the point of doing it, when he saw something coming. Worth a try, he thought, and waved vigorously at it. It slowed, then stopped. It was a Jeep.

Chapter Fifteen

"Okay," Bart said, looking at the list. "Beef, onions, garlic, peppers, rice, soy sauce. I asked about the bamboo sprouts and water chestnuts, but they don't have any."

"Then I'll improvise," Jamaal said. "Broccoli, that'll work." He disappeared in the direction of the Post Office/grocery store's produce section. Tomorrow it was back to Clemson; tonight, it was teriyaki stir-fry. Jamaal claimed he knew how to make it. Bart had offered to help, boil the rice maybe. Jamaal had been diplomatic, at least by his standards. "Oh hell no," he had said. "Nothing against you personally, but you stink as a cook. The whole cabin stinks when you cook." Earlier in the week, Bart actually had boiled rice, but he had tried to work on the puzzle at the same time and had let the rice boil dry. The smell of charred rice had lingered in the cabin for days.

Spring break only lasted a week, but except for the burnt rice it had been a fine week. They had planned to do very little, and had managed to do even less. In general, they had relaxed. Two days of rain had given Jamaal time to finish the course material he had brought, and Bart had expanded the puzzle by at least two inches.

The stir-fry was everything Jamaal had said it would be. "You cook almost as well as Arnold does," Bart told him, which Jamaal took as high praise. Earlier in the week, Bart had dragged his roommate out of bed with no explanation, and had driven him down to the Diner. Jamaal's plate ended up as clean when he finished as it had been when Arnold took it off the stack, the last of his biscuit having sopped up the last of the milk gravy. "We will be coming back here," Jamaal had said as they left. "I won't say he cooks better than my mama—you don't get to be my size on bad cooking—but he's good."

On Friday, they packed to go back to Clemson. Their choice was breakfast at the cabin, or breakfast at the Diner, and Jamaal made the choice easy. "We've got no bacon left, and no butter. We're out of bread. What we have is eggs and Spam." Bart made a face. "Actually," Jamaal said, "I can work with Spam. Slice it thin and fry it crisp, then do the eggs in the Spam grease: not half bad. But if the choice is between that and breakfast at the Diner, I vote for the Diner."

Bart agreed. They left the Spam in the cupboard, but the eggs would go bad before they came back, so they took them along. At the Diner, Bart had the Country Breakfast, but Jamaal had asked Arnold what else there was.

"Whatever you want," Arnold said. "I can make most anything. You hungry?" Jamaal was. "Okay, then. What you need is what I call the Special Breakfast. It's not on the menu board, cause I ran out of letters, but you'll like it." He went back to the grill before Jamaal could ask him what the Special was, but in a few minutes he brought it out: a slab of country ham with a sunny-side-up fried egg on top of it, grits with a puddle of red-eye gravy in the middle, and a biscuit. "That suit you?" It did. In a stage musical, the Jamaal character would have burst into song. There would be another clean plate when he was finished.

Not everyone at the Diner that morning was so thorough. At a booth nearby, a man saw a dark car go past, then he and his companion left their breakfasts half eaten, paid their tabs, and went out to a red Ford pickup.

◇◇◇◇◇◇◇◇◇◇◇◇◇◇◇◇●◇◇◇◇◇◇◇◇◇◇◇◇◇◇◇◇

Bart didn't usually stop for hitchhikers, but these two were pitiful, all dusty and beat-up looking. He wasn't sure there was room for them, but their FBI badges and their assurance that they didn't mind riding in back with the duffel bags, won him over. Neither Bart nor Jamaal saw the man who had climbed up the slope from the red truck, but Bragg did. He was at the point of yelling 'Get down!' when he saw that instead of pointing a gun at them, the man was trying to flag down a ride, just like they had done. The chase was apparently not over. "Son," he shouted to Bart over the wind noise, "would you pull over up here?" Bart did. "I think we're about to have hostile company." He gestured at

McIntyre. "Special Agent Adams here is trained in defensive driving. Would you mind swapping places with him?" He had considered having the boys simply get out, but he didn't want to risk their being found by the pursuers. The bad guys might think they had seen something, and he didn't think they would want to leave witnesses. Bart came around back, where Bragg was stuffing the boys' duffel bags up against the tailgate. Then they were back on the road.

The man who had been driving the red truck watched as another car blew past. People who knew him called him Dock, and he was a wheel man. Slim, his passenger, might have been called a button man, but Slim didn't like labels. He was just Slim, and that was all anybody needed to know. Today the job was two nosy government types; tomorrow it would be somebody else. Slim didn't think of himself as cold; he thought of himself as practical, and right now the practical problem was that they needed a car.

Dock had made it up to the road first, but his attempts to flag down a ride had been total failures. It didn't occur to him that he wouldn't have picked up somebody who looked like him, but it did occur to Slim. "Lie down in the road, there beside their car," he said. Dock did as he was told. People who dealt with Slim generally did as they were told, sooner or later.

The South is the Bible Belt. Everyone knows the story of the Good Samaritan and the others, the not-so-good ones who passed by on the other side. The man in the silver Lexus may have been thinking of that very story when he stopped for Dock, but Slim didn't ask, and by the time Dock had gotten up off the road, Slim had lowered the man's body down into the wrecked car. "Get in and drive," Slim told him. Dock got in and drove. Slim was almost certainly a sociopath, which gave Dock some misgivings, but except for that Dock thought they made a pretty good team.

Up ahead was a line of traffic, following a tractor that was doing maybe 15 miles an hour. If the man on the tractor thought it was safe to pass, he would gesture to the car behind him to come around, but on the curvy road, that didn't happen very often. The Jeep was the fourth in line, just behind a motor home that was too high and wide to see around except briefly on some curves. The eighth in line was the silver Lexus. "Peek-a-boo," Slim whispered when he spotted the Jeep. "I see you."

McIntyre had been keeping track of what was behind him. "Car just joined the line, and I count two heads in it." The three cars immediately behind him looked all right, but that newest car might be the enemy.

"Assume it's them," said Bragg. "And if it is, we've got problems. If they can pull up beside us, they'll spray us like they're watering a garden." He got one of the duffel bags. "Son," he told Bart, "I want you to hug this like it was your sweetheart. I'll be over here," indicating the area behind McIntyre. The cloth top was down; they had lowered it right after they had joined the parade. To Jamaal, he said, "If you'll get yourself down on the floor in front of the seat, you'll be a little safer. I hate you boys had to be part of this." He stood up and drew his Glock, to the puzzlement of the people in the car behind them. "Do you think you can pass?" he asked McIntyre.

"I can try, but we'll be hung out there a long time." Jamaal said something to McIntyre, who looked puzzled. Jamaal made a gesture that looked like a stone skipping off a pond. "Brace yourself, sir," said McIntyre. "He says we're in for a surprise." He swerved the Jeep partway left, enough to see if anything was coming at them, and then he stomped on the gas. The Jeep's engine gave out a roar, and despite McIntyre's warning Bragg was almost pitched out of it. By the time they cleared the tractor they were doing sixty and getting faster.

Dock had been watching to see if the Jeep made its move, and now he saw it. "So you want to race, do you?" he muttered. "All right then, let's do it." No way some pissant Jeep was going to smoke him. No way.

The Lexus was fast, and it should have been a short race. It wasn't. It took the better part of five minutes for Dock to close the distance, giving Jamaal time to talk McIntyre out of his Glock. He knelt in the passenger seat, facing backward. Bragg was on his back, feet against the tailgate, using his knees as a tripod for his own Glock. He told Bart to stay low. The Lexus had been driving straight toward them, but when Dock saw the pistols aimed at him, he started weaving erratically, trying to close the distance without getting shot. "Okay," he told Slim. "I'm going to go left and then hold it straight for a second or so." Slim nodded, and the Lexus went left. Slim stuck his gun out the window and fired off a burst. From the Jeep, Bragg and Jamaal returned fire, and one shot put a hole in the Lexus's windshield on Slim's side. It missed Slim, but he ducked down; Dock let off the gas and began to weave again. "New plan," Dock said, sliding down in his seat until he could just see over the dash. "You stay down, and I'll ram the damn thing."

"Do it quick," Slim said from the foot space. "I think they got the radiator." There was steam coming out from the edges of the hood, which probably meant the engine would overheat and seize in a couple of minutes, maybe less. It was time to make the kill. Dock quit weaving and gunned it.

Moving the duffel bag had uncovered the carton of eggs that the boys hadn't wanted to leave at the cabin. That gave Bart an idea. When Slim had slipped down out of sight, and the roar of the Lexus's engine had signaled Dock's new plan, Bart reached around the duffel bag and begun lobbing eggs at the Lexus. There were only four eggs, and the first two missed, but the next two hit right where he wanted them, at the bottom of the windshield.

All of a sudden instead of a clear windshield, Dock had a sunlit blob in front of him. The Lexus swerved sharply as he hiked himself up in the seat, trying to see around the glowing white and yellow mess. Bragg and Jamaal had used a lot of bullets during the first attack, but each had a few left, and now they used them, aiming for the driver. The Lexus suddenly went sideways in the road, and started rolling.

Hitting something at ninety-plus miles an hour is almost always going to be fatal. A rolling wreck at ninety is sometimes survivable, depending on the vehicle. In the red pickup, Dock and Slim would have been roadkill, but tumbling along in the Lexus, nestled in its airbags, they somehow survived, and by the time the Highway Patrol came to investigate, they were gone. Their job had been to protect the break-in crew from the government snoops, and they had chased the snoops out of town. It was a good story, and by the time they were back in New Jersey, they actually believed it.

Chapter Sixteen

According to Winston Churchill, there is nothing more exhilarating than to be shot at without result. Bart had read that somewhere, and when he had read it, it had seemed plausible. Now that he had actually been shot at, twice, he knew better. He thought that maybe the first time hadn't been a fair test, since Churchill had specifically said, "without result," but after being shot at from the Lexus, he decided Churchill had simply been wrong, unless "exhilarating" was British slang for sick-to-your-stomach.

The Jeep pulled onto a side road and stopped. For a while, they just sat there, then everybody got out. McIntyre spoke first. "I believe," he said, "that I need to rethink my opinion of Jeeps." He looked at Jamaal and gave him a nod, which Jamaal returned along with McIntyre's Glock.

"You shot like a soldier," Bragg told Jamaal. "Where did you learn to do that?"

"My papa taught me," Jamaal said.

Bragg's expression said he would have to think about that. When fathers teach their sons to shoot, it's usually to plink with a .22. What he had seen Jamaal do was combat-style shooting. Interesting. Of course, if Bragg had had a son, that was exactly what he would have taught him. "Quick thinking with the eggs, too," he told Bart. "Good use of available materials."

Bart wasn't sure if the man was being sarcastic, but he seemed sincere. "Is it over?" he asked.

"Almost," Bragg said. "We'll need your names and addresses for our report, but they won't be made public." Because, he thought, that kill team might have survived, and we don't want them to know who you are.

McIntyre had been on the phone. "Sir? I've got the location."

"Good," Bragg said. "Let's get there and get done so our friends can get back on their way."

The location, as McIntyre called it, had once been a

working farm. Now its fields were grown up in weeds and its driveway needed gravel. There was an ordinary-looking barn, a little bit out of plumb but otherwise more or less intact except that it badly needed paint. There had once been a farmhouse near the barn, but it had long since lost its battle with kudzu. "Are you sure this is right?" Bart asked. Several of Jamaal's horror movies started out with people driving up to places like this.

"They weren't going to be coming by road," Bragg answered. "Follow me," They got out of the Jeep and walked around the side of the barn. At the far end, they were able to see what the barn had hidden: a large gray-green helicopter.

Jamaal was starting to get a bad feeling. Bart didn't know what the helicopter meant, but he did. "Oh my god," he muttered. Bart gave him a quizzical look. "It's a Blackhawk variant. It's not something civilians use." He looked at Bragg, then at McIntyre. "Just out of curiosity, who the hell are you guys, really?"

Bragg was thinking he might still salvage the FBI story when a man in a sergeant's uniform came from around the corner, saluted him, and said, "Captain Bragg? The colonel wants to see you." The sergeant noticed Bart and Jamaal, but a raised eyebrow was his only comment.

Bragg nodded to the two boys. "That's right. My name is Steven Bragg. I am a captain in the U. S. Army. This is McIntyre. His rank is...well, it's complicated. Officially, he's a lieutenant, but he's more of a...I suppose you could say, technician."

"J. B.," said McIntyre, holding out his hand. His parents had named him Junius Brutus McIntyre, but for years he had gone by J.B. Some of his colleagues had tried to find out his full name, but they hadn't succeeded. Messing with records was what McIntyre did best, and he had done a good job with his. To the waiting sergeant, McIntyre said, "Does the colonel want to see me, or only Captain Bragg?"

"Only the captain, for now," replied the sergeant, "but I would appreciate it if you would stay close by, so I won't have to hunt you up if she decides she wants you too."

That got Bragg's attention. "She? I was expecting Colonel

Salinger." The sergeant shrugged, and Bragg sighed. "Okay, then. Take me to your leader."

"Thank you, sergeant; see that we are not interrupted."

"Yes, ma'am." The sergeant left, closing the door behind him. The room they were in was upstairs in the barn. It was empty, except for a card table and a folding chair. On the table was a file folder, and in the chair sat Colonel Elizabeth Menendez.

"At ease, captain," she said. If Bragg relaxed, it didn't show. "It appears that you and Mr. McIntyre have been making a mess of things, and it has fallen on me to straighten them out. So let's start with the basics: What are you doing in South Carolina? The file doesn't say."

No, he thought, it wouldn't. "Ma'am, we were gathering information for an aspect of Project Clevis."

The colonel pursed her lips. "That tells me next to nothing, captain. What information were you looking for?"

"Ma'am, by the terms of our assignment to Clevis, my team and I have a degree of autonomy, such that..."

"You are being evasive, captain," she said with icy calm. "Answer my question."

"...such that," he continued, "in furtherance of the project, I am permitted to choose the ways and means without clearance from Colonel Salinger. Our presence here represents one such choice, and that is as much as I will be saying on the subject."

She let that hang in the air for a few seconds. "Before I call the sergeant back in to arrest you for insubordination," she said, "let me remind you that a subordinate must obey a direct order from a superior. I am a colonel. Colonels outrank captains, and this is a direct order: Tell me your team's specific objective in South Carolina."

Using his finger and thumb only, Bragg drew out his Glock and laid it on the table. "Ma'am, I guess it's time to call in your sergeant. I report to one specific officer, and you are not him. I must therefore decline to answer your question."

"If you mean Randy Salinger," she said, mockingly, "I have news for you: he's been transferred to Fort Polk, Louisiana, and his career is as dead as Clevis. So let's try this again, one last time: What were you looking for?" She stood up and locked eyes with him.

Bragg stared back, but stood silent; he had said what he had to say, and there was nothing to add. After what seemed like almost a minute, Bragg heard the door behind him creak open. "Well, ain't this a pretty sight!" said a voice that was not the sergeant's. It had a distinct Texas drawl, and a purist might have heard purty instead of pretty. Bragg knew that voice, but he never moved. "Sergeant? Find us a couple more chairs." The man with the Texas drawl walked over to where Bragg could see him. "I honestly believe a piece of paper held up between the two of you would catch fire. I only wonder which side would char first. At ease, both of you." He wore a combat uniform like the colonel's, but instead of an eagle, his had a star. The sergeant appeared with two more chairs. "Thank you, sergeant; that'll be all." He took the chair behind the desk, and motioned the other two to sit down. "Steve, right off the top of your head, give me your first impression of Colonel Menendez."

"Clear and direct," Bragg said stiffly.

"Uh huh. Elizabeth, first impression of the captain?"

"Loyal to his mission." The way she said it, it didn't sound like a compliment.

"You are damned liars, both of you. Steve, I figure you've decided she's a castrating bitch," he looked at Bragg, who avoided eye contact, "and Elizabeth, you're pretty sure he's a stiff-necked pig." The Colonel examined her nails. "All right then, it's time I introduced you. Steve, meet Colonel Elizabeth Menendez. I expect her to replace me one day. She could do it right now if she had to. She's got good sense, and I trust her, and from now on, if she tells you a thing, she speaks for me. Oh, and she's only a castrating bitch if you piss her off, so you might want to not do that," he paused, "again."

"Elizabeth, meet Captain Steve Bragg. If a job needs doing, he can do it. He'll do it legally if that's the best way, but if you're squeamish, don't ask him for details. If he comes across as a stiff-necked pig—and he surely can—it's cause he takes his job seriously. After a couple of beers, he's a hell of a nice guy. I've offered to promote him, and he's told me—how did you put it, Steve?—to stick it up my wrinkled old ass? Yeah, I think that was it. Tell Colonel Menendez why."

Bragg looked uncomfortable, but this was the man he took orders from. "Ma'am, captains get to go out in the field and do what soldiers do. From what I've seen, colonels and generals just sit on their duffs and read reports. Oh, and colonels do occasionally jerk captains around." How she reacted to that would tell him exactly how much of a bitch she was.

Her eyes widened, then she smiled, just a little. "Jerking captains around is not my idea of fun," she told him. "Where's the challenge? Actually, though, I have heard that generals enjoy it. Some of them," she glanced over at the general, "even order their subordinates to do it."

The general wagged his finger at her. "Don't start. You're the one who told me he'd fold at showdown, and now you know better. Sorry about that Steve, but Elizabeth needs to know who she can rely on, and I think now she does." She gave him a nod of grudging agreement. "But before I drag my wrinkled old ass back to the Pentagon, there's a whole bunch of things I need to know, starting with something Sgt. Barnes just mentioned. Why are there two civilians out in the yard, and why is McIntyre trying to buy a Jeep off one of them?"

"Well, sir," Bragg began, "it happened like this..."

When Sgt. Barnes went down to get McIntyre, he had found Jamaal and Pvt. Cox, facing each other in a wrestling stance, surrounded by the other three privates. The sergeant stepped up behind one of his men, got his attention, and asked in a low voice, "Winston, you want to tell me what's going on?"

Winston whispered back. "That fellow McIntyre said that Jeep would do zero to sixty in five seconds, and Cox called bullshit on him. The skinny kid said McIntyre was right, so Cox said they were both full of shit. Then the big kid said Cox looked kind of scrawny to be using grown-up words like that, and Cox told him he'd be scrawny too, if he lost all that baby fat. That's when we drew the circle, and, uh, here we are."

"Uh huh. Who'd you bet on?" the sergeant asked. He didn't have to ask if there was betting. When Army guys draw a circle, there is always betting.

"I went with the big kid. Something about the way he smiled when Cox made that crack about baby fat. Got good odds, too." Winston had been dividing his attention between his sergeant and the two in the ring, but he decided the sergeant was through with him and he went back to watching. The sergeant was about to put a stop to it—it really wouldn't do to have one of his men beat up a civilian—then he saw what Winston had seen: the big kid wasn't worried. He decided to wait; he could always call a stop to it if it got too ugly.

The match didn't take long. Cox made his move, a faked attack to the right, followed by a leg sweep to catch Jamaal off balance when he adjusted his stance. Or at least that was Cox's plan; Jamaal's adjustment was faster and closer in than Cox had thought possible, and suddenly Cox found himself flying through the air toward his sergeant, who stepped politely out of the way. The team's medic ambled over to see if Cox was all right, decided he was, and went back to the group. Money changed hands.

Sgt. Barnes found McIntyre and sent him upstairs. He told the rest of his squad to find useful work or he would find some for them, and in a moment all that remained were Bart, Jamaal, and the sergeant. "That was a slick move," Barnes told Jamaal. "The Army used to teach that move, but they had too many injuries during training, so they quit. And I know for damn sure they don't teach it in college wrestling. Would you humor a broken down old sergeant and explain how you happen to know it?"

Jamaal looked at the Sergeant. He looked at the name on the uniform. Then he changed angles and looked some more. Finally, he was sure. "I learned it from my papa," he said. "Same as you did."

Sgt. Barnes now gave Jamaal the same once-over Jamaal had given him. "That was, let's see, eight, nine years ago, special training at Leonard Wood. So you'd have been about what...ten? Well I'll be a son of a bitch; are you Ron's boy? You are! You're Jamie Sheridan!"

Bart took notice. "Jamie?" he said delightedly. "They called him Jamie?"

Jamaal gave him a dark look. "You never heard that. Remember, I know where you sleep." To the sergeant, he said, "Yeah, that's me, the little kid watching from the sidelines."

"Not so little, even then. What are you doing now?"

"Freshman at Clemson. This is my roommate, Bart. We were coming back from spring break when your guys flagged us down. That's when McIntyre found out what the Jeep would do." There was a crunch of gravel behind the sergeant and Jamaal's eyes got wider. He had grown up around sergeants, but his social circle hadn't included officers.

"Andrew Compton," said the general. "Relax son, I don't bite. I've just had two of my men tell me the same story, about how they hitched a ride in a magical Jeep. Before I call in the shrinks I wanted to see exactly how crazy they are. Is this it?"

It was Bart who answered. "Yes, sir."

The general walked around it. He squatted down and looked at the tailgate. "Uh huh, they said the man got off one burst, and I see the marks. I ought to be seeing holes," he mused, "and I'm not." He tapped on the tailgate. "Solid. And thick. Interesting."

Jamaal thought he should explain. "I think it's to counterweight the engine, sir. It's a big engine."

Bart had a thought. "Uh, general, can you drive a stick shift?"

Jamaal winced. Among Army people, generals are always called sir, and they don't get asked questions. They especially don't get asked if they can or can't do something. He was about to apologize for his roommate's ignorance when the general laughed out loud. "Hell, son, I was driving a stick long before you were born."

Bart gave the combination of a nod and a shrug that says, I hear you but I'm not sure I believe you. "In that case it's been a while." He held out a key. "Think you still can?"

The general looked at the key. "Sergeant, what do you think; can the old man still drive a stick?"

Sgt. Barnes knew his general. "I can't say, sir. He's right; it really has been a while."

"Oh, so it's like that, is it?" He snatched the key and slipped into the Jeep. "Sergeant, get in and buckle up tight. I'm about to give you a driving lesson." To the boys he said, "If anybody asks, tell them I'm out in the field, pretending I'm a captain." With a shower of gravel, the Jeep was gone.

Jamaal gave Bart a squinty look. "You just pulled something, and I'm not sure what. How did you know he wouldn't bite your head off?"

Bart was watching the Jeep disappear in the distance. "I've never met any generals, but I've read about them. Check me out on this: They mostly give orders. They want a car, they tell somebody, bring me a car. I knew he was curious about the Jeep, just from the way he looked at it, but I'm not military; he can't give me orders, and I didn't figure he'd want to ask, so I baited him a little. The sergeant understood."

Jamaal grunted agreement. "Sergeants understand a lot. Staff sergeants understand a heck of a lot."

"What do colonels understand?" Bart asked casually. He was facing the barn, and had seen Col. Menendez walking toward them.

"Colonels don't..." Jamaal began, until he noticed that

Bart was looking past him, then he added, "...miss much either."

"Nice save," said a voice behind him "There are so many other places that sentence could have gone. Elizabeth Menendez." She held out her hand. Jamaal took it, but couldn't think of anything more to say.

"Bart Phillips," Bart said when it was his turn for the hand shake. "My friend with the look on his face is Jamaal Sheridan. He's an army brat, if that tells you anything. I guess I'm just a regular brat."

She looked them over. "An egg throwing brat, from what I hear." She nodded at Jamaal. "So that would make you the sharpshooter. There are a couple of things we need to ask you two, but I don't see Gen. Compton. He came down to find his sergeant, and now they're both gone."

Jamaal recovered the power of speech. "They, uh, had to go somewhere, ma'am, but he left a message. Something about pretending to be a captain."

"A captain."

"Yes, ma'am."

She looked at the place where the Jeep had slung the gravel, rolled her eyes, and went back into the barn. The boys went to look at the Black Hawk. A half hour later, the Jeep was back, announced by a loud "Yee-ha." The general parked it by the copter, and Sgt. Barnes eased himself out. Then he got down like he was going to do a push-up, and kissed the ground. "Stop that," the general growled. "You know it wasn't that bad." The sergeant stood up, looked at Jamaal, and made a face that said yes, it really had been that bad. "Come on, all of you," the general said. "I'm afraid we've kept the colonel waiting."

◇◇◇◇◇◇◇◇◇◇◇◇◇◇◇◇●◇◇◇◇◇◇◇◇◇◇◇◇◇◇◇◇

The boys' debriefing was almost over when General Compton asked about the Jeep. Just out of curiosity, where had it come from? Bart said his great uncle Wade had died and left it to him.

"Wade," the colonel said, looking through her notes. "What was his last name, if you don't mind my asking?"

"Dawson. Wade Dawson."

The colonel looked up from the file. "Did your uncle leave you anything else, besides the Jeep?" she asked casually.

"I have a scholarship he arranged for, but no, except for that, only the Jeep." He didn't think of the puzzle as an inheritance; it was a graduation present.

"Do you know if there was anything else in his estate? Buildings, machinery, anything like that?"

"There were a couple of bells. Other than that, I have no idea. Mr. Schroder would know; he's the executor."

The Colonel was looking at her notes again. "Emmett Schroder?"

"Yeah. Do you know him?"

"Not personally," she said. "Do you know him well enough to ask him about the estate? I think it may be important."

"Sure. I've got his number." The call took longer than Bart had thought it would, and when it was through, he had a couple of questions of his own. "Did your two guys piss off Mr. Schroder's secretary, by any chance? Because somebody sure did, and her description fits them."

The general answered. "That's not exactly how the captain described their, ah, interaction, but it has the sweet ring of truth. He does need to work on his people skills, particularly with women." He glanced at Colonel Menendez.

"Well, from what Evelyn told me, he's had one lesson already, and if he needs another one, she'll be glad to give it to him. It wasn't his people who broke into the office, was it?" That got their attention. Neither Bragg nor McIntyre had said anything about a break-in.

Colonel Menendez shook her head. "They were the only ones of our people down here, and they didn't do it. Was anything taken?"

"No, whoever it was didn't steal anything. In fact, all they did was look in one file, the one with Uncle Wade's will in it. Does that matter?"

"Yes," said the colonel, "I think it might." She glanced at her watch, and turned to the general. "The law office will probably be closed in an hour, and if they need to go back for a second look, they won't waste any time, not after what happened today. I recommend we post the squad there." The general agreed. "Sergeant?" the colonel called toward the door, which opened immediately. "Dust off the van. Everybody except the copter crew, equip for close-quarter night work. We leave in twenty minutes." To Bart and Jamaal, she said, "Gentlemen, it has been a pleasure meeting you. I'd appreciate it if you didn't discuss what happened today with anybody." She waited until the general had gone down to the Black Hawk, then took Bart aside. "We may have seen the last of that crew," she told him, handing him a card, "but if something comes up, call that number and mention my name. You helped some good men today, and we don't forget who our friends are. Oh, and thank you for letting the general unwind for a few minutes. He doesn't get to do that very often."

By the time Bart and Jamaal got downstairs, a very forgettable van had appeared in front of the barn. Men who, a few minutes before, had been dressed in camo were climbing in, dressed now in black. Bart didn't recognize their equipment but Jamaal did. "Battle gear," he said. "It looks like somebody's kicked a hornet's nest, and the hornets are about to kick back."

Chapter Seventeen

The ancient Greeks taught speaking and music as one subject. Anyone who has listened to recordings of Adolf Hitler's speeches will understand why. On paper, the Fuhrer's rants are the usual political nonsense, but his message was not in what he said; his message was in how he said it. Foreigners who were there, people who understood not a word of German, have told of being caught up in the same emotions as the rest of his audience. It was the delivery that spoke to them, not the words. Music does not have to be sung, or played on a guitar, or indeed on any instrument at all. Pitch, tone, stress and rhythm are what music is made of, not just notes and chords and rests; a good speaker knows that. And if German—arguably the least musical of the Western languages—can sing to the emotions, how much more is that true of languages which are naturally poetic, such as Arabic. A skilled speaker of Arabic can combine the words and the poetic rhythm of the language into a message that speaks directly to the heart. Dr. Ziya's brother Mehmed—or, as his congregation knew him, the Imam Muhammad—was such a speaker.

The sermon his son Murad had prepared for him was a competent piece of writing, but Murad had no ear for poetry. "*The tombs of the so-called Sufi saints are as much idols as were the images of wood and stone, in the time of Confusion,*" Murad had written, and that was all right. The references to wood and stone were good visual images; he would keep them. But, "*Their veneration is error, and that error must be driven from our house,*" that was clumsy; he could do better. He scratched through that line and wrote in its place, "*If an ugly woman disgusts the village, she can be driven away. Perhaps another village will see her differently. But if the ugliness is sin itself, sending it elsewhere accomplishes nothing. Idolatry is an ugly blemish on the face of the world, and driving it away simply moves the blemish from one part of the face to another. Whether near or far, the veneration of tombs is an insult to God, and if we tolerate it, our fate will be the same as that of any other worshipers of idols: to burn forever in the righteous fire.*" Yes, that was better. Murad would probably have edited out the reference to the ugly woman, but Murad had the soul of a bureaucrat. This sermon was not the one that really mattered anyway. That would come next week. That was when the program required him to send the faithful out to start that righteous fire, led by himself as their commander.

Commander of the Faithful; he liked the sound of that. It was an old title, a heroic title. It was almost as old as that other title, the one he intended to use in earnest: Caliph, the Successor to the Messenger of God. Murad was right, though; it was still too early in the program to mention the New Caliphate. Later, after he led his followers to the Sufi shrine, after they dipped their swords in the blood of the sinners... No, that wasn't quite right; the imagery was dated. His sons' warehouses were not full of swords, and no one dips an assault rifle in blood. So how should he phrase it? Perhaps this: When they have seen the blood of the sinners soaking into the desert sand, sinking toward Hell like the souls of those same sinners. Yes, much better. He added that to his notes for next week. The blood was the key image anyway, not the weapon. Once their hands were red with the blood of the Sufis, it would be much easier to turn them against the Shi'ites, and the Hindus, and whoever else refused to submit. The first blood did not have to come from the Sufis, of course; any minority would do, but from the standpoint of the program the Sufis were ideal: their doctrines were not widely understood, so any vile practice he attributed to them would be believed. And better yet, they were pacifists, so there was no risk of the attack failing. Best of all, one of their shrines was conveniently close, the tomb of their blacksmith saint at Wadi Qadr. Their destruction would be the decisive act that would cement his followers' loyalty to him, and it would tell all the others, "If you fail to heed the righteous will of the Faithful, you will surely taste the fire." That was another good phrase, he thought, and added it to his notes.

Chapter Eighteen

The safe in Emmett's office had once belonged to a jewelry store. When it was new it had been state of the art, but so had black-and-white TVs; the safe had been around a while. The short man in the ski mask had made note of its make and model during their first visit, and a little research had told him how its lock was designed. Using listening gear undreamed of when the safe was made, he quickly had it open. He took pictures of its interior, from several angles, so that he could put each thing back exactly where it had been. Then he took everything out, including finally the leather-bound book on the bottom shelf, identified only with the letters WD. He needed almost a half hour to shoot its pages, but he knew he had found something. No one would have taken the trouble to encrypt that much text if it weren't something important, something he wanted kept secret. When the man was through, he put everything back where it had been and closed the safe, even resetting the dial to the number it had been on. During all of this, his taller partner had simply stood by, watching and listening; he was the security half of the operation. They were supposed to have two more lookouts outside, but either they hadn't shown up or they were really well hidden.

The short man sent the pictures to a number he had been given, then watched the progress bar on the screen as the data went wherever it went. Exactly where that was, neither of the men knew or cared. To do the job, they didn't need to know; they only needed a number to call. When the send was complete, the man re-formatted the phone's memory card several times, then signaled his partner that it was time to go. The partner eased open the back door, listened, then slipped out, followed by the short man. They were almost to the street when four shadows converged on them. "Freeze," said a voice.

In the early days of prohibition, when the revenue agents found a moonshiner at his still, they would burst out of the woods, yelling. After a while, they noticed that if they yelled "Don't move," or "Don't run," the moonshiner would almost always run,

148

but if they yelled "Freeze," he wouldn't. A startled, frightened man doesn't know what to do, and doesn't have time to make a plan. So, if he hears "move" or "run," he is going to run. He hears the command, and ignores all the rest. "Freeze" works a lot better. The glowing green dots on the burglars' legs probably helped too. Green dots meant military laser sights, and legs as targets meant, "We've done this before: if we shoot, we're not going to hit each other; we're just going to hit you." The men froze. A van with its lights off came around the corner, and in less than a minute, the street was empty.

◇◇◇◇◇◇◇◇◇◇◇◇◇◇◇◇●◇◇◇◇◇◇◇◇◇◇◇◇◇◇◇◇

The two burglars had concerns about legality. The military, they said, could not arrest civilians, and that was only the first of a long list of their sacred constitutional rights that they said were being violated. They no longer wore ski masks, but the other man in the back of the van did. He told them that they were not, in fact, under arrest, that they were free to leave any time they wanted. He even opened the van's rear door and offered to assist in their departure. The burglars stayed, but their attitude remained poor; they complained that jumping out of a speeding van would involve injury and pain. The man in the ski mask mentioned the common belief that suffering improves one's character, adding that, in his opinion their characters had ample room for improvement. The burglars took that as a slight, and sulked in silence for the rest of the trip. That is how the ride to the barn went, or at any rate that is how the man in the ski mask described it when he wrote his report.

At the barn, the burglars' attitudes were still poor. The shorter man's phone yielded the number he had called, a throw-away phone in New York City, but that was all the information anyone got from them. The colonel kept up with the questioning from a monitor upstairs in the barn, but the burglars were professionals, and they knew the drill. "You ain't got nothing on us," the taller one kept saying. "Where's your evidence? You gonna testify? I don't think so. Our lawyer's gonna have a field day with you idiots," and on and on.

Colonel Menendez turned off the sound and looked at Bragg. "Captain, I think we have gotten all we are going to get, and those two have begun to get on my nerves. What do you think we ought to do with them?"

Bragg was surprised, and that didn't happen very often. Ranking officers don't usually ask for advice from their subordinates, which is why so many lieutenants get the reputation of being idiots: their sergeants know a lot more than they do, but the lieutenants don't want to look weak, so they don't ask. Bragg thought for a while. "Ma'am, do you appreciate irony? Because there is a way..." He let that hang in the air.

"Do it. Do I want to know details?" She remembered what the general had said.

Bragg gave her a look of bland innocence. "Details of what, Ma'am?"

◇◇◇◇◇◇◇◇◇◇◇◇◇◇◇●◇◇◇◇◇◇◇◇◇◇◇◇◇◇◇

They took the burglars back to Larson. The men's car, which they had parked a block away from Emmett's office, was now parked behind Larson's liquor store. After Sgt. Barnes had demonstrated the proper way to render a man unconscious with a choke hold, twice, the burglars were laid out on the floor of the store at the end farthest from its jimmied-open back door. The store had security cameras, but men dressed exactly like the burglars had covered the lenses with squares of duct tape, on which were clear impressions of the thieves' fingerprints. A few seconds after they started to stir, the store's alarm went off, and the police arrived just as they came staggering out the back door. Between the store's opened safe, the listening device, the money in their pockets, and their fingerprints on the duct tape, it wasn't a hard case to crack. Their story, that the government had sent men in black to kidnap them and plant them there, reminded the police of a tale that one of the local thieves had told, years before, about how he had been taken up in a UFO, forced to drink until he passed out, and then left in that same liquor store beside an open bottle of Jim Beam. If you're going to lie to us, they told the burglars, you should at least try to be original.

◇◇◇◇◇◇◇◇◇◇◇◇◇◇◇◇●◇◇◇◇◇◇◇◇◇◇◇◇◇◇◇◇

In 1915, the Union Traction Company had a problem. It made trolley cars, and trolley cars weren't selling well. So the company made a calculated wager. President Wilson said he could keep the country out of the European war; Union Traction bet that he couldn't. It retooled, and then got rich making railroad cars for troop trains. The armistice in 1918 put an end to the troop train business, but by then the company had branched into other areas of military supply, making parts for aircraft, ships, and tanks. To assist it in selling to the rapidly-rearming Europeans, Union Traction merged with a Belgian arms company, Armen-Alliance, and became Traction-Alliance, a name which in due course became Traxell International.

The lobby floor of Traxell's New York headquarters was a triumph of the atrium school of interior design, a bright, high-ceilinged plaza where tropical plants, elaborate fountains, and smiling receptionists made the visitor feel welcome. Elevators from the lobby went up ten floors, all except for one elevator, which went to eleven if you had a security card. The eleventh floor had no fountains, no plants, and no smiling receptionists. In fact, the lobby on eleven had no people at all. You left the elevator, went through a screening gate, looked into a retinal scanner, and then got on a different elevator, which took you up to the floor you really wanted. Unless, of course, you hadn't done well on the security scans. If that happened, the elevator took you to thirteen, and nobody wanted that. If it turned out that you were what you should be, going to thirteen still meant delays and inconvenience. And if not...well, there were rumors.

Harold "Hal" Stasevik's office was on twenty-three. Within Traxell, the higher the floor, the higher the status, and twenty-

three was respectably high. Outside the company Hal was
unknown. He had never been interviewed by a business magazine,
and neither his name nor his department ever appeared in the
annual report to shareholders. That the department even had a
name was a concession to convenience; Hal had a seat at board
meetings, and they had to call him something, so he was vice-
president in charge of Research Liaison. Hal's people sometimes
did actual research, but usually they looked for research that
somebody else had done. That sometimes involved spying, perhaps
stealing, and occasionally a little bit of what they called
interrogation. Few people on the board knew everything that
Research Liaison really did, and absolutely no one wanted to know
how it did it.

One way Hal kept his department out of public notice was
to find people who could focus on details and not worry about the
big picture. The man in front of his desk at the moment was the
very model of a detail person. His name was Nelson, and he was
the senior member of the Information Technology team. He was,
by his own description, a computer geek, and he was a good one.
"Do you have anything yet on that decryption problem I sent
down to IT?" Hal asked him.

"Not yet," Nelson replied. "We're pretty sure it's a public-
key encryption. Some of those can be broken, some can't. The one
we use in house isn't breakable by any attack I've ever heard of,
but this one looks like it might be vulnerable. I want to try a power
fault attack, even though it'll take a couple more hours on Big
Mama."

"If that's what it takes, I'll get it approved," Hal told him.
Time on the company's supercomputer was precious; some of the
most vicious fights at executive board meetings were over which
department got how much time. Hal didn't know what a power
fault attack was, and he didn't care. If it worked, he could read the
coded book; if it didn't, they would try something else. That book
might be nothing—some small-town tax cheat's second set of
accounts, maybe—but it was their best hope of finding the Dawson

process. The process wasn't patented, so if they found it, they could claim it, and it was potentially worth billions.

The book had been in the probate lawyer's safe, but that didn't mean the lawyer knew the key to the code. Still, he might, and if the mainframe failed, they could always interrogate him. Best to try IT's way first, Hal thought. If that worked, there would be no corpse to dispose of.

Chapter Nineteen

The Sufi compound at Wadi Qadr sits by itself in the desert. There is a central domed shrine and a few smaller buildings, all surrounded by a wall. The man in the white Mercedes had parked it some distance from the compound's wooden gate, possibly out of respect, or possibly so that anyone watching him walk toward the gate would see that he was unarmed. In a loud voice he called out the bismillah, the formula spoken before any special undertaking: "In the name of God, the merciful and compassionate."

A man's head appeared over the top of the wall. He called to the man on the ground, "Do you come in peace?" Someone wearing a suicide vest would of course say he did, but to tell the lie following the bismillah would damn him twice, once for the suicide, and again for the sacrilege.

The visitor had expected that question, or another like it, and he had his answer ready. "I come in peace, but death follows close behind me. I would speak with Sheikh Hamid." Several moments passed, then there was a muted clunk and the gate opened. The visitor went into the courtyard, where he was met by a guide who took him toward one of the smaller buildings. The visitor looked at his guide's face longer than was strictly polite, and finally said, "You are the Sheikh's son, Abdullah, are you not?"

"You know me?"

"Only from photographs."

Abdullah found that surprising. The visitor could have said he had made a lucky guess, but instead he had said something both informative and disturbing, as Abdullah had not known he had ever been photographed. "Your business with my father, is it such that I might be present?" he asked.

"You are in day-to-day charge of the shrine, are you not?" The man did not wait for an answer. "If it would not have been disrespectful to your father, I would have asked to meet with you instead of him; so yes, you should be present." They had arrived at their goal, and Abdullah opened the door for the guest. Inside, an elderly man at a writing desk rose to meet them. The stranger bowed respectfully. "Sheikh Hamid, I am Fareed, the son—the younger son—of Mehmed Ziya. You may know him as the Imam Muhammad."

The walls of the room were lined with books; the room itself was furnished with rugs and cushions in the desert fashion. The old man gestured for them to be seated. "I know of the famous Imam," he said after he had seated himself. "He says he would rid the world of idols." He paused for a moment, in thought. "Are you acquainted with the Western philosopher Nietzsche?" Fareed was not. "*If you contend with monsters,* Nietzsche wrote, *you must take care that you do not become one.* Do you know what the West calls someone who seeks notoriety and achieves it? I am told they call him a media idol. When your father comes to visit us, perhaps I should warn him not to look in any mirrors."

"He seldom gazes into mirrors," Fareed said. "He finds his voice more interesting than his appearance. Tomorrow, at the Friday prayers, he will use that voice to lead the people here to Wadi Qadr to, as he will put it, 'rid our land of the scourge of idolatry.' I have heard him rehearse his sermon, and I myself was almost inspired to pick up a gun and come here."

Abdullah leaned forward. "And yet, you did not. May I ask why?"

Fareed looked him in the eyes. "Can you recite the shahadah?"

"Of course," Abdullah replied. The shahadah, the statement of faith, is the central precept of Islam. "There is no god except God, and Muhammad is the Messenger of God."

"Exactly so," said Fareed. "From childhood, I was taught that anyone who freely recites the shahadah is a Believer. I was also taught that one Believer does not kill another. I was not taught that respect for pious men is wrong, even if they are dead, and yet now I am assured that it is idol worship, and that you and everyone else here must be killed. I do not know whether you are a good Muslim or a bad one; that is for God to say, not me, and not my father. That is what I believe. What I know is that if you and your people are here after Friday prayers, you are marked for death, and I wish not to have your blood on my hands."

Abdullah was about to say something, but his father gestured him to silence. "We knew of your father's intentions; we did not know his schedule. For that, I thank you. As for the blood, it will flow if God wills it, but only if. I think it would be best if you were not at Wadi Qadr when your father comes to visit. Now, may I offer you some coffee?"

The Imam was well pleased. This was the crucial sermon, and it was the best he had ever written. Starting with themes his listeners had heard from infancy, he built to a thundering conclusion: "*You know what must be done, for God has willed it. You can adopt His will as your own, or you can set your will against His, but in the end it is all the same: the outcome has been ordained since the first day of creation, and your will, your choice, cannot change it. Your choice is between seeing God in Paradise, or carrying your stubborn pride with you to Hell, where it can feed the fire under your spitted soul forever. My friends, the time to make that choice is now. Today, I go to the serpents' den. Today, I will give the Sufis one last chance. Renounce your idols and rejoin the community of Believers, I will tell them. And today, if they persist in their blasphemy, I will cleanse the earth of their stench! The time has come, and the means are at hand! I go to do God's will; will you join me? Will you join me? Will you join me?*"

By the time he had made the third and loudest call, the crowd was on its feet, screaming its agreement. As the Imam strode toward the door, his white robes swirled around him. It had required several rehearsals and some subtle tailoring to get them to do that, but the effect was exactly what he had wanted. Like a billowing white cloud, he swept out the door toward the waiting trucks, then took his place in the open bed of the one at the head of the line. There were already men in that truck, men who had not been inside for the sermon. Their job was to distribute the guns, and then to distribute themselves among the crowd, so that the initial gunfire would seem to come from everywhere at once. His son Murad had been very clear on that point: if several in the crowd opened fire at the appointed time, everyone else would follow. But those first shots had to be fired, and that must not be left to chance.

It was all scripted, all rehearsed. He would leap from the lead truck, march grandly forward and pound on the gate, calling on those inside to open it in the name of God. If they did, he would urge the mob to follow him inside, where his planted gunmen would begin the slaughter. If the gate stayed shut, the lead truck would ram it open. Either way, the work would be finished in a few minutes. Murad would be shooting too, but in his case it would be video. The more heroic-looking moments would adorn the news broadcasts that evening, along with the call to the faithful throughout the land to rise up and complete the cleansing.

The Imam was disagreeably surprised to find the gate already open, blocked only by an old man in a plain brown burnoose, holding a large book. This was not according to the script: it would be foolish to pound on an open gate. As the Imam wondered what he should do, the old man spoke, in a voice audible to all. "I am Hamid, son of Issa. I am the eldest of those you have come here to kill. Tell me, will you perform this valiant deed yourself, or will you trick these others into doing it for you?"

The Imam was a talented writer, and with a good text he was a gifted speaker, but he was not a good improviser. He fell back on a line from his sermon: "I call upon you to renounce your idols and rejoin the community of Believers," he bellowed. Somehow, yelling at one old man was not nearly as grand as it would have been if he were shouting it at a closed gate.

The old man smiled. "I worship no idols, as you well know. I testify that there is no god except God, and that Muhammad is the Messenger of God. And I honor the Book." He held it out toward the Imam. "Can you show me where it says you may lawfully slay a peaceful Believer? For if it does not, you are leading these people into Hell for your own profit. Or do the people not know what the family business is?" There was some murmuring in the crowd, as those who did in fact know, told the others.

The Imam held one of the assault rifles. It was for appearance only, of course; he had never actually fired one, but like all the others, it was loaded. Nothing he could think to say would sound right, and yet he had to do something; the situation was getting out of hand. He pointed the weapon skyward and pulled the trigger. Nothing happened, and he thought he heard some sniggering mixed with the murmuring behind him. He saw a little lever on the side of the gun, flicked it down, then pointed the weapon at the old man. This time it worked. He held the trigger and played the stream of bullets up and down the old man's body, both while it collapsed and afterward, until the magazine was empty. Only then did he see how many of the bullets had torn into the Book. The murmuring stopped; the crowd was deathly silent. Raising the empty gun over his head, he shouted "Follow me," and ran into the walled compound. No one followed. After a moment, a few of the men from the lead truck straggled in behind him, but there was nothing for them to do. The courtyard was empty. The Imam ran into the nearest building, but no one was there either. It was the same everywhere. The old man had been the only one, and when the Imam came back through the gate, the crowd was gathered around his corpse.

A flock of birds can be flying along when, for no obvious reason, every bird will suddenly change direction. Schools of fish do that too, all together and all at once. Anyone who thinks man has risen far above the beasts has never seen a mob in action, because like the birds and the fish, a mob can change from this to that in the blink of an eye. The sight of the Qur'an, bloody and torn, still clutched in the dead hands of the harmless old man, was all it took. Someone yelled out "Demon!" Others took up the cry. A stone was thrown, then another. The Imam stepped back and called to the men he had hired, "Kill them!" The men looked at the crowd, which far outnumbered them, and which was armed exactly as they were, then they dropped their guns, turned their backs, and walked back toward the trucks. The Imam ran into the compound and slammed the gate, but the latch inside had been dismantled, and the crowd quickly poured in behind him. There were only a few stones in the courtyard so they dragged him outside the walls, where there were more than enough.

They buried the old man where he had stood his ground against the demon. The damaged Qur'an they also buried, as custom dictated. The broken body of the demon they left for the carrion birds. Murad rode back to town with the peasants, trying to look like one of them. He had dropped the video camera and moved to a different part of the crowd when he realized what was happening, but even there he had gotten some dark looks, so he had done what he had to do. No, the people thought, he could not possibly be the evil Murad. Not even a demon's son would help to stone his own father.

Chapter Twenty

The puzzle was finished. During the first weeks back at school, Bart hadn't made much progress with it, but then one day Tori noticed it and asked if she could work on it. That was fine with Bart. For him, a puzzle—even this puzzle—was just a problem to be solved. The more challenging it was, the more interesting the problem, but that was all. For Tori, it was different. For her, a puzzle was a gauntlet, flung at her feet by the puzzle maker, a duel to be won or lost, and Tori hated to lose. The first time she saw the puzzle on Bart's desk, it had been like the scene in old western movies, where the sheriff and the villain square off and it's time to get the little children off the street. "Oh my god," she had whispered. "Is that a Stave?" Bart told her it was, but the lack of awe in his voice surprised her. "Do you know what those things cost? They're like, the gold standard of crazy-hard puzzles. Can I touch it?" Jamaal had faked a coughing attack to cover his laugh; he figured that was the first time any girl had asked Bart that question. Bart didn't notice. Tori did, but despite the look she gave him, Jamaal didn't transform into a toad.

The first time Dee had brought Tori over, the excuse had been that they were out shopping, and needed Bart's shirt size. That, and she said her roommate had wanted to meet the blushing Ninja. Bart had turned sunburn red when she said that, and so had Tori, which Dee took to be a good omen. Jamaal had grown up with a sister and knew—at least he knew better than Bart did—how girls think, and he had given Dee an inquiring look from across the room. Her reply, a wink, was all the answer he needed. He nodded his approval.

Jamaal had grown up on army bases, and army brats don't end up shy. Plus, he had played team sports ever since he could walk. Maybe being part of a team makes a boy outgoing, or maybe being outgoing makes a boy a good team player. Whichever it was, Jamaal wasn't shy, and Bart was: too shy for his own good, Jamaal thought. Bart could talk to strangers—that's how he and Dee had met—but he didn't go places just for the fun of meeting new

people. Jamaal told him he was antisocial; Bart replied that half
the strangers he had met lately had tried to kill him, which Jamaal
said was an exaggeration; it hadn't been as many as half, but he
conceded Bart might have a point. Still, if Dee thought the green-
haired girl had friend potential, Jamaal was all for it.

Bart had started on the side of the puzzle with the sketch
of Larson on it, the sketch that had shown where the bells were.
From working the puzzle, he knew that the other side had
something on it, too, but he hadn't gotten any idea of what. They
talked about how to flip the puzzle over without it coming apart,
and the best way to do it, they decided, was to slide it onto
something stiff, hold it down somehow, and then flip it over.

They were about to try pillowcases, stretched tight like a
trampoline, when Jamaal had an inspiration. "Smith and Jones,"
he said. Bart thought about that, realized what his roommate was
saying, grinned, and high-fived him.

Tori raised an eyebrow. "Smith and Jones?"

Jamaal answered. "They live down the hall. That's not their
real names, but it's what we all call them. They go out on
weekends and come back with stuff. They don't say where they get
it, and we don't ask."

"Cause we don't want to know," added Bart. "But up on
their walls they've got more road signs than Highway 28 has. Two
of those would be perfect." With that, they were off down the hall.

Like so many great ideas, this one had a flaw. Smith and
Jones didn't lend out their treasures. The guys came back to their
room defeated, which triggered Tori's problem-solving instincts.
"Do either of them have a girlfriend?" she asked. Jones did. Tori
got her name and went to work. First, she found out that the girl
was a Kappa Delta, then she called a friend of hers in KD. Within
five minutes Jones was at the door with a chastened look and two
metal signs. Both signs said the same thing: "Trustee Parking
Only," but one was from Georgia Tech and the other was from
Florida State.

Jones gave Tori a look of mixed resentment and respect. "I don't know who you are, but I'd hate to be on your bad side," he grunted.

"Why, whatever do you mean?" she said innocently. The boys promised to bring the signs back tomorrow, and Jones went slouching back to his room. Flipping the puzzle over was easy, now that they had the right tools, but the back side was not the revelation they had hoped it would be. It was a very loose sketch of a cat in a basket. Below the basket, in Wade's shaky writing, were two words: *Look here.*

◇◇◇◇◇◇◇◇◇◇◇◇◇◇◇◇●◇◇◇◇◇◇◇◇◇◇◇◇◇◇◇◇

The next morning Bart and Jamaal cut class and drove to Larson. It didn't take long to find the sewed-up slit in the bottom of the cat's basket, where a small, flat notebook had been slipped into a cavity in the basket's stiff base. Emmett was amused. "That is so like the old rascal," he said. "It was hidden in plain sight, but only the right person would find it."

Jamaal waited until they were back in the Jeep. "So what do you think is in it?"

Bart had opened the front cover just long enough to read a line in Wade's shaking writing: *...you will need to put aside some received truths,* it said, *and let some disquieting possibilities take their place. If that prospect disturbs you, go no further.* "Back at the farm, they asked me if Uncle Wade had left me anything besides the Jeep, and they seemed disappointed when I said no. I think this is what they were talking about, and I think it's something we should all talk about."

◇◇◇◇◇◇◇◇◇◇◇◇◇◇◇◇●◇◇◇◇◇◇◇◇◇◇◇◇◇◇◇◇

"Do you think your uncle was in the CIA?" Tori asked when they showed her the notebook. "I mean like, he could have been one of the ones they gave the LSD to. That would explain a lot."

Bart had actually considered something like that, but then he remembered what Ahmed, the foreigner at the wake, had said about the iron bell. "No," he finally said, "I think it's a lot stranger than that. Jamaal, do you remember what I told you about Uncle Wade's wake?"

"You mean, about the food and the fireworks? Sure."

"Well, all that was true, but there was more. There was a big bell, and a little bell, and a fellow named Ahmed. I didn't think anybody would believe it if I got into all that, cause I don't really understand it myself. It's like a giant riddle. I thought solving the puzzle would solve the riddle, but now I think it's bigger and stranger than that, and I'm going to need some help with it. Are you interested?"

Jamaal gave him a funny look. "You mean stranger than that trip in the Jeep?" Bart knew which trip he meant. Tori wondered, but she decided it could wait.

"Yeah," Bart answered. "A lot stranger than that. Maybe scary strange. So, in or out?"

Jamaal didn't hesitate. "I'm in."

Tori had a question. "Can Dee help too?" Bart said sure. "Then we're in."

A half hour later, he had told the story. It wouldn't have taken that long except there were a lot of questions. The last one came from Jamaal. "Those Army guys we met on the road, they never said why the bad guys were after them. You really think it was this?"

Bart thought about that. Wade was his only connection with Emmett, and when he had mentioned Emmett to the colonel, all of a sudden her squad had jumped into action. That didn't feel like a coincidence. "Yeah. I think so."

Tori was by now feeling totally left out, because Bart's story hadn't included anything about the Army, or bad guys. Within a few minutes she had wormed the rest of the story out of them. "Remember how I said we were in?" she asked. "Well, you can tattoo that on your forehead, cause we're totally in."

Bart asked her to find Dee. "We need to know what's in

the notebook, and if we're going to be in this together, I think we should find that out together."

Chapter Twenty-One

The notebook turned out to be mostly text, but there were sketches scattered through it. The Introduction, however, was all text:

When I was in North Africa, I saw some amazing things, things which I knew to be impossible. I have spent the remainder of my life trying to understand those things, and in some measure I have succeeded: I am able to do what I saw done there. I am also able to whistle, but I once tried to teach that art to a friend, only to meet with complete failure. Perhaps my student was inept, but I suspect the problem was my teaching. I do not believe you truly understand a thing unless you can explain it to someone else, which makes me think that I don't really understand whistling; I simply know how to do it. It may be the same with what I saw in North Africa, but in the hope that a lifetime of study has not gone completely to waste, I am going to try. I hope you will approach this project with an open mind; you will need to put aside some received truths, and let some disquieting possibilities take their place. If that prospect disturbs you, go no further; you would not like where the journey ends up. But if exploring a new world appeals to you, I invite you to come along with me now.

The gifts that Uncle Wade had sent every year had been a little odd, Bart knew, but so had Uncle Wade, so he hadn't given them much thought. The books, the puzzles, the kits with no directions, they were simply the sorts of things that an odd uncle sends. It was only later that he found out most kids didn't have odd uncles, and that fringe science wasn't what most of them grew up reading. Looking back, he realized Uncle Wade must have been preparing him for something, and now he hoped he would find

166

out what it was. The book of old sayings had a Chinese proverb: "When the student is ready, the teacher will appear." Was he ready? He hoped so, because it looked like the teacher had appeared.

Chapter One: Useful Lies

I had never been out of the country until the Army sent me to North Africa. I didn't know very much about the place, and apparently the generals didn't either, because they thought the Vichy French forces would come over to our side. They were wrong; we had a hell of a fight. My unit was scattered, and I ended up wandering alone in the desert, eventually ending up at an old Sufi shrine called Wadi Qadr where the Sufis took me in. It was at Wadi Qadr that I saw what I saw, and learned some of what I have learned.

The Sufis are Muslim, in much the same way that Pentecostals are Christian: their faith is more personal, more mystical, and sometimes more emotional than is true of the general run of believers. We had been told a little about them before the invasion, just as we had been told about the French, and when I stumbled through the gate of their compound I expected to find a ragged band of ignorant fanatics. Instead, I found some of the kindest, most interesting people I have ever met, several of whom spoke excellent English. There was one in particular, Hamid, the son of old Sheikh Issa, who took it upon himself to educate me in their customs.

Hamid knew Islam inside and out—his father was the master of the shrine, after all—but he knew next to nothing about Christianity and the West. I learned from him, and I think he learned from me; I don't know which of us got the better of that bargain. My chief challenge was to convince him that Christians worship only one God. The one-ness of God is the central tenet of Islam, and to Hamid the Trinity—the Father, the Son, and the Holy Spirit—added up to three gods, not one, which he said was two gods too many.

Our unit had shipped out from Boston, and the trip across took ten days. Ten days is a long time to be cooped up on a ship. We exercised, we played cards, we watched movies, and we talked; that was pretty much it. We talked about home, family, girlfriends and baseball, and we talked about religion, since some of us would be making the trip home in a box. The chaplains earned their pay on that trip. I got to know one of them—he was Catholic I think, though it didn't seem to matter—and I had asked him about the Trinity. "You have to remember," he said, "the New Testament wasn't written in English. The word 'person' back then didn't mean exactly what it means in modern English, even though that is how it gets translated. A persona was the mask that a Greek actor wore on stage. Their plays used stock characters, and the mask told the audience which character the actor was playing. That cut down on the number of actors they needed, since the same actor could come on stage at different times wearing different personas. One way to think of God in three persons, or three personas, is to think of Him as the Actor, appearing on the stage of the world, wearing whichever of His masks is appropriate. Three masks, but only one Actor."

"Huh," said Jamaal. "They sure didn't teach that in Presbyterian Sunday School. Or much else either; I remember thinking for a long time that God was an old white guy with a beard. Like Santa Claus only, you know, not jolly."

"Yeah, I know," Bart said, remembering the lake of fire. The four of them were sitting around a table at Clemson's cyber café, Java City. Bart had taken a phone picture of each page of the notebook and encrypted the folder they were in. The book itself he had wrapped in brown paper and placed in his campus mailbox. Reading Wade's shaky writing from the little screen wasn't easy, and the introduction had taken a while. "Do you want to hear any more of it?" he asked. They were almost the last ones left in Java City. "We're almost at the end of this part." They told him to get serious; if there was more, they wanted to hear it. He flicked to the next page and read:

I told Hamid what the chaplain had said about the masks. He said it was an interesting viewpoint, one he would have to ponder. After a few days, he still wasn't sure how he felt about God putting on masks, but in the course of thinking about it, he had come up with a question of his own. "Would you say," he asked, "that we perceive the world as it is? What we see and hear, feel and smell, our image of reality, is it accurate, do you think? Are we really seeing the world or, as when we look at an orange, are we seeing only the rind, but not the part that matters? To use your chaplain's term, are we only seeing the mask the world wears?"

I had run into that question before, in an undergraduate philosophy course. I told him what I remembered, which wasn't much because the philosophers couldn't agree on an answer. Berkely had said one thing about it, Kant had said something else. Hegel had said quite a lot, though what he meant is anybody's guess. My own feeling, then and now, is that we see the mask. I recalled that in the Bible, Moses did not see God; he saw the burning bush. In receiving the

Qur'an, Hamid told me, Muhammad did not see God either; he saw the angel Gabriel.

I asked Hamid what he thought. "I do not know," he said. "That is why I must think about the masks. Our order teaches that God is present in everything, so perhaps you could say the universe itself is the mask that He wears." He paused, then added, "Perhaps many masks, layered, like an onion. A long time ago, the founder of our order accomplished a thing, something I will one day show you. Perhaps you could say he lifted one corner of the topmost mask, and saw what was behind it. Since then, based on his teachings, successive masters of the order have done the same. But the founder went deeper into whatever it was that he found, deeper than anyone else has. Another of the masters tried to follow his path, years later, and whatever he found there deranged him. I think that if God does wear masks, it is for our benefit, not His."

In the end, Hamid didn't completely accept the Greek theater explanation of the Trinity, although he did admit it was intriguing. He talked it over with his father, who suggested that God shows us as much of Himself as we are capable of understanding, and our imagination fills in the gaps. I have thought about masks quite a lot since those days at Wadi Qadr, and I believe Hamid was right: masks are a good thing, as a rule. I never worked with the world's first big computer, ENIAC, but I saw it in operation once, after the war. ENIAC wore no mask; its blinking lights showed what it was doing, and to its priesthood of technicians, the lights made sense. To everyone else, watching the lights was like trying to read tea leaves. Computers today are much more accessible; they hide what they do behind a colorful, helpful interface, which is to say, a mask. Take the mask away, show only the zeros and ones that they actually work with, and almost nobody would be able to use them. Algebra is another mask. Apples and oranges are an untidy mess, but you can make X and Y perform like ballet dancers.

We still teach the Bohr model of the atom, with its little electron balls orbiting around a nicely defined nucleus. We now know that an atom isn't really like that: instead of the little balls there are probability waves that are maybe here, or maybe there, or maybe not. We can visualize little balls; we cannot visualize probability waves, so we still teach the little balls. If the student takes quantum physics, we can teach him about electron clouds and probability waves. If the student majors in, let us say, economics, the Bohr model will do nicely, better than the truth, actually. Like any mask, it sacrifices strict accuracy for ease of understanding, but that illustrates my point: if the choice is to see the mask or to look directly at what seems to be utter chaos, the mask is usually the better choice. It isn't actually chaos, by the way, but that is a subject that must wait until later, after some special principles have been mastered.

"That's it," Bart said. "That's Chapter One." Now they really were the last ones in Java City, and the place was closing up. They were all starting to wonder, what sort of trip had they signed up for? And when they got where they were going, where would they be?

Chapter Twenty-Two

Wade's notebook was not an easy read. The first chapter resembled a journal, but then came seven chapters on the structure and what it called the "personality" of metals, one metal per chapter. The personality of a metal seemed to have something to do with linkages between its various attributes. "Tin has a loose K link," the notebook said. "If it slips, tin is no longer a metal." That didn't sound right, but when Bart looked it up in a chemistry text, sure enough, if you chill tin, it becomes a gray, crumbly something that is not a metal in any sense of the word. The chemistry text said nothing about any K links being involved, though. He hoped the notebook would explain that later.

The other metal chapters were like the one about tin: characteristics of atoms, observations about crystal structures, and notes about linkages. Each metal chapter included a sketch that looked like a set of mangled monkey bars, each with its lines connected differently. The metal chapters were tin, lead, zinc, gold, silver, copper, and iron, and as he digested each one, Bart had to keep going back over the earlier ones, just to keep straight the distinctions the book had made between them. He made a set of cards, and Jamaal quizzed him on them, asking questions neither of them understood, such as "Which end of copper's Green link detaches?" The answer, according to the book, was "The end that joins the H link." Whatever that meant.

Here and there in the notebook, there were odd comments, apparently offhand, and never discussed in depth. One of the more cryptic ones had said, "Einstein was no fool. If he had meant E equals m, he would have said, E equals m." That seemed obvious, until Bart asked a teaching assistant in the physics department about it. "Yes, E equals m, that's what it boils down to," said the TA. "Energy equals mass, and mass equals energy."

"What about c-squared?" Bart asked. "I mean, everybody knows Einstein's equation is $E=mc^2$."

"C-squared simplifies out," the TA explained. "The c term is the speed of light, so many miles per second. Only it doesn't have to be miles, so if we define how far light goes in a second as, say, one lightmile, then we have light going one lightmile in one second. One divided by one is one, and one squared is one, giving us E equals m times one. So you see? The c term goes away."

Bart thought that was too easy. The quantity went away, but what about the units? One distance divided by one second was one, true enough, but if you squared it, it was one square distance divided by one square second, and those survived. Bart knew about distance squared; it was area. But what was time squared? The TA said not to worry about it. "Trust me: it doesn't matter." Maybe not, Bart thought, but what Wade had said still nagged him: if Einstein had meant to say E equals m, Einstein would have said, E equals m. And he hadn't.

Bart was taking Introduction to Philosophy, and one day after class he decided to ask the professor about squaring time. "Alas," said the man, an amiable old German named Ritter, "we know almost nothing about regular time, and nothing at all about time squared. We know, or think we know, that the present moment exists, and that it necessarily has to have some duration, but we don't know how long that duration is. Some say the merest instant, some say as long as two seconds. And when the present moment is over, does it stop all at once, or does it taper off? Does the present moment continue to exist, fossilized, so to speak, as the past, or does it simply evaporate? What do you think, Mr. Phillips?"

Bart had never thought about it that way. "I honestly have no idea," was the best he could do.

"Nor do I. Luckily, it does not matter."

"I beg your pardon?" Bart thought he might have misunderstood, although Dr. Ritter's accent was not all that strong. "The past doesn't matter?"

"Not in the least," the professor said jovially, "nor the future either. Let us say you go to a Gypsy fortune teller, and she says you will die tomorrow. If she is right, if the future is already determined like what is on the next page of a book, there is nothing you can do, so you need not worry about it. If, on the other hand, what the Gypsy told you is not a necessary truth, only a possibility, more or less likely depending on what you do, and—what is crucially important—what everyone else in the world does, the future would be an example of mathematical chaos: impossible to predict. So you need not worry about that either. Since the Gypsy is either right or wrong, and since either answer leads to the same conclusion—don't worry about it—yes, I would say the future doesn't matter. And the past matters even less."

The next time the group got together, Bart reported what Dr. Ritter had said. Jamaal shook his head. "No, I'm not buying that," he said. "If you know about a danger ahead of time, you can take precautions. Knowing matters."

Dee looked thoughtful. "Perhaps," she said. "But I see Dr. Ritter's point. If you see what only might happen, that is one thing. But if you see what absolutely is going to happen, your precautions will only take you to Samarra." None of the others had any idea what she meant by that. "It is a very old story, from the Book of the Thousand and One Nights," she said. "A man's servant meets Death in the market at Baghdad. The servant runs home to tell his master he is afraid, because Death gave him a strange look. To hide the servant from Death, the master sends him to Samarra, a half day's journey from Baghdad. Then the master goes to the market and confronts Death, saying "Why did you give my servant a look?" Death explains that his look had merely been one of surprise. He had not expected to see the servant there at Baghdad, he said, because their appointment, later that evening, was at Samarra."

Jamaal made a face. "That's really dark," he said. "I thought those stories were about Ali Baba and Sinbad the sailor, not people seeing Death at the mall."

Dee laughed. "You are thinking of the short collection, the 'Arabian Nights.' Those are the stories we tell to children. The full collection has the other stories: the dark ones, the funny ones, and the ones that are, as you would say, for adults only."

The others made mental notes to see which version the library had. "This is just gloomy," Tori said. "What does time have to do with the problem anyway?" They had started to refer to the book and its subject, whatever that was, as "the problem," which seemed like as good a label as any. "I mean, it's about melting stuff, not about time, right?"

Bart had no idea. But, he said to himself, I'll bet it matters. Wade was no fool either.

◇◇◇◇◇◇◇◇◇◇◇◇◇◇◇◇●◇◇◇◇◇◇◇◇◇◇◇◇◇◇◇◇

Nelson stood up, stepped away from his monitor, and did a little dance. It wasn't a ballroom dance, more of a jig, and his execution showed more enthusiasm than skill, but it got its point across: Nelson was happy. The mystery book had been yielding to his final assault, one letter at a time, and a text of some sort was beginning to take shape. "It's in German!" he shouted. "Change the letter-frequency tables from English to German, and see if it doesn't all fall into place." His assistant, Singh, changed an instruction and suddenly whole words were appearing on the monitor. In a few minutes, they had it all. "Now, let's see what the translator can make of it." The translator was a language interpreter program, and on Big Mama it took it only an instant to convert the German text into English. Ordinary translator programs do reasonably good work on easy texts, but Big Mama was as good as the humans at the UN who translate speeches. Or usually it was. This time, though, what it showed on the monitor made no sense. The assistant read two sentences of it aloud:

```
Understanding pursues its own
nature in isolation, so it follows
that consciousness has no part in
understanding's process of free
realization, but simply observes
and apprehends it as an unadorned
fact. Thus it must necessarily be
our initial task to step into its
place and to be the concept which
shapes what is contained in the
result.
```

"That can't be right," the assistant muttered. "Maybe it's one of those codes where you only read every third word or something. I hope so, because this is nonsense."

Nelson stared at the emerging text with a curious mixture of déjà vu and horror. "No, I've seen that sort of thing before," he said gloomily. "If I'm right, it's why I changed my major from Liberal Arts to Information Tech. I think it's Hegel." He took the German text to a terminal with outside access and pasted it into a search page. In a moment, the answer appeared: G.W.F. Hegel, *Phänomenologie des Geists*, 1807. "Do you know," he said to no one in particular, "how much time we've used on Big Mama, deciphering this garbage? This is bad, this is really, really bad." He seriously considered taking the elevator down to the lobby, leaving the building, and walking away. Except he couldn't walk far enough, and he knew it. Traxell would find him. Traxell could find anybody. He felt like he was scheduling his own hanging, but putting it off wouldn't help. He called 2300 and asked the secretary when he could see Mr. Stasevik. No, Nelson assured her, it wouldn't be a long meeting.

Hal Stasevik leaned back and closed his eyes. He looked exactly like what he was: an angry man counting to ten before he said something. "Wilson," he said at last, "I cannot tell you how unhappy I am right now." Nelson squirmed in his chair, wondering if he should correct his boss. Before he could decide, Hal held up a hand. It looked almost exactly like a priest's gesture of benediction. "No, this isn't on you. I'm a son of a bitch, but I try to be a fair son of a bitch. I gave you a problem to solve, and you solved it. I can't ask more than that." He sent Nelson back to IT, and stared off into space. No, this pile of crap wasn't Wilson's fault. But by God it was somebody's fault, oh yes it was. Somebody had cost him time, and somebody had cost the company money, but most of all somebody had played Hal Stasevik for a sucker, and nobody was going to do that and get away with it.

◇◇◇◇◇◇◇◇◇◇◇◇◇◇◇◇●◇◇◇◇◇◇◇◇◇◇◇◇◇◇◇◇

The office of Traxell's chief of Security used to be on twenty-four, but when the former chief retired, Roland Bathori had moved the office to thirteen. He needed to be near his people, he said. None of the other VPs had had a problem with that; the move freed up some prime office real estate, and they didn't really think of Security as a proper department anyway, at least not in the sense that each of theirs was. It was, they thought, more of a service agency, like IT. Hal Stasevik had never been to thirteen; non-Security people didn't go there if they didn't have to. Hal knew a VP who had gotten new contact lenses, colored ones, and when the retinal scanner on eleven hadn't recognized him, the elevator took him to thirteen. There were a few polite questions, a retinal scan without the contacts, a re-scan with the new contacts to update their records, and he was on his way. Not a big deal, the man admitted, except that the entire time he had been there, he had not seen another human being; it had all been done with speakers and cameras. And no, he didn't ever want to go back.

"This is Hal Stasevik," Hal told the voice that answered Security's number. There was no immediate response, so he added, "VP of Research Liaison. I understand Mr. Bathori needs to speak with me." With any other VP, he would have asked for Rod, or Bill, or Stu, but Roland Bathori didn't have a nickname. He was, in a word, cold. Not surprising, Hal supposed, for someone in that line of work.

"That is correct. Mr. Bathori would like to see you at 3:45, Mr. Stasevik." The voice reminded him of a scene from any of several disaster movies, where a calm voice would pleasantly announce that self destruct would occur in this or that many minutes. It wasn't a computer, he felt sure, but it might as well be. "And when you come, please allow a few extra minutes," the voice continued, "so that your identity can be confirmed." The line went dead. When you come? Hal had planned to invite Bathori up to twenty-three, maybe offer him a drink. This wasn't good. In a world where status is judged by subtle cues—where your office is, where you park, where you sit at board meetings—it mattered who came to whom. Hal didn't know why the head of Security wanted to see him. The message had been phrased as a request and not as an order—one VP does not give an order to another, after all—but declining a request from Security was not a step he wanted to take. Not yet; he needed a few more operatives of his own, before he was ready to take on Roland Bathori's team.

He got off the elevator at 3:42. The elevator lobby on thirteen was small, about twelve feet by fifteen, and it was empty. The wall facing the elevator was blank, except for a retinal scanner and a hand plate. From a hidden speaker came that cold, uninflected voice: "Please look into the scanner, and place your palm on the hand plate."

Hal located the security camera and faced it. "I already did this when I came in this morning," he said to the camera. "Why do I have to do it again?"

"This morning's scan told us that Harold Stasevik came to work. This new scan will tell us if you are Harold Stasevik, or someone else."

"And if I were someone else, what then?"

"We would find that disappointing," said the voice, "and I am afraid we do not take disappointment gracefully."

Hal put his hand on the plate and looked into the scanner. There was a click, and the door to his left opened, revealing a hallway. "Suite 1320," the voice said. Hal half expected it to add, "Have a nice day," but it didn't.

Like the floor it was on, Roland Bathori's office suite deviated from the rules of executive status. Hal's office on twenty-three had a huge antique walnut desk, comfortable chairs, a few tasteful ceramics, and a somewhat primitive watercolor landscape. The anteroom of Suite 1320 had a desk equipped with a computer monitor, a keyboard, and an anonymous-looking young man in a gray suit. There was no chair for visitors; apparently they didn't get drop-ins. The young man spoke, and at last Hal had a face to go with the voice. "You may go in; Mr. Bathori is expecting you." Hal went in. Ordinarily, he made small talk with receptionists, but not this time. What do you say to someone you thought might be a machine, when you're still not completely sure?

The office he entered had no art on the walls, and of course no windows. No office on thirteen had windows. The architect had decided that a dark band midway up the building would be attractive, so twelve and thirteen had no glass. Add a bunk bed and a metal toilet, Hal thought, and the Security chief's office would look just like a prison cell.

"Ah, Harold, I'm glad you could make it." Roland Bathori rose and extended his hand, but whether he was offering a handshake or simply gesturing to the one guest chair was unclear. Hal shook the hand. It was cold. "Please, have a seat."

Hal had a seat. "Let's get this over with," he said. "I assume Security is concerned about something." Security was always concerned about something, he thought. You'd think the company was a nation at war.

Bathori nodded very slightly. "You are pursuing a project, we understand, in connection with the Aero division's Feathercopter. Is our understanding correct?"

Hal almost asked why that was any of Security's business, but decided not to make an enemy he didn't have to make. "Substantially correct. We are researching a supply issue having to do with the sensor array."

Bathori nodded again, but his face betrayed nothing. "Aero tells us that the Feathercopter has been shelved, and that the Army has abandoned the project they called Clevis. Were you aware of that?"

"We don't do research for the Army," Hal said. "We do research for Traxell. This particular area, amorphous metals, has the potential to make the company a lot of money." He stressed the word 'lot'.

"Perhaps so," Bathori said, "but your inquiry has another potential as well. We believe it has the potential to harm the company. We would request—for now, let us call it a request—that you abandon the project before it generates even more problems.

Or did you think we didn't know about the business in South Carolina?" That was exactly what Hal had thought, but he didn't say it. He didn't say anything, and neither did Bathori. The two of them sat silent for almost a minute, then Bathori nodded. "I see. Jason?" The office door opened. "We seem to be finished. Would you show Mr. Stasevik out?"

◇◇◇◇◇◇◇◇◇◇◇◇◇◇◇◇●◇◇◇◇◇◇◇◇◇◇◇◇◇◇◇◇

The bartender called down to the man on the end stool. "Slim, it's for you." It was three in the afternoon, and they were the only ones in the place.

"Well bring it over here man, it ain't like you're busy or nothing."

"No, but it ain't like you tip good, either," said the bartender, as he brought the phone.

"Slim?" It was Dock on the phone. "Got your message. What's happening?"

"Got work. You interested? Usual arrangement." The usual arrangement was that the button man got two thirds of the fee, and the wheel man got the rest, less expenses.

"Sounds good. Close by, or road trip?"

"Road trip. Meet me in an hour, usual place and I'll give you the details." Slim didn't like to give details over the phone; you never knew who might be listening. The way he saw it, he was a professional, and you don't get to the top of your profession by being sloppy. Slim had known since the eighth grade, what that profession would be, ever since a stray dog had wandered into his yard. The dog was rough looking, and Slim decided the world would be better off without it, so the dog had been the next hour's entertainment. Within a few years, he had graduated from animals to people, and by now he was very good at what he did, which was to find whoever he was hired to eliminate, and then to eliminate them. Ordinarily, he worked alone, but for out of town work he needed a wheel man, and Dock was his favorite.

Slim hung up the phone and drained his bottle of beer. It

would be his last beer for a while; he never drank during a job. "Put it on my tab," he told the bartender, and headed for the door.

"No tip?" asked the bartender, not sounding surprised.

"Sure, I'll give you a tip," Slim said as he reached the door. "Always get your beer in an unopened bottle, so you'll know the bartender hasn't pissed in it." Then he laughed. Out on the sidewalk, he was still laughing. A tourist, passing by in a taxi, thought how nice it was to see such a happy man on the streets of New York.

Chapter Twenty-Three

They had settled into a routine. On Wednesday mornings, none of them had to be in class before ten o'clock, so at eight thirty they would gather at Java City for coffee and muffins and an update on the notebook. Sometimes Bart would summarize what he had been reading, but one of the early sections he had read verbatim:

The first time I saw it done, I thought it might be an elaborate hoax, a way for the Sufis to have fun at the expense of the stranger. Except that by then I wasn't really a stranger; I knew them, and they knew me, and while we would joke and jest, to have made a fool of me would have violated their customs of hospitality. Arab hospitality is a source of pride for them, as well it should be. I am told that one of their early notables once found that a bird had made its nest in his tent. He slept elsewhere until the bird had raised its young and left, rather than inconvenience a guest. The story is perhaps a fable, but it illustrates the point.

They all gathered in a circle around Abdullah, who would be attempting his first melt. His grandfather, Sheikh Issa, sat cross-legged on a cushion beside him, maybe for moral support, I don't know. In front of Abdullah was a wooden bowl. An ingot of bronze, warmed briefly on a brazier, was placed in the bowl, but Abdullah showed no sign that he noticed it; he was meditating, they told me later. Sufis very often meditate on the name of God, but that was for spiritual journeys. For a purely material task like metal work, some other path must be found. One of the Sufis began to hum, and the bronze took on a wet look, as if it was sweating. A second hummer joined in and then, all at once, the ingot slumped into a puddle in the bowl. At the others' invitation, I put my hand in and stirred it. The metal was as liquid as mercury, and cool. I removed my hand from the bowl, and the two hummers ceased their drone. Abdullah opened his eyes and smiled. Sheikh Issa said something in Arabic, which Hamid translated as, "Welcome back."

Again, they invited me to touch the metal in the bowl. It was solid, and it was warm again. They weren't sure why warmth was needed, but they assured me that unless the metal is warmed first, the heat it needs will be taken from something nearby, perhaps even from the practitioner. One of them told me the story of an over-confident novice who had tried to melt a large piece of copper without first warming it. From the way my friend described the man's corpse, I would guess that his brain froze. To avoid having your mind quite literally turned to mush, remember to preheat the work.

"Oh yuck!" had been Tori's comment on that. "Can you imagine what that must have felt like?" The others gave her a collective look. "Oh, right, you really wouldn't..." her voice trailed off.

Today, the topic had been some properties of silver, and it hadn't taken long. "I've been wondering about something," Jamaal said when Bart was through. "If this is as easy as just sitting down and thinking deep thoughts, how come it hasn't, you know, caught on? I mean, you'd think it would be like a cottage industry."

"Perhaps the charcoal lobby has suppressed it," Dee said. "In Turkey, they say there was once a camel that could go a hundred miles on a gallon of water, but the water sellers bought it and ate it." She waited a few seconds while the others tried to decide if she was serious. Dee had a sense of humor, but her friends usually didn't understand her jokes, any more than she understood theirs. "I am kidding," she finally said. "You know, like the miracle carburetor that the oil companies supposedly smothered?" There were a couple of forced laughs as the others looked for the humor. "But Jamaal is right, it makes no sense. The first one to do it was a metal worker, but he was also a Sufi. Surely in five hundred years someone who is not so mystical has learned it. Unless..."

Bart finished her sentence for her. "Unless having your brain frozen isn't the only danger." He remembered how Ahmed, the Sufi visitor at Wade's wake, was surprised that Wade had been able to do iron, because of something bad that had happened to the last one who had tried it.

"Perhaps if the choir hums the wrong tune, something bad happens," Dee said. The others thought it was more Turkish humor, but she was serious. "Each metal has had a musical note as part of its personality, has it not?"

Tori thought for a second. Dee was right: in the metal chapters, there was always mention of a note. "What is bronze made of?"

"Copper and tin," Dee told her. "So you see? Two metals, two people humming."

"Yeah, it did say humming," Tori finished. "I wonder if it has to be guys." She looked at Dee, and Dee looked at her. "No, notes are notes." She looked at Bart. "You just got yourself a backup group."

None of them knew anything about meditation, but to no one's surprise Tori knew someone who did. Her friend, whose name was Anna but who called herself Raven, had been a big help, but she hadn't said very much about the void. The first time Bart had gone there, the void had been a surprise, and the surprise had ended the session. "You reacted," Raven explained afterward. "You have to accept what you find. Don't expect anything, don't hope for anything; just be willing for whatever happens to happen." The next time—not the next time he tried, but the next time he succeeded—he wasn't surprised. "You must let go of here, and let go of now," Raven had told him. "You must simply be." Bart accepted the void. After a few more tries, the transition came naturally. The void was neither dark nor light, neither roomy nor cramped. It was nowhere and nothing, but Bart found that if he accepted it, it accepted him, and he could float in it, simply being.

But there would be no floating this time; he had work to do. In Wade's notebook, tin had come first, but in a small town, pure tin is hard to find. Lead, on the other hand, is easy. Every sporting goods store has plenty of it, in the form of sinkers and loose buckshot. So there they were, Bart sitting cross-legged on the floor, with a bowl of lead shot in front of him, still warm from the water bath it had been in. Jamaal stood behind him, Dee and Tori in front. They were in one of the music department's windowless, soundproof rehearsal rooms, the quietest place any of them could think of except maybe the cabin in Viney Cove. They had talked about going to the cabin; the girls really wanted to see it, but it had one big drawback: if something went wrong, the cabin was a long way from help.

Gently, without disturbing the void, Bart shaped a thought. Everything the book had taught him about the personality of lead, he brought to the front of his mind, and the void changed. It became a landscape of hills and valleys, features that might be forces and fields, or not; he didn't care. He didn't have to understand what he saw. The notebook had said the tone for lead was the b-flat below high c, so Jamaal tapped a b-flat tuning fork against his shoe. The girls had good musical memories, but they didn't want to take a chance on a wrong note. Tori took up the note, humming it, and in the void the landscape became more and more defined, more angular, until it became a lattice of rods and angles, the monkey bar design the notebook had shown for lead, only more detailed. The lattice floated in the void, its geometry both beautiful and alien. Bart willed himself closer to it, and it grew larger. He saw the link the book had said he should look for, exactly where it should be. He grasped it—that was how he thought of it, a grasping—and pulled it from where it was toward where he wanted it to be. The link moved a little, then slipped out of his grasp and went back to where it had started out. He let the structure recede from him, and opened his eyes.

Jamaal bent over him, looking worried. "What went wrong?"

Bart shook his head. "I don't know; I had it, but then it got away. How long was I gone? It seemed like about five minutes."

Dee shook her head. "Ten seconds, perhaps less." The others agreed. Then Tori glanced at the bowl.

"Uh, guys?" The little balls of lead were gone, and in their place was what looked like frozen gray soup. Nobody said anything for a while, then Tori broke the silence. "I don't think anything went wrong. I think the world just changed, and we weren't looking."

Zinc was next in the journal, and when Bart tried it, he found that moving its melt link took a little more effort than lead's had. He thought that zinc's higher melting point might be the reason, but when they tried getting it hotter beforehand, nothing had changed. It was still, as Bart put it, "kind of stiff." He hated to think what it would be like toward the end of the list.

I have left iron until last, and for good reason. I have seen the nickel and cobalt lattices, but only with great effort, and I could not work with them; their linkages are too strong. Iron is barely within reach, but it differs from the other metals in some fundamental ways. One of those ways concerns its melt link, which is not where the others are. To reach it, you must go past the outer linkages, which is easily done, but once you are inside, the path back out is not obvious. By the purest accident, I had a guide when I first went in, and if you found the clue I left, you know what that guide was.

"Okay, now that was obscure even for Wade," Jamaal said. They had convened for their usual meeting in Java City.

"The puzzle was the clue to finding the notebook," Bart mused, "but maybe it's also the key to unlocking it. Maybe there's something else on the map that we need to look for."

Dee shook her head. "No, the map served its purpose. But there is something on the puzzle that has not been useful until now. The cat."

Jamaal was skeptical. "No, the cat served its purpose too: finding the notebook."

Dee shook her head. "No, the clue to the notebook was written on the puzzle, after Stave made it. Your uncle could have hidden the notebook anywhere, and written in a different clue. But the cat was actually printed on the puzzle."

Bart had a thought. He found the box where he kept papers he didn't want to lose, and in it was the first letter Emmett had ever sent him. "Yeah," he said after he had re-read it. "I thought that's what it said. Wade died sitting in his favorite chair, with his cat in his lap."

"From the way you've talked about him," Tori said, "I didn't think of your uncle as a cat person."

"He didn't think so either, until one moved in on him. The cat he had when he died is an orange tom. Emmett's been taking care of it."

"I like cats," Dee said. "What is the cat's name?"

"According to Emmett, Wade never named it; he just called it Orange Cat."

Dee frowned. "No, that will never do. A cat deserves a name. We must meet this cat."

Tori agreed. "Yeah. You two keep saying you'll show us the

cabin; well, it's time. How about this: We cut class Friday afternoon, go meet your Mr. Schroder, check out the cat, and spend the weekend at the cabin. Dee and I can cook, so we won't have to live on Slim Jims."

"Hey," Jamaal protested, "I can cook." The girls just looked at him. "No really. Ask Bart."

Bart remembered their last stay at the cabin. "He does a great stir-fry. And I cook some, too." Jamaal remembered the burned rice, but said nothing. You don't rat out your roommate.

"Okay then," Tori said. "We'll take Friday, and you two can cook Saturday." She looked at her watch. "Gotta run." Apparently, both girls had to run, and in a moment Bart and Jamaal were alone at the table.

"What just happened?" Bart said to no one in particular.

"If you'd had a sister, you'd know," Jamaal said. "They wanted to go to the cabin, they asked about going, you never said yeah, sure, but now, somehow or other, they're going."

"So you're saying we got played."

"Yeah, that's pretty much what I'm saying. We need to start planning a menu, cause there's no way those two are going to get bragging rights on cooking."

Chapter Twenty-Four

Slim had opinions on everything, and he believed in sharing them. Over the course of their trips, Dock had heard what Slim thought about, among other things, women with ankle bracelets ("whores, every one of them"), men with mustaches ("fags, I guarantee it"), and lawyers ("crooked sons of bitches"). Now it was time to hear about businessmen. "You give a guy a suit, he thinks his shit don't stink," Slim said. "They never look a working man in the eye, you know what I mean? Once you got that figured out, you can go anywhere. You put on a work shirt, and the suits just see a blur."

Dock grunted.

"I had a job one time," Slim went on, "big labor lawyer over in Queens. The word came down to do him, and do him in public, you know? So it'd make the six o'clock news. I think maybe he'd been talking to the feds, and the boys wanted to make an example out of him. Easy enough, you say, but the guy was never alone. There was always a bunch of other suits around him, like he was some kinda rock star. You wanta know what I did?"

Dock grunted again. It wasn't a yes grunt or a no grunt. It said, I'm with you so far; tell me more. Slim used to ride with a guy named Tony, and one trip, Tony didn't come back. Nobody ever said why, but Dock figured Tony hadn't grunted enough, and that Slim had stopped talking. A long drive with a sullen, brooding Slim was like lugging around a bomb with a loose wire: you never knew what might set it off. Dock didn't have much education, but he wasn't stupid. If it took a grunt every now and then to keep Slim talking, he figured grunts were cheap.

"I'll tell you what I did," Slim went on. "I dressed up like I was one of them guys that works on traffic light controls, you know? Found a control box out front of where the suit worked. There I am, first thing in the morning, poking around in the box with this long screwdriver, only it ain't a screwdriver, see? I've ground it to a point, like an ice pick. Here come the suits, and when the guy gets almost past me, I turn around and put it in him,

190

just under the breastbone, right into the heart. I say "Oh, 'scuse me," and walk away. The guy takes two more steps and drops dead, and by then I'm around the corner. It was all over the news. And you know what?"

Grunt.

"I'll tell you what. One of them suits looked right at the TV camera and said it was some Mexican that done it. Another one said it was some guy with a gang tattoo. It's just like I was saying: they don't see past the shirt."

"That's sure what it sounds like," Dock said, thinking it was time for more than a grunt.

The subject of businessmen seemed to have played out, so Dock turned on the radio and set it to scan. Hard rock, easy listening, top 40; he changed to AM, where the scan found a farm report, then a country preacher bellowing and gasping, and finally a call-in show about politics. Slim reached over and switched it off. "All I wanta know about politics," he said with a growl, "is who gives a flying fuck?"

"Superman," Dock blurted out. He had learned that one in ninth grade.

"Huh?" Slim snapped. "Why would Superman care about politics? Sometimes I wonder about you, man."

They were still three hours from Greenville, where they would get off the Interstate and find a motel. Three hours was too long to ride in silence, so Dock watched the billboards for inspiration. He saw one that was advertising some light beer. "You ever try any of that?" he asked.

Slim made a rude noise. "I can piss better beer than that," he snorted. "I remember one time a waitress brought me some of that light crap after I said bring me a beer. You know what I told her?"

Dock grunted. Life was back to normal.

The man who called himself Sanchez ran his boat gently

onto the sandy beach. It was the same beach he always used, isolated and unwatched. Aside from some seaweed that had washed ashore, there was nothing to see in either direction but sand. "We are arrive, Señor," he told his passenger.

"You said there would be a car."

"We are early. The car will be here," the boatman assured him. He was lying. There would be no car; there was no road. The beach was a sand bar. At high tide it—and his passenger—would be under water, but by then he would be back in Tampico, lining up the next one. Truly, the gringos should give him a bounty on each of them: one fewer illegal for them to whine about. "See," he said, nodding toward the shore, "over there it is." His right hand eased down toward the holster on the hidden side of his seat. He was not watching the passenger's hands; why should he? He had frisked the man before they set sail. It never occurred to him that the fishing knife he had lost a month ago might have been where the man would find it.

Police trainees have to be taught just how dangerous a knife is. A man with a knife can close a thirty foot gap before an officer can even draw his weapon, let alone aim and fire it, and the passenger was only three feet from the boatman, whose hand was still groping for his pistol when he felt the sting of the blade across his throat. He heard the passenger saying something, but the words were strange, and he had no time to think about them.

The passenger heaved the man's body into the water, then backed the boat off of the sand. He found the man's pistol, a cheap little .32 automatic, and tossed it overboard. Better no gun than an unreliable one. A knife does not misfire, or jam, or—as Fareed's had—snag on your pocket when you try to draw it. Fareed had died entirely too quickly, he had thought at the time; there were so many questions he could have answered. Was it you who got me on the Americans' no-fly list, brother? Was what happened at Wadi Qadr your fault, brother? Does it hurt when I do this, brother? None of that mattered, of course. When he remembered, later, who he was, he also realized that no man was his brother.

During the ride back from Wadi Qadr, Murad had not

known what he should do next. Could the program be salvaged? Perhaps; he had the sermons already written. But it had taken his father years to establish himself as an Imam, and his father had had the gift of oratory. No, he had decided, he would dispose of his inventory and live the life of a prince. It was only when the trucks approached the city, and he saw the column of smoke rising from his warehouses that he realized the full extent of Fareed's perfidy. And it was only as he watched the life drain out of Fareed's face that he finally remembered who he really was. It was all so very clear; how could he have forgotten? A man does not stone his own father. A man does not butcher his own brother. But someone does, and for him it is no sin, because God himself wills it. He was not Murad the patricide; he was Azrael, the Angel of Death.

He steered north, keeping the land just in sight to his left. The boat had enough gas to reach one of the coastal towns, some place where that he could get a car and be about his task. He finally beached the boat near a glow in the night sky, a parking lot, he thought, perhaps for a shopping center. He was wrong; it was an airport, on a spit of land just across the bay from Corpus Christi. He waited, crouched among the parked cars until a woman came past, dragging a wheeled suitcase. The last words she heard in life were *Salaamu alaykum*, peace be upon you, the words Azrael always speaks to the one whose name has reached the top of his list. The woman's car smelled strongly of cigarettes, but it was not for him to question what God had provided. Within minutes he had it on I-37, headed north. At San Antonio he would turn east, toward the place these people called Clemson.

Chapter Twenty-Five

"Hal Stasevik; we spoke on the phone. I'm glad to finally meet you, Tom. Or should I call you Major?"

Tom Harper thought about it. "Tom, I suppose. I'm through with the Army."

"You didn't like life as a soldier?"

Harper's jaw tightened. "You know, and I know, that the next war will be won, if it is, by technology and not by soldiers," he said. "But they still let the soldiers run the Army, and they don't know a quenched field from a ripe quince." Tom Harper wouldn't have known a quince from a plum, but he thought his comparison had a nice ring.

"Oh you don't have to convince me," Hal told him. "But if the Army doesn't want your talents, we do. We sell to any number of armies, and some of them understand the world the way you do." That was a test. If Harper flinched, the interview was over. Harper nodded agreement, and Hal went on. "You recall the Clevis project? There was a supply problem, you might recall. We believe we may have a solution for that, but there are still some, shall we say, technical hurdles to be surmounted. That is why I wanted this meeting. We will appreciate any assistance you can give us. Our appreciation would take the form of a very substantial consulting fee." Hal had chosen his words carefully. He might just as easily have said that Traxell would bribe a man handsomely to forget about secrecy laws and loyalty oaths, but that would be crude, and in any event, he felt sure Harper understood what he was saying.

Harper understood. "Mr. Stasevik, I look forward to working with you." He stared directly into Hal's eyes when he said it. Offer made, offer accepted.

"Excellent," Hal said. "What we need, my technicians tell me, are the answers to a few questions."

"Fine; ask away."

"Oh they aren't questions for you, Tom. There are people we think may know how to make the alloy Carlisle needed, and we intend to, ah, ask those people. If you had access to someone who knew how to make that alloy that Carlisle needed, what would you ask him?"

Harper thought about that for a moment. "Would the person want to be helpful?"

"Helpful might be an overstatement. Let's say he would be willing to answer direct questions, but he might not volunteer anything he wasn't asked."

Harper mulled that over. It sounded like somebody was in for a bad day. "I would want to construct a question flow chart, to allow different follow-ups depending on what direction the answers took. How soon do you think you'll need it?"

"As soon as you can do it."

Harper thought about that. "I can have the critical issues nailed down in under an hour."

"Excellent. Let me find you a workspace."

"I am a little curious about one thing, if you don't mind my asking."

"Ask away," Hal said. Was this the flinch he had been watching for?

"Does any of this have to do with Greenville, South Carolina?"

Hal nodded. "Not Greenville, but not terribly far from there, either. Why do you ask?"

"The Clevis operations team lost a man in Greenville, somebody named Travis. I never knew why Travis was there, but Captain Blood seemed to be really upset when he heard his man had died."

"Captain Blood?"

"Sorry, Capt. Bragg. He was in charge of the non-technical operations team of Clevis. Captain Blood is what my staff called him."

With your tacit approval, I'm sure, Hal thought. "I take it you didn't get along with the captain."

"He's an arrogant ass. And stubborn. If the Clevis team hadn't been broken up, he might have been a problem for you.

Not to imply, of course, that Traxell had anything to do with that death in Greenville." Not that I care, he thought.

"No, of course not. I appreciate your concern, Tom, but I wouldn't worry. The Army is, I think, not going to be a problem."

Willie Sutton supposedly said that he robbed banks because that's where the money was. Nathan Huntsinger, the CEO of Traxell, visited D.C. from time to time because that is where the politicians were. Senators weren't too bad, but meeting with congressmen always made him feel dirty. Senators were at least indirect when they asked for a bribe; the House members came right out and said, "Money talks, but so far yours is just mumbling." Greedy, clumsy idiots. But, he thought, you do what you have to do. What he had to do this trip was to smooth out a little issue for Research Liaison, something about interference Hal Stasevik thought they might get from the Army. The senator who could take care of that little issue was chairman of a committee the Army couldn't afford to offend, and Huntsinger's people knew where that senator usually went for lunch. Nathan got there early, and nursed a salad until his prey arrived.

"Jimbo," he said heartily, rising from his chair. "What a pleasant surprise. Good to see you!" He pumped the senator's hand.

Jimbo's given name was James; nobody except other Harvard grads ever called him Jimbo. He probably would have recognized Nate eventually, but he didn't have to; his earpiece told him. It looked exactly like a hearing aid, but it let the aide behind him discreetly tell him things. *Nathan Huntsinger*, the aide murmured. *Goes by Nate. Traxell CEO. Big contributor. Wife's name is Judy.* Aides who remember details like that will never be unemployed, no matter how the elections go. "Nate," Jimbo said with apparent pleasure, "you're looking good. How's Judy?"

"She's taken up watercolor painting," the Traxell man said, "and she seems to have a knack for it." Actually, her paintings were dreadful, but if he hadn't told Judy that, he certainly wasn't going to tell Jimbo. "Say, how is that boy of yours, the one who went to MIT?" Nate's people kept a file on everybody in government, and he was a quick study; he didn't need an earpiece.

"About to graduate. After that, we'll have to see." He was tempted to ask if Traxell was hiring, but that would be in poor taste. Anyway the boy's grades were mediocre, and Traxell only hired the best of each year's crop.

"Have him give me a call," Nate said with a smile. "We've got some projects in the works that would benefit from some fresh thinking. In fact, one of them is related to that Clevis project the Army used to be working on."

"Oh? I thought your guys had given up on that. Something about a supply problem?"

"We never give up when the nation's security is involved." Mention national security if you can, his briefing notes had said. "There was a supply issue, but my tech people say they may have found a workaround. Which reminds me, my guys say the Army is still looking into that supply thing. Didn't the Clevis team get broken up and re-assigned?"

"That's what they reported to the committee. I can check to make sure."

"Would you do that? I'd sure appreciate it. We can't really justify putting our people to work on the sensor problem if the Army still thinks it's their baby." Or in other words, we won't need Jimbo Junior if we don't do this project.

Jimbo understood. "If they haven't dropped it, they will, I can promise you that."

Nate adjusted his glasses, a cue for a young man to walk up and say, "Mr. Huntsinger, your car is here." With apologies for having to leave so soon, Nate hurried out. The car would take him to the airport where the corporate jet was waiting. It had, he thought, been one of his better performances.

General Andrew Compton looked around the table where his colonels met for their weekly staff meetings. "I just got a memo from the office of the Secretary of Defense" he said, "saying that interference with a certain well-connected defense contractor would be contrary to the national interest. I just thought I should pass that along. Dismissed, except Menendez." When they were alone, he motioned her to a chair. "That little matter in South Carolina, has anything come of that yet?"

"The Dawson thing? No. We have a team ready to go down there if things start to pop, but nothing has so far."

General Compton had graduated from the University of Texas, where ROTC had given him his start in the Army. But even without a West Point ring he understood how Washington worked. "If I've got this thing figured right, something is about to pop, and we represent a complication. So somebody has pulled some real expensive strings to get us ordered to stand down."

"Yes, sir. Is there any wiggle room?"

"Given where this memo came from, I would have to say no. Your team is to take no further action on the Dawson matter. But if you should just by accident happen to hear anything, keep me up to date."

"Just because you're curious, of course."

"That's right." He smiled innocently. "Just because I'm curious."

Chapter Twenty-Six

"I think you should retire and write a book," Hal Stasevik's wife told him. He tried to look interested. "You could call it *My Rules of Life and Business,* or something like that." He told her he would think about it. "No, you won't," she chided him. "I know that look. But even if you don't write the book, you ought to think about retiring. I mean really, what are you going to get if you put in forty or fifty years at the company? I'll tell you what you'll get: some dinky plaque from a trophy store, in recognition of the long and faithful service of Insert-Name-Here. If you didn't have to go in every day, we could travel, we could see the world. We could, I don't know, buy a vineyard or something."

"We don't know anything about running a vineyard," Hal told her.

"We could learn; that's not the point. The point is, between your pension and the stock options and all the rest of it, you don't need to work another day. We've got enough; let's enjoy it."

Hal sighed. Enough? Of course they had enough, if money were what mattered. And yes, he supposed they could travel, but he knew how that would go. They would be standing in line to see the Pope or some such thing, and his wife would strike up a conversation with some tourist from Nebraska. "You simply must meet my husband," she would say. "He used to be somebody." Actually, she wouldn't say exactly that; she wasn't an idiot or he wouldn't have married her, but no matter what she actually said, that is what he would hear, that he used to be somebody. Well, he was somebody right now: he was a player. If a player cashes out of the game, that's exactly what he is: out of the game. The game isn't about money; it's about where you get to park, where your office is, and how many windows it has. It's about who has to kiss who's ass. The game isn't about money; it's about winning, and for those who love the game, there is no such thing as enough winning.

And as for writing a book, that was a really bad idea. Hal was a realist. He was only a somebody inside the world of Traxell;

outside, he was just another suit. Oh sure, he could pay some hack to ghost-write him a book, but it would be on the discount tables the day it hit the bookstores. The only ones who would read it would be the other players at Traxell, and he could just imagine how that would go: "Hey," one would say, "you're going to love this. Hal says it's crucial to put honesty and integrity ahead of corporate profits." Then they would laugh their asses off.

Of course, he wouldn't have to have it ghost written; he could write it himself. A list of his actual rules of life and business would be an instant best-seller, except that writing it would violate his first rule of life and business: *Do not put anything in writing that can get you sent to prison.* He could spend ten minutes talking with his wife about vineyards without getting indicted. Those same ten minutes, spent with a grand jury, would end very differently. *Here on page 48,* the prosecutor would say, *you write that witnesses should never be left alive. Would you like to explain that?* Hal didn't think he would like that at all. He agreed with a comment Calvin Coolidge had once made: 'You don't have to explain what you don't say'.

"I really will think about it," he lied, "but I've got to run. The limo is here."

She gave him a peck on the cheek. "Well anyway, have a good day. And remember," she said with a little laugh, "don't leave any fingerprints." She always said that before he left for the office; she thought of it as her little joke. Hal thought of it as rule number five.

◇◇◇◇◇◇◇◇◇◇◇◇◇◇◇◇●◇◇◇◇◇◇◇◇◇◇◇◇◇◇◇◇

The station manager looked around his office. On the wall where all the Broadcast Excellence awards should be, was the station's FCC license and nothing else. On another wall was a little shelf that was going to hold all the broadcast awards he thought the station was going to win, back when he had taken the job. It held one award, a cheesy little trophy of a football player throwing a ball. *For Excellence in Sports Broadcasting*, its plaque said. A trophy like that was given out every year by the regional high-school athletic conference, and each of the local stations had one. It looked stupid up there, all by itself on that shelf, but taking it down would be bad for morale so he left it alone, literally and figuratively.

Sweeps week was coming up. The network had been losing viewers, which meant they couldn't charge as much for ads. Less ad money meant less money for programming, which meant more second-rate shows, more recycled old sitcoms, and even fewer viewers: a death spiral, in other words. But this time the network execs said they would be coming on strong: new programs, cliff-hanger episodes, the works, and they expected the local stations to get with the TV program. They actually said that: get with the TV program, as if the play on words would fire up the troops. He thought about the station's troops, and he didn't like his prospects. Normally, local programming would stay pretty much the same during sweeps week. Weather is usually boring. Sports can be exciting, but only if the games are exciting, which the station couldn't control. That left the news operation. If there isn't any real news to report, something would have be stirred up and called news. "Come up with something for sweeps week," He told the news director. "I don't care what, and I don't care how, but I want something we can stretch out for five days during the ten o'clock news slot."

The news director was, in his own opinion, far too good for this Podunk station. All he needed was a chance to show what he could do, and now he had that chance. This would be his masterpiece: an exposé on how corporations buy influence on Capitol Hill. The money shot would be an ambush interview of some fat-cat CEO trying to dodge questions from the virtuous corruption-fighting reporter. That was always great television. To decide which CEO to ambush, he checked with the advertising department to see who didn't buy air time. The name Traxell practically stood up and waved. Traxell, he found out, spent millions on advertising, but they ran it in trade publications and on the walls of the D.C. Metro, where their target audience would see them. The news director got the Traxell CEO's name and address, then sent a reporter and a camera crew out to make news. The quarry lived in a gated community, which was good; the segment could open with the gate guard, telling the reporter—the personification of the People's Right to Know—that he wasn't welcome there. Then they would slip in some other way and set up the ambush. It was a great plan, the news director thought.

The gate guard was a new hire. He looked at the crew's press credentials, asked where they were going, and waved them on in. They parked a block away from the Huntsinger house, hid in the bushes until a limo pulled up, and then when Nate came out the front door of his house, they pounced. "Mr. Huntsinger," the man with the mike cried. "We're from Eyewitness News, and we'd like to ask you some questions. Let's start with your influence on the Hill; how much money did it take to buy it?" According to the script, Nate would either duck back inside, get in the limo and race off, or threaten to call the police, any of which, with the right commentary, would be visual proof of another corporate villain's guilty conscience.

"The best laid plans of mice and men," wrote Robert Burns, "gang aft agley." The reporter had actually read that line in high school English, but it hadn't registered, largely because he hadn't known what ganging aft agley meant. He was about to find out. "Eyewitness News?" Nate Huntsinger said with apparent delight. "Hey, you guys do great work!" He gestured toward the waiting limo. "Jerry, come back in an hour; the meeting can wait." To the reporter he explained, "They can't very well start without me, now can they, and I am always glad to talk to the media." All of that was a lie, of course. The chauffeur's name wasn't Jerry; Nate had no idea what it was. There wasn't any meeting to cancel, and he had never heard of Eyewitness News. Nathan Huntsinger had an MBA from Harvard, but his job was not to administer the business; Brussels took care of all that. Nate's real job was public relations, and he was good at it. By the time the news crew had packed up and gone back to the station, Nate had worked his magic. A corporation, he had explained, was nothing more than a lot of good citizens, banded together for a common purpose. They could lobby their congressmen individually, couldn't they? Of course they could. So why not collectively? People do that all the time. Working people do it through their unions, retirees do it through the AARP. Why shouldn't ordinary people, shareholders, be able to do it through their corporations? These are decent, hardworking people, Nate said, who just want what everybody else wants: a fair hearing for their concerns. Surely there was nothing wrong with that.

The reporter hadn't thought he would actually be doing a real interview, so he hadn't done any real research. The more he listened to Nate's spiel, the more plausible it sounded. Nate was careful. He never actually said that Traxell's shareholders were decent, hardworking people, or even that they were U. S. citizens. For the most part, Traxell's shares were owned by other corporations, which were in turn owned by yet other corporations. At the far end of that maze there were fewer than a hundred actual people, and of those, perhaps a dozen lived in the United States.

The reporter swallowed it whole. He also swallowed a plate of cookies that Judy Huntsinger brought in. "They're just out of the oven," she told them. The reporter hadn't gotten the story he had gone to get, but he thought what he did have was pretty good. The news director apparently disagreed, to judge by his first question: "What the fuck were you drinking?"

"Uh, I think it was buttermilk," the reporter replied.

"Buttermilk. Are you insane?! Have you looked at your tapes?! All you need is a hospital scene and a dog, and Hallmark could run it as a feelgood movie! Well, guess what: we're not Hallmark. Our public doesn't want milk and cookies; it wants somebody it can hate. It wants a villain. And do you know what villains don't do? They don't serve cookies!" He sent the reporter away, then he walked over to his scheduling chart. Hurricane season was coming up. The public wants villains, but they also want to see some poor sap standing outside in the worst of the storm, holding onto a pole for dear life while trees blow past him. On the scheduling board, opposite the words Storm Chaser

Report, the news director wrote in "Cookie Monster," a nickname that would follow that reporter the rest of his television career.

The cookies really had been a nice touch. Nate's wife hadn't made them, but she had picked them out at the bakery. Plus, she had taken them out of the freezer, microwaved them, and brought them out just when she thought the interview had needed interrupting. "You always were good on your feet," she told Nate, "but I think that was your best performance ever. I listened from the hallway, and you almost had *me* convinced."

Scheduled interviews were supposed to be pre-cleared with Security, but ambush interviews obviously couldn't be. When Nate reported the interview to Bathori, he added what his wife had said. "From what you've told me, I agree with her," the Security chief said. "There was no harm done. I do think we might want to take steps to prevent it from happening again."

"I don't think it will," Nate replied. "I had a talk with the head of the gate guards, and as for that TV station, well, I know the chairman of one of the broadcast oversight committees. The FCC is going to be, shall we say, encouraged to review their broadcast license. Very thoroughly. Just to make sure they're devoting enough resources to the community they serve."

"In other words, to let them know they should mind their own business, and not ours."

"In other words."

◇◇◇◇◇◇◇◇◇◇◇◇◇◇◇◇◇●◇◇◇◇◇◇◇◇◇◇◇◇◇◇◇◇◇

There had never been an ambush interview of Roland Bathori. A few people outside of Traxell knew that the company had its own Security division, but none of them could name its chief. A reporter who showed up at the Information desk and asked to see the head of Security would be told that the chief did not give interviews. If the reporter persisted, he would be shown the door, politely if possible. A reporter who wanted to catch Bathori at home would first have to find who he was, and then find where he lived, and not even Nate knew that second detail.

He thought he knew, since Traxell paid for an apartment for Bathori in a lower Manhattan highrise, but if Nate had dropped by for a visit, he wouldn't have found Bathori home. Ever.

Bathori paid a Ukrainian woman to come in once a week to dust, and to replace the older food in the refrigerator with newer items. She always got things her family liked, things that wouldn't go bad in a week. The pay was good—more than good, really, since it was in cash, and therefore, as she thought of it, tax free. It was a very good job, and why her client wanted it done was not her concern. She knew about the wall safe behind the ugly watercolor painting, but whatever he kept in it was not her concern either.

The apartment's door was solid, and its lock was reasonably good. It would defeat an amateur, but a skilled burglar would have no trouble with it. The safe, like the door lock, was designed to delay a thief, not defeat him. In the safe was a pistol, a stack of hundred-dollar bills, and a passport. The thief would think he had found an emergency get-away kit. He would be wrong.

Coal miners in the old days would take a canary down into the tunnels with them. Canaries are delicate creatures, very sensitive to bad air, so if the bird dropped dead, the miners would know it was time for them to leave, lest they be next. The safe was the canary in Roland Bathori's coal mine. If it was opened, a tiny switch in the hinge would send a signal to the Traxell Building, a signal that meant someone was prying into his business.

When Bathori had moved his office from twenty-four to thirteen, he told the board it was to be near his people. The old chief had dropped in occasionally, but when he was upstairs his staff could easily imagine him sipping single-malt with the VPs or golfing with the CEO. Now they saw the boss daily, and they knew he worked as hard as they did. He was always the first one there, and he was always the last one to leave.

At least they assumed he left. He did leave his office, but except for an occasional restaurant meal, he seldom left the building. During the office move, he had brought in a crew that worked at night, installing a stairway from a coat closet in his office down to a utility closet on twelve. The change never showed up on the building's schematics. After the stairs went in, a different crew went to work on an unused area on twelve, converting it, they were told, into a guest suite for visiting executives. The schematics never showed that change either. They still showed that space as "reserved for records storage" but it would never be needed for that. Traxell stored its records in Big Mama's memory cores, and sent the paper originals to the incinerator.

Some companies still have water coolers, where the staff can swap gossip, spread rumors, or even get water, but more and more the water cooler is being replaced by the break room. People hang around a little longer in a break room than they did at the water cooler, but the company recoups some of that lost productivity by the profit it makes from the vending machines. At Traxell, each of the bottom ten floors had a break room, but the executives had something better: they had the Executive Dining Room on twenty-six. All of the VPs took their lunches there, including Roland Bathori. Unlike the others, he didn't socialize. He ate alone, and he left when he was done. Some of the executives wondered if Security had the room bugged, but their bug detectors couldn't to find anything. Not trusting his detector, one of the VPs had let an outside security firm check it out. "Top of the line," their technician assured him. "State of the art." What the tech didn't mention was that the art assumed certain things, such as solid-state bugs. Bug detectors can sense transistors and diodes. What Security had in fact installed in the EDR was old-style vacuum-tube equipment, with nothing solid-state about it. The system wasn't as sensitive as the newer equipment, but a bug detector wasn't going to find it.

Corporate executives aren't expected to know about that sort of thing, and the Traxell VPs thought they could speak freely in the EDR. They talked about who might or might not be looking at a promotion. They talked about whose wife might or might not be shopping for a divorce lawyer. They talked, in other words, about whoever wasn't there at the moment, which meant that they frequently talked about Roland Bathori: what they thought he did, how they thought he did it, whether his assistant, Jason, was actually human, and on one occasion a year or two back, what his home might be like. "Fairly plain, I would think," was one man's opinion.

Someone else disagreed. "I understand Huntsinger gave him one of his wife's paintings, and that Bathori told him he would hang it in his living room."

The first speaker shook his head. "I said that too, when he gave me one, then I took it straight to the attic. What do you think, Hal? Chez Bathori: plain or fancy?"

Hal gave it some thought. "Plain, bare. No, more than bare. Empty, like him; nothing, not even furniture. Just the coffin he sleeps in." Everybody laughed, and even Roland Bathori, who was monitoring the conversation from his office, smiled briefly. The smile wasn't for Hal's clever quip, but for what it revealed. It is always useful to know what someone really thinks of you, even— or maybe especially—when what he thinks is dead wrong.

The air in the hallway on twelve was cool, for the benefit of twelve's only official resident, Big Mama. The air that met Roland Bathori when he opened the door marked Records Storage was warm and damp, almost tropical. The ceiling was a softly glowing expanse, unblemished by ductwork or conduits or anything else that would scream, "This is not a sky." His anteroom was, in essence, a greenhouse. As he walked by the various colonies of shrubs, flowers, vines and vegetables, Bathori gave them their daily inspection. "And how are we doing, children?" he asked, pausing at a row of bell peppers. He picked a red one. "Zigeuner sauce over veal tonight," he told it. "You will look very handsome in it."

The air in his living quarters was cooler and dryer, more like what Big Mama breathed, but the ambiance was nothing like the stark, bright, angular world of the supercomputer. The floor was carpeted, the walls were of dark wood, hung here and there with tapestries. There was a small table beside a comfortable leather chair, a writing desk near a bookcase, and a large, freestanding antique globe. More than anything else, the room resembled a London gentlemen's club from the late 1800's. A computer terminal in an alcove was the only concession to technology. The kitchen was more functional, and the bedroom almost met Hal's description, having a bed and a straight-backed chair as its only furniture.

Bathori took the pepper, and an onion he had teased out of the ground in the root-crop section, and set to work on his sauce. Then, while it simmered, he brewed a cup of tea which he took over to the leather chair. "Marta," he said to the room, "Music. Sebastian Bach, the Musical Offering." He closed his eyes and sipped the tea, letting the music carry him away from the world of dog-eat-dog executives.

Dinner was satisfactory. Zigeuner sauce is either satisfactory or it isn't; it is never spectacular. Spectacular was for weekends, although some weekends he would venture out into the streets of New York, to see what passed for edible at the better restaurants. Nearly always, he could do better, but on those rare occasions when some chef did impress him, he would experiment until he had figured out what the secret was, and add it to his repertoire. If toads like Harold Stasevik wanted to scoff at how he lived, let them scoff. Stasevik would go home to an unhappy wife, eat a forgettable meal, and go to sleep in a generic house on a street where he couldn't name the neighbors. That, Bathori thought, was a life suitable for cattle. As for himself, he preferred to live like a human being. If that required, as it sometimes did, that he do questionable things, then that was simply how it was. He took a stem glass out of a cabinet. Which wine after dinner? After a moment's thought, he decided on a Tokay. As he settled into the leather chair, he thought of how Stasevik had described Chez Bathori: plain, bare, and empty. No, he thought with a smile, not even close.

Chapter Twenty-Seven

Slim had a list, and the first name on it was Margaret Adams, Wade Dawson's former housekeeper. She lived in a small brick house on Hampton Street in Larson. The mailbox hadn't been painted in a long time, but when it was new it had said George Adams, which Dock noticed right away. "So, what are you going to do if George shows up?" he asked.

"Not real likely," Slim assured him. "George got sent to 'Nam in '72 and never came back. They checked." That was one of the things Slim liked about working for Mr. S: his people sweated the details. "Okay then, let's do this. Drop me off, go see the sights, then come back in a half hour. I'll meet you at the corner." As Dock pulled away, Slim went up the walk and rang the doorbell. "I hate to worry you, ma'am," he said to the gray-haired woman who came to the door, "but I saw smoke coming out of your eave vents, and I thought there might be a problem."

"Smoke? Oh dear," she said, coming out onto the porch and looking up. That moment of inattention was all Slim needed. He had her gagged and taped into a chair in thirty seconds. Then he got to work.

Dock picked him up right on schedule, and asked how it had gone. Slim told him it had gone all right. "Mr. S is looking for a factory he says the dead guy had. He's working on finding it from his end, but he said if the old lady didn't know—and she didn't— that I should check with the dead guy's lawyer. I'll bet if I ask him real nice, he'll tell me. Maybe not right away, but that's all right; I got lots of time. Lots more than he's got, anyway." Slim laughed; he was looking forward to doing the lawyer. "The lady in there," he jerked his head back toward Mrs. Adams's house, "told me the dead guy used to play poker; she even knew who he played with. Would you believe, one of the players is that lawyer? The next game is tomorrow night, and I think I'll drop by."

"Well now, that's a shame," Emmett said into the phone. "Would you let me know when the service is? Thanks, Fred." He hung up and sighed.

"Somebody die?" Evelyn asked.

"Yeah, Margaret Adams. Fred says it was a heart attack." Fred was the county coroner.

"Where?"

"At home. She hadn't picked up yesterday's mail, and Clyde got worried." Clyde was the mail man. "The police found her on the floor in the kitchen. Apparently, it was a real mess. She had been opening a can of peas when it happened, and they spilled everywhere."

Evelyn chuckled sympathetically. "She would have hated that. Her kitchen was always spotless."

"Was she a good cook?" Emmett asked casually.

"Judging by what she used to bring to the church pot-lucks, I would say she was."

He thought for a moment. "Didn't we draw up Margaret's will, a couple of years ago? Yeah, we did. Who is the executor, do you remember?"

"I think you are, but I'll check." Evelyn spent a few minutes in a side room lined with filing cabinets, and returned with a folder. "Uh huh, it's you. Why?"

"Because as executor, I can go into the house without being a trespasser, that's why. There's something I want to check on." He stood up and headed for his back door.

"Well don't think you're going without me," Evelyn announced as she marched up the hall to lock the front door.

"And you're going, why?"

"Because even if it occurred to you to clean up her kitchen—and it wouldn't—you would do a half-assed job of it. Margaret was a friend of mine, and no friend of mine is going to her reward knowing her kitchen is a mess."

As Evelyn had expected, Margaret Adam's kitchen was clean and tidy, except for the peas. Most of them she swept up with a little whisk broom she had brought from the office, and the rest—the ones that had been stepped on by the police or the coroner—she scraped up with a pancake turner she found in a drawer. While she worked, Emmett poked around. He looked in the refrigerator, he looked in the sink. Then he started to pace, silently cross-examining an imaginary witness. It was a method he very often used before a trial, to probe for flaws in a theory. 'Now you say she was opening a can of peas,' he said to the witness. 'What do you imagine she was going to do with them? Was she going to eat them straight from the can, with a spoon?' In the courtroom he wouldn't have gotten away with that; it called for the witness to speculate, but in Emmett's mental trials there were never any objections. The witness answered that Mrs. Adams wouldn't have eaten cold peas from the can, so she was obviously going to heat them up, maybe as a side dish, maybe to add to a stew. 'What would she cook them in?' Emmett asked his witness, who thought a saucepan would do the job. 'All right, so where is it?' Emmett asked. The witness didn't know. Perhaps there had been one, and the police had put it away. 'The same police who not only left the peas on the floor, but the empty can too? You're saying they would have put a pot back on the shelf?' Emmett said, pointing at the offending can.

Evelyn noticed the gesture. "I'll get to that," she said, "or you can pick it up."

"I'm arguing with a witness," he told her, "and the son of a bitch is hiding something." Evelyn didn't say anything, but her look invited an explanation. Instead, she got a question. "When you cook something canned, do you get out the pot before you open the can, or after?"

Evelyn considered that. "Before. I guess you could open the can and then get out the pot, but I never do."

"My guess is, most people don't." Emmett struck a pose, holding up a finger the way he did in front of a jury. "Ladies and gentlemen," he said out loud, "I submit that the State's theory is absurd. We are told that this woman—a good cook, by all accounts—was opening up a can of peas with no pot to pour them in. We are told, that this good cook was going to use canned peas when..." he walked over to the refrigerator and opened its freezer door, "she had two packs of frozen peas that she could have used. I ask you, how likely is that? And I submit, not very. I suggest that it is much more likely that the peas were opened and scattered by someone else, someone who wanted the death of this healthy woman to look natural, when in fact it was anything but." He closed his hand into a fist, a subliminal cue to tell his mental jury that he had clinched his argument.

His real jury frowned. The peas had struck her as odd, but she couldn't have said why. "So you're saying what? Burglers? Somebody broke in, she had a heart attack, and they did this to cover it up?"

He shook his head. "A burglar would just leave her where she fell. Unless she didn't really die of a heart attack. Autopsies cost money. Nobody would order one if it was obvious how she died. I think that whoever broke into our office is still looking for something."

"But why Margaret. I mean, I know she was Wade's house-keeper, but what could a housekeeper tell anybody?"

"Other than who Wade's friends were? I can't imagine."

"His friends," Evelyn said, thinking. "You mean like, you?"

"Me, and some others. I think I'd better make some calls."

◇◇◇◇◇◇◇◇◇◇◇◇◇◇◇◇●◇◇◇◇◇◇◇◇◇◇◇◇◇◇◇◇◇

Bart knew it had to be there, somewhere, and sure enough, there it was. The little card had gotten cupped and dog-eared, but everything in a guy's wallet gets like that after a while. On it was a telephone number; no name, no extension, just a ten-digit num-ber. After two rings, a teenage girl's voice answered: "Hello?" He could hear music playing in the background, one of the new boy bands.

He was about to say "Sorry, wrong number," but he was

sure he had gotten it right. "Col. Menendez, please," he managed finally.

"And like, who is this?"

"I'm, uh, Bart Phillips."

"Bart? Hey, how's it going?" the girl asked. Then the music stopped and a man's voice said, "Sorry, I forgot to switch off the voice module."

Bart knew that voice. "McIntyre?"

"J. B., at your service. You need the colonel? She's in a meeting right now, but I can slip her a message."

"No, I don't even know if she's who I need. She just said if I ever called this number I should mention her name."

"What do you need? Maybe I can handle it."

"I don't really know if I need anything. I just got a call from Mr. Schroder. He's a lawyer who—oh, yeah, you've been to his office. Anyway, those people who broke in? He thinks they're back."

"That would be very interesting, if true. Why does he think that?"

"Well you see, Uncle Wade had a housekeeper..."

The drapes were open. Through the picture window Slim could see the four poker players, sitting around a table. There were only four chairs and the cards had been dealt, so nobody else was expected. In other words, there weren't going to be any interruptions. He would need to close those drapes, of course; his kind of business needed privacy. He slipped up to the front door, rang the doorbell, and waited. When one of the players opened the door, he said "Hey, I've run out of gas and my phone has gone dead. Do you mind if I come in and use yours?"

Calvin Zorn looked him over. "No, that's all right; you stay there, and I'll call somebody for you."

"Think again, Gomer," Slim said, bringing his pistol from behind his back and pointing it at Calvin. "You just raise your hands and back up, over there toward the others, and nobody has to get hurt." Not yet, at any rate, he thought. That part comes later. "Oh, and the rest of you? You can raise your hands, too. You, chubby," he nodded toward Jim Perkins. "Close the drapes. And don't do anything heroic. I'm watching you."

Jim did look a little on the chunky side, but they all did. A ballistic vest under the shirt will do that. Jim closed the drapes. "Now what?" he asked, to keep Slim's attention focused on what was in front of him and away from Bud, who had slipped out from behind the door.

"Okay, now I want you to..." Two Taser darts hit Slim from behind, and after a few seconds of making animal noises, he fell to the floor. Bud stood ready to give him another jolt if he needed it, but the others had Slim disarmed and duct-taped before he started to wiggle on his own.

"Wow, I know what I want for Christmas," Bud said, as he handed the Taser to Emmett, "unless I can keep this one."

Emmett shook his head. "No, the Sheriff wants it back." He went over and closed the door. "If there's any more of them out there, we want the coast to look clear."

Slim lay on the floor, his ankles and wrists taped together. He glared at the five men, but didn't say anything. Arnold walked over to him, squatted down, and shook his head sadly. "You in a heepa trubba, boy," he said in what he thought was an Alabama accent. "I've always wanted to say that to somebody. Mr. Schroder, just offhand, how much trubba would you say this boy is in?"

Emmett pretended to ponder the question. "Well now, let me see," he said. "If you really wanted to lay the wood to him..."

"Let's say that we do," Arnold said.

"All right, then. Mr. Zorn: Can you testify of your own knowledge that he entered your dwelling without your consent, and with the obvious intent of committing a crime?"

"I can indeed, Mr. Schroder. I told him to stay outside and he forced his way in."

"And at night, too. Dear me. Do you recall, sir, if he had a firearm?"

"Why yes he did. And he pointed it right at me."

"I see. Well then, to answer Mr. Devore's question, that would make him guilty of first degree burglary, several different ways. Would you like to know what first degree burglary carries, Mr. Devore?"

"I believe I would, Mr. Schroder." They were both enjoying this.

"As I recall, it carries fifteen years to life." Emmett went and stood over Slim. "And when a South Carolina judge says 'life', there ain't no good time or gain time. Life means 'until you die'. Oh, and by the way, you're under arrest."

Slim finally thought of something to say. "This is bullshit, this is—what do you call it?—entrapment. Anyway, you can't arrest me; you got no warrant."

Arnold looked at Emmett. "Oh dear. Mr. Schroder, do we need a warrant?"

Emmett pursed his lips as if he were thinking about that. "Well now let me see. As I recall, the law of South Carolina is that, if a person breaks into a home at night and without permission, any citizen can arrest him by any effective means. That's a quote, by the way: 'any effective means'." He squatted down and looked Slim in the eye. "And we won't have to pour a can of peas on you to make it look natural, either. Welcome to South Carolina, you murdering son of a bitch."

For the fifth time, Dock cruised past Calvin's house. Slim's signal that everything was all right was to turn the porch light off, and it was still on. Something had gone wrong. He drove to another part of town and got out the phone Slim had left in the car. Slim hadn't wanted to risk getting caught with that phone, because the first number on speed dial was his contact. Dock wasn't supposed to use it, except in a real emergency. This, he decided, was a real emergency. A voice answered: "Yeah?"

"Uh, yeah, this is, uh, I mean, I'm the driver for Sli...for the guy who..."

The voice cut him off. "We know who you mean. Why are you calling and not him?"

"Uh, I'm pretty sure the, uh, the man with me has gotten caught."

"Caught. Do you mean captured, or do you mean killed?" Earlier, the voice had sounded irritated, but now it sounded interested. Very interested.

"I don't know. All I know is, he went in, and he never came out."

"Went in where?"

"A house where some guys were playing poker. He was supposed to, uh, ask one of them some questions. Or something."

There was a long pause, then the voice said, "I see. Leave the neighborhood, but don't go far. Keep the phone charged; I'll be calling back with instructions." The man Dock had called hung up, and walked across the hall to Harold Stasevik's office. "The South Carolina thing has blown up," he said. "The driver thinks DiSantis has been captured."

Hal stared off into space for a moment. "Then our asset has become a liability. Clean it up; do it yourself. I want it done right this time, and I want it done fast."

"What about his driver?"

"Him too. We have to assume he knows too much."

Everyone on Traxell's upper floors thought of the man as just another one of Hal's flunkies. Slim would have known better, if he had ever met him. It was something in the eyes, Slim had once told Dock. You look into a killer's eyes, and you just know. "I understand," the man said, with a slight smile. "Consider it done."

◇◇◇◇◇◇◇◇◇◇◇◇◇◇◇◇◇●◇◇◇◇◇◇◇◇◇◇◇◇◇◇◇◇◇

Bart was in the shower and Jamaal was at the gym, so when Bart's phone started saying "Intruder alert! Intruder alert!", The phone said the number was blocked, but Tori answered it anyway.

She figured Bart wouldn't mind, since nobody called him who didn't know her too. Or almost nobody; she had answered it one time, and it had been a pollster who had wanted Bart's opinion on some candidate. Instead, he had gotten Tori's opinion of pollsters, and he hadn't ever called back. This time, though, it wasn't a pollster. A girl—judging by her voice she couldn't be more than sixteen—asked if Bart was there. Tori almost told her that Bart was in the shower, but then she thought no, if the caller really was some high-school sweetheart, she could work up her own fantasies. "I'm afraid not," she said, as nicely as she could manage. "Could I take a message?"

"Would you?" the nymphet said. "Just tell him Jaybee returned his call, and could he call me back, okay? Same number as before." Tori muttered that she would be sure to tell him, but Jaybee had already hung up. Jamaal had been trying to educate Bart on how girls think, but he hadn't gotten to the part about sudden mood swings. When Bart got back to the room, he learned that on his own.

"You have a message," Tori said. The words dripped icicles. "Lolita said for you to call her," she paused, "like you did before."

"I don't know any Lolita," Bart told her, not getting the reference. The librarians hadn't put Nabokov on his reading lists.

"No? Then how come she said you had her number, just tell me that."

"Now wait, wait; some girl named Lolita said I called her? This is somebody's idea of a joke." And a really bad joke too, he thought.

"I didn't mean her name was Lolita, I meant she *was* a Lolita. Her name is Jubie, or Jerri, or something else cutesy like that."

It struck Bart that 'Jerri' was no cutesier than 'Tori' but before he could get himself into real trouble he realized what else she had said. "J.B. Is that who called?"

"She might have said Jaybee."

"Okay now, calm down, I can clear this up in a second." Bart dug the card out of his wallet.

"You carry her number around with you?"

Bart decided that saying anything else would only make it worse. He tapped in the number and waited.

"Hey, that was quick," a girl's voice said. "Who was that who answered before?"

"That was my, uh, that was a really good friend named Tori, and you have gotten me into a lot of trouble. She thinks you're somebody named Lolita. Would you mind straightening things out while I've still got all my body parts?"

"Sure thing. Is she still there? Put her on." Bart handed the phone to Tori. "Tori?" the Lolita voice said. "Bart says I got you upset. I am so sorry. Now I want you to listen carefully, because this is really really important." As he spoke, McIntyre gradually moved a slider control on a touch screen. "That mental picture you have of me? You may want to rethink that, just a little." Word by word, his voice had become less like a teenage girl's and more like a grown man's. "Now could you put Bart back on?" McIntyre asked, in his normal voice. Tori handed the phone back to Bart. "Are you out of trouble?" McIntyre asked him.

"I don't know," Bart said. "Let me check. Am I out of trouble?"

"Maybe," she said, then took the phone back. "You, on the other hand," she said to McIntyre, "deserve to be tied down and whipped."

"Und vot makes you sink I vudent like dat, Liebchen?" the phone purred, this time in a warm contralto.

Tori's face turned bright red, and she tossed the phone back to Bart as if it had suddenly gotten hot. "I think I'm out of trouble," Bart told McIntyre, "but if she ever sees you, be ready to run. Anyway, I've got news for you. That thing I told you my friends were worried about? Well, it turned out all right: they caught the guy."

"Wait, you mean the one they think killed the housekeeper? Who caught him?"

"My friends did. They set a trap for him and they got him. At least they're pretty sure it's him. Mr. Schroder says he can get him put away for life, even if they can't prove he killed Mrs. Adams."

"Where is he now?" McIntyre asked, trying to hide his excitement.

"The county jail, there in Larson. They're holding him as a John Doe cause he won't tell them his name. He's got a preliminary hearing day after tomorrow, but Mr. Schroder says his chance of getting out on bail is, and this is a quote, exactly zero. Anyway, I thought it might be important."

"The day after tomorrow," McIntyre said as he wrote it down. "You have no idea how important, but I've got to run. I will definitely be back in touch." His voice changed back to its teenage girl version: "Oh, and tell Tori bye for me."

"Lolita says bye," Bart told Tori, who pitched a pillow at him.

Chapter Twenty-Eight

General Compton was in a sour mood. This was his morning to read reports, and he had a basket full of them. Most were routine, but he still had to read each one, initial it and add an occasional comment. What was it Bragg had said, something about captains going out and having fun while generals sit on their duffs and read reports? Uncomfortably close to the truth, he thought. The report in front of him was typical, setting out in tedious detail what the cafeteria was doing to comply with the agriculture department's latest theories of proper nutrition. "Meat, starch, bulk, and something green, that's all you needed to know when I was a pup," he growled at somebody who had just appeared in his doorway, "and yet somehow my generation survived." He added his initials to the others on the report, tossed it into his Out basket, and looked up to see Elizabeth Menendez. "Hell, when I was in Guangxi I lived for a week on nothing but mung beans and dog meat. Where's that on their damned pie chart?"

"Guangxi?" Had she heard that right? "When were we in south China?"

"Hmph. Officially? Not since '49. Forget I mentioned it. Want to read some reports? I'll share."

"I've got plenty of my own, thank you. No, I'm here about that matter you were just curious about. Are you still curious?"

"Affirmative. You've heard something?"

She closed the door. "Do you remember that road race that Bragg and McIntyre got into down in South Carolina? The one where that stolen car got all torn up?"

"The one with the Jeep. Oh yeah, I remember that."

"Uh-huh. Well, with a little off-the-record encouragement, the state police hauled the Lexus down to Columbia and took it apart. Long story short, they found something: a fingerprint, one that didn't belong to the car's owner. It belongs to one Andrew DiSantis."

"Ah," the general said, "And what do we know about Mr. DiSantis?"

"Street name is Slim. According to New Jersey, he's just a punk. New York thinks he's more than that. They can't quite pin anything on him, but they think he's a killer."

"And what do you think? Is he the one who killed Travis?" The murder of Mr. Travis was something the general never mentioned without his jaw clenching up.

"Maybe, but I think I know why New York can't nail him. They've got a list of the jobs they think he's done. Some were shot, one was drowned, and a couple were done with an ice pick. There was only one broken neck, so you can't really say Travis fits into a pattern. This guy doesn't seem to have a pattern. But the victims do. I put my best analyst to work on them, and guess what? If you dig deep enough, there is the hint of a pattern. The ones that weren't obvious mob hits, were almost all people who were inconvenient to Traxell, one way or another."

"Now that is interesting."

"I thought so. Oh, and there's one more thing."

"You are a tease, you know that," the general grumbled.

She shrugged. "It's how I train to be a general. McIntyre got a call from that Phillips boy yesterday, about the death of a woman in Larson. He thought there might be a connection with the break-in at the lawyer's office. Anyway, now they think they've caught the man who did it. He's being held in the county jail. His fingerprints haven't come through yet, but if there's a chance he's DiSantis, I thought you ought to know."

The general stared off into space for a moment, then nodded. "Get a team down there. If it is our guy, and if he was looking for somebody in Larson who has something on Traxell, I want to know who that somebody is, and I want to know what they've got."

"I would swear you told me our hands were tied." the colonel said.

"You have an inconveniently good memory," the general replied. "Yes, I did tell you that, and yes, we're still under orders to leave Clevis issues alone. Officially, what I have in mind has nothing whatever to do with Clevis. Our mission relates to the murder of Mr. Travis. He was one of mine, and if those SOBs think I've forgotten about him, they've got another think coming. Because, just to be clear, hell no, I have not."

◇◇◇◇◇◇◇◇◇◇◇◇◇◇◇◇●◇◇◇◇◇◇◇◇◇◇◇◇◇◇◇◇

"Do we have a problem here?" There was no one else in the office, but Roland Bathori often spoke to himself. He found that it crystallized his thoughts and helped him focus. "Let's find out, shall we?" He called up an employee file. "Ah yes, I believe we do." A woman had announced on Facebook that her husband, 'an important executive at Traxell', was about to get a promotion because of his outstanding work on a very important project. That, the Security chief thought, was wrong on so many levels. The man was an eighth-floor worker bee, the project had been fairly routine, and his contribution had merely met expectations. Apparently, though, he had done some bragging at home. And that was all right, as far as it went. What was not all right was that it hadn't stayed at home. The company's rule was quite clear: say nothing about your work to people who cannot keep their mouths shut. If your spouse is a gossip or your child is a babbler, then tell them nothing. "A promotion?" Bathori said to himself as he made a notation in the man's file, "No, I don't think so." The man wouldn't be fired, but he would never rise above eight. There was a discreet tap on his office door. "Come," he said, only a little louder than when he had spoken to himself. He knew Jason's knock. "Yes?"

"Something of concern," his assistant said, in his soft, uninflected voice. "Research Liaison has been using an outside man named DiSantis for their—as they call them—interrogations. According to our source at NYPD, Mr. DiSantis left a fingerprint in a car during his last assignment in South Carolina. No warrants have been issued, but that can only be a matter of time."

"A fingerprint. That would seem to be...careless." Bathori said the word as if it tasted bad, the way one of the old Grand Inquisitors might have said 'heresy'. "I have wondered when this project of theirs would go from a potential concern to an active one, and I believe it now has. Notify Mr. Stasevik that he is to recall his man, immediately."

"For retirement, I take it?" Jason glanced downward, toward the floor below: twelve.

Bathori nodded. DiSantis's exit interview would indeed be on twelve. Not in Records Storage, of course. Twelve wore, as it were, several hats. It was home to Big Mama the supercomputer; it was where the building's air handlers sat, rumbling away, and where the building's back-up generators waited for the city's power grid to go down. But more to the point, twelve housed the big incinerator, the one that was, its installers had joked, so much like the ones the crematoriums use.

◇◇◇◇◇◇◇◇◇◇◇◇◇◇◇◇●◇◇◇◇◇◇◇◇◇◇◇◇◇◇◇◇

The jailer tapped his baton against the bars. "Hey, you, your lawyer's here to see you."

Slim sat up. "About damn time," he muttered. He hadn't called a lawyer, but he wasn't surprised. Dock must have let Mr. S know there was a problem. Slim feared no man and respected very few, but Mr. S was one of those few. Mr. S knew how to take care of problems.

The jailer let Slim into the visitors' booth, where he sat on one side of a plastic window. On the other side was a tall, silver-haired man in a dark pinstripe suit. What he had signed in the jail's visitor logbook wasn't his real name, but it was the name of a real lawyer. His own law license was, technically, in a state of suspension because of a disagreement with the Georgia bar. They took the position that taking trust account money to cover gambling debts was unprofessional conduct. He had tried to explain that he wasn't taking the money, he was only borrowing it until his luck changed. At worst, he had told them, it had been an error of judgment, but they wouldn't listen to reason. He was, as he saw it, simply the victim of bad luck. He had been one card away from a big score in Atlantic City, and if that last card had been a spade instead of a heart, he could have put all the money back and no one would ever have been the wiser. Then he wouldn't need to act like he cared what happened to this nasty little man in front of him.

"Listen," Slim told the man, "you've got to get me out of here."

The man held up a hand and shook his head. "I will handle that, you may rest assured, but from this moment on, I don't want you to speak another word. Use hand gestures. The police aren't supposed to listen in on attorney-client conferences, but they do. Nod if you understand." Slim nodded. "Good. Now, have you made any statements since they brought you here?" Slim shook his head. "At the time and place where you were arrested, did you say anything that might be twisted to sound incriminating?" Slim liked the way this man thought. He tried to remember what he had said to the poker players, decided it wasn't anything bad, and shook his head. "All right, I believe that is all I need for now. There will be a bond hearing tomorrow. You are to say nothing, not a word. I will do all the talking. Do you understand?" Slim did. "Excellent. I will see you then. My theory of the case is that you went to that house for assistance in an emergency, that you were set upon and robbed by a group of drunken gamblers, and that they have concocted this charge to cover up their own misbehavior. I don't see this case going to trial, but if it does no jury will convict you. Keep your mouth shut, and you won't do any time for this; I guarantee it." Slim nodded, and the visit was over.

The lawyer strolled casually back to his car. The phone in his coat pocket was the best available, but the phone he used for the call he made to his real client was on a cheap throw-away that he had bought that morning. "I suppose a jury might take as long as twenty minutes to convict him," he told the man who answered, "but only if one of the jurors needs to use the john. The locals haven't sent his fingerprints off yet, but if he turns out to have a record—and he looks like the kind who would—I would say he's looking at a minimum of twenty years. At tomorrow's bond hearing, I think he might start to see how bad his prospects really are, and after that I cannot guarantee his silence. Bond hearings are set for ten o'clock, and the jailer says the prisoners are brought over just before the hearings." A lawyer isn't supposed to sell out his client, but since the Georgia Bar said he wasn't a lawyer, and since Slim wasn't really his client, those were mere quibbles; they didn't matter. What did matter was that his real client paid real money. He thought how happy his favorite dealer would be when she saw him, back at her table, with an armload of chips. And this time he would walk away a winner; he could just feel it.

◊◊◊◊◊◊◊◊◊◊◊◊◊◊◊●◊◊◊◊◊◊◊◊◊◊◊◊◊◊◊

"Bart?" said a familiar voice. "Steve Bragg. From the Jeep ride? I was, uh, going to be in the area this afternoon, and I wondered if you could spare me a few minutes."

"Yeah, sure. I get out of my last class at four."

"Yes, I know. I'll see you then." The call ended. He hadn't had time to say which class or in which building, but when he came out into the sunlight, there stood Bragg. They walked to the end of the block, where McIntyre was waiting in a car. In a few minutes they were cruising along Highway 28. "We have been thinking," Bragg began, "about that fellow your friends caught. We think we should have a talk with him, and wondered if your Mr. Schroder could help us do that. The problem is, we may not have the, ah, best rapport with his secretary, and we thought you could help with that."

"Because we don't want it to end up like last time," came McIntyre's voice from the front seat. Bragg had used his two days in jail to work on his unarmed combat skills. McIntyre had spent the time watching a prisoner with bad breath and worse teeth, who might or might not have winked at him.

Bart thought it might be better not to ask what McIntyre meant. "Sure, I can vouch for you. When do you want to do it?"

"In about a half hour. That's where we're going now."

◇◇◇◇◇◇◇◇◇◇◇◇◇◇◇●◇◇◇◇◇◇◇◇◇◇◇◇◇◇◇

The law office normally closed at five, but Evelyn told Emmett he had a late appointment. She didn't elaborate, since Bart hadn't said why he was coming, only that it was, as he put it, "kind of important."

McIntyre got them there right at five. They would have been a few minutes earlier, but Bart had insisted they stop at a florist shop. He went in first and held the door for Bragg and McIntyre, each of whom carried a vase of long-stem roses. "Right there," Bart told them, pointing to Evelyn's desk. They put the flowers down, then stood facing the secretary. "All right," Bart said, nodding at them. "Now."

In unison, the two men said "We're sorry." They had practiced that on the way over. Evelyn wasn't struck speechless very often, but her mouth was still open when Emmett came down the hall.

Emmett, like most men, saw little point in cut flowers. They were pretty for a while, then they wilted and died. That made them, in his opinion, very appropriate for funerals, but not much else. He looked at the two bouquets on Evelyn's desk. "Who died?"

Bart gestured to the two penitents. "Mr. Schroder, I want you to meet two friends of mine, Mr. Bragg and Mr. McIntyre."

Evelyn came back to life. "Wait a minute, that's not who you said you were, that other time."

Bart gave them another nod. "We're sorry," they said again.

"Hmph," she said, but it was hard to stay upset with two such contrite wretches.

"We need to see you for a few minutes, Mr. Schroder," Bart said. "It's about those recent break-ins you had."

"Break-in," Emmett corrected him. "There was only one."

"No sir," Bragg said quietly. "There were two, and we think they still haven't found what they wanted. They may not have gotten it from Mrs. Adams either, which is why we're here."

Emmett gave them a long look. "I think," he said, "that we had better go on back to my office. Evelyn, would you lock up?"

"Sure, unless you mean lock up as I leave, cause that's not what's about to happen."

Emmett was going to say something when Bragg interrupted. "What we have to say may affect both of you, so I think Ms Pitman should hear it."

Nobody called Evelyn "Ms Pitman" without getting a lecture, and she had one on the tip of her tongue when something occurred to her. "How do you know my last name?" She turned toward Bart. "Did you tell him?"

Bragg looked at McIntyre. "Show her." McIntyre took out his phone, tapped it a couple of times, and showed Evelyn the screen. There was her driver's license photo, her full name, her date of birth, and her Social Security number. "Would you like to see your high school transcript?" Bragg asked. "We are not with the FBI, Ms Pitman, but we do work for the government. We believe that someone very much wants to know about Wade Dawson, and that it may have occurred to them to ask Mr. Schroder about him. If he can't give them what they want, they're likely to ask you, and if they find out from either of you about Mr. Phillips here, they're going to want to ask him."

"When you say ask, you mean something else, don't you," Evelyn said. It wasn't a question.

"Yes ma'am, I mean drug or torture, question and kill. Just like what they probably did to Mrs. Adams. Now, Mr. Schroder, we need to know about what happened at that poker game. Shall we get started?"

◇◇◇◇◇◇◇◇◇◇◇◇◇◇◇◇●◇◇◇◇◇◇◇◇◇◇◇◇◇◇◇◇

As he did on every criminal court day, Emmett visited the jail. If a client had a hearing coming up, he made sure the client knew what was about to happen and more important, what had better not happen. If the client hadn't already heard it, Emmett told him the story of Rance Dugan. Rance had been on trial for three felonies, and he had left enough evidence behind that acquittal was not a realistic possibility. Emmett explained to Rance that he couldn't keep him out of prison, but he might be able to cushion the blow if Rance would say he was sorry, and had learned his lesson. Just those two things: sorry, lesson learned; nothing more. Rance, however, hadn't gotten where he was in life by doing what he was told, and when the jury foreman had read out the verdict—guilty on all three counts—Rance had stood up and told the jury they could all get fucked. The bailiff expected Judge Cressy to throw a fit, but he didn't. "Mr. Dugan," he said patiently, "it is rude to interrupt, and we aren't quite finished." Then he very calmly gave Rance the maximum on each charge, with the second and third sentences to run consecutive to the first, and consecutive to each other.

Today, Emmett's only client on the calendar was one of his regulars, a man who had been to court almost as often as Emmett had. He didn't need to have his hand held, but Emmett's jail visits served two purposes. As often as not, there was somebody in jail who didn't have a lawyer, and Emmett ended up with a new client. As a rule, Emmett came to the jail alone, but this time he had a man with him, a lawyer friend from out of town, he told the jailer. If the jailer thought the friend looked a little like a recent guest of his, he didn't say anything. A lot of people came through his jail, and the one-timers didn't make much of an impression.

"Let me know when you're done," the jailer told them. He went back to his magazine, and the two visitors went back to the cells. In a big city jail, leaving a lawyer alone with the prisoners would get a jailer fired. Larson is not a big city. Duane Glaspy, the day jailer, had done the job for twenty years, and he knew who he could trust.

If it had been a Monday, the jail would have been full of the weekend drunks, but today only two cells were occupied. Emmett went over to talk to his client, and Bragg strolled down to the cell at the far end. "Good morning," he said. Slim gave him a glare, but didn't say anything. "I know, you want a lawyer present during questioning. Well, that's fine, there's not going to be any questioning; I'm just going to tell you things. Let's start with your name: Andrew, only I'm told you prefer Slim. Yeah, Andrew, I know who you are. These people here don't, but I do. I know who you are, and I know what you do. I was in that Jeep you chased, after you killed a man and stole his Lexus. I'm sure you remember the Lexus, Andrew. There wasn't much left of it after the wreck, just a lot of broken glass and jagged metal. My guess is, you were wearing gloves, and that one of them snagged on something sharp. But I could be wrong; you could just be losing your edge. You see, you left a fingerprint."

Slim's eyes widened a little, but still didn't say anything. He hadn't been wearing gloves in the Lexus; he never wore gloves—they dulled the feel of the trigger—but he was always careful not to touch anything without wiping it clean. There hadn't been time to do that when the Lexus wrecked, but he hadn't thought anybody would find any prints. He could feel sweat starting to form on his forehead.

Bragg noticed the sweat, and shook his head in mock sympathy. "Oh dear, I've upset you, haven't I. But the news isn't all bad, Andrew. The good news is, we want your employers more than we want you. Think about that, and then you can think about this: if you clam up, and they convict you of even one of the hits that we both know you've done, South Carolina lets you choose which way you want to die: the poison needle, or the electric chair." He glanced at his watch. "Time for me to go. I'll be out there when they bring you over; give me a wave if you want to talk. If not, I'll give you one, only it'll mean bye-bye."

◊◊◊◊◊◊◊◊◊◊◊◊◊◊◊●◊◊◊◊◊◊◊◊◊◊◊◊◊◊◊

The Keowee County courthouse sits in the middle of town, alone in its own block: Courthouse Square, they call it. There had been a time when every teenage boy in the county would spend the week polishing his car so that when he went cruising around the Square on Saturday night, the girls would see how cool he was.

Like all customs, that one eventually died out. Now, the only people who cruised the Square were looking for parking places.

The Sheriff's Office is a two-story building across the street from the courthouse; the upstairs part of it is the county jail. Bringing a prisoner to court in some counties means taking him to the sally port, loading him in the prisoner van, driving across town, letting him out at the security entrance of the courthouse, then marching him in. In Keowee County, there is no sally port, no prisoner van, and no security entrance. Duane brings the prisoners downstairs in leg irons, and walks them across the street to court. Security consists of Duane telling them, "If you run and make me chase you, I will flat lay a hurtin' on you." Nobody ever took Duane up on that. Running in leg irons is slow, and Duane is, as they say, a big old boy.

They all paused at the crosswalk: Duane, Emmett's regular, Slim, and the man they thought was Slim's lawyer. Slim whispered to the man, "I'm getting a bad feeling about this. I want you to make a deal. I know things, big things, but I want the deal in writing first." He could do prison time; he'd done it before, and he knew how to handle it. But he didn't like needles, and riding the lightning didn't appeal to him either. He had heard that when the juice hit you, your brain would fry inside your head, and you could hear it. The man in the dark suit nodded as if in agreement, but he edged a little farther from Slim than he had been. Slim saw Bragg on the other side of the street, and his hand was starting up to wave when, two blocks away, a set of crosshairs settled on his chest. If someone had been near the shooter, he would have heard a fairly loud *whump*. That is the best a suppressor can do to silence a .308, but it is good enough. A .308 bullet travels faster than sound; it leaves a little sonic boom all along its flight path, a hard crack of a sound that seems to come from everywhere. If the muzzle blast is softened to a whump, nobody can be sure where the bullet came from, and the shooter can simply walk away.

Slim stopped, literally dead in his tracks. Then he fell back onto the sidewalk and lay still. There was a hole in his chest no bigger than a pencil might have made, but there was no hole in his back; the expanding bullet had spent all of its energy making mush out of his heart and lungs. The lawyer wasn't really surprised; Slim had known too much. It didn't occur to him to think, in the two seconds he had left, that he knew too much too.

◇◇◇◇◇◇◇◇◇◇◇◇◇◇◇◇◇●◇◇◇◇◇◇◇◇◇◇◇◇◇◇◇◇◇

They sat around the table in Emmett's conference room. Emmett had found some clean glasses, and the bottle of Jack Daniels that he kept in the office safe was no longer full. "They found the rifle," Evelyn said. She had been monitoring the police radio. "A sniper rig, they're saying. It was under a parked car. They're going to dust it for prints."

"Waste of time," Bragg muttered. He was in a gloomy mood. Slim had been ready to deal, he just knew it. To come that close was frustrating, but what was really galling was that somebody had read the situation as fast as he had, and had gotten a shooter into position. "Whoever took that shot knew his business," he said. "There won't be any prints."

Evelyn disagreed. "He left the gun, didn't he? That was sloppy. That doesn't sound like something a professional would do."

Emmett took a long sip of the whiskey. "I had a client once who told me a curious thing. Nehamiah Pinckney Hayes, his name was. Went by Pink. You remember him, don't you Evelyn?"

Evelyn remembered. Pink Hayes's father was a state senator who was being talked about for governor, and none of the criminal lawyers in three counties had wanted to risk defending his boy and losing. Having a friend in high places has a lot of perks for a lawyer, and the opposite is true too. Emmett wasn't looking for any favors from Columbia, so he had agreed to take the boy's case. "Uh-huh. What about him?" Emmett hadn't ever said much about the case, which was unusual for him.

"He killed three people, one a month. That was the summer of what, '95? Somewhere back there. Anyway, he used the same gun each time, a big Ruger Blackhawk. That's what finally got him caught: they found the gun and matched it to the killings. I asked Pink why he hadn't got rid of it, and he told me he couldn't, that a gun that has killed somebody is special, and the more kills it has, the more special it gets. The way he said special was...well, it was creepy. I figured he was crazy, but since then I've noticed something: if you ever see a murder gun up for sale at an auction, you can count on it, it'll go high. I don't think a regular murderer would have left his gun behind."

Bragg nodded. "I know a lot of military snipers. They'll use the same gun time after time. They'll tell you it's because it's zeroed in just right, or that they like the weight of it or something like that, but deep down, I think it's what you said: a gun that has killed is different. But a professional killer is different, too. He'll use a gun one time, and walk away from it. Are you a betting man, Mr. Schroder?" Emmett allowed as how he was. "I have twenty dollars that says the rifle they found has no prints on it, and no serial number, and no ballistic history."

Emmett thought about it. "I don't believe I will take your wager, sir, unless you're offering some pretty steep odds." He examined the bottle of Jack, which had a couple of inches left in it. "Would any of you care to finish this off?"

"Better not," Bragg said, standing up. "We've got to catch the red-eye out of GSP." With that, the party broke up. Outside, it was dark, but that was as it should be; anything else would have clashed with the general gloom.

◇◇◇◇◇◇◇◇◇◇◇◇◇◇◇◇●◇◇◇◇◇◇◇◇◇◇◇◇◇◇◇◇

The voice on the phone told Dock he should be out on the sidewalk when the prisoners were brought over. "Be where your man can see you," he had said. "Oh, and do you have a bright colored shirt?" Dock told him he had a red one. "Good. Wear it. It will help him see you. When he does, give him a thumbs-up. That's the signal he's looking for. It means we're taking care of everything, and not to worry."

Dock had looked for his red shirt, but it turned out he

hadn't packed it after all. He thought about buying one, but decided against it. Slim didn't need a signal. After so many road trips, Dock knew every thought in Slim's head, and one of those thoughts was that if there was a problem, his precious Mr. S would take care of it. He went on upstairs to the courtroom, and had just found a seat when he heard three sharp cracks from somewhere outside, followed by voices yelling. The bailiff got on his radio and relayed to the crowd what he heard: three men down, one of the prisoners, a out-of-town lawyer, and some guy in a red shirt.

It took Dock about two seconds to realize how right Slim had been: Mr. S really did know how to take care of problems, and apparently he had decided Dock was a problem. His thoughts began to race. If they thought they had killed him, all he had to do was go get back to the car and drive away before they found out different. Unless they had already realized their mistake and then they'd be watching the car. He left the courthouse on the side away from the gathering crowd, and got almost as far as the Confederate memorial when inspiration struck: everybody was rushing to see what had happened, leaving the cars parked around Courthouse Square unwatched. He took a stroll, and sure enough, midway down the block was a nondescript Toyota with its keys dangling in the ignition. Just as he was about to get in, another thought struck him: Slim's phone. Could it tell them where he was? He didn't know, but if it could, those people would know how to do it. He tossed the phone under a bush, got in the Toyota, and in a few minutes he was out on the highway, headed for home.

◇◇◇◇◇◇◇◇◇◇◇◇◇◇◇◇●◇◇◇◇◇◇◇◇◇◇◇◇◇◇◇◇

"Hello?"

"Hi Becky, it's me."

"Floyd, are you drunk again? My protective order says you're not supposed to talk to me."

"Aw come on, Becky. That just means face to face, not over the phone. And anyway I didn't call up to bother you, I just called to say I love you, baby."

Becky hung up, but Floyd had said what he had to say, and he could always call back. He was feeling mellow, and it wasn't just from the weed. He had been making his usual rounds that afternoon, looking for bottles and cans and whatever else might bring in a little cash, when he had struck gold, at least by his standards: somebody had tossed away a perfectly good cell phone.

Chapter Twenty-Nine

Nathan Huntsinger looked around the boardroom. "I see that we are all here, so the meeting will come to order." The room was already in order, but the formula had to be spoken, like some ancient spell, so that the minutes would reflect that the meeting had officially started. If it had been up to Nate, he would simply have said, "Okay, let's get going." Nate prided himself, he had told a Forbes interviewer the year before, on the informality of his board meetings. Entirely too many CEOs thought they were royalty, he had said, and they treat their executives as if they were peasants. He preferred to think of himself not as a king, but as first among equals.

The first-among-equals model sounds good in theory. In practice, it has a flaw, summed up in the old saying: "No man is a hero to his own valet." The old kings—the real kings—knew that. Their castles might be cold and drafty, but a castle did more than just keep the enemy out: it kept the peasants out, too. If the peasants found out that the king snored and belched and had yellow toenails, just the way they did—if, in other words, they found out he was just a man—nothing good would come of it. In ancient China, when a ruler no longer inspired awe, they said he had lost the mandate of heaven. In France, when Louis XVI turned out to be just weak-chinned fat guy, they said, "Louis Capet, how do you plead, guilty or not guilty?" Different cultures, different words, but the meaning was the same: put your head on the block, and say goodbye.

Nate Huntsinger's board knew him for what he was: a silver-tongued glad-hander. That knowledge didn't put his crown in jeopardy, because they also knew it was only a cardboard crown. The real power lay in Brussels, and none of the New York executives mistook the company's chairman, Henrik Verhoeven, for his equal. On those rare occasions when Dr. Verhoeven's jowly face appeared on the boardroom's wall-size monitor, they all sat silent and gave due attention, the way loyal subjects should.

One by one, the department heads gave their reports. The

reports had a certain amount of variety, but basically they were of two kinds. If a project was going well, its success was reportedly due to the brilliant leadership by the VP in charge. But a project that was over budget, or behind schedule, or in some other way was not meeting expectations, was always the victim of intra-service rivalries at the Pentagon, or unstable economic conditions in Europe or, if all else failed, a deplorable lack of cooperation from some other division within the company itself. Blame-shifting was never listed on the board's agenda, but it might as well have been; every meeting seemed to include it, and like any blood sport, those who weren't involved secretly enjoyed watching it.

One of the VPs was finally wrapping up. His department's latest project was on schedule and within budget so, predictably, his report had largely consisted of self-congratulation. "All right, it sounds like that's going well," Nate said. He had only a vague idea what the project was supposed to produce, but its numbers were what they were supposed to be, and if the metrics were right, he saw no need to dig any deeper. "Hal, let's hear about your mystery project. I see in last month's minutes that you said you thought you would have something to report. Do you?"

Hal had thought he might get a pass this time, but he had an answer ready, just in case. "I still think we are close to a breakthrough, although our timetable has had to be adjusted because of a security issue. An issue," he added, "that we have handled." He didn't know if they were anywhere near a breakthrough, but then, neither did Nate.

Nate looked at his Security chief. "A security issue. Roland, should we be concerned?"

Bathori stood up. Some of the VPs reported from a sitting position, but he preferred to stand. "Risk is part of business. We understand that. Risk in pursuit of profit is to be expected, and we are prepared to deal with it. Risk does begin to concern us when it is incurred unnecessarily. Our colleague's quest is, I believe, for an industrial process, and our concern is that the process may not be exploitable. The inventor of the process lived very simply, in a rural backwater. That is hardly what one would expect from the discoverer of a potential goldmine. That suggests to us that the process, or formula, or whatever it is, either doesn't exist or cannot be exploited, for some reason. The profit potential, in other words, appears to be questionable. The risk to the company, on the other hand, we believe to be substantial. Our colleague mentioned, a little too casually I think, a security issue. That reference was to a contractor of his who required retirement, and while I concede that the retirement was well handled by our colleague's own people, the fact that it was necessary at all is worrisome."

Hal bit his lip. Everything Bathori had just said was true, except the part about the profit potential. Of course there was profit potential. This thing was actually was a goldmine. To abandon a goldmine just because it might cave in was stupid, but that was exactly what Bathori seemed to be recommending. He rose to his feet. "The risk, as my colleague has so generously noted, has been handled." That wasn't strictly true. When the police had released the names of the shooting victims in Larson, the third one turned out to have been a retiree named Sigman when it should have been a wheel man named Dockery. That had most definitely been a loose end, until the phone they had given DiSantis had suddenly come back to life. The loose end was about to be snipped off. "According to our analysis in Research Liaison, the process has enormous profit potential, and minimal risk. I can assure the board that there is nothing it needs to be concerned about."

Information Technology did not have a seat at the board meetings. IT was, as the company saw it, a service agency and not a company division. But the board meetings had to be recorded, and somebody had to set up the equipment. Several of the VPs could have done it, but none of them wanted to be tagged as Nate's AV boy, so they let IT do it. Security always did a bug sweep before a board meeting, but the recording equipment wasn't a bug; it was supposed to be there. All of which is to say that IT listened in. They told themselves that by knowing the board's concerns, they could anticipate what they needed to prepare for, but in fact, spying on the bosses gave them almost the same thrill that their multi-player computer warfare games did: they were doing something adventurous without running any real risk. Most of the time, the meetings they listened to were routine, but not always. If a department was having serious problems, a curious procedure would sometimes be invoked. The VP with the problem would be asked to step out of the room and a vote would be taken: retain or retire.

"What do they mean when they talk about retirement?" Singh asked. He was the department's newest member, fresh out of grad school, and this was his first time listening to a board meeting. "Does it mean somebody gets fired?"

"In the meetings I've listened to," Nelson replied, "I've only heard them vote to retire someone one time. That was when the Missile division built a guidance system that was so flimsy it couldn't survive launch. The company took a huge loss on that one, and the board voted to retire the VP in charge."

"How did he take it?"

Nelson frowned. "Not well, apparently. He stepped in front of a truck later that day. Everybody says it was suicide." Singh wondered what Nelson meant by "everybody says," but decided not to ask. Some things, it's better not to know.

Chapter Thirty

Azrael looked in the mirror, and frowned to see the face of Murad Ziya looking back at him. So many years lost, he thought, so much that he should have been doing, while instead this delusion had strutted and preened, plotting its meaningless little schemes. And even now, with Murad gone, the body was still wasting his time: it required food, it demanded sleep, and its strength was barely equal to the tasks he required of it. The brown little man at the convenience store, for example, had almost gotten a pistol from under the cash register before he took his final journey. Getting shot would have been inconvenient, Azrael thought. Obviously he couldn't be killed, but the body he wore could be damaged. He had found out last month when a woman had stabbed him in the shoulder. The wound had hurt, and it had bled. Not as much as she had, of course, but her blood was of no consequence; her work on earth was finished. His was not, and the time he had been forced to spend in this seedy motel waiting for the wound to heal was time that could have been better spent. Not to speak of the money it had cost. Each of the ones whose lives he had completed had contributed something toward his expenses, but none of them had had very much, and the one time he had tried to use a credit card, the gasoline pump had asked him for some kind of code number, and had refused him fuel when he had not known it. His shoulder had healed nicely, though, and at last he felt strong enough to drive. It was time to finish the task that God had given him, and to be rid of this contemptible body.

Second-semester history, Europe Since 1500, met on Friday afternoons, so Thursday nights were trivia nights. First semester, there had been just Bart and Jamaal, but Tori and Dee had decided Jamaal needed a cheering section, so now they sat in too. As the semester drew toward its close, Bart's questions got harder, and sometimes trickier. The last one this evening was the most devious yet. "What war started because of Bad Ems?" That was what Bart said, but what Jamaal heard was, "What war started because of bad M's?"

Jamaal closed his eyes and thought. Bart had fooled him last week with a question about Prince Albert, Queen Victoria's consort. Albert was a German, and didn't pronounce some words the way the British did. Instead of saying "either" with a long E, he said eye-ther, and so naturally the upper classes had to start saying it that way too. But even a German could pronounce M, Jamaal thought. He was almost ready to admit he was stumped when he realized his mistake. "France against Germany," he said, "the Ems Dispatch."

"Close enough," Bart conceded. "France against Prussia."

Jamaal grinned. "I remember what I see a lot better than what I hear, so I've started looking up pictures. I remembered Ems because of that Frenchman, the one who looked like Snidely Whiplash, and how sad he looked in that painting of him after he lost that war, sitting there with old Bismarck like a riverboat gambler who just lost a big hand. But what was his name...?" His face suddenly brightened. "Napoleon the Third," he declared, to which he added, "You know, the French are fucked up."

Dee made a face. "Jamaal," she said, "you should not say that. The French are not fucked up. The Greeks, perhaps, but not the French."

Jamaal stood his ground. "No really, they are. Think about it. There was Napoleon, and then after a while there was Napoleon the Third, but there never was a Napoleon Jr. There was Louie the Sixteenth, but the next Louie up at bat was the Louie the Eighteenth. It's like every once in a while they lose count or something. You can't tell me that's not fucked up."

Bart was going to explain about royalists and their lost heroes when Tori decided to weigh in. "If we're talking about what's fucked up, I've got a candidate: copper. I've been working on it for a week now, and I'm no closer to melting it than I was when I started." They had been going through the seven metals the journal listed more or less in order, except they had had to skip gold. The girls had some jewelry, and Jamaal had his high school ring, but all of what they had was alloyed, and they weren't ready for alloys yet. They had done silver, though. They found a little one-ounce ingot at a coin shop. Jamaal had been the first to try it, and according to him it had put up quite a fight. Copper had been Tori's project, and it was making her crazy. Anyone else would have given up, or asked for help, but not Tori. The contest had become personal, Tori versus a cheap little copper bowl, and right now the bowl was winning.

The guys had learned through painful experience that if Tori didn't ask for help, Tori didn't want help, so on that note the meeting broke up. Dee, though, was protected by the roommate rules; on the walk back to their dorm, she offered a suggestion. "What if we both went in," she asked, "and pulled on it together? Do you think that would work?" Tori hadn't thought about that. The journal hadn't said anything about tandem melts, but at least so far it hadn't warned against them either.

Always before, when one of them had gone into the melt trance, the other had been there to do more or less do what athletes do in a weight room when they have someone spot them. The spotter's task is to deal with whatever goes wrong, and in the girls' case that meant making sure the one in the trance didn't fall over and hit her head. If they were both going into the void, they needed something to prop themselves up. Luckily, they had pillows. The first time Jamaal had seen their room, he had wondered out loud if four dozen pillows was enough, and he had quickly learned two things: they didn't think they had too many pillows, and they knew sarcasm when they heard it. They didn't actually have four dozen, but they had enough to thoroughly pummel Jamaal and Bart, who protested that he hadn't said anything. Tori set him straight. "He's your roommate," she said, "and roommates share." That didn't make sense to Bart, but it seemed to make sense to Dee, who threw another pillow at him. He understood better when, later that evening, Jamaal explained his father's theory of collective punishment. Bart had his own theory, which was that the girls just liked to throw pillows.

When they had the pillows arranged to suit them, Dee warmed the bowl with a hair dryer while Tori called up a music app on her phone, and played the note for copper. Then, with that note humming softly in the background, they closed their eyes and entered the void.

Tori willed the melt link to move, and as usual, it wouldn't. She couldn't tell if Dee was present or not, but suddenly the link came free. She, or they—she still couldn't sense Dee—pulled it almost to the next junction, then held it there, just to show it who was in charge. Finally, she, or they, let it go back and they left the void. At first Tori wasn't sure she really had left it. The void had been dark, and now their room was dark, too. As her eyes adjusted, she realized the dark wasn't total, the way it was at first in the void. A little light was coming in the window from outside, but it was dark enough. "Hey, what's the big idea?" she called out to Dee, thinking her roommate had turned out the lights, but Dee was just starting to sit up, and obviously hadn't done anything. Tori went over to the light switch. It made a crunching sound when she flipped it, but the lights didn't come on. Tori explained to the switch, in language Jamaal's father would have recognized, that it wasn't behaving the way she wanted. Dee found a candle. It didn't give much light, but it gave enough for them to take stock.

One of the historical figures on Dr. Ziya's first-semester exam had been the Greek king Pyrrhus, of whom Jamaal had said, "He called a play that gained yardage, but that got his quarter-back's leg broken." In terms of gained yardage, the melt had been a Pyrrhic victory: the copper bowl was now a copper disk. The quarterback's leg consisted of everything else made of copper within about a twelve foot radius of where the girls had sat: the wires in the walls, the contacts in the switches, everything. "A freak electrical surge," was how Maintenance explained all the melted wires, switches and sockets. Maintenance didn't know about the rest of the damage. When Tori tried to call Bart to tell him what had happened, her phone wouldn't work. Neither would Dee's. When Dee tried to unplug her hair dryer, the plug had no prongs and the wires inside the cord were crisp and hard. Their computers fared no better, but at least they were under warranty. The factory techs had never seen a computer with intact plastic, but with all of its wires and circuits melted. What could do that? "Maintenance says it was a freak electrical surge," the girls told them. The techs scoffed at that, until they tried to come up with a better explanation. "Freak electrical surge," they eventually wrote on their reports, since it couldn't be anything else.

"So where are you going to live?" Bart asked. Maintenance had told the girls that the rewiring job would take several days, maybe a week, and that no, they couldn't just camp in the room in the meantime. The job would have to be finished and inspected before they could move back, and the inspection might take another week.

"The school offered to put us up in a motel," Tori told him, "but the one they said they would pay for wasn't any good. I Yelped it. Somebody said there were bedbugs."

Jamaal had a thought. "Hey, I know: you could stay with Dee's father."

Dee looked around for a something to throw at him, but Cyber City didn't have any pillows. "Papa lives in a tiny little apartment," she said, "just big enough for him and his books. And anyway, he goes to bed very early. He probably thinks that I do too, and he can go right on thinking that; we cannot stay with Papa." She and Tori gave Bart the pitiful lost-kitten looks that they had practiced for the last hour. "So could we stay at the cabin? Please?"

That had already occurred to Bart, but he had decided it wouldn't work. "It's an hour's drive, at least," he pointed out, "and you don't have a car."

"No, but we will," Tori said. "The school says they'll spot us the cost of a rental car, but we're too young to rent one, so Dee's father can rent it, and we'll drive his." She glanced over at

Dee, the signal that it was time to close the deal. "Please," they both said together, holding the word for a long two-count.

When poets write about power, they usually mean the power of love. Only a few of them have tried to describe the other forces that rule the world. Congreve mentioned music, which he said could bend a knotted oak. Schiller wrote of stupidity, against which, he said, the very gods contend in vain. Both of them wrote a long time ago, and the world has changed. A modern poet, looking for an example of mind-boggling power, would find no better example than teenage girls. Bart didn't think Dee and Tori should be alone in an isolated cabin for even one night, let alone for a week or so, and he laid out his reasons. Dee and Tori wanted to go, and for all the difference Bart's reasons made, he might just as well have argued with Congreve's knotted oak.

◇◇◇◇◇◇◇◇◇◇◇◇◇◇◇◇◇●◇◇◇◇◇◇◇◇◇◇◇◇◇◇◇◇◇

Any old cabin, closed up for a while, gets a musty smell, a mixture of wood smoke, mildew, and time. After their first visit to the cabin, the girls had washed all their clothes to get the smell out. The guys hadn't washed anything. The way they saw it, if something didn't show dirt, and didn't stink, it had another wear or two left in it. "Your shirt still smells like the cabin," Tori had told Bart one day the next week. "What did you wash it in?"

"I didn't wash it in anything. It wasn't dirty."

Tori had made him take off the shirt and smell it. "You don't think that needs washing?"

That was, in fact, what he thought. "Here," he tossed the shirt to Jamaal, "does this stink?"

Jamaal knew nothing about the scent industry, but he did a fairly good imitation of a perfumer testing a new formula. He inhaled here, sniffed there, closed his eyes, held his breath, and finally gave the verdict. "Little bit of smoke, the way stuff smells after a camping trip. It's a good smell: woodsy. Nothing wrong with the shirt."

Tori couldn't believe what she had just heard. "You don't smell the mustiness?"

Jamaal said he didn't, but Bart admitted that yeah, there might be a slight musty note, like the way an old library book smells after being opened for the first time in decades. For him, that smell brought back good memories. Tori let it drop. She hadn't read Schiller, but having grown up with brothers, she was acquainted with, if not stupidity, at least male stubbornness. For her, the smell of the cabin wasn't nostalgic at all, it was just musty.

This trip, she and Dee had come prepared. By the time the guys drove up the next weekend, there wasn't a shelf in the cabin that didn't have at least one scented candle on it. The effect was noticeable. "Whew!" Jamaal said when he opened the door. "It smells like a French cathouse."

"You insult the cat," Dee protested. "He is a very clean cat." They had borrowed Orange Cat from Emmett, in case there were mice at the cabin. As if he realized he was being talked about, the cat uncurled from his chair cushion, stretched, and curled back up. Tori explained what Jamaal meant by a French cathouse, but Dee held her ground. "It does not matter," she told Jamaal. "You are still wrong. The smell in a French bordel is much more floral, with just a hint of musk. The scent from our candles is more spicy than that."

There was an awkward silence while the others wondered if this was yet more Turkish humor. Tori was sure that one of the guys would rise to the bait, but for once they knew better. She stood it as long as she could, but finally she had to know. "Uh, Dee, how do you know what a cathouse smells like?"

"I know because I have been in one, of course. There was a very nice house across from our apartment in Marseille when Papa and I lived there. That was," she thought for a moment, "eight years ago. Papa would go to his boring diplomatic receptions and leave me at home alone with no one to talk to, so I would slip across the street and play Belote with the ladies. I will never forget the smell, but it did not come from candles; it came from perfume." She stuck her tongue out at Jamaal. "So there."

While Jamaal tried to think of something to say, something that wouldn't put pillows in the air, Bart decided to change the subject. "The candles might come in handy if you try another team melt." They hadn't talked much about that; the girls were embarrassed by the damage they had caused, but also a little proud of it, and they hadn't quite come to terms with the contradiction. "You might not want to try it with iron, though, unless you want to melt all the nails in the cabin." That was a joke. They hadn't done the iron chapter yet. Bart had glanced at it, but they had agreed to master each metal before going on to the next one. So far, copper was as far as anyone had gotten, and none of them had managed a solo melt of copper yet. And, all joking aside, they didn't want to do another two-person melt until they figured out what had gone wrong with the last one.

Bart had worried that the drive time between campus and the cabin would be a problem, but there turned out to be a compensating advantage. Exams were coming up, and the cabin was the perfect place to study: no dorm noise, no friends dropping in for entertainment, and no telephone distractions. There was, of course, the issue Jamaal had brought up when Bart had stayed there the first time: Leatherface coming to the door with a chainsaw, but Bart didn't think he ought to mention that, not directly anyway. "I wonder if you could borrow your father's pistol," he said to Dee, "just to be on the safe side."

Tori didn't think so. "Why would we ever need it?" she asked. "Nobody ever comes around the cabin, Mr. Schroder said so. Anyway, I've never fired a gun, and neither has Dee; if we had one, we'd probably just shoot Bambi by accident."

"Or shoot you, the way Papa did," Dee added. They would be fine, they told him, and again, arguing the point got Bart nowhere.

◇◇◇◇◇◇◇◇◇◇◇◇◇◇◇◇●◇◇◇◇◇◇◇◇◇◇◇◇◇◇◇◇

"You really think they'll be okay?" Bart asked Jamaal during the ride back to Clemson.

Jamaal thought they would. "No worse than anywhere else, I guess. I mean, where is anybody really safe? Take that woman in the news yesterday. She stopped at a rest area off I-85. Public, well-lit, and yet somebody just walked up to her, cut her throat, took her purse and stole her car. She probably thought she was safe. Which reminds me: just to be safe, we both need to wash our shirts when we get back to the dorm. I don't want to have to explain to Coach why I smell like a bayberry candle."

◇◇◇◇◇◇◇◇◇◇◇◇◇◇◇◇●◇◇◇◇◇◇◇◇◇◇◇◇◇◇◇◇

"Could you perhaps direct me to Enver Ziya's office?" the tall man asked, when the faculty secretary finally looked up.

"Professor Ziya?" she said. "Certainly. Do you have an appointment?"

Azrael nodded. "Of course."

He spoke with calm certainty, a nice contrast to the students who so often tried to bluff their way past her. That, and something about his accent, said that he was a man who could be trusted. Still, "I don't see an appointment on his calendar."

"A mere oversight, I am sure," he said pleasantly. "The appointment was made some time ago." Quite a long time ago, he thought. When the world was made, in fact. This day, this hour, this place.

"Well I suppose it will be all right," she decided. "Go down that hall, to the last door on the right."

"Thank you ever so much," he told her. "You have been very helpful." He gave her a slight bow as he said it, little more than a nod of the head, but it confirmed her opinion that she was dealing with a gentleman. Azrael, for his part, walked purposefully down the hall, gave the last door on the right a light tap, and went in.

The office was empty. That was all right; his task was practically over, and he could afford to be patient. He walked over to look at the books that took up most of one wall of the office. Histories mostly, or commentaries on history. There was also, he noticed, a book on the desk, but it didn't come from Enver's bookshelves; a label on its spine said it was from the university library: *The Rubaiyat of Omar Khayyam.* Azrael leafed through it. Rubbish, he thought, some fool of a poet babbling about love, and wine, and clay pots. Then he saw a verse that made him think he might have judged the poet too harshly.

> Whether at Naishapur or Babylon,
> Whether the cup with sweet or bitter run,
> The wine of life keeps oozing drop by drop,
> The leaves of life keep falling one by one.

Well yes, exactly; the poet had at least understood that much. There are only so many leaves on each man's tree of life, and when his last leaf withers, it is time for him to drop what he is doing and get on with his journey. And yet, no one ever seemed to be ready. It was very sad.

As he put the book back where it had been, he noticed what had been under it: a note, in very neat handwriting. "Papa," it said, "There is no phone at the cabin, but an attorney that Bart knows, Mr. Schroder, says you can leave messages with his secretary. I will check with her every day before we go up to the cabin. You wanted to know where the cabin is, so I have had Bart draw you a map. D." He tore a sheet from a pad by the telephone, and wrote down the lawyer's name. Then he copied the crude map. Azrael smiled. Only God is perfect, he thought; even an angel can make a mistake. The next name on his list was not Enver Ziya after all; it was Enver's daughter, Dilara.

◇◇◇◇◇◇◇◇◇◇◇◇◇◇◇◇●◇◇◇◇◇◇◇◇◇◇◇◇◇◇◇◇

The faculty secretary glanced up to see who was trying to slip past her this time. "Oh, Professor Ziya; I thought you were in your office."

"No, I went out for a walk." He had slipped out the building's rear exit, and had planned to come back in the same way, but the door had locked behind him. The smokers on the faculty liked to prop it open with a rock, but this time the rock had been gone. Probably the Dragon Lady had taken it away, to make people come back in the front door the way they were supposed to. Enver knew he shouldn't think of her as the Dragon Lady—it was a term he had picked up from Dilara—but it actually did seem to fit her.

"You have a visitor," she told him, adding, when he looked around, "Oh, not here; I sent him on back to your office. He said he had an appointment."

"I must not have written it down," he said. "Who is it? I have already made him wait, and if I can't greet him by name, that would be twice that I have been rude."

She pursed her lips. "I, um, I forgot to ask. But I'm sure you'll recognize him; he called you by your first name."

"Can you describe him?"

"Tall, neatly dressed, early thirties I would guess. Oh, and he has a little bit of an accent. I couldn't place it at first, but I finally remembered who he sounds like: Yuri Zhivago."

He had heard that name. "Was that not a character in a book?"

"I don't know about any book," she said. "I saw a movie on the classics channel the other night, and your visitor sounds just like the main character." She did something on her computer, then nodded. "Omar Sharif; that's who played him."

"Enver was surprised to find that he knew who she meant. He watched very few movies, but even he remembered Egypt's best-known movie star—the one best known in the West, at any rate. He started toward his office.

"And come to think of it," she called after him, "you even look a little like him, through the eyes."

He paused, then smiled. "You think I look like Omar Sharif?"

"Oh no," she said. "I meant you look a little like the man in your office, like you might be related."

Enver took one more step, then stopped. A chill ran down

his spine. Except for Dilara, he had no living relatives. His brother and his two nephews had been the last, and they were all dead. He had gotten word of his brother's death several weeks after it happened, from an old friend in Tunis. His friend had called him about something else, and only when Enver had asked for news of the famous Imam Muhammad had he heard the story of the sermon, and the stoning, and the rumors of who had cast some of the stones. The mob had apparently then come to the city, butchering the Imam's son Fareed in his office, and setting fire to a warehouse where, the police were sure, the Imam's other son, Murad, had also died. That had seemed plausible at the time, but now, walking down the hall to meet a perhaps relative who spoke English with an Egyptian accent, Enver was beginning to wonder if they were wrong. He decided he was probably being paranoid, that this was most likely an old colleague of his, dropping in for a surprise visit. He opened his office door, but the room was empty, with no sign that anyone had been there. How odd, he thought. How very odd.

Chapter Thirty-One

Floyd was pretty sure he was dreaming, because this sort of thing didn't happen except in dreams, or when he had done a lot of weed, which he hadn't because he was almost out. He liked dreams, but this was looking more and more like one of the ones he would wake up from in a cold sweat. A man was standing over him and saying something, saying it like it was important, but Floyd didn't know what it was because he hadn't been paying attention. In a dream, you didn't have to pay attention; stuff just happens, and it either makes sense or it doesn't, so you don't have to worry about it. That was pretty much Floyd's philosophy: don't worry about it. The man didn't seem to agree. "Something something," he was saying. Apparently this was going to be one of the dreams where nothing made sense. Luckily, Floyd was used to those too.

The man's words began to sort themselves out. "Something listen something not joking do you understand?" Floyd didn't say anything. The man drew back his leg and kicked Floyd hard in the nuts. Floyd hadn't been kicked in the nuts since grade school, but some memories you don't forget, and this felt exactly like he remembered. The man spoke again. "Okay, good; I have your attention," he said, probably thinking Floyd was listening to him, which Floyd wasn't; he was looking at the man, who was not, he decided, really a man. He looked like a man, but he had dead eyes, so even without horns and a tail, Floyd knew who he was. He was the Devil, come to take him, just the way Becky always said he would. Was he a he, or was he a He, with a capital He like the other biggies got. Is that what the H in Jesus H Christ stand for, he wondered; He? "Pay attention," the Devil said. "I am looking for a man who calls himself Dock. Tell me where he is, or you'll get more of that."

Floyd tried to focus, but then he thought how funny it would sound in a big-box store for the Devil to get on the P.A. and announce, "Shoppers, hurry over to aisle six where we're having a two-for-one special on nut-kickings." Really funny, he decided.

Then he realized what else was funny. The Devil didn't even know Doc Dawson was dead. "You missed him," Floyd said with a giggle. "He must have got past you."

The Devil took that in stride. "Do you know where he went?"

Floyd thought about that. Was this a multiple-choice test? Okay, fine; what were his choices? If it was just Heaven and Hell, that was one thing, but a hippy who had camped with him in the mill for a week had told him about reincarnation. Floyd could sort of remember stuff that he didn't think had happened, at least not to him, so there might be something to the reincarnation thing, unless it was from that time he had smoked some Jimson weed. That had been some bad shit. What was the question? Oh yeah, where had Doc gone. Not enough information, he decided. "All I can tell you is, Mr. Schroder took him out to the fairground, and there was a big party, and then he was just gone."

The man cocked his head to one side. There had been a Schroder on the list DiSantis had been given. "Emmett Schroder?" he asked.

For a moment, Floyd was surprised. "You know him? Oh, yeah, he's a lawyer, so I guess you would, but he's not like most of them, so you can't have him either." Speak the truth and shame the Devil, Floyd's mother used to tell him, but he never thought he would actually get to do it in person.

"You're sure about that: Schroder took Dock somewhere?" the man asked softly.

"Of course I'm sure. I wouldn't lie to you." Or should it be You with a capital Y, Floyd wondered, enlarging on his earlier mental debate about the H.

"And that's all you know?"

Floyd tried to remember what he had said, and what he had only thought about. "About Doc you mean? Yeah, I guess I'm done."

The man raised the silenced .22 pistol he had been holding. "Yeah," he said, "I guess you are."

◇◇◇◇◇◇◇◇◇◇◇◇◇◇◇ ● ◇◇◇◇◇◇◇◇◇◇◇◇◇◇◇◇

Evelyn was in the back, filing some papers, when the bell over the office door dingled. She came out into the waiting room to find a tall, well-dressed, pleasant-looking man waiting by her desk. "Yes sir?" she asked. "Can I help you?"

"Perhaps you can," Azrael told her. "I am looking for my daughter, Dilara. I understand that she comes here in the afternoon before she goes to the cabin where she is staying. May I stay and wait for her?"

"I'm afraid you've missed her. She and Tori were here about a half hour ago, but they've already gone on up to the cabin. Do you know where it is? I can draw you a map."

Azrael pulled out a sheet of paper. "Thank you, but Dilara made a sketch for me." He gave Evelyn a little bow and left. She went back to her filing, but a few minutes later the door dingled again, this time for Bart and Jamaal.

"No roses?" she said in mock disappointment.

"Not this time," Bart told her. "We're just taking some groceries and stuff up to the cabin, and thought we'd drop by to say hello."

"Groceries and stuff," Evelyn said. "You're not lonely for your friends, or anything like that are you?"

"Well, maybe, a little," Bart said, trying to sound casual. Behind him, Jamaal gave Evelyn a nod and a wink. Technically, that violated the roommate rule, except that everybody in their dorm knew how lonely Bart was. They had gotten used to hanging out with the girls in the evenings, and as the repair work on the dorm dragged on Bart was starting to wilt, like a plant that hasn't been watered.

Jamaal had stood it as long as he could, then he suggested they surprise the girls with the makings of a cookout. "You could surprise her even more," he added, "if you told her you missed her."

"I'm not ready to get shot down just yet," he told Jamaal.

Jamaal didn't want to hear it. "Listen, I've lost more

girlfriends than you've ever had, and I know what I know: If you're ready to be more than just friends, a girl wants to hear you say it."

"That sounds a lot like betting the ranch on the turn of the next card. Suppose it's a bad card."

"Then you start work on a new ranch. But come on, it's not like you're holding an inside straight and you lose if you don't fill it. I've seen you two together, remember? You're holding at least three of a kind, and no card you can draw will change that." Bart told him he would think about it.

Evelyn saw Jamaal's wink and understood. "All right then. Oh, and I hope you got enough stuff; there's going to be five for dinner. Dee's father was here a few minutes ago, and he's on his way up to the cabin too."

"I hope he likes bayberry," Jamaal muttered.

As they pulled out of the parking lot, Bart had a thought. "When I picked you up, you'd just gotten out of Dr. Ziya's class, right?"

"Uh-huh,"

"Did he leave class early?"

"No." Jamaal began to see where this was going, and didn't like it.

"And we came straight here." Jamaal nodded. "So how did he get here ahead of us?" Neither of them said anything for a few minutes. As a rule, Bart drove just under the speed limit—"like an old woman," was the way Jamaal described it—but by the time the Jeep reached the edge of town, it was living up to its potential.

◇◇◇◇◇◇◇◇◇◇◇◇◇◇◇◇●◇◇◇◇◇◇◇◇◇◇◇◇◇◇◇◇

Evelyn answered the phone on the second ring. "Emmett Schroder's office."

"Yes, hello," said a man's voice. "My name in Enver Ziya. My daughter has said I should check with your office to see if she has any messages."

Evelyn frowned. "Uh, no, she hasn't left any messages. Sorry." After she had hung up, she went back to Emmett's office.

"Dr. Ziya just called. Only, it wasn't the same Dr. Ziya who was here a little while ago."

Emmett thought about that for a moment, then frowned. He picked up his phone and punched in a number. "Janet? Emmet. Is Harley there? Yeah, I'll wait." A minute passed, then, "Harley, do you still keep that little revolver in your desk drawer? I wonder if I could borrow it for a while. Great; I'll be right over." To Evelyn, he said, "Cancel my appointments. You know where I'll be."

By the time he got back from Harley Bishop's office, Evelyn was waiting for him by her car. "Get in and buckle up. You didn't really think I'd let you go up there alone, did you?"

Chapter Thirty-Two

The orange cat had decided he liked Dee. If she sat down for more than a few minutes, the cat would curl up in her lap, and he would stay there until she stood up. If she had a book to read, she could turn sideways to read it, or she could rest the book on the cat; he didn't seem to mind, but he wasn't going anywhere. That suited Dee, who liked cats, but Tori took it as a snub. "What's wrong with my lap?" she asked the cat after the pattern had developed. The cat had glanced at her briefly and then given himself a tongue bath. That, apparently, was all the answer she was going to get.

The first time the group had gone up to the cabin, there had been a lot of bragging about who could cook. Bart had held up Jamaal's teriyaki stir-fry as the standard to beat, and when Jamaal made it, it actually had lived up to the hype. When Tori's turn came, she had done what she could with some fish they had gotten at the Post Office/grocery store at Oak Grove, but even she thought the stir-fry had been better. That would never do. Dee had cooked last night, so tonight was Tori's turn, and she was going to try her hand at stir-fry. It was, she promised Dee, going to be spectacular, but good intentions, as Cookie Monster the reporter had found out, gang aft agley. The soy sauce Jamaal had bought when the guys spent their first weekend at the cabin was down to about a tablespoon, and Tori needed a lot more than that. A web search would have told her to try Worcestershire, but with no web access at the cabin, she fell back on instinct and came up with a mixture of salt, garlic powder, and coffee, which ended up looking a lot like soy sauce. She was letting her concoction simmer in the pan when there was a muted thock-thock-thock sound from the direction of the cabin door.

Like the rest of the cabin, the door had been built after the Civil War, when roving bands of bushwhackers were a fact of life, and it had been made strong: two-inch-thick oak, with massive hinges. The sound Tori heard was Jamaal, pounding on it as hard as he could. He had just raised his fist to give it another wallop when Dee threw back the bolt and opened the door. She looked at the fist, frozen in the air. "If you hit me," she told Jamaal, "I will tell your sister. I have friended her on Facebook." Then she saw Bart climbing the porch steps with two grocery bags. "Is that food?" she asked. Jamaal said it was. "God is merciful," she said very softly. The smell from the frying pan had begun to concern her, because if it tasted the way it smelled, it was going to be really bad.

Tori was having misgivings of her own. She had tasted her concoction, and it wasn't even close to what she had hoped. Salt, garlic, and a burnt flavor were all she could taste, so she had added some sugar, and then a tablespoon of ginger. The worst that could happen, she had thought, was that it wouldn't be edible, and then they could fry some burgers. The guys would never know, because neither she nor Dee would ever tell them

"He's not here yet?" Jamaal asked.

"Who isn't here?" Tori responded, glad he hadn't asked what she was cooking.

Bart answered. "Dr. Ziya, except maybe the boogyman." He explained about the man who had visited Emmett's office before they did, but who shouldn't have been able to get there ahead of them.

"Papa drives faster than some people," Dee said, making a point not to look toward Bart. "In the parts of Europe where there were no speed limits, he would drive very fast."

That made Jamaal feel better. "I guess he might have passed us on the way to Larson," he said. "Everybody else did." He didn't look at Bart either.

"Well, nobody passed us between Larson and here," Bart muttered.

"I will give you that," Jamaal said. "You made me proud."

No longer worried about the boogyman, Bart had walked over to the stove and looked into the pan. "Stir-fry? Can I taste it?" Before Tori could say no, he had taken a spoon and put a dollop of the stuff in his mouth. Then his eyes got wide and his jaw started to tremble, but finally he swallowed it. "It's a little, uh, intense," he said.

"You just don't like spicy food," Jamaal said, taking a spoonful for himself. Immediately, he was faced with a dilemma: run out to the porch and spit the horrible stuff as far as he could, or match what his roommate had done and swallow it. As usually happens when machismo battles good sense, machismo won; with an effort, he choked it down.

The agonized looks on their faces didn't impress Tori. "You two are such liars," she told them. "Nothing could be that bad." She took a spoonful, and found out that yes, something could be. Her face took on the exact expression of a Greek tragic mask, and she lunged for the door. Bart and Jamaal gave up their fight to keep down what they had swallowed, and ran after her. All three of them were leaning over the porch railing before they realized that someone else had arrived on the porch, someone who now stepped inside and shut the door. The last thing they heard before Dee's scream was the scraping sound of the door's latch, sliding shut.

Azrael had not driven fast. During the years when he had thought he was Murad, it had been different; Murad had wrecked more than one expensive German car on the sand-swept highways of North Africa. His wrecks had simply joined all the other wrecks. People felt that it either was their day to die, or else it was not, and if it was not, speeding would not kill them. Speeding was not going to kill Azrael either, but there was no need to hurry; what he had to do would happen exactly when it was fated to happen, no sooner, no later. Also, speed draws attention, and the car he was driving belonged to someone else. So he kept up with traffic, but did not pass anyone. Shortly after going through Oak Grove, someone did pass him: a boxy little car with two boys in it. He expected to see them wrecked in a ditch somewhere along the way, but he never did.

The sketch he had made showed the road he needed to take, on the right, just past a bridge. And suddenly, there it was, a one-lane gravel road going into the woods. The woods, and in fact this whole part of the world, felt wrong to him. Everything was too green, too damp, and this tunnel through the woods was too dark. Driving in the desert, everyone wears sunglasses, all the time, and Azrael did not think to remove his when he took the road into Viney Cove. Before long, he steered too wide on one of the road's shadowed curves and got his car stuck in a ditch. He wondered how much farther the road went, but then shrugged. It didn't matter. The end of the road marked the end of his mission, and however far he must walk to reach it, that was how far he would walk.

◇◇◇◇◇◇◇◇◇◇◇◇◇◇◇●◇◇◇◇◇◇◇◇◇◇◇◇◇◇◇

Standing now with his back to the cabin door, Azrael held up a calming hand. "There is nothing to fear, Dilara," he said. "You are about to meet God, the merciful and compassionate. That should be cause for rejoicing."

Dee stopped screaming. In part it was the gesture, in part the fact that he wasn't coming at her, but mostly it was the way he spoke, like an uncle reproving a naughty niece. Except this wasn't her uncle; this was her cousin.

"Murad? What are you doing here?" From the door came a muted *whump*.

He shook his head, either sadly or pityingly, she couldn't tell which. "No, child, I am not Murad. I am Azrael, and I have come to help you on your way. Come." He gestured for her to move toward him, but she stayed where she was. He sighed. "The infidels have all resisted me, which was to be expected given where they are all going. But you, Dilara? From you I had hoped for a Believer's acceptance. Let me ask you plainly: Will you now submit to the will of God and come with me, or must I take you?" There were more sounds from the door.

"What are you talking about?" Dee shouted at him. "You are my cousin Murad."

"There is no Murad," he said, a little angrily. "You had a cousin, Fareed, but he is dead, as is his father. Their times came, and I took them. Now, your time has come, and I will take you. You can be my guest on our journey, or my prisoner, it is all the same to me."

She tried to think of a stinging reply, what Tori called a zinger, and she remembered an expression her father had begun using. "You are as crazy," she said, "as a dead cat! It is not for you to say when anyone's time has come."

Azrael shook his head, again either sadly or pityingly. "Then your choice is to go as a prisoner. Know, then, that your choice defines your destination as well: the fire. So be it." He stepped forward and she backed away, but he wasn't trying to reach her. From a table near the door, he took one of the burning candles, then bent down and used it to light a corner of the cushion of the cabin's only upholstered chair. The foam in the cushion accepted the fire greedily, and in a moment the entire chair was ablaze, soon followed by the table next to it. Azrael stepped back, drew his knife, and again blocked the door. All he had to do now was wait.

Outside, they heard most of the exchange in the cabin, and when Dee started screaming again and smoke started coming out of the windows, they knew what had happened. Jamaal had given up trying to batter the door down, and had run over to the Jeep, looking for a tire iron. Tori thought of the woodpile; maybe a piece of firewood would work as a battering ram. Bart stayed where he was, thinking about how the door was mounted. Big hinges, top and bottom, and a heavy sliding latch, all made of iron.

Chapter Thirty-Three

"Until you have mastered the lower metals," Wade had written, "do not attempt the higher ones." Bart had found out what that meant when, early on, he had tried reading a couple of chapters ahead. In the later chapters, he had come across references to things that hadn't been mentioned in the earlier ones, things that had to be experienced to be understood, because there were no words for them. Tori's struggle with copper had been an example of that. The chapter before copper had been about gold. They only had alloyed gold, and fine gold was too expensive, so they had read about it, and then skipped on to copper. It was only after Dee had wheedled an old gold-plated tie-tack from her father that they had made any progress. The melt link in gold, they discovered, didn't move in the obvious direction. The alien geometry of its lattice meant that moving the link from Point A to Point B was much easier if it went around a place they came to call Point Not. They called it that because it wasn't there, except that it apparently was. Dee found it one place, Jamaal found it somewhere else. What they finally decided was that Point Not's location depended on who was looking for it. When that principle had sunk in, copper became much more cooperative.

Bart had read the iron chapter, but he hadn't tried to do iron yet. "The path back out is not obvious," Wade had warned, and the key to finding that path was apparently the cat, or at least a cat. The journal had elaborated on that, but not by much. "You must take the guide along," it said, adding that the student should practice the technique with one of the simpler metals before attempting iron. That had been on Bart's agenda for the weekend. Right now the cat was in the cabin with Dee and a maniac.

He set his phone to play the note for iron, slipped it into his shirt pocket, and closed his eyes. It seemed to take longer than usual to enter the void. Hearing Dee's screams might have been why, or it might have been the thought of his brain freezing. Bart centered himself on the note from his phone, and finally the void accepted him. First there was the landscape of features and properties, then the lattice. Wade's journal had said that iron's melt link, the one that meant solid here, liquid there, was not on the surface, so Bart didn't waste time looking for it. He moved past the surface bars, into the structure itself. Two levels in, there it was. He gave it a tentative pull, trying to find the route around Point Not, and after what seemed like forever, he found it. Moving the link to its liquid position, he held it as long as he could, hoping that would be long enough. When he could hold it no more, the link slipped back and he relaxed, waiting for whatever came next, no longer focusing on iron and its properties. The latticework around him faded, and he was back in the void.

Except that it wasn't a void. It wasn't dark, and it wasn't featureless. He was surrounded by light, extending as far as he could see, sparkling and shimmering in subtle shades of red and green, changing to islands of blue that soon became something else. It was, he thought, like visible music, and it was easily the most beautiful thing he had ever seen. "Thank you for letting me see that," he thought, not knowing or caring who he was thanking. Some gifts you just have to acknowledge.

"*You are quite welcome,*" a voice replied, from no particular direction.

Except for the sparkling points around him, there was nothing visible, no white light to go toward, no loving relatives waiting to receive him, and no bearded saint at a pearly gate. Bart formed a thought. "Where are you?"

"*We are all around you,*" said the voice.

"All right then, where am I!"

"*If you mean, where is your material body, we do not know. We know, of course, which planet you came from, but we do not know where on that planet you left your body. If, on the other hand, you mean, where is your consciousness, the question is meaningless.*"

If Bart had been able to kick himself, he would have. Of course it was meaningless. He had left the world of where behind. "Sorry," he thought. "How about 'Who are you?' Does that have any meaning?"

"*Quite a lot, but you lack words for the concept. We can bypass words and give the answer to you directly, but the one time we have attempted to do that, it was not a success.*" Bart thought of the Sufi master that Ahmed had mentioned, the one who came back insane. "*Yes, that was the one. We did not intend him any injury, but we could not undo it.*"

Bart thought about the first Sufi master, the one who had made the iron bell. He had probably believed he was talking to God, so he had felt no need to ask.

"*At first that is what he believed, but we explained that we were created and not creators. He then decided that we were what he called djin, creatures of smokeless fire, and that explanation seemed to satisfy him. In your world, you know us as iron, but that is, to oversimplify, merely the shadow that we cast. For the purpose of addressing your question, let us say that we are the essence of your universe.*"

Bart recalled the introduction to Wade's chapter on iron:

Stars run on fusion: their gravity and heat fuse the light elements together, and from that process they draw yet more heat. When the light, fusible elements are gone, the supply of heat stops, but gravity remains, and the star collapses. The energy of that collapse creates the heavier elements, and among them, iron. Iron is peculiar, in several ways. The elements lighter than iron can be fused to make heavier ones, and the elements heavier than iron can decay to make lighter ones. All of the other elements are subject to change, but once iron is created, it remains iron forever, so as time goes by, it accumulates. It could be argued that the universe is nothing more or less than a machine for turning hydrogen into iron, because that is essentially what it does and what it will do until, at the end, iron will be all that there is. Some have called that final condition the iron death of the universe, but I am told that the

exact opposite is true. I cannot say that I
understand what that means, but I can say this,
and say it with great confidence: those who told
me, would know.

When he read that last sentence, Bart had wondered who
Wade was talking about. Now he thought he knew. He found that
the voice didn't seem to mind answering questions, if the
questions made sense. He still couldn't think of the voice as iron,
and conversing with the universe was too weird, so he just thought
of it as the voice. "Do you ever get involved with what goes on in
my world?" he asked it.

"*As a rule, we do not.*"

"But you can?"

"*To some extent, yes. Your time stream has only one dimension;
ours has two. To enter a world like yours, even if only to observe, is quite
difficult for us.*"

"A world like mine. Do you mean our planet?"

"*Your world has many planets, and there are many worlds. Some
are very similar to yours. Some are not.*"

"How many?"

"*Larger than any number you can conceive, although the exact
number continually changes, as new worlds branch off, and others
converge.*"

That raised a question, but he felt like he wasn't going to
like the answer. "If I were to go to one of those others..." he began.

"*You might not find it congenial, as there would be no material
body waiting there to receive you. The same would be true if you returned
to the wrong place on your own planet.*"

Not finding his body, Bart thought, would probably be
worse than just not-congenial. It was time to change the subject.
"If you don't visit my world, how do you know English?" In
Jamaal's space-alien horror movies, the aliens tended to speak
English, and that had always seemed strange.

"*The one who came before you, the one whose words you recalled a moment ago, visited us many times, and we learned a great deal from him. His thoughts were well formed, and his words were a close match to his thoughts, which made acquiring his language quite easy. Your thoughts are less well focused than his were, and your words only partly reflect your thoughts."*

Hey, give me a break, Bart thought; I've got a lot on my mind. He didn't give that thought the push that he gave to the words he wanted heard, but to the next one he did. "The one you just spoke of, was he here when he died?"

"During his last visit, he told us that his physical body had become unreliable, then he sent his guide home and proceeded, as he put it, onward. We have assumed that his body perished, as he has not visited us again. That is a pity; he was always a welcome guest. His motives were pure."

Now that was interesting. "Have you had visitors with impure motives?"

"From time to time, yes. Some of them thought they were wizards, who thought they could force us to serve them. Others were trying to turn our shadow into gold, which even we cannot do. None of them brought a guide, or found the correct return path. There have been no visits of that nature for hundreds of your years. Perhaps their examples may have discouraged others from following them."

Their examples? "What happens to the ones who don't find their way back?"

"If a visitor stays with us too long, a necessary connection seems to be lost, and the visitor fades away. Beyond that, we do not know."

Bart didn't ask how long was too long. It would be better, he decided, for it to come as a surprise.

Jamaal found a lug wrench in the Jeep, but not the tire iron he had hoped for, something he could pry with. Tori fared no better at the wood pile. What little of the firewood was left was too short and too light. They came around to the front of the cabin from opposite directions, to see Bart sitting on the front porch, leaning against one of the posts. In his pocket was his phone, still quietly humming a low note. Then, much louder than the phone's note, there was another noise, at first a grating sound like a hundred fingernails scraping across a blackboard, then a clinking crash as the slates on the porch roof came sliding off.

Jamaal scrambled over the pile of slates. He could guess what Bart had tried to do, but had it worked? Only the slates above where Bart sat had slid off, and the cabin door was still closed. Okay, Jamaal thought, let's find out. He squared off with the door, and charged.

Coach Edmunds had a rule about tackling: "When you hit a man, don't just jostle him. Hit him hard!" Jamaal applied that rule to the door: he hit it hard, and it toppled inward. The cabin was filled with smoke, but Jamaal thought he could see Dee at the far end of the room. "This way!" he yelled.

Dee couldn't see her cousin in the smoke, but she knew she was safer out than in. She ran. Tori was dragging Bart down the porch stairs, and when Jamaal saw that Dee was safely out of the cabin, he helped with the dragging. In a moment they were all out in the yard. Only then did Dee remember the cat. "We have to go get him," she wailed. "We can't let him burn in there!" Tori didn't say anything; she simply pointed toward the Jeep, where the orange cat was sitting on the hood.

"He was out of there like a shot, as soon as the door was gone," Tori said, "He's a pretty smart cat."

◇◇◇◇◇◇◇◇◇◇◇◇◇◇◇◇●◇◇◇◇◇◇◇◇◇◇◇◇◇◇◇◇

If I were that lawyer, Hal's man thought, and I wanted to hide Dock, where would I put him? At my office? Probably not. At my house? Maybe, but the neighbors might see him. No, the more likely place would be that cabin in the woods that the computer jockeys had found. That would be the place to start.

He had to walk the last part of the way; some idiot had parked in the ditch and blocked the road. That was probably a good sign, though; it meant somebody was in there. When he reached the edge of the clearing, he saw them: three kids, gathered around a fourth one on the ground. He thought about firing a shot in the air to get their attention, but he heard somebody say something about a shot, and that gave him a better idea. "Since you bring up the subject of shots," he shouted, "I need for you all to sit down and shut up, or else you *will* get shot." They sat down and shut up. Seeing a man with a gun has that effect on people, he had found. "I am looking for a man named Dockery," he told them when he was closer. "You may know him as Dock. You have ten seconds to tell me where he is, or I will shoot the fat kid. Then I will start a new ten-count, and so on until somebody tells me, or none of you is left." He waited. No one spoke. "I see. Then we may as well begin. One."

Lying under the heavy oak slab that had been the cabin door, Azrael tried to make sense of what had happened, and the more sense it made, the more uneasy he felt. It had been his moment of triumph; his quest was over, its success assured. The fire was spreading toward the girl, who had fallen to her knees. "There is no god but God," she was saying, when suddenly the flames disappeared. Smoke remained, but the fire was gone. Then he noticed the girl. She was looking wide-eyed at something to his right. When he glanced that way, he saw what she had seen: the wide wrought-iron door hinges had turned to wax, and the wax was running down the door. He looked to his left, and saw that the latch and its brackets were doing the same thing. The blade of his knife wilted and dropped off. That was when the door had burst inward. Now he lay on the floor, the heavy door on top of him, thinking about that wax.

The wax was important, he thought. The wax meant something. Then he realized why the wax mattered. The Evil One can tempt the faithful by lies and deceptions, but only God can create, and making iron into wax is, without question, an act of creation. He, Azrael, was there to kill the girl, and yet God had willed that the girl live, and the Angel of Death does not disobey God. But if he was not Azrael, who was he?

He heaved upward with all his strength, and the door fell to one side. As he stood, a drop of blood hit the floor, followed by another; the blow from the door had ripped his scalp, and it was bleeding freely. No matter. Nothing mattered now.

◇◇◇◇◇◇◇◇◇◇◇◇◇◇◇◇●◇◇◇◇◇◇◇◇◇◇◇◇◇◇◇◇

"Two," the man said. He wondered how many of them he would have to shoot. Only one, he guessed, and then somebody would start to sing. "Three." From the cabin came the sound of something heavy crashing to the floor. He glanced in that direction, to see a man staggering out of the cabin door, his face a bloody mess. "Dock?" the man shouted. "Come on down here. I've come to take you back."

Murad came down the cabin steps, walking like a man carrying a heavy weight. He had thought he was Azrael, but now the real Azrael had come to take him. "I understand," he said. As he passed Dee, he said something the others couldn't make out, then he walked on. He had an appointment to keep.

"That's far enough," the man said when Murad was about ten feet from him, but Murad just kept walking. The man preferred a head shot, but his target was getting too close for that; the angle was wrong, so he put one in his belly. Murad flinched, but kept walking. The man shot again, then again, but Murad didn't seem to feel it. "Die, damn you!" the man said through gritted teeth, firing as fast as his gun would cycle, until Murad's knees finally buckled, and he fell at his killer's feet.

Jamaal had been around pistols all his life. The one in the man's hand was a model he knew, and he knew how many rounds it held: ten in the mag, one in the pipe. As the walking man absorbed shot after shot, Jamaal kept count. By the time the death walk was over, the count had reached eleven.

◇◇◇◇◇◇◇◇◇◇◇◇◇◇◇◇●◇◇◇◇◇◇◇◇◇◇◇◇◇◇◇◇

The man with the gun believed in trusting his gut. People in his line of work have to do that, or they don't survive long. In his once-over of the group outside the cabin, he had seen a pair of schoolgirls, a fat kid, and a boy who was either dead or unconscious. No danger there, his gut told him. Now that Dockery was dead, it was time to finish the others. He had just ejected the pistol's empty magazine and reached for the spare he kept under his belt when, out of the corner of his eye, he saw the fat kid spring to his feet. Good, he thought; now I won't have to choose who goes first. Not much of a challenge, though. From forty feet away, the kid wouldn't be halfway to him by the time he had a round chambered.

In an XXL sweatshirt, Jamaal did look a little on the plump side. As for whether he was slow, opinions might differ. Jamaal thought he was. His best time in the 40 yard dash was 5.3 seconds, and he thought it should be under 5. Of course, time trials are run in full equipment, which in Jamaal's case averaged about twenty pounds. Without the pads and helmet, he covered the 40 feet between him and the gunman in just over a second and a half. To a man standing on the gallows waiting for the hangman to release the trap, a second and a half can seem like—and actually is—a lifetime. But to a man who has to slam a magazine into a pistol, chamber the first round and bring the gun to bear on his target, all while that target is charging toward him with violent intent, a second and a half is not long at all.

Emmett hadn't planned on walking to the cabin, but that was what he was having to do. Somebody's car had gone halfway into the ditch, and another car was parked behind it, and the road was well and truly blocked. "Remind me...I need...to walk more," he gasped.

"I remind you of that all the time," Evelyn told him. "I need to remind you to listen when I give you good advice." She was about to give examples when, off in the distance, came the sound of shooting: pop, pop-pop, and then eight pops close together. A few seconds later, there was one more, but only one.

"Harley took this in on a fee," Emmett muttered as he drew Harley Bishop's revolver. "I wonder if he's ever fired it."

"You're saying you don't know if it works?"

He handed it to her. "What I'm saying is, I hope to hell you don't have to find out."

Chapter Thirty-Four

The man got the magazine inserted and a round chambered before Jamaal reached him. He even got a shot off, but there wasn't enough time to line it up, and he thought he had missed. He hadn't. The shot hit the middle toe on Jamaal's right foot, but by then Jamaal had already committed to a diving tackle. The impact would have made Coach Edmunds smile. When the man opened his eyes he saw Jamaal bending over him, holding the pistol. "You may be thinking about running," Jamaal said. "Go for it. You shot my toe; I can't chase you," he raised his right foot, where blood was starting to drip from a hole in the shoe. "You never know, I might miss you." He sighted the pistol at the man's head. "I've got two shooting medals that say different, but that's what makes life interesting. You know what I'd really rather, though?" He laid the gun on the ground behind him. "I'd rather you tried to fight me, right here, right now, just you and the wounded fat kid." The man stayed where he was.

Jamaal noticed somebody coming out of the woods, and had picked up the pistol before he saw who it was: Evelyn, holding a little revolver. Jamaal couldn't believe his eyes. "Did you bring a stopwatch too?" he called out.

She looked puzzled. "Why in the world would I need a stopwatch?"

Jamaal shrugged. "Well, you brought a starter pistol. I figured maybe you were going to run a track meet."

Evelyn gave the gun a disapproving look. "Do you mean to tell me..."

Tori interrupted her. "Do you know what to do? Did Emmett tell you? He won't wake up." The girls had laid Bart out on his back. He looked asleep, or dead.

"I know some first aid," Evelyn said. "Did one of the slates hit him?"

"No," Tori moaned. "He did that thing Wade used to do, but he did it with iron and he didn't have a cat."

Evelyn tried to make sense out of that. "Emmett never

talked about Wade's business," she said, "so if this has to do with that, you'll have to ask him."

"Where is he?" Jamaal asked.

"Sitting on a log midway up the driveway. He said he had to catch his breath, and that I should take the gun and go ahead without him."

The others stayed where they were, all except Dee. First she went over to the Jeep, where the cat let himself be gathered up. Then she slipped Bart's still-humming phone out of his shirt pocket, and sat down cross-legged beside him, making a nest in her lap for the cat. She told Tori, "Spot me." Tori opened her mouth to protest, but Dee cut her off. "The cat will not sit with you, and anyway, I am alive because of him. Spot me."

"But we don't know how it works," Tori said, trying to think of some way for this not to happen.

Dee didn't want to hear it. "Wade did not know either, the first time he did it. Remember? He said he found the guide by accident. Perhaps he went in when the cat was in his lap, and that is all that is required. I hope so, because that is what I am going to do." She placed Bart's phone on the ground beside her, stroked the cat one last time, and closed her eyes.

◇◇◇◇◇◇◇◇◇◇◇◇◇◇◇◇●◇◇◇◇◇◇◇◇◇◇◇◇◇◇◇◇

Bart was trying to think of another question, but he couldn't ask what he really wanted to know: Would he feel it when he started to fade away? Or would it be like going to sleep? He was about to ask about those other worlds when he heard a different voice. "Bart? Bart? Are you there? Where are you?"

The new voice, like the one he had been talking to, wasn't made of sound; it was words in his mind, but it still sounded familiar. No, it couldn't be. "Dee? Is that you? I'm over here." He tried to kick himself again. He didn't know where here was, so he couldn't tell anyone else. But, somehow, it worked. Her voice seemed to get nearer.

"Oh, there you are," she said. "I have come to bring you back."

Bart couldn't help himself; he had to say it: "I hope that counts as a pure motive."

"And what is that supposed to mean?" She sounded a little bit miffed.

"*It means he is as concerned for you as you are for him,*" said the voice.

There was a moment of shocked silence. "Uh, Bart, that was not you, was it."

"No. That was..." He groped for a short way to describe it—or them; the voice always said we. "Do you see the spread of sparkles?"

"The what? Oh!" She hadn't taken it all in until he had called her attention to it. "It is almost painful, it is so beautiful. What is it?"

"It is...or they are...the voice you heard. They live here."

"Oh," Dee said. "Hello. Is my motive pure?"

"*It is. We would have expected no less from a daughter of Knirra.*"

Bart sensed confusion from Dee. "I am the daughter of Enver Ziya. I do not know anyone named Knirra."

"*Perhaps daughter is not the best word, but it is the closest that you have. Knirra was your mother's mother, one hundred and eighty three iterations ago.*"

That made Bart curious. "I thought you didn't get involved with what happens in our world."

"*We need not visit your world to know your friend's heritage. She carries it with her. Her ancestor was the senior priest at a place she called Thera. She and three others came to us together, the only time such a group has ever done that. They thought we could save their land from some peril, but we could not. Indeed, according to the one you call Wade, their visit may have amplified the peril they feared.*"

"What happened to them?" Dee wanted to know.

"Uh, Dee, I hate to interrupt, but I don't think I have much time left before..."

"Oh. Yes, that is why I have come. I have the cat in my lap, or I did when I came here. But I do not know what I should do next. Can you help?" That last seemed to be directed toward the voice.

"We can. Your guide is still with you, and can find the path back; it is the gift of his kind. But for you both to accompany him, you must first merge."

"Merge? I do not understand."

"It is done like this." They felt a sensation of movement, then of nearness, until suddenly there was no sense of me-and-you, but only a sense of we. The voice spoke again. *"Hrrlle, mmrrau'sst"* but the sound was mixed with a feeling of warmth and a slight whiff of cream. Judging by what happened next, the combined meaning was, *"Hrrlle, take them home."*

Bart opened his eyes to see Jamaal, Tori, and Evelyn looking down at him. "Did Dee make it back all right?" he asked, then he noticed her, sitting cross-legged beside him with the cat in her lap. He reached over and squeezed her hand. "Thank you," he whispered. The cat squirmed around and nuzzled their clasped hands. "And thank you, Hrrlle," Bart said to the cat, giving it a long stroke. The cat purred happily. Finally, somebody knew his name.

◇◇◇◇◇◇◇◇◇◇◇◇◇◇◇◇●◇◇◇◇◇◇◇◇◇◇◇◇◇◇◇◇

When Emmett reached the clearing, the first thing he noticed was the heap of roofing slates. "Who did that?" he asked no one in particular. Everybody looked at Bart, everybody except the gunman, who stared sullenly off into the distance. "And who is this?" He pointed to Murad. At Dee's request, they had laid her cousin on his back, and she had done what she could to clean off his face.

"He was the one who came to the office saying he was Dee's father," Evelyn answered.

"He tried to kill Dee," Jamaal added, "and that one over there killed him."

Emmett walked over toward the shooter. "And yet they're not treating you like a hero," he said thoughtfully, staying a safe distance from the seated man. "You want to tell me why?" The man didn't say anything.

"On come on, you can tell him," Jamaal told the seated man, speaking the way someone would speak to a small child. The man's only response was a hard glare. "Okay, then I will. He held us all at gunpoint and said he'd kill us one by one if we didn't give up somebody named Dockery. Then that other one came out of the cabin, and this one shot him to death."

"Self defense," the man growled. "He came at me. Just like you did."

"Oh right, you were going to shoot the fat kid on ten, and then you had to defend yourself against his toe. Who's going to believe that?"

There was no answer, but Emmett nodded thoughtfully. "A jury would, if there isn't anybody left to contradict it." He strolled around in front of the seated man. "That's what you think, isn't it? Lawyer up, hunker down, and wait for your friends to whittle down the witness list? Again."

The man's mouth twisted itself into a sneer. "I guess you'll just have to find out."

Emmett nodded affably. "Maybe. Maybe not." He turned to the others. "I've done my exercise for the day already, but you're all in good shape." He looked at Jamaal's bloody shoe. "Most of you, anyway. Who wants to dig a grave?"

They picked a place partway upslope behind the cabin. Tori dug a while, then Bart, then Dee. Jamaal wasn't able to dig—his toe was beginning to hurt him in earnest—so he made himself useful by trussing up the gunman with some duct tape he got from the Jeep's emergency box. Emmett volunteered to help dig, but nobody wanted this to be, as Evelyn put it, the day his head finally blew off. "Well then, I've got some business to take care of," he said. He got the Jeep's keys from Bart and disappeared down the road, with Evelyn riding shotgun.

"What am I missing?" she asked him, as he jockeyed the Jeep around the cluster of parked cars. "That body is evidence. If we hide it, what's to prove he's a murderer?"

"At a trial, you mean? Whether we bury it or not, there's not going to be any trial. If we report it, the Sheriff will have to arrest him, and right then we'll all get targets painted on our backs. No, I've got a better idea." He took out his phone, checked for coverage, and got two bars. Then he took out his wallet and dug out a card he had gotten from Bragg. "Take your car back to town," he told Evelyn. "I've got something in mind for our shooter, and it's probably better for you if you don't know anything about it."

◇◇◇◇◇◇◇◇◇◇◇◇◇◇◇◇◇●◇◇◇◇◇◇◇◇◇◇◇◇◇◇◇◇◇

Dee washed the blood from Murad's body as best she could. After that they lowered him into the grave. Dee consulted an app on her phone. "It uses GPS to show the direction to Mecca," she explained, then she turned Murad's head so that he faced that way. Finally she covered the face with a cloth, and they filled in the hole.

They stood around for a few minutes in respectful silence. Finally, though, Jamaal asked a question that had been troubling him. "I don't get it," he said. "I mean, he was your family, so I guess you had to bury him, but you were his family too, and he tried to kill you. Why? What had you ever done to him? Did he tell you?"

"No," Dee said. "He told me my time had come, and that as the Angel of Death, his duty was to take me."

"Maybe that was how he was able to take all those bullets," Jamaal mused. "I mean, if he really thought he was an angel, maybe he couldn't feel pain."

Dee shook her head. "I believe he felt every one of them. As he walked toward the man with the gun, he told me something.

He said..." then her voice faltered, and a tear ran down her cheek. "He said, *Üzgünüm, kuzeni.*"

No one said anything for a moment, then Tori said softly, "I don't understand; what does that mean?"

Dee didn't say anything. She had held it together as long as she could, but now the tears came in earnest. In a low voice, Bart answered the question, "It means, 'I am sorry, cousin'."

There was a long moment of silence. Tori opened her mouth, but nothing came out. Dee stopped crying. "Eğer Türkçe konuşabiliyor musunuz?"

Bart looked confused. "No, I don't speak Turkish. Why would you think..." Then he stopped. "Oh."

There was another long silence. "Oh?" Tori finally said. "That's it? You know what uzi-guzi-kuzi means, and all you can say is Oh?"

"Yeah, 'oh' is about it," he said. He closed his eyes and thought back. "How long was I in there? It felt like a long time, and there was a lot of stuff I don't understand, but I'm sure there weren't any language lessons. On the way out, Dee and I got sort of smooshed together, so I guess if I picked up some Turkish, that was when it happened." He wondered if Dee had picked anything up from him. Probably not, he decided. She already spoke English.

Chapter Thirty-Five

About a half hour after he and Evelyn had left on his mysterious errand, Emmett drove the Jeep back to the cabin. He still wouldn't say what the errand had been, but when it was clear that it didn't involve killing the shooter, the man got a lot more vocal. Mostly, what he had to say was veiled threats—and some not so veiled—about how they didn't know who they were dealing with, mixed with speculation about how each of them would get what was coming to them. Jamaal finally got tired of hearing it. Duct tape, it turned out, made an excellent gag.

"We've got places to go and things to do," Emmett told them. "First, we've got to get the road unblocked." He did not, it developed, mean they should just move the cars to the side of the road. He meant something more like a caravan, and he had already worked out the details. He had sent Evelyn back to town in her car. "I don't want her involved in this," he explained. Nobody asked what 'this' was, and Emmett didn't offer details.

The car Dee and Tori had borrowed from Dee's father was a two-door Boringmobile, as Tori put it, but it could seat five. They put the gunman in the trunk and headed down the road. When they reached the parked cars, Emmett gave out their assignments. First, they had to get Murad's car out of the ditch, which took everybody pushing together, except Jamaal, who steered it. Then Emmett lined up his parade. Calling it a parade was Jamaal's idea, but the word fit. Emmett would be in lead car, the one Murad had come in. It had a Georgia license plate and was, Emmett figured, almost certainly stolen, so Dee and Tori would follow close behind it in the Boringmobile, so nobody else could get behind it and read the plate. Dee asked where they were going, but all Emmett would say was that it was a place he knew about. The gunman's car was a rental; they found the papers in the glove compartment. Bart and Jamaal were to take it to the airport and leave it at the rental-return lot. As for what would happen after that, Emmett just said to trust him.

It took a little over an hour to reach Greenville and there

the parade split up, the girls following Emmett and the guys going to the airport, where they dropped off the gunman's car. Then they just hung around feeling conspicuous until the B-mobile pulled up. "Hey sailors," Tori called out to them. "Need a lift?"

Emmett was in the back seat. Dee offered to join him there so that Jamaal could ride shotgun. It might be easier, she said, for him to get in and out of the front seat with his injured foot. "Plus," she told Jamaal, "you're big. If you sit in back, everybody else will get smooshed up."

Tori gave Bart a look. "Yeah, we don't want any more smooshing."

"So where did you guys go?" Jamaal asked.

"I think it was a bad part of town," Dee answered. Tori nodded in agreement.

"I had a client once," Emmett said, "who had an interesting business. People with car payments they couldn't afford would pay him a little money and give him their car keys. Their cars would get 'stolen', insurance would pay it off, and everybody was happy, except maybe the insurance company. Anyway, what he would do was bring the car to Greenville, park it where I parked that one, and walk away. After a while, the car would disappear. He didn't know where it went, and he didn't care, but I figure there's a car crusher somewhere around there that pays so much per pound and doesn't ask questions."

"Okay, so what do we do now?" Bart asked.

Emmett took out his phone. "Now we follow some directions I got," he said, looking at the screen. "Get on I-85 and go south to the Powdersville exit. Then take 153 north toward 123. After that, we'll be on some back roads for a while." He put the phone away.

"And then?" That was Tori.

"And then, we'll have to see."

◊◊◊◊◊◊◊◊◊◊◊◊◊◊●◊◊◊◊◊◊◊◊◊◊◊◊◊◊◊

They had been on a deserted stretch of two-lane highway

for what seemed like a long time. "Okay, now slow down," Emmett told Tori. "There's supposed to be a side road up here somewhere."

Tori could see for a mile down the highway, and there wasn't any side road. "I think you should just admit that you're lost," she said.

From the back seat, Emmett sighed. "You sound just like Evelyn," he said. "I may not know exactly where we are, but I have followed the directions to the letter, and I am emphatically not lost. Just keep an eye out for a side road."

Jamaal noticed something. "You see where there's a gap in the fence?" he said. "I'll bet the road you're looking for goes through that."

Tori wasn't buying it. "Uh-huh. If I turn there and we go in a ditch, are you going to pull us out? I don't think so. And I don't want to have to explain to some guy in a tow truck why there's a man in the trunk." But sure enough, right where Jamaal had said, the ditch went over a culvert, and there were vague signs of a road across a weedy field. Tori eased the car off the highway. "I hope it's a better road than it looks like," she muttered.

"It is," Jamaal said. Up ahead was a kudzu-covered mound that had once been a farmhouse, and next to it, a very ordinary-looking barn, still needing paint, still a little out of plumb.

They heard the helicopter before they saw it. Jamaal cocked his head to the side and listened. "I thought I knew all the military birds," he said, "but I don't recognize that one. It's not a Blackhawk, I know that much." He was still trying to guess when the machine landed. It was a black civilian model, without numbers. Out of it climbed three men wearing business suits. Two of them were carrying Uzis.

As soon as the whine of the copter's engine died, the man without an Uzi shouted, "Raise your hands and don't move!" His two companions kept the group covered while he frisked everybody. He found the gunman's pistol that Jamaal had brought with him. "You won't be needing this," he said, then he stepped away from them. "You were expecting somebody different, I expect. Well, they couldn't make it. Now, where is he?" Nobody said anything. The man raised Jamaal's pistol and clicked off the safety. "I will ask you again: Where is he?"

Emmett jerked his head toward the car. "In the trunk."

The man opened the driver-side door, pulled the handle for the trunk latch, and looked inside. "Fritz," he called to one of the guards, "come help me with this. Mark, if anybody moves, shoot them all." He and Fritz pulled the gunman out of the trunk and cut the tape off of him. They tore the mouth tape off last, and once he could talk, he talked a lot, mostly about how he was going to kill some fat kid. The team leader slapped him across the mouth, hard. "You need to shut the fuck up," he said. "You have no idea what kind of favors we had to call in just to rescue your sorry ass. And it's all because you bungled a simple cleanup. Now get in the copter. We'll take care of them." He nodded toward Emmett and the others. The gunman started to say something, which earned him another slap. "I have apparently not made myself clear," the leader said. "I wanted to take you up to a thousand feet and see if you could fly. Oh no, they said, you're 'too valuable'. Well you know what? You'll be just as valuable without your teeth. Now shut your damn mouth and get in the copter." The gunman gave him a scowl, but he didn't say anything. As soon as he was inside the helicopter, the leader stepped back. "Finish it," he told the two guards in a loud voice, then climbed in after the gunman.

For the last several minutes, Bart had been trying to decide where he had seen Fritz and Mark. Jamaal had figured it out already. One was Private Winston, and the other was Private Cox. Cox raised a finger to his lips and winked. The message was unmistakable: Don't make a sound. Winston fired five short bursts into the ground, then they both ran for the copter, whose main rotor had already started to turn. In a minute, the yard was empty. Emmett started toward the car. "Is anybody else hungry?"

he asked. "Arnold said he'd keep the Diner open late for us. Come on, I'm buying."

Tori saved her thunder until she had gotten the car back on the highway, but then the storm broke. "You planned all that?" She couldn't decide if she was more angry, incredulous, or astonished. "I have sweated through everything I'm wearing—and some of it may not be sweat—because of some scheme you cooked up? You..." she couldn't think of anything harsh enough, "...are a very bad man."

Emmett shrugged. He had been called worse. "It had to look real," he said. "If you hadn't looked scared, he might've figured out what was going on."

Jamaal turned around in his seat. "Okay, I'm game. What *was* going on?"

Emmett smiled his Buddha smile. "Two things. Or maybe three, depending on how something else plays out. First, we're rid of him without having to explain things to the Sheriff. You know, things like why all those slates came off the roof. Second, their man thinks you're all dead, so they won't send anybody else to clean up his mess."

"Who are 'they'?" Dee asked.

"Ah, now that is the question, isn't it," Emmett said. "People better informed than I am think it's a corporation called Traxell, but they haven't been able to prove it. So that's the third thing. They're going to turn the horse loose, and see whose barn he runs to."

They were the only ones in the Diner, so Arnold gave Emmett the key and told him to lock up when they were through. The first order of business, everybody assumed, would be that Tori would light into Emmett again. Everybody assumed that except

Tori, who had something else on her mind. "I want to know," she said, "just what went on in there, in the iron matrix." Jamaal didn't say anything, but he cocked his eyes over toward the counter, where Emmett was assembling a stack of plates. The message was clear: how much do we want to tell him about what we do?

Emmett brought the plates to the table, then went back for a pie that Arnold had left for them. "Uh-huh," he called back over his shoulder. "I've been wondering about that, too. Did they say anything about Wade?"

They. The word hung in the air for almost ten seconds, until Bart broke the silence. "You know about...them?"

"Them?" Tori asked it before Jamaal could.

Emmett brought the pie to the table, with a knife and a handful of forks. "Them," he said. "Or, 'the others'. I've heard Wade call them that, too. Did they say whether Wade made it through all right?"

Bart nodded. "They, uh, said he went..." What was the word they had used? "Onward."

"Good. I had worried about that. One other question, and then I'll let you explain what the hell we're talking about. When you met them, do you remember your first impression?"

Bart did. "Music. Deep, wide, massive music, but silent; it was made out of color."

Dee gave Bart a puzzled look. "But it wasn't like that at all. It was like a huge sunlit field of flowers, made of all kinds of jewels, sparkling in the sunlight."

Emmett nodded. "Uh-huh. Wade told me he saw an n-diminsional manifold in flux. I never understood what he meant by that, but he said it was breathtaking. I think it all depends on you. That's a guess; I've never been there. I used to help Wade with the lower metals when he did three-metal alloys, but I never did iron. He said it might be too dangerous for me."

"He was probably right," Bart said. "They put a high value on pure motives, and sometimes yours are..." he groped for a nice way to put it, "open to question."

"No, sometimes they just plain suck," Tori said. She still shivered when she thought about the men at the barn with the Uzis. "Let's get back to who 'they' are."

Bart repeated what he had heard them say, and Dee added what she could. In the end, though, it was Emmett who best summed it up: "God only knows."

Dee's father offered them coffee, but Dee said they would all prefer tea. She puttered around in his kitchen making it, then reappeared with a pot and five cups. Now for the hard part.

Between the fire, the shooting, and the rest of it, there hadn't been much time for the four of them to talk privately, and what little time they did have, they spent worrying about what to tell Enver. They thought about not telling him anything, but in the end they knew they had to, or rather that Dee had to. "Papa," Dee rehearsed, "your dead nephew Murad showed up at the cabin where we were staying, out in the middle of nowhere. He said he was the Angel of Death and that my time had come, then he locked himself in the cabin with me and lit the cabin on fire. But it turned out all right because Jamaal kicked in the door and I escaped, and when Murad came out of the cabin, a stranger walked out of the woods and shot him to death, and then went away." They saw no need to mention distracting details like falling slates, melting hinges, and black helicopters.

Tori didn't feel good about the official storyline. "I mean, don't get me wrong, I was there and that's what happened, but when you lay it out like that it really does make you sound, oh I don't know, crazy? Just saying." They sat in the Jeep a while longer, hoping for inspiration, but they kept coming back to the nub of the problem: the story wasn't believable. "Maybe you could get your father drunk before you tell him," Tori suggested.

"The strongest thing Papa drinks is coffee," Dee said gloomily. "Oh, and if he offers you any, don't take it. You won't sleep for days." Finally, having put it off as long as they could, they went up the door, feeling like prisoners walking to their own hanging.

It didn't go as badly as they had thought it would. When Dee got to the part about Murad, Enver had interrupted. "Ah! So it was him!"

"You knew?" Dee asked.

No, Enver explained, he hadn't really known, not for sure, but now he didn't have to wonder if a ghost had come to his office. "But I do not understand how he could have found you."

"Evelyn—Mr. Schroder's secretary—said he had a map, like the one I drew for you."

Enver thought about that and bit his lip. "I had that in my office. I am so sorry. But I interrupted. Please, continue."

Dee continued. The part she had particularly worried about, the part about how the mystery man had come out of the woods, and how Murad had marched calmly to his death, went better than she had hoped. Instead of asking awkward questions about what had happened to the shooter, or to Murad's body, Enver's thoughts took him in another direction entirely. "Even on the back side of the world, a man's destiny will find him," he said, his voice a mixture of sadness and awe. "A family's destiny as well, it would seem. Whatever else all of this means, Murad's death means the end of the house of Ziya."

Dee thought about that, and about a line of mothers and grandmothers extending back to...how long ago? "Papa? Have Turks always traced our families through the father?"

"I believe so. Why do you ask?" Enver was surprised at the change of subject, but also a little bit relieved. He hadn't really thought about being the last of his line until now.

Dee hesitated a moment. "I have a reason. Has anyone ever done it the other way?"

"Through the mother, you mean?" Enver thought back through history. "Yes, I believe the Lycians did, and also the Carians." That got him a blank look from everybody. "Ancient kingdoms, in the southwestern part of what is now Turkey."

"Wasn't that where mother's family was from?"

Enver looked puzzled at yet another change of subject. "She was from Fethiye, and yes, that is quite near the old Carian port of Kbid."

"Was it also near a city called Thera?"

"Thera? No, I do not recall a..." Then he remembered. "Ah. You mean Santorini. The Christians renamed it, but long ago, long before the Common Era, it was called Thera."

Bart didn't wait for Dee to ask the next question. "Uh, Professor Ziya, did anything...interesting...ever happen on Thera?" He remembered what the others had said, how they had had four visitors from Thera. *They thought we could save their land from some peril, but we could not.*

Dr. Ziya nodded gravely. "The island was volcanic, and the volcano erupted, except that 'erupted' is a very poor word for what happened. Santorini today is a mere crescent of land, around the eastern edge of a four-cornered crater. That crater is where the greater part of Thera once was. So, to answer your question, yes, I would say that something very interesting happened on Thera: perhaps the greatest volcanic explosion to occur since man has walked the earth."

Chapter Thirty-Six

McIntyre read the text for the third time, and then hit Send. The message, ostensibly from one division in the Justice Department to another, read as follows:

```
The Keowee extraction went as
planned, so our man's cover should
still be good. As far as the target
knows, their operation went off
without a hitch.
```

◇◇◇◇◇◇◇◇◇◇◇◇◇◇◇◇●◇◇◇◇◇◇◇◇◇◇◇◇◇◇◇◇◇

Along with the usual morning reports, Jason brought a single sheet of paper into Roland Bathori's office. "This came in on our DOJ feed," he said. "It may mean nothing, but the Keowee reference brings Mr. Stasevik's operation to mind."

Bathori read what Jason had brought him, then stared at the ceiling for nearly a full minute. "I believe we have to assume so," he decided. "I had hoped Harold's project was nothing worse than a potential risk disguised as a real opportunity. I stand corrected. It was a genuine risk, and it has matured into a present danger. Whether he knows it or not, it appears he has brought a spy into our midst."

"Will we be notifying Mr. Huntsinger?"

"No, not yet. He would try to have one of his tame congressmen shut down their investigation, and that might make Justice wonder how we found out about it. That data feed is too valuable to lose over something we can handle in-house."

"Yes sir." Jason's face didn't actually smile, but the edges of his mouth rose a millimeter or so. Matters handled in house were his specialty.

"Make the entry monitors aware of what to look for, and if anyone who even might be this person tries to access the executive floors, have him brought to twelve and let me know. We will want to interview him, at length and in depth."

◇◇◇◇◇◇◇◇◇◇◇◇◇◇◇◇●◇◇◇◇◇◇◇◇◇◇◇◇◇◇◇◇◇

The black helicopter set down at an abandoned strip mall outside Jersey City. A waiting car took the gunman into lower Manhattan and dropped him off near, but not directly in front of, the Traxell Building. "They're waiting for your report, and they want it in person," the driver said. He didn't say who was waiting; the Army's lawyers had warned him about not suggesting where the man should go, or whom he should see. He has to make those choices on his own, they said.

The driver pulled away from the curb and disappeared into city traffic. It wasn't his job to watch the man. That task went to a bag lady on the opposite side of the street, who watched as the man strolled casually past the big glass doors that led into the Traxell lobby. "He went on by," she said into a hidden mike. "He's looking around. Okay. He's coming back. He's in, he's in."

Another woman, dressed in an expensive business suit, followed him in. She timed her stroll through the lobby so that, by the time the man had spoken with the girl in the information kiosk and gotten some sort of card, she was already in the elevator. She held the door for him, and when he got on, she hit the button for 10. The man thrust his card in a slot, and pushed an unmarked button. The woman got off on ten, looked at the office directory, shook her head as if she hadn't found what she was looking for, then caught the elevator as it came back down.

"He went on up," she reported after she had left the building.

In a van outside the federal courthouse, Bragg thanked her and hung up. "How are you coming?" he asked McIntyre.

"Almost finished." McIntyre was putting together the evidence chain for the federal prosecutor. "Okay," he said after typing for another minute, "I think that's got it."

"Walk me through it," Bragg said.

"We start with the killing of Raymond Travis. He was an Army officer on Army business; that makes his murder federal.

Then we add the attack on two more Army personnel, you and me, when we went down to investigate Travis's death. The fingerprint in the Lexus tied DiSantis to that attack, so by catching the man who shot DiSantis, and tracing him back to Traxell, we've connected Traxell to Travis."

Bragg held up a hand. "Okay, pause it right there. What connects the guy we picked up, with the one who shot DiSantis? What tells us they're the same?" Bragg hoped McIntyre had seen something he hadn't.

McIntyre stared at the ceiling while his hands traced shapes in the air. When the shapes fit together the way he wanted, he spoke. "Travis was investigating this Dawson person when he got killed. The lawyer who drew Dawson's will got his office broken into. We started investigating Dawson, and DeSantis tried to kill us. In all of that, Dawson is the common element. Now, Dawson's nephew—or grandnephew, whatever Bart is—he and the lawyer were both at that place in the woods where our shooter shows up. That can't be a coincidence." He frowned. It didn't sound as good when he said it out loud as it had looked when he sketched it in the air.

"It's a weak link," Bragg said. "Too weak."

"Maybe," McIntyre mused, "maybe the man said something. You know, like 'This is from your friends at Traxell'. That would be nice."

Bragg rewarded him with a sour look. "Yeah, and a videotaped confession would be nice too, but we don't have that either. I think you may be onto something, though. When Schroder called, all he said was that they had caught the assassin. After that we talked about what to do with him, and I didn't ask how he knew that's who they had caught. I think it's time I did."

"Mr. Schroder? Steve Bragg here, and I've got McIntyre on speaker. Let me get right to the point. The man we took: did he ever say anything about why he was there, or who had sent him? Anything like that?"

Emmett thought back. "He told me he was going to claim self defense. After that he said a lot about how sorry we'd all be, and how we didn't know who we were messing with, but he never said who that was. Let he rephrase that. He never said it while I was there. I got there late. If he said something earlier, the others would know. Except Bart; he was unconscious when...well, he was unconscious."

Bragg heard the word 'when,' but decided it could wait. "The other ones there, were they the ones you brought to the barn?"

"Yeah. Bart and Jamaal you already know. The tall girl is Tori and the shorter one is her roommate, Dee. They might know something."

"Tori," McIntyre leaned in toward the table mike. "She's what, Bart's girlfriend?"

"That's what Evelyn thinks. She's a likeable girl, but I'm high up on her shit list right now. Something about getting the pee scared out of her by two guys with Uzis."

McIntyre smiled. You might be high on her list, he thought, but I've got permanent dibs on the top slot. Later, Bragg asked him about the smile. "I was recalling a personal best," McIntyre told him, and described the Lolita conversation. "And judging by how she reacted when another girl called Bart, I would say Ms Pitman is right on the money. Our boy may not know it, but yeah, he's got a girlfriend."

◇◇◇◇◇◇◇◇◇◇◇◇◇◇◇◇◇●◇◇◇◇◇◇◇◇◇◇◇◇◇◇◇◇◇

Emmett had said Bart couldn't help them, but Bart was the one McIntyre felt most comfortable calling. "Sure," Bart told him. "I'll check and see if anybody remembers anything." It didn't take him long to call back. Jamaal, he had found out, had been paying attention to the man's gun, and not his words. Dee had just escaped from the cabin and wasn't sure what else was happening right then. She thought the man had said something but, like Jamaal, she couldn't remember what.

Tori could. "Dockery," she said. "That was the name of this kid in eighth grade who used to snap my bra strap, and I remember thinking, if it was Butch Dockery this guy was looking for, I'd help him look." She thought for a moment. "Dock; he said that too. He was looking for somebody named Dockery, but we might know him as Dock. Say, you're not asking this for that Jaybee character, are you? Cause I've still got a bone to pick with him."

Bragg watched as McIntyre did things on a computer. Bragg was not anti-computer, by any means, but he didn't enjoy using them the way McIntyre seemed to. He had tried out one of the combat simulation games, but he lost interest after a few minutes. "That's not how it is," he said. "When they come out with one that ruptures your eardrums when a grenade goes off, or where you can smell the blood if your buddy takes one to the chest, you let me know." Compared with Gen. Compton, though, Bragg was an enthusiast. Col. Menendez had heard some cursing from the general's office one day that was several degrees worse than usual. His computer, it seemed, wasn't obeying orders.

"I told it to print, and it didn't do it. Now it wants me to push a button that says it's OK for it not to print." He pointed to a little box on the screen. "Well, it's not OK, and I'm not going to push the button, but it won't do anything else until I do." He hunted around in a drawer until he found what he was looking for: a hammer. Menendez persuaded him not to kill the offending machine, but the next day she saw a tech carrying it away. "It broke," was all the General would ever say.

"Anything yet?" Bragg asked McIntyre.

"I'm in the NYPD database, cross-referencing the names Dock and Dockery with known associates of Andrew "Slim" DiSantis," McIntyre said, the way someone else might have said he was multiplying seventeen by three. A name appeared on the screen. "Timothy Dockery," McIntyre said with a smile, "come on down."

◇◇◇◇◇◇◇◇◇◇◇◇◇◇◇◇●◇◇◇◇◇◇◇◇◇◇◇◇◇◇◇◇

The man in the chair was conscious again. "All right, good, let us continue," Bathori said to him. "We have reached the clearing in the woods. What do you see there?" It had taken a while for the inquiry to reach the clearing. The man had had to be revived every now and again, but mostly the questioning had dragged along because Bathori wanted to know everything about each detail of the narrative before going on to the next one. That had meant spending a long time on what had happened in the Hutton mill, since the man's recollection of what Floyd had said was apparently a paraphrase, and Bathori insisted on the actual words. They had finally gone on to other things, but only because Bathori wanted the man to survive a while longer. He still didn't believe that Floyd had said what the man remembered.

"There was a cabin," the man said. "It was made of big rocks. There might have been a fire. The roof looked like it was falling in, and there was smoke coming out the door. There were two cars parked beside the cabin: a gray two-door sedan and an old Jeep. There was a cat on the hood of the Jeep. An orange cat."

"We can skip the cat," Bathori said. "Tell me about the people. Start with how many there were."

The man hesitated. "There were four. Two girls and two boys, but one of the boys was stretched out like he was hurt or something. Then Dockery came out of the cabin."

"You recognized him?"

"No, his face was all bloody, but after I told the kids to give him up or I'd shoot the...that I'd shoot one of them, that's when he came out of the cabin, so I knew it was him. I told him I had come for him, and he said he understood."

"All right. What happened next?"

"I killed him."

"Are you sure?" That was the crucial question.

"Listen, he took eleven hollow-points to the gut, so yeah, I'm sure." Even now, the man had some professional pride.

"And then?"

"My gun jammed while I was reloading, and they rushed me." No amount of torture was going to make him admit that a fat kid had done it all by himself. "Then some woman came out of the woods, and later a man came along, and the man said to put me in the trunk of the car."

"Did either man or the woman see you shoot Dockery?"

"No, it was all over by then. All they saw was his body."

"And the four who did see you shoot him?"

"Your guys lined them up and shot them. You don't have to worry about them." The man looked down at his wrists, taped to the arms of the chair. "You don't have to worry about me, either. You know that, don't you? I'm loyal to the company."

"I am sure you are loyal," Bathori said, "but only you know who you are loyal to, and that is a problem." He nodded to Jason, then walked toward the door. Before he left the room, he paused. "Loyalty of any kind is a rare trait, however, and it should not go unrewarded." He nodded again toward Jason. "Make it quick and painless." Then he went out and down the hall, to make sure the incinerator was ready.

Chapter Thirty-Seven

They found Tim Dockery's address, a run-down residential hotel in a seedy part of town, but they didn't find Tim Dockery. "I ain't seen him in a while," the desk clerk said. Did the clerk know where he might have gone? He shrugged. "I mind my business, and they mind theirs." After some discussion, the clerk accepted a hundred dollar inspection fee, in exchange for which he agreed to continue minding his business while they checked out the room. It contained an unmade bed, a chair with some clothes thrown over it, an empty dresser, and a little TV set. That was all. "I should have more tenants like him," the clerk said when he came back to lock up. "You wouldn't believe what I've had to clean up in some of these rooms. There was this one couple: they had this thing they liked to do with marinara sauce, you know, like you'd put on spaghetti, only what they would do was...well, you don't wanta know."

Finding a good picture of their man was another problem. "He's a driver," Col. Menendez had pointed out to Bragg when he phoned in his report. "Drivers need to have driver's licenses. It looks like you could get a license photo from DMV."

"Good idea," Bragg said, as if he hadn't already looked into that. None of the New York drivers named Dockery matched the desk clerk's description of his model tenant. He glanced over at McIntyre, expecting to see eye rolling, but the technician's thoughts were obviously somewhere else, and when the call was over, McIntyre likewise went somewhere else: back to his own motel room, and the equipment he had set up there.

The first thing McIntyre had done when he checked in, even before he unpacked, was to put out the Do Not Disturb card. For one thing, he kept house better than the housekeepers did, but mainly he didn't want them wondering what all his equipment was for. In particular, he didn't want them to see the machine that made ID cards, which he was using when Bragg came to check on him. "Okay, who are you this time?" Bragg asked.

"William Anders," McIntyre said, "Probation Officer."

"You think our man is on probation? We'd have found that already."

"No, but when the colonel mentioned DMV, the V made me think of juvie. Mr. Dockery has stayed under the radar as an adult, but what about before then? Maybe he behaved himself until he was eighteen, but I'll bet you he didn't, and if I'm right, he has a juvenile record. It won't be online from that far back, but somewhere in some filing cabinet is a folder with his name on it, and if we're lucky, a picture. Juvie records are sealed, but a P.O. can pull them."

Bragg thought about that. "Let me guess: you'll age the picture like they used to do with the kids on milk cartons."

McIntyre smiled and nodded. With a decent picture, they could comb the DMV database for similar faces, and find out what name the driver was using. Then it was just a matter of legwork and time, and they would finally meet the elusive Mr. Dockery.

◇◇◇◇◇◇◇◇◇◇◇◇◇◇◇◇●◇◇◇◇◇◇◇◇◇◇◇◇◇◇◇◇◇

According to the sign over its lobby door, the hotel was called the Montabella. Nobody actually called it that; it was the Monty, and it was a flophouse. According to the desk register, the man in 6-D was named Tim Johnson, but he was wrong; it was Dock. Times were tough, or he would have been staying somewhere better. He had had a couple of little jobs since he gotten back, barely enough to pay the daily rent on his room. He would like to have gone back to his old place to get his TV, but if anybody was watching for him, that was where they'd be watching, so he hid out at the Monty.

The Monty wasn't much, but it did have an elevator. It creaked and groaned whenever anyone used it, and it smelled like piss, but it worked. The stairwell smelled even more like piss, and so did the crew that liked to hang out there. They didn't care what they smelled like. In fact, they didn't care about very much of anything, except getting more of whatever their drug of choice was. They cared about that a lot, so Dock used the elevator.

He waited to get in until there wasn't anyone else around. The way he figured it, nobody gets mugged by an empty elevator. He didn't hate the muggers; a man does what he has to do to get by, after all, but muggers got upset it if you didn't have anything to give them, which right now Dock didn't. The elevator made its usual noises, but it eventually made it up to his floor. The doors opened, Dock stepped out, and suddenly he found himself back in again, this time in the company of Steve Bragg. "Congratulations," Bragg told him. "You're invited to a come-as-you-are party. In fact, you're the guest of honor."

Dock had two options, they told him: talk to us, or we'll have you arrested on some charge—we'll find something—and get your name in the papers. Your real name, not Johnson. Do you remember what happened to Slim? Do you think they won't do that to you? So here it is: talk or die. Choose now.

Dock talked. For as long as she could stand it, Menendez listened in while an Army interrogator tried to question him. She stood it for all of five minutes, and then she gave up. It wasn't that Dock wasn't cooperating, but the way he remembered things was by topic, and the interrogator kept asking questions by subject, which wasn't quite the same thing. The Army man would suggest a subject—Slim's methods of killing, for example—and Dock might start with a throat-cutting in Jersey that Slim had told him about during a trip to Chicago. That the killing had happened in Jersey didn't matter anymore; the topic had shifted to Chicago. He remembered what Slim had said about Chicago-style pizza, and Polish sausage, and that led to what Slim had said about Polacks. At first the CID man tried to channel the answers back onto what he thought was the subject, but after a while he surrendered to the inevitable and let the flood of words go where all floods go, which is mostly downhill. Everything was being recorded anyway; the computer would transcribe it and highlight the important details:

the dates, the places, and what they particularly wanted, the names.

The transcript wasn't as much help as Menendez had hoped. Slim hadn't been a name dropper. She skimmed the transcript looking for useful facts, and didn't see any. It wasn't until she read it line by line that she saw something. Dock was rambling on about the last trip he and Slim had made. "There was this old guy down in Larson," he said. "He wasn't the target because he was already dead, but Slim's mistress thought the dead guy's lawyer might know something about a workshop he had. Slim found out the lawyer would be at a poker game, and that's where he figured to snatch him. Then he was going to, you know, sweat him. He was looking forward to that. Did I mention he really hated lawyers? He told me about this labor lawyer up in Queens that he had done with an ice pick or something. You should have seen him when he talked about that, the way his face lit up." He had more to say on the topic of lawyers, but by then Menendez had quit reading. Two words had caught her attention: Slim's mistress.

◇◇◇◇◇◇◇◇◇◇◇◇◇◇◇◇●◇◇◇◇◇◇◇◇◇◇◇◇◇◇◇◇

The interrogator had gone back to wherever his office was. Menendez's mental picture of that office was a beehive, out of which CID men came, all dressed alike, all thinking alike, and if she had known that he worked in a square cubicle instead of a hexagonal cell, it wouldn't have altered her opinion in the slightest. The thought of calling him back in to explore a detail he had missed the first time, didn't appeal to her. She sent Bragg to talk to Dock.

He got right to the point. "Tell me about Slim's mistress."

"His what?"

"His mistress."

"You mean, like, a personal whore? That kind of mistress? Slim didn't do that. He got off on hurting people. He wouldn't have known what to do with a woman that he wasn't hired to, you know..."

"All right then, some other kind of mistress. Whips and chains, that sort of thing?"

Dock shook his head. "Torture? No, except..." He thought back. "There was one time he said he had stretched a job out for a couple hours and videotaped it, only it wasn't a woman. It was a cop that had roughed up somebody important's kid. The client wanted to know the cop had suffered, you know? But he didn't use whips or chains; he used the guy's own night stick. He tied him down, then started breaking bones, fingers and toes first, then legs and arms, ribs—you know, from the outside in. He saved the guy's skull for last so he'd feel it all. Got a real good bonus for that one, he told me; it made the client happy."

"He worked for more than one client?"

"Oh sure, he didn't care."

"So which one of them did he call his mistress?"

"You still on that? Then let me say it again, real slow this time: Slim didn't have no mistress."

Bragg sighed. It was a good thing, he decided, that he didn't have that cop's night stick right now. "Then why," he finally said, "did you tell Agent Whatsisface that Slim's mistress thought the lawyer in Larson would know something?"

Dock gave him a pitying look. "You people need to get the shit out of your ears," he said. "I never said nothing about a mistress. I said Mister Ess. He was Slim's favorite client."

Bragg knew he had hit paydirt, but he tried to sound casual. "Did he ever talk about this Mr. S?"

"You mean like, what did the S stand for? Nah. He didn't really talk about his clients. Well, he did say stuff sometimes, you know, like how one was a big shot in the Jersey mob, or how another one thought he was a big shot in the mob, but was about to find out different. But you know, he did say one thing about Mr. S; he said it a couple of times. If he ever got in trouble, he said, Mr. S would take care of him. I'd say he got that right."

◇◇◇◇◇◇◇◇◇◇◇◇◇◇◇◇●◇◇◇◇◇◇◇◇◇◇◇◇◇◇◇◇

"Rich? Andy." Only close friends knew Gen. Andrew Compton as Andy, but one of those friends was Richard Clevenger. Rich was a spy, but not in the old sense of the word. NSA doesn't have spies in the old sense. Their people don't skulk in the shadows, or wear trench coats, or hide microfilm in hollow rocks. For the most part, they sit in cubicles and listen. Or rather, their equipment listens, and they monitor the equipment.

In the early days of the twentieth century, the United States had one of the best code-breaking departments in the world, but at the end of the Great War, the Secretary of State ordered it shut down. Gentlemen, Secretary Stimson said, should not read each other's mail. The Great War turned out to have been merely the first World War, and by the time WWII rolled around, Henry Stimson had become the Secretary of War. The times had changed, or he had, because intercepting and decoding enemy messages became central to the nation's war effort, and this time the Black Chamber, as they once called it, did not close at the end of the war; it became the National Security Agency. NSA does not have a motto, but if it did it would probably be, "If we haven't heard it, it hasn't been said." In Latin, of course.

"Andy, always good to hear from you. What do you need?" Rich sounded happy. Andy Compton never called unless he had something interesting.

"I need a name."

"What's wrong with Andrew? I've always thought it fit you."

"Ass. I need somebody else's name. Somebody inside Traxell."

"Okay. Tell me what you know, and I'll find out what I can."

"Andy? Rich. That name you needed? I don't have it, but I know where you can find it."

"You have my full attention."

Rich didn't say how he had done it, and the general didn't ask. Rich didn't say because it had been embarrassingly easy—easy for NSA, anyway—and there is no mystique in doing easy tasks. Gen. Compton didn't ask because he knew it had involved computers, and he didn't want to admit that the evil devices did occasionally have their uses.

Rich had started with a question. If Traxell really had been involved in burglaries and killings in South Carolina, how had their people known where to go, and who to look for? Somebody, presumably the mysterious Mr. S, had known about Schroder's connection with Viney Cove, so somebody—maybe him, maybe his IT people–had done a lot of research. Had any such searches been made in the time frame in question? It turned out that several had been. Most of them had been done through a server in Connecticut that might or might not have a connection to Traxell, but one, a map search for Viney Cove, had not. That search had been done at a coffee shop two blocks from Traxell's New York headquarters. Security cameras on the street had captured the face of the person who made the inquiry, and facial recognition had given him a name: Tanvir Singh.

Singh lived on the nineteenth floor of his building. As New York apartment buildings went, it wasn't great, but at least no one pissed in the stairwells. On weekends Singh actually used the stairs; it was good exercise, but nineteen was too many flights to climb at the end of a long work day, so today he used the elevator. There was one other passenger, but Singh had learned New York etiquette: no eye contact, no conversation, just pretend the other person isn't there. That became harder to do when the other man pushed the red button and the elevator jerked to a stop between floors. "Good evening, Mr. Singh," Steven Bragg said, almost conversationally. "Do you have a minute?"

Singh might have replied, but all the spit in his mouth had chosen that moment to dry up. He had friends who had been mugged, so this wasn't a total shock, but it also wasn't quite the way his friends had described it. The man was relaxed, his hands were empty, and he wasn't angry, the way his friends always described their muggers. By the time he had worked up enough spit to say something, he realized that the man had used his name, and that the red button hadn't started the alarm bell the way it was supposed to. "Who...who are you?" he finally managed.

"Do you know the riddle about the tree falling in the forest?" Bragg said. "If a man walks into an elevator and no one sees him, is he really there? And if he isn't really there, there isn't really an answer to your question, is there? Perhaps you should have asked who I am not. I am not from Traxell. I am also not from South Carolina, although some friends of mine are. You did some research recently that almost got those friends killed, Mr. Singh, and that is, shall we say, unacceptable. That valley you were interested in—Viney Cove—can you tell me why you looked it up? That would make the next few minutes go so much more smoothly." The team had discussed going straight for what they really wanted, the payroll data, but had decided the direct approach was too likely to evoke company loyalty. Interrogating a man, or corrupting him, for that matter, is done best when it is done gradually.

Across the street from the building, in a parked van, Col. Menendez gave McIntyre a nod. "I didn't think the captain was the best choice for this," she said. "I stand corrected. That's damn good acting. Just the right hint of menace, without saying anything overtly menacing." McIntyre nodded back, which the colonel mistook for agreement. You only think he's acting, McIntyre thought. And if you can feel the menace through a speaker, imagine what it's like in person.

In person, it was brutal. "Am I..." Singh swallowed, suddenly having entirely too much spit. "Am I under arrest?"

"Why no, Mr. Singh," Bragg said softly. "Among the many things I am not, I am not a policeman. If you don't want to discuss this with me, I'll get out on the next floor and the elevator will take you the rest of the way up. Of course, there may be someone waiting for you there, someone with a badge, and a warrant, and handcuffs. Do you want to find out?" Bragg put his finger back on the red button. "Or do you have a minute?"

From the building's lobby they went to the van, where Bragg introduced Singh to Menendez, except he called her something else. Her ID said she was a federal prosecutor. "We don't bring charges until we know we can win," she told Singh. "In your case, we have more than enough. You did a computer search that was used to target a killing. At the very least, that puts you in a criminal conspiracy. We could probably get you thirty or forty years for that, if you were the one we wanted. You are not. We want to know where you got your assignment."

Singh saw a ray of hope. "If I tell you, will I then not go to prison?"

Menendez nodded. "Our policy is that the first one on the bus gets the best seat. If you talk to us now, that first one will be you. It somebody else talks before you do, then he would get the best seat, and you would get...well, there's only one best seat."

"So...no prison?"

"No prison."

Singh didn't say anything for almost a minute. "My father was a shopkeeper in Lahore," he said at last. "I learned at his knee when to haggle and when to accept an offer. I want the best seat. The search request came to us from one of the department heads."

Menendez took out a notepad. "And his name is...?"

"I do not know his first name, but his last name is Stasevik."

Menendez looked gloomy. She had just gotten off the phone with the federal prosecutor. "I honestly believe," she said, "that if the streets of Heaven really are paved with gold, that man will complain about the glare. He says we still don't have enough."

Gen. Compton accepted that calmly. Decades in the Army had taught him to suffer fools, if not gladly, then at least stoically. "Did he say why not?"

"He says we've got proof that Traxell is curious about our dead professor, and that somebody at Traxell has a name starting with S, but that only shows that Stasevik could be Mr. S, not that he has to be. We still need a link between the shooter and DiSantis or Dockery, to cast a sinister light—those are his words—on the computer search that Stasevik had our IT guy do."

The general cocked his head to one side. "Don't we have that? Bart's girlfriend said the shooter asked about Dockery. What more do we need?"

"According to the prosecutor, we need for her to say it under oath. We need for her to come to New York and testify."

Chapter Thirty-Eight

Colonel Menendez stared at her phone in disbelief. She couldn't remember the last time someone had hung up on her, but she knew that she hadn't liked it then, and she found that she still didn't like it. She was thinking about what she ought to do about it when Capt. Bragg had the bad luck to walk past her office. He hadn't actually intended to walk past; there were things he needed to discuss with the colonel, but one glance at her face told him this wasn't a good time. He hadn't quite made it to the next turn in the corridor when the sharp spear of her voice impaled him. "Captain, I want to see you. Now."

She got right to the point. "I want to know what Mr. McIntyre did to Tori Lasker."

"Did, ma'am? As far as I know, they've never met." He hoped the evasion would buy him some time. It didn't.

"Then he did it from a distance. We need Miss Lasker to come to New York to talk to the grand jury, but when I called to tell her, I only got as far as hello when she said, and I quote, 'You're not fooling me again J.B.' Then she told me that if she ever met me, and again I'm quoting, "Even you von't like it." Then she hung up on me. Now, unless you know another J.B., McIntyre has done something, and I want to know what it was."

There was no way out. "Ma'am, if you have a few minutes, it would be a lot easier to show you than to tell you." She didn't reply, but she didn't refuse, so Bragg took out his phone and called McIntyre. "Are you in your office? Good. Stay there." He made a courtly gesture to the door and said, "Ma'am, after you."

◇◇◇◇◇◇◇◇◇◇◇◇◇◇◇◇●◇◇◇◇◇◇◇◇◇◇◇◇◇◇◇◇

Every year, millions of high school students take trigonometry and calculus. Some of them will have careers where trig and calculus are useful, but most won't, and in a few years, the great majority won't know cosine theta from f of x. McIntyre had gone through basic training because Army regs said he had to. He had learned to march in cadence, and to run obstacle courses, and how to make a bed that a drill sergeant could bounce a quarter off of. Since then, he hadn't done any cadence marching, or run any obstacle courses, and nobody cared how he made his bed. When his two immediate superiors suddenly appeared in front of him, he didn't jump to his feet and salute the way they had taught him in basic, although he did sit up a little straighter.

The colonel was past caring about salutes. "Soldier," she snapped, "You tell me why Tori Lasker would call me J.B. and then insult me in a bad German accent and hang up on me, and you do it now."

McIntyre thought fast. "I've, uh, only spoken with Miss Lasker one time, ma'am, and it was over the phone. I suppose she could have gotten the impression that...but I didn't actually..."

Menendez leaned a little toward him and made a snapping-shut gesture with her thumb and fingers. McIntyre shut up. "You're weaseling, McIntyre. Get to the point. What did you do?"

McIntyre swallowed again. He had been working on his voice-and-accent program for months, but he hadn't wanted to demo it until it was perfect. Not that it mattered what he wanted; he remembered at least that much from basic. In a contest between what he wanted and a direct order from a colonel, the direct order won. "Ma'am," he said, "if you will bear with me for a moment, I think I can show you." He touched an anonymous-looking icon on his screen, then another one labeled LL. It had originally been TG, for Teenage Girl, but after talking with Tori he had tweaked it a little and renamed it LL, for Lolita. When the program came up, he typed a number in each of two boxes, and picked up a microphone.

In the colonel's pocket, her phone started to buzz. It was, it said, from Gen. Compton. "I'd better take this," she muttered, and answered it. She saw McIntyre's lips move, but what she heard on the phone was a teenage girl saying "Oh wow, I think I've, like, got the wrong number. Woopsies." McIntyre tapped a control and in his own voice said, "In my defense, I didn't call her; she called me. And I didn't say anything bad." Then he remembered another of the voices he had used. "Well, not really bad. And not in that voice."

"Explain." The word hung over him like a storm cloud, full of dark potential.

"Um, you see, after she found out I wasn't what she thought I was she, ah, told me I needed to be tied up and whipped. So I thought that, well..." He tapped a different icon, this one labeled CO, the Countess Olga voice. It was, he thought, going to be a long morning.

◊◊◊◊◊◊◊◊◊◊◊◊◊◊◊◊●◊◊◊◊◊◊◊◊◊◊◊◊◊◊◊◊

"Bart? Steve Bragg. How're you doing? Great. Say, if you don't mind, I need a favor."

"Uh, sure," Bart said, but with mixed feelings. So far he had done the captain two favors. There was the time he had helped patch things up with Evelyn, and that had been fun, but the time before that—the Jeep race—had been really exciting but it hadn't been fun at all.

"Great. I need for you to ask your, ah...to ask Miss Lasker to call Col. Menendez."

"Is that all? No problem. I've got the number in my wallet."

"I'll need to give you a different number, one that doesn't go through the, uh, switchboard."

"Switchboard? You still use a switchboard?"

"Not the old kind, no. I meant McIntyre. Apparently he and Miss Lasker have...issues. Anyway, if you could have her call this number," he read it off, "it would be very helpful."

"Yeah, I can do that. When should she call?"

"As soon as she can. It's kind of important."

Bart wondered why Bragg hadn't called Tori himself, but he didn't ask. Probably it was something to do with rank, he thought. It wasn't. Bragg had offered to make the call, an offer the colonel had thought funny enough to share with Gen. Compton. "Oh God no," was the general's reaction. "Now, if I had an ultimatum I wanted delivered, Steven would be my first choice. Or if I needed a second for a duel. But as you may have noticed, diplomacy is not his strong suit."

"And you're saying it's mine?"

"I'm sure you can be tactful when you want to be," he said carefully. The colonel's willingness to call stupid ideas stupid had offended more than one of his colleagues.

"An interesting theory," she said. Her phone had started to vibrate. It was a South Carolina number. "Shall we test it?"

Chapter Thirty-Nine

Hal Stasevik was angry. He was, in fact, somewhere past angry. Roland Bathori had just called to say that the Larson matter had become an active danger, and would have to disappear. Hal had told him, again, that everything was under control, and that the operation had been a success. Bathori's response had been cryptic. "No operation should be called a success," he had said, "if the patient dies." Then he had hung up.

Hal wondered if throwing his phone through his office window would make him feel any better. Probably it would, he decided, but it wouldn't be worth the other problems it would cause. He stared out the window for a few minutes, clenching and unclenching his fist, then he made a call he had wanted to make for some time. Finally, still angry, he went to the office where he had put Tom Harper. "When you were in the Army," he said, "did you ever get the feeling that you were surrounded by idiots?"

"Every day," Harper replied, with an emphatic nod.

"I have a job for you. It is time for the idiots of the world to find out they don't always get what they want."

Roland Bathori reread the exchange on his computer monitor, emails between an office worker on six and his wife:

Are we still having dinner at your sister's tonight?

No, you're taking me out, LOL. Sis is still on that grand jury and says until it's over she can't talk to you. You're not involved in lasering research are you? Or maybe its research lasering. Anyway, she says we can come over tomorrow night. They only have one more witness.

He cleared the screen and summoned Jason into his office. "Sometime, perhaps as early as tomorrow, we will be getting some visitors with papers. The subject of the papers will almost certainly be Harold Stasevik's project. Get Morrison and Fuller. Go up to twenty-three, and gather up everything—files, phones, anything connected with the project—and bring it all down to twelve."

"And if Mr. Stasevik objects?"

"As far as I am concerned, you can bring him too." He dismissed Jason and tapped in the number for Nathan Huntsinger's office. "I need you to call an emergency board meeting," he told the CEO. "Yes, immediately. I have a retirement motion for the board to consider: Mr. Stasevik."

"I see," Nate said with a sigh. These sorts of meetings were always stressful, and this one was going to be more so than usual. As soon as he was finished with Bathori, he called the first number on his speed dial. It wasn't the first because he called it a lot; he almost never did. It was first because of who it was. "Dr. Verhoeven?" he said when the call finally went through. "Nathan Huntsinger in New York. Fine, thank you. We have an issue I thought you should know about. Or, I suppose you could say, two issues. Mr. Bathori, our chief of Security has just asked for the retirement of Mr. Stasevik. That's right, Research Liaison. I agree, very awkward, and all the more because Mr. Stasevik, had just made the same motion regarding Mr. Bathori. I have scheduled the meeting for tomorrow morning. Yes sir, I agree. I will see to it."

◇◇◇◇◇◇◇◇◇◇◇◇◇◇◇●◇◇◇◇◇◇◇◇◇◇◇◇◇◇◇

Tori was trying not to seem nervous, but she was. What she knew about criminal prosecutions, she knew from TV, and on TV a lot of prosecutors are savage beasts, using their grand juries as their fangs and claws. She had worn her hair blond for the hearing, which had drawn a compliment from Emmett. "Yeah, well I think of it like your necktie," she explained. "You wear it to show which team you're on. Purple hair today would be like a lawyer coming to court in a sweatsuit. You are going to be in there with me, aren't you?"

"I'm afraid not; they don't let lawyers go in with witnesses. If you need me, ask for a break, and they'll let you come out in the hall and talk with me."

"Well that bites. What if they try to trick me?"

"They're not going to trick you. The prosecutor already knows what you're going to say. He'll ask you what the man did, and what he said, and that'll be that. In and out in ten minutes."

"But what if they ask what we were doing up there at the cabin? Do I tell them about Dee's cousin and all the other stuff?"

Oh hell no, he thought. "That would be when you would ask for a break and talk to me. I don't really see that happening."

"Ten minutes. In and out. You're sure."

Emmett smiled his best trust-me smile. "Ten minutes. I'm sure."

◊◊◊◊◊◊◊◊◊◊◊◊◊◊◊◊●◊◊◊◊◊◊◊◊◊◊◊◊◊◊◊◊

Executive board meetings were usually a curdled mixture of tension and boredom. This time it was all tension and no boredom. While it was possible that no retirement would be approved, none of the division heads believed that would happen. Somebody was going to die today.

Hal went first since his had been the first motion, if only by a few minutes. He painted Roland Bathori as a paranoid obstructionist, a man whose over-blown worries about imaginary dangers stood in the way of profits the like of which the company hadn't seen since the end of the Cold War. It was not, to judge by the looks on his colleagues' faces, an easy sell. Security was supposed to be paranoid, wasn't it? Then came Bathori's turn. The questioning and death of the man Hal had sent to clean up after Slim was news to Hal, but to the others it was at best only mildly interesting. These things happen. That the man might have been a Justice Department plant was more interesting, as was the idea that Hal had somehow gotten an Army team ordered to stand down while his own people did a helicopter rescue. Bathori emphasized that. "Do you really want every division to have its own little private army?" he had asked, "Or do you want Research Liaison to have the only one? Security works for all of you; Harold Stasevik's force works only for him, for his projects, and for his goals. My own goals are simple: keep the company safe. Do you know what his goals are? If the answer is no, then I tell you the man is a danger, if only for that reason. But there is another reason. Even as I speak, a grand jury is meeting to investigate the company, because of something Research Liaison has done and is still doing. This is the sort of crisis that Security knows how to handle. Ordinarily it is, but when I sent a Security team to gather up the remnants of Harold's mess so the matter could be properly sanitized, it seems he has hidden them away. It is time to retire him."

Hal had expected to be attacked, but not outright lied about. That was going too far, even for a retirement hearing. "I don't know what the hell he's talking about. I have no pull with the Army—I look to you for that." He gave Nate a nod. "And my private army, as he calls it, consisted of one man, a trusted assistant who was retired without my consent. But since my colleague has posed the question to you this way, I will do the same. Do you want a Security division that feels free to send its tentacles into your departments, plucking out any of your employees it wants and then lying to cover it up? Because that's what you have right now."

Hal paused. He had spoken in anger, and while he thought he had done all right, it was time to return to the presentation he had planned. He had given Harper the Larson files, as he called them, and sent him out of the building, but Harper was too valuable to use only as a courier. Harper knew people, retired military people. One of them, a man skilled with locks, had gone to the highrise where Bathori had his apartment, to look for anything incriminating. Just before the meeting started, Harper had sent Hal a text. In a hidden safe, they had found money, a pistol, and a passport. "If my colleague is so avid to serve the company," Hal asked when Bathori sat down, "why does he have a false passport and a stash of cash, hidden in a safe in his apartment? Planning to disappear, Roland? Were you even going to say goodbye to us?"

Bathori had been on his way to the meeting when Harper and his crew had broken into his dummy apartment. If he had been in his office, he would have seen the background on his monitor's desktop go from medium red to blood red, the signal that his safe had been opened, but he knew now that it had. "Helicopter extractions, and now burglaries, Harold? Who else's home have you violated? William's, perhaps?" He pointed to one of the VPs. "Paul's? Even Nathan's? Gentlemen, I run a tight ship, but I cannot protect the company if you allow this loose cannon to roll around on deck. His recklessness is a danger to all of you. That said, I believe you have heard enough to make your decision."

"The man is a snake," Hal said in reply. "It is the nature of snakes to bite. If you let him bite me, which of you can be sure he won't be bitten next?"

On that note, Nate said it was time for discussion among the board members, and sent the two potential retirees to wait in their offices. Then he pushed a button on the video console, and the big screen at the end of the room lit up. "Dr. Verhoeven, do you have anything you'd like us to consider?"

The Chairman looked sad. "The retirement of a senior executive is never pleasant, but in this case, I think it cannot be avoided. One of the two gentlemen is clearly delusional, and it is our task to determine which one. Nathan, do you have available the witness I requested?"

"Yes sir." Nate opened a side door, and made a gesture. "Mr. Ross, would you join us?"

The IT geeks had been very quiet as they strained to hear. Nelson broke the silence. "They're really going to do it. They're really going to retire a VP."

Singh nodded. "Which one, do you think? Or might they do both?"

"I don't know. There's never been a double hearing before, at least not while I've been here. Just be glad they're not talking about us."

"I wonder," Singh said to no one in particular. "I wonder if they would need a meeting in order to retire us. Or would Mr. Huntsinger simply tell someone, Do it." He thought for a minute, then asked casually, "If we needed to leave quickly, what would be the best way to do it? I tried to use the fire stairs once, but the door between twelve and eleven is locked. A sign said Security will unlock it if there was a fire. I would think that violates the fire code." No one bothered to respond to that. After what they had heard, a fire code violation was a minor concern. Right now, their major concern was to hear who this mysterious Mr. Ross was, and what he had to say.

They didn't have to wait long. "Goede morgen, Dokter Verhoeven," said Jason's bloodless voice. "And good morning to you, gentlemen as well. How may I serve you?"

◊◊◊◊◊◊◊◊◊◊◊◊◊◊◊●◊◊◊◊◊◊◊◊◊◊◊◊◊◊◊

"Are you done, or just on a break?" Emmett asked Tori.

"Done. It went exactly like you said it would: What did you see, what did you hear, thank you very much."

Emmett dug out his phone. "Mr. McIntyre? Emmett Schroder. You wanted to know when the testimony was finished. Well, it's finished. Yeah, that quick." He turned to Tori. "Ready for lunch?"

She couldn't believe it. "You could eat, with all this going on? The tension is killing me."

Emmett chuckled. "I suppose it all depends on what you're used to. More times than I like to think, I've sat by a client waiting for a murder jury to come back. That's my idea of tension. Come on; I saw an Italian deli down the block. Whatever else you want to say about New Yorkers, they do know how to build a sandwich."

"Mr. Ross," the Chairman said, "are you familiar with the events surrounding the retirement of Mr. Stasevik's man?"

Jason nodded. "I am, sir. His, as we call it, exit interview was somewhat protracted, and I conducted portions of it myself."

"Excellent. Mr. Bathori has given us the man's account. Were you able to listen in on that?"

"I was. I agree with the substance of his account."

"The substance. But not the details?"

Jason hesitated. He knew exactly what he was going to say next, but the hesitation implied that he had qualms about saying it. "First of all, I believe you know that Mr. Bathori hates Mr. Stasevik, though I am not sure why. When it occurred to him that Mr. Stasevik was building a private army—an absurdity, in my opinion—he essentially abandoned the inquiry into whether the employee was a government spy, which I believe he was. I have checked on the details of the man's rescue story, and they do not stand up to scrutiny. In particular, he said the team that rescued him killed five witnesses. If that many people from one community were to disappear at one time, there would be news reports about it, and there have not been. If bodies had been found, there would be police reports, and there have not been. I conclude that the man's story of killings was a fabrication, and that the helicopter rescue was, likewise, a fabrication. I believe that line of inquiry should have been pursued in depth, but instead of doing so, Mr. Bathori accepted the story as true, because of the bad light it cast upon Mr. Stasevik."

The Chairman gave one of his ponderous nods. "Thank you, Mr. Ross. I have only one further question. If the board should decide to retire Mr. Bathori, are you capable of heading the Security division?"

Again Jason hesitated, and again it was an act. "Yes sir," he finally said. "I am."

The discussion began with the least-senior VP. Not wanting to take the losing side, he spoke very cautiously. "From what I've heard, the issue seems to be risk tolerance, and Hal's appears to be higher than Bathori's." By the time the comments had worked their way up to the most senior of the VPs, the issue had evolved into, "There are no risk-free opportunities, at least not ones that make any money." When everyone else had spoken, it was the Chairman's turn, but all he had to say was, "It appears to me that we have a consensus. Shall we vote, then?" Without waiting for an answer, he continued, "All in favor of retiring Mr. Stasevik?" No one moved or spoke. "Very well, the motion fails. All in favor of retiring Mr. Bathori?" Several hands went up, then all of them. The Chairman nodded. "Nathan, would you ask Mr. Ross to join us again? I believe we have an assignment for him."

Chapter Forty

The guard knocked lightly on the office door. "Mr. Bathori? They need you back in the boardroom." Nothing happened, so he knocked again, then after what he hoped would seem like a respectful pause, he opened the door. The office was empty. He closed the door again, and paged Jason. "There is a problem." He might as well have said "I have a problem" because, as the one who had escorted the—as he now knew—fallen Chief to his office, he was the one who would answer for it if the man had escaped.

Jason got there in half a minute. He had been at the elevator, waiting to give his former boss his retirement package. He got right to the point. "State the problem."

"He went in, he never came out, and he's not there now."

"Let me see." Jason went in and verified what the guard had told him. He couldn't imagine his old boss curled up in a fetal position under his desk, but he looked there anyway. Finally he stood before the only remaining hiding place, a closet he had seen every day, but had never really noticed. He tried the knob: locked. Tapping on the door, he called out, "Sir? We need to get back to the board meeting." Getting no answer, he took a key from his pocket, the master key for everything in the building. With a gesture, he let the guard know he was to turn the lock and jerk the door open on a count of three. Then he drew the pistol he had planned to use in the elevator, and went down on one knee, to present a smaller target if his quarry shot back. He signed three, two, one. The door flew open, and there, in the darkness of the closet, stood his target. Jason fired five times, as fast as he could work the trigger.

There was no return fire. The man in the closet was an overcoat, whose hanger had been twisted so that it hung facing forward. Otherwise, the closet was empty. That made no sense at all; people don't simply disappear, not without help from the incinerator anyway.

Jason's phone buzzed in his pocket. It was Bathori. He

listened for a moment, then broke the connection. Angrily shoving the wounded coat to one side, he searched the closet for a hidden door. There wasn't any sign of one. Glancing down he saw, set into the floor of the closet, a fold-down handle, and with it as a clue he was able to trace the outline of a hatch. "Open it," he ordered the guard, but no amount of tugging would budge it. Several more of his trusted men had arrived after they heard the shots, and in a voice that was now anything but emotionless, Jason gave them their orders. "Have the lobby guards clear out any visitors, and then seal the building. No employee leaves until I say so. You," he pointed to one of the new arrivals, "guard the hatch. The rest of you, come with me." This could have been done with some dignity, he thought, but if the old man wants it long and painful, then long and painful it will be.

◊◊◊◊◊◊◊◊◊◊◊◊◊◊◊◊●◊◊◊◊◊◊◊◊◊◊◊◊◊◊◊◊

Gathered around Nelson's monitor, the IT team had gotten a fairly good sense for how the board meeting was going, so the Chairman's final question to Jason hadn't been a surprise. Jason's unequivocal answer, on the other hand, had been. "Even you, my son?" Nelson muttered, which earned him several quizzical looks. "Caesar's last words to Brutus," he explained, "and you all know what happened after that." Some of them didn't, but they didn't say so. It had apparently been something bad, and that was enough.

It was more than enough for Singh. "I have always thought of Mr. Bathori as cold," he said, "but I have at least thought of him as human. About Jason, I am not so sure, especially now. It has been a pleasure working with you, but I am, as they say, out of here." He started toward the elevator.

Like the Chairman's question, Singh's decision wasn't a complete surprise. The group had even discussed whether, if an evil time came, they should leave as a group, or trickle out individually. Melissa, one of the newer hires, decided Singh was right. "I think I hear my mother calling," she said, as she followed him toward the elevator. The others looked at each other, and without another word being said, they followed her. The elevator held them all, barely.

The crossover on eleven was where there might be a problem. And in fact, the man watching eleven's monitor did think it was odd for the entire IT staff to take a break at the same time. But he wasn't under orders to stop them, and Mr. Bathori's office didn't answer when he called to ask if he should, so he didn't. They got to the ground floor and crossed the main lobby without incident, getting almost to the street door before a guard blocked their way. "Sorry," he said. "The building is locked down until further notice. Nobody enters, and nobody leaves."

"But you let them leave," Singh protested, pointing through the glass wall at several people who had just left the building.

"They came in off the street. You came down in the elevator. Don't get your shorts in a wad; this shouldn't take long." By now, several more guards had joined the one at the exit. If pushing their way out had ever been an option, it wasn't any more.

"Can you at least tell us what the problem is?" Nelson asked. He knew he wouldn't hear the truth, but he might find out what the official line was.

"We think an intruder got past eleven. Until we know for sure, nobody leaves. Now I need you to move back from the door please." Then, remembering his instructions, he added, "Oh, and we are sorry for any inconvenience." Nelson didn't think he sounded very sorry.

◇◇◇◇◇◇◇◇◇◇◇◇◇◇◇◇●◇◇◇◇◇◇◇◇◇◇◇◇◇◇◇◇

The Security team had done their usual pre-meeting sweep of the board room, and as usual they had found nothing. In particular, they hadn't found the bug that Bathori had smuggled in, shielded in a little wire mesh pouch. He hadn't switched it on until after the sweep was finished. As soon as he got back to his office, he got the bug's companion earpiece out of his desk and began listening to the board's discussion. He had nothing else to do, since his computer was off the network. That was surprising, he thought, but only because it was good procedure. For a potentially condemned man to have high-level access to the company network would have been idiotic, but that didn't mean Huntsinger would have thought of it. The idea had to have come from Brussels.

The longer the meeting went, the more it was obvious how it would end. He knew he had enemies on the board, but he also knew the limits of what an individual enemy can accomplish. Like a lone wolf, an isolated enemy can cause trouble, but it is manageable trouble. The subject the board was discussing had let the lone wolves find each other, and now a pack was forming. Alone against a pack, there is only one defense: find cover. Bathori took a last look around his office. There was nothing there that he would miss. He lifted the hatch, went down six or seven steps, and locked it shut behind him. After a few minutes, he heard the distant sound of five shots. They must have unlocked the closet, he thought, and there was only one other person who had a key that could do that. He took out his phone, and called Jason. "You might want to reload," he said. "If it took you five shots to kill a coat, imagine how many it will take to kill me." There was no reply, and his phone said the call had ended. That was all right. He hadn't called to make small talk; he had called to make Jason angry. Angry people make rash decisions. Bathori had been angry too, at first: angry at himself for having misread the situation, and angry at Jason for having turned traitor. He had savored the anger, but then let it go; it served no useful purpose.

It took him only a few more seconds to reach his home. Here, there was quite a lot that he would miss. Very soon, Jason and his barbarians would be coming here, defiling his belongings, profaning his home. It would be, he thought, a crime against beauty, but then he was about to commit one himself. He smashed the antique globe to pieces and retrieved the passport he had hidden inside it. The one in his apartment safe had been a forgery. This was his real one, the one he would need for his trip. He thought about what he would say at the ticket counter if they asked if he was going to Brussels for business or pleasure. Pleasure, he would tell them. Not for everyone, of course; not for Henrik Verhoeven, the head barbarian. But for Roland Bathori, his trip to Brussels was going to be pure pleasure.

Was there anything else he needed? Ah, yes; from his kitchen he got a toothpick. He gave Marta instructions for music, took one last look around, and left. He was in a hurry. No one at Traxell had ever seen Roland Bathori in a hurry, but this was not the time to worry about his image; he had work to do.

Jason's men stood with guns drawn. Facing them was an unmarked door in a side hallway on twelve. Finding the door hadn't taken long; a few minutes with the building's schematics had shown them what was directly below Bathori's closet. Getting in, though, had proved to be more of a challenge. Jason's master key wouldn't even go in the lock, so they had sent for a drill. Two broken bits later, they had the door open, but all they found was the bottom of a set of stairs. The next several doors they tried opened easily enough, but Bathori wasn't behind any of them. Then they came to a door marked "Records Storage," and again, Jason's key wouldn't fit. Again, they drilled.

They expected to find a large open space; that was what the schematics showed. Instead, the door opened on a jungle. It was a very odd jungle—well-tended paths curling between islands of greenery—but to the Security men, used to the concrete canyons of New York, it was straight out of a Tarzan movie. Once they had verified that Bathori wasn't crouching behind some bush, they squared off opposite the door at the far end of the greenery. This door had no lock, and opened easily. "Damn," one of the searchers muttered when he looked inside. "What is this place?"

Jason came in last. One look around told him he didn't like it. The room was dark and old-fashioned, but more to the point, it wasn't something he had known about, and that was

328

disturbing. In the background, he heard a chorus, not quite singing but not quite speaking either. "Anybody know what that is?" he asked.

One of the men cleared his throat. "It's Gregorian chant, sir. I was raised Catholic, so I..."

"Yeah, yeah. So what are they saying?"

The chanting had stopped, but now it started over again. The man closed his eyes and listened, moving his lips with the chanters. "It's the Dies Irae."

"The what?"

"It's from the Mass for the dead, but I don't think they use this part any more. It's about how the world ends."

Jason had a horrible thought. "How do they say it ends?"

The man silently mouthed the old words: *solvet saeclum in favilla.* "In ashes," he said. "Dissolved in ashes."

When Traxell's New York headquarters was new, the PR people had bragged about how Green its design was. They were especially proud of the sod roof. In reality, the roof was nothing more than Nate Huntsinger's putting green, but to the PR people, anything green was Green. Another much-bragged-about feature— the term the brochures used was 'eco-friendly'—was the building's supposedly smaller-than-average carbon footprint. All of the heating and cooling systems, the flacks pointed out, were powered by clean, Green, natural gas. Of course, between the people, and the office equipment, and Big Mama, the building generated more than enough heat, even in winter. It used gas to heat the water for the showers and Jacuzzis next to the executive gym, and it used gas for the air conditioning system, enough at any rate to justify PR's Green claims, but in fact the building ran mainly on electricity, not gas. There were times, though, when it used quite a lot of gas, such as when the big backup generators kicked on, or the incinerator was fired up. That was why, just in case the power went off on a very cold day and, for whatever reason, something needed to be disposed of in a hurry, the architects had specified a three-inch gas line to run from the city main up to the mechanical room on twelve. From there, branch lines led in several directions. Usually they did. Right now, one of them didn't.

Even outside the door to the machinery room, Jason's men heard the roaring noise. The first man in the room saw the reason for it. "He's unbolted the pipe to Generator One," he said. This wasn't a man who would ordinarily know that, but since one end of a black pipe with 'Generator 1' painted on it was hanging loose, it wasn't a bad guess. The noise they had heard was coming from the pipe it had once joined, as gas roared out of it.

"Cut off the gas!" Jason yelled over the roar. One of the men pointed to the main valve and shook his head. Where there should have been a handle on a shaft, now there was only a shaft. Jason pointed to the hanging pipe. "Put it back!" The men were able to raise the pipe back into position, but the pressure of the outrushing gas was too great; they couldn't force the pipe end back into its mate. "Get out!" Jason bellowed, and they all went back to the hallway and shut the door.

Everyone looked scared, but one of the men looked puzzled too. "Sir," he said, "shouldn't the gas smell be stronger?" Jason thought about that. The man was right. The room they left should have been full of gas, and they should smell it in strongly the hall. He looked back in the machinery room and saw the answer. A panel had been removed from one of the air system's main return ducts, and it was sucking the gas in.

Jason took out his phone. "Sir, we have to evacuate the building. Yes sir, immediately."

In the boardroom, Nate put away his phone. "Gentlemen, I am told we need to leave the building, and that we should hurry." Several of the members had been sniffing the air, and the rest of them now noticed the smell. They hurried. By the time they reached the elevator, an alarm was hooting, and the elevator buttons were blinking red. "You'll have to use the stairs," Nate told them, pointing the way. For overweight, overdressed men, they made surprisingly good time, until they reached fourteen.

There, the way was blocked by people solidly packing the stairwell, and not moving. "What's the problem?" one of the VPs asked the woman in front of him, a data analyst from Sales.

"They can't get the door unlocked at twelve," she said. "They say somebody broke a toothpick off in the lock."

Chapter Forty-One

"What the hell could possibly be taking so long?" Bragg asked the FBI man next to him. They were sitting in a car, in a parking garage several blocks from the Traxell Building, waiting for the go-ahead. They had been sitting and waiting for almost two hours, which was almost two hours longer than Bragg liked to sit anywhere, for any reason. What made it especially galling was that when the time did come, he would only get to watch; the Army team would not be going in.

"If we're not involved," he had asked Col. Menendez, "then why do we need to be there at all?"

The colonel had asked her boss the same question. The answer she got—and the answer Bragg now got—was that they were there to observe and if the need arose, to act like Boy Scouts. "I asked the general what he meant when he said that, and he just laughed. 'Ask a Boy Scout', he said. So I'm asking you: what do you think he meant?"

"What makes you think I was a Boy Scout?"

"Oh please. It's written all over you. I don't know what happened to friendly, kind, cheerful, and reverent, but you're a walking example of the rest of the Scout Oath."

"It's the, ah, Scout Law, actually," he muttered.

"Whichever, you're busted. So how do we act like Boy Scouts? Help old ladies across the street?"

Bragg thought it over. "All I can come up with is the motto: Be Prepared." In the hours since then, he still hadn't come up with anything better. Be prepared. No problem; he was always prepared.

The FBI man cocked his head to one side, listening to his earpiece. "It looks like it'll be a while longer," he said. "The Assistant U.S. Attorney who's handling the case is in chambers with the judge. Some RICO case they're trying to settle. His office doesn't know how long it will take."

"So get a different DA."

"It doesn't work that way. Just relax; it'll all work out

eventually. I figured it up once, and two-thirds of my job is just sitting and waiting. You get used to it."

Bragg knew about waiting. He had done a lot of waiting when he was in basic training, and he never had gotten used to it. "I need to stretch my legs," he told the FBI agent. "If anything happens while I'm gone, don't wait for me." The agent had no problem with that. Waiting alone in the car was boring, but waiting with an impatient fidget in the car was actively stressful. He got enough stress during the part of his job that didn't involve waiting.

Walking the sidewalks of New York requires a degree of common sense. Gawking at the tall buildings, for example, is a mistake. Half the people on the sidewalk are in their own private ear-bud-isolated world. They instinctively match the walking speed of the people around them, but they won't see some Kansan who stops dead in his tracks to gawk at the Chrysler Building. They won't apologize when they run over the Kansan, either.

Avoiding eye contact at intersections is another important coping skill. If a pedestrian in a crosswalk makes eye contact with a driver, the driver has won. He knows he can come right on through, and that the walker will jump out of the way. But if the driver can't be sure the walker sees him, he will usually hesitate, and then the pedestrian wins. Either way, of course, somebody gets yelled at.

Avoiding eye contact with the street people is also a good idea. The crazies take it different ways, but none of the ways are good. The non-crazies take it as an opportunity. They are a varied lot. Some of them are homeless, some of them aren't; all of them claim to be. Some really are injured veterans, but some of the amputees are dopers who stuck the wrong thing in the wrong place. Regardless, each of them has a pitiful story, and if a pedestrian slips up and makes eye contact, he gets to hear it. The details of the stories differ, but all of them end the same way: "So, can you help me out?"

Bragg made his way toward the block Traxell stood on, hearing the listless chants of "Spare change? Spare change?" and the more ambitious "Psst, hey mister!" One or two barked out, "Hey, look at me, why don't you look at me!" It must work occasionally, he thought, or they'd try something else. Just as he rounded the last corner, one of them did try something else. A raspy voice floated up from a pile of clothes slumped against a building. "Hey, you, Mr. Bigshot. Yeah, you. C'mon, peel off a buck for your fellow man. I know you've got it." Bragg ignored the man, as he had all the others, but this one didn't give up. "I got this way serving my country," he said loudly as Bragg passed him, and when that didn't get a response, he added, "Cheap son of a bitch."

The rule is, if you look, you have to listen to the story. The exception to the rule is, if they cross the line, the look is free. The SOB crack crossed the line, so Bragg gave him a hard, disapproving stare. A filthy and, to judge by appearances, smelly McIntyre stared back at him. "Where's your chaperone?" Bragg asked in a low voice.

McIntyre tilted his head sideways. "He used to be right over there," he said without moving his lips. "He's gone to take a leak."

Bragg turned and watched traffic, or seemed to. "He's never heard of adult diapers?"

"Apparently not, and I'm not going to tell him. He might ask how I know."

"Anything going on over there?" Bragg made it a point not to look at the Traxell Building.

"Doesn't look like it. Mostly...no, wait; that's new."

With an effort, Bragg resisted the urge to look across the street. "Describe."

"Bunch of people being hustled out the door, and a guard locking it behind them."

"Oh hell, they know." Bragg sprinted across the street. Through the lobby's high windows, he saw a line of guards with their backs to the door. Facing the guards was a small group of people, one of whom saw Bragg and waved frantically at him. It was Singh, and when he saw he had Bragg's attention, he went from waving his arms to clasping his hands together in a pleading gesture. Silently he mouthed one word, over and over: *Please.*

"O'Malley, we got a problem. Or maybe I should say, you got a problem. Your report looks like some pothead wrote it. Why don't you just tell me what happened."

"Yeah, sure Sarge. Where you want me to start?"

"Start with you in your patrol car."

"Okay, well I'm driving down the street, keeping an eye on things, see? And the light turns red a couple of cars in front of me so I'm just sitting there, you know, waiting for the light to change, when all of a sudden this bum comes up and busts out my car window with his elbow."

"A bum. Can you describe the bum?"

"He was a bum, what else can I say? Clothes all ragged and dirty, hair kind of greasy. He looked like they all look."

"Uh-huh. So you exited the vehicle."

"Well, yeah."

"Tell me why."

"Whadda you mean why? Why do you think!"

"You don't want to know what I think. You said you exited the vehicle, and your report doesn't say why. So tell me."

"So I could arrest the bum who broke my window, that's why."

"Okay, I'll write that in. Did you arrest him?"

"He got away."

"That's it? 'He got away'? That's what you want the report to say? How did he get away? Did he run?"

"Not then. First he, uh, he resisted."

"He resisted. You mean he fought you? What did he do?"

"Okay, now right at first he didn't do nothing; he just stood there. Then when I got my piece about halfway out its holster, he sort of reached out and took it away from me."

"You're not going to believe this, but you left that out of

your report too. Tell me how a bum disarms a New York cop."

"Hey, it's not like I'm proud of it, you know? All I can tell you is, he was quick, and it happened real fast. His hand just kind of snaked out and gets my piece, then he tosses it down a storm drain, sticks his tongue out at me, and runs away. Well I ain't letting that happen, so I take off after him."

"Leaving your cruiser there in the street."

"Hey, it was just gonna be for a second, okay? I mean, how fast can a bum run? How am I supposed to know some suit is gonna get in my car?"

"Uh-huh. And what happened next?"

"Well naturally I leave off chasing the bum, and yell at the suit to get the hell out of my car, only he don't pay no attention. He jerks the wheel around, and then guns it hard until it's sideways in the street. Then he aims it straight at that big building on the corner, the one where, you know... Anyway, he bumps the doors, but they must have been locked or something, cause they don't open. So he backs off and this time he rams them real good, and then he just drives on in, like it's a car wash."

"And all this time you're doing what?"

"Hey, we're only talking a couple of seconds here. I run into the building, figuring to put the arm on the guy."

"Did you see him?"

"Yeah, him and a bunch of others. I mean, the place was a madhouse. There were alarms going off and lights flashing, there were guards running everywhere, and people standing around, and other people running out of the fire stairs, and all of them were yelling and screaming."

"How about the guy in the suit; did you see him?"

"Just for a second. He'd gotten out of the car and was standing over by the door. He looked right at me, and then he made a funny kind of gesture."

"A gesture. You mean like he gave you the finger, or what?"

"No, it was like a salute, but with three fingers. By then, everybody was getting the hell out, and he just sort of flowed out with them. I chased after him, but I only got a little way up the block before...well you know what happened next."

"Yeah. I know what happened next."

Nate hadn't quite made it to the fire stairs when he had a better idea. Instead of going down, he could go up, to his rooftop putting green. The air on the roof was clean and pure, and whatever happened inside wasn't going to affect him. He pulled out his phone and called his travel agent. "I need an air taxi sent to the Traxell Building. Yes, immediately. No, a small one will do." Then he tapped in a different number. While I'm waiting, he thought, I might as well be helpful.

In the sub-basement of the Traxell Building, a telephone rang. The telephone sat on the desk of the head of Maintenance. Like IT, Maintenance had no seat on the executive board. The board handled matters of great importance; Maintenance only handled window washing, plumbing, housekeeping, heating, cooling, and whatever else needed doing.

Maintenance got a lot of memos from the executive floors, but not many calls. What few they did get were usually complaints, or demands that somebody be sent, right now, to fix a dripping faucet or wash a smudge off an Important Person's window. The man on duty took his time answering, figuring it was one of those. It wasn't. "They've got a gas leak on twelve," the phone said. "Cut it off at the main valve. ASAP!" The caller didn't bother to say, "This is Nathan Huntsinger." Employees shouldn't have to be told who he was; they were simply supposed to know.

God-damned stuff-shirted know-it-alls, the man thought. Whatever it was, they always wanted it ASAP. He ambled casually over to the big main gas valve and gave the wheel a turn, then another, and gradually the hiss of gas in the pipe faded to silence. Back in his office, he wondered what they would want next, and he didn't have to wait long to find out. This time Mr. Guess-Who-I-Am didn't sound as urgent, but he was just as peremptory. "Is the gas off? All right, now shut off the electricity. The gas got into the air system, and the blowers are spreading it everywhere."

"Uh, you do know that..." the man began.

"I know what I want done," the voice interrupted, "and that is all either of us needs to know. Now do as I told you, and cut off the power."

"Yes sir," the man said, "I will get right on that." Idiot, he muttered as he trudged back down the hall toward the main switch. He had tried to tell him: You don't have to cut off everything in the building just to cut off the blowers; there are separate breakers for the blowers. But no, he says. Do as I told you. Idiot.

He opened the cover on the main switch and pulled the big lever from ON to OFF. In the now-empty lobby, the lights went out, all except the flashing, emergency-warning lights. They, like the alarms that kept on hooting, were powered by the banks of batteries on twelve. The backup system wasn't there just to power the alarms, of course. It was there so that Big Mama would never go down. The batteries couldn't carry Big Mama indefinitely, but they didn't have to; that was what the generators were for. Of course, the generators ran on natural gas, the same gas that had now been cut off, so they weren't going to start, no matter how long the batteries cranked them. But batteries are nothing if not persistent; they would keep trying, over and over, until they went dead or the world ended, whichever came first.

◇◇◇◇◇◇◇◇◇◇◇◇◇◇◇●◇◇◇◇◇◇◇◇◇◇◇◇◇◇◇

Natural gas is a wonderful fuel. Clean, cheap, easy to transport, it has only two real drawbacks. One is its smell. Out of the ground, natural gas has no smell, so the gas companies add an odorant to it. The other drawback of gas is the reason they add the smell: to warn people. If enough gas gets into the air—enough being about over one part in eighteen—the mixture goes from being a fuel to being an explosive. By the time the man in the basement turned off the gas, there was already enough.

Gas won't explode just because it can; it needs a spark. The spark in this case may have come from the relays in the battery room, slamming open and shut as they tried, over and over, to get the generators started, or it could have come from something else entirely. Whatever it was, and wherever it was, the gas found it.

◊◊◊◊◊◊◊◊◊◊◊◊◊◊◊◊●◊◊◊◊◊◊◊◊◊◊◊◊◊◊◊◊

"There's a car in the lobby," McIntyre's chaperone radioed in. "People running out. Don't know why." He was going to ask if he should go check when the top half of the Traxell Building erupted in a huge fireball.

The voice in his earpiece asked, "Pearson? Are you there? What just happened?"

Pearson stared openmouthed several seconds before he answered. "I don't think we're going to need that search warrant anymore."

◊◊◊◊◊◊◊◊◊◊◊◊◊◊◊◊●◊◊◊◊◊◊◊◊◊◊◊◊◊◊◊◊

Nate was about to call the travel agent again. Traxell was a good client, and he expected better service than this. Then the pressure wave from below reached the underside of the sod roof, lifting it and him into the air. He floated weightlessly, but the street beneath him was rapidly getting larger. In some corner of his mind it occurred to him that he was having a falling dream. When he was younger, falling dreams had scared him, but now he almost enjoyed them. It would be interesting, he thought, to see how this one ended.

◊◊◊◊◊◊◊◊◊◊◊◊◊◊◊◊●◊◊◊◊◊◊◊◊◊◊◊◊◊◊◊◊

The woman had worked for the phone company a long time ago. She was dead now, but her voice—recorded in 1976—hadn't aged a day. "We're sorry," she said placidly, "your call did not go through. Would you please try your call again." This was the third time Tom Harper had tried his call again, and the fourth time the woman had said she was sorry. Whatever else dead people are, they are patient.

The living are not as patient. "Can it, bitch," Harper told the recording. This was starting to piss him off. Two calls to Stasevik had both gone to voicemail, and Traxell's main number was out of service. Not getting Stasevik didn't surprise him; cell coverage in New York is a lot spottier than any of the companies like to admit. But he had a good signal at his end, and Traxell was on a land line, so bad coverage didn't explain that. Somebody had probably dug a hole and cut a cable. That meant a couple of hours' wait, at least.

Tom Harper had one thing in common with Steve Bragg: he hated to be kept waiting; it was almost a personal insult. Not that he was calling about anything important; he just needed to know what to do with all those files Stasevik had had him cart out of the building. He wondered if Stasevik would care if he took a look through the files. Probably not, and it would give him something to do while he waited for this phone mess to clear up. He pulled out the bottom file, and saw a familiar name on the tab: CLEVIS. Well now; this might not be so boring after all.

Chapter Forty-Two

The flight from LaGuardia to Atlanta was either un-eventful or boring, depending on whether Emmett or Tori was describing it. Changing planes at Atlanta went smoothly enough, as far as the passengers were concerned, although there had been a minor problem in the baggage area. The routing tag on a crate had somehow gotten mangled. Its bar code was an indecipherable mess, and only two letters of its airport code had survived. Originally, the tag had said GSO, the code for Piedmont Triad airport at Greensboro. Now, it just said GS. The baggage guys looked around, and the only bags they saw with GS-anything tags were for GSP, so they sent the crate there. Problem solved, probably. And if not, it was Greenville-Spartanburg's problem now.

When the plane landed at Greenville, Emmett, Tori, and the dozen or so others on the connector flight from Atlanta did what passengers always do, despite knowing how futile it is: they hurried to the baggage carousel. Once there, they stood and waited. After quite a while, a man came out of an Employees Only door. He set a crate down beside the carousel, went back where he had come from, and the passengers resumed their vigil. Finally, a bag tumbled out of the inner sanctum, to be snatched off the conveyor by its owner, then one by one, bags plain and fancy appeared, until only Emmett was left bagless. The airport man who had brought out the crate now appeared again, hugging a suitcase. Looking at Emmett, he said, "You belong to this antique?"

Emmett tried to look offended, but Tori had already commented on his suitcase at some length, and antique was almost a compliment compared to what she had called it. "Yes," he said with exaggerated dignity. "It's mine. Is there a problem?"

The man shrugged. "Yeah there is, but now it's your

problem. The handle broke off." He looked at the crate he had left earlier. "That yours too?" It was a natural question; they were the only ones left.

Tori had wondered about the crate, and while Emmett told the man that it wasn't his, she walked over and took a look at it. "M'rrau?" said the crate, sounding at the same time unhappy and hopeful. Stickers on the crate explained: LIVE ANIMAL, they said in inch-tall letters. Tori couldn't see well enough through the air holes to tell what kind of animal, but when she squatted down beside the crate, a long furry white leg came emerged with a cat's paw at the end of it. "M'rrau?" it said again.

"Poor lonely thing," Tori said, and stroked the paw. Her reward was a loud purr from the crate. To the baggage man she said, "If nobody claims it tonight, what happens to it?"

"We'll put it with all the other unclaimed luggage," he said. "Somebody'll call animal control on Monday, I guess. You sure it's not yours?"

The way he said it, she knew that if she said yes, he wasn't going to ask for proof. She stroked the paw again. There would be papers in the crate, she thought, with the owner's name and address, maybe a telephone number. As if sensing opportunity, the cat in the crate gave out a very loud purr, and that tipped the scale. "Maybe it is," she told the man.

"Good. Take it."

The man was back through his door before Emmett could do more than open his mouth, but when they were alone by the carousel, he said casually. "I didn't remember that you had a cat. Is it a he cat, or a she cat?"

"I don't know, but it's pitiful and it needs me," she said. "And I think it likes me. Never mind why, but I need a cat that likes me, and Hurl doesn't." She had dropped Spanish in high school because she couldn't roll her r's, and she still couldn't. She called the orange cat Hurl because she couldn't say Hrrlle the way Dee and Bart did. She thought was close enough, but whenever she said it, the cat turned his back and flicked his tail.

Emmett nodded thoughtfully, but he had long ago learned

not to say everything he thought. "Well, all right then. Let me go get the car." He found a cart for his handle-less suitcase, then headed for the exit. "I'll meet you and your, ah, new friend at the curb."

The first thing Tori did when she got in the car was to call Dee. "We're back! It's over!"

"I would say so," Dee replied in an odd tone of voice.

"I can't wait to see what happens now. Has anything happened while I was gone?"

Dee thought her roommate might be joking, but finally she said, "You really don't know? It's been all over the news!"

"Oh, I don't pay any attention to the news; just tell me." Her phone gave a little beep. "Oh darn, it'll have to wait. I played games on my phone all the way from New York, and it's about to die."

"Okay, I'll tell you later. Maintenance said we could go back to the dorm, so that's where I am now. And..." She realized she was talking to herself; the call had gotten dropped. Jamaal brought in another armload of pillows. "Over there, for now," she told him, ignoring his rolled eyes. "I'll arrange them later."

The drive from GSP to Clemson takes about 45 minutes. Tori spent the first half hour of it in silence, but as they were passing Easley, she spoke up. "Uh, Mr. Schroder? I wonder if you could do me a really, really big favor."

"Well certainly, if it's something I can do."

"Dee—my roommate—told me we're back in our dorm room. And that means...I mean, we can't..." She wondered if pitifulness would work on Emmett, and decided on truth instead. "They don't allow cats in the dorm. Would you mind taking care of this one, just until we can find its owner? I'll pay for its food and everything, if you'll just...I know you're already taking care of Hurl, but if you could just..."

He let her go on for a minute or so more, but he had already decided he would do it. Emmett considered himself a connoisseur of good arguments, and while hers lacked polish, she at least hadn't gotten all weepy on him. He saw enough crying in court, most of it manufactured, that tears didn't impress him. Sincere distress, on the other hand, appealed to his sense of chivalry, and Tori did seem to be sincerely distressed. He just hoped the orange cat wouldn't react badly to a competitor.

◇◇◇◇◇◇◇◇◇◇◇◇◇◇◇◇●◇◇◇◇◇◇◇◇◇◇◇◇◇◇◇◇

"Good morning," Evelyn told Emmett when he came in the next morning. Then, still without looking up, she added, "And just what have you got there?"

Emmett had taken the cat home with him after dropping Tori off. Being around the orange cat had taught him something about cats. When it came time to get the white cat back into its crate, a little canned tuna had done the trick. "It's a crate."

She gave him a critical look over the top of her glasses. "I can see that. I can also see something inside it, and I'm guessing it's an animal. You want to explain now, or after coffee?"

"It's a cat, but it's not mine. It lost its routing tag and got abandoned at the airport, and Tori temporarily adopted it. She couldn't take it to the dorm, so I agreed to keep it. Just until we find its owner, of course."

"Of course." She peered at the carrier. "So what is it, male or female?"

"I don't know. Aren't most cats female?"

"Did you even take biology? Let me see that cat." He set the crate down and released its latch. One long silky white leg stretched out of the opening, followed by another, and then a head. Evelyn reached out to pet it, but she was too slow. The cat stepped forward and ground its head against her hand, then looked up to see who whose hand it was using. One of its eyes was sky blue, the other was sea green. "Well," Evelyn said as she scratched the cat's ears. "Aren't you special! Whose cat are you, anyway?" She asked Emmett if he had checked the carrier for papers, but he hadn't, which didn't surprise her. She looked in the carrier and found the shredded remains of the luggage routing tag, and what might have been the thoroughly-chewed remains of an address label. "You did that," she told the cat. "You're another tomcat, aren't you! A lady cat would be better behaved." Emmett objected, and a quick look under the tail sustained his objection. "Well then, that was very unladylike of you," Evelyn told the cat. She went to work, piecing together the shreds of the tag. When she was finished, she looked up the number for Piedmont Triad and called the service desk there. Was anybody looking for a cat that hadn't arrived?

The woman at the desk didn't know anything about a missing cat, but she took Evelyn's number and promised to pass it along if anyone asked. "I wouldn't count on it, though," the woman said. "Usually we would have heard something by now."

While Evelyn was on the phone, the cat explored the waiting room. She checked out the chair cushions, sniffed the door jamb, then went down the hall toward Emmett's office. Almost immediately there was the sound of a cat fight: hissing, spitting, loud yowling; but when Evelyn tiptoed down the hall, she found Emmett at his desk making notes in a criminal file, and the two cats, tangled together, each giving the other a tongue bath. Evelyn shook her head. "I don't think I understand cats," she told Emmett, and went back to her desk.

◇◇◇◇◇◇◇◇◇◇◇◇◇◇◇◇●◇◇◇◇◇◇◇◇◇◇◇◇◇◇◇◇◇

"Nisa, I think it's for you."

"What do you mean, you 'think'? Who did the person ask for?"

"I couldn't tell. It's some old guy, and I can't make out what he's saying, so I know it's not for me, and nobody but Freddie ever calls Jordan, so it's not for her. That leaves you."

Nisa took the phone. "Hello? This is Nisa Shahin."

"Nisa!" It was her father's voice. "Happy birthday. How did you like my little surprise?"

"You mean this call? It is a very nice surprise." To her housemates, she mouthed "It's my father."

"No, of course the surprise is not this call. Did no one from the airport call you? I sent you a...a package. Oh this is not good, not good at all." He sounded crushed.

"What have you sent me? Oh you have to tell me. Please?" She had wheedled her father into sending her to college in Greensboro, she had wheedled him into letting her live off-campus; wheedling him into giving up a secret shouldn't be hard at all. She widened her eyes and gave the phone a pleading look, which entertained her housemates but which also, she knew, helped give her voice just the right pitiful note.

It didn't work. "I cannot tell you. If it did not arrive, I must find out why. I will call again when I have straightened this out. Oh, and that girl who answered the phone? Thank her for me, but you might want to speak slowly; she sounds like she might be a little bit simple. Did I tell you happy birthday?"

He hung up and called in his secretary. "Nisa did not get the package I sent. This is a disaster."

His secretary waited for details before she declared an emergency. Mr. Shahin was a good boss, but he tended to be somewhat loose with his use of the word 'disaster'. "What did you send her?"

"Her kitten, Minnosh. It was going to be a surprise."

"Is that legal? I didn't think they could be sent out of the country."

He winced. "I said she was a Persian. Perhaps the customs people found out the truth, and they are holding her in some horrible cell somewhere. Or she could be in a warehouse for unclaimed luggage. If anything happens to that cat, Nisa will die of sorrow. We have to find her."

All right, the secretary thought, this might actually qualify as a disaster. Nisa had practically grown up in the office; everybody there thought of her as family, and yes, the child did love that cat. There were invoices to be entered, and tax reports to be filled out, but they could wait; family came first. She got out a steno pad and made a list of places to call. When the first call yielded nothing, she marked a name off the list and called the second one. By the end of the hour, she had crossed off an entire page of possibilities, but that was all right; she hadn't gotten where she was by giving up easily, and she had a lot more steno pads if she needed them.

Chapter Forty-Three

Tom Harper had introduced himself to Evelyn as Mr. Thomas, which all by itself was enough to get on her bad side. As Evelyn saw it, only a complete ass introduces himself as "Mister." Emmett hadn't heard the introduction, but he noticed that Evelyn seemed a little cool toward the client when she brought him to the back office, and wondered which of her etiquette rules the man had violated. Emmett had his own set of rules, one of which—"Get to the point!"—the man proceeded to ignore for the next fifteen minutes. Mr. Thomas would not have been the first client Emmett had told to get to the point, but this time he resisted the urge. The man reminded him of a poker player, trying to take the measure of a new opponent. That suited Emmett all right; he knew what to show and what to hide. What he showed Mr. Thomas was what he thought Mr. Thomas probably expected to see: a small town nobody, easily impressed by an expensive suit and a smooth line of patter.

As a cadet, Harper had played barracks poker from time to time, but his luck hadn't been any good, or he hadn't been, and he had written the game off as a waste of time. He wasn't so much sizing Emmett up—he already thought of Emmett as a small town nobody—as he was trying to find out what Emmett knew about his former client, the deceased Wade Dawson. Dawson was the key to the amorphous metal puzzle; that much was obvious from Hal Stasevik's files. But Stasevik's plan, to snatch the dead man's lawyer and sweat him for information, had been idiotic. You don't have to kidnap small-town lawyers. All you have to do is pay them. Or say you'll pay them

Eventually, he did get to the point. Dawson was dead, and so he wasn't a client anymore. If Emmett wanted to make a quick five thousand dollars, all he had to do was to turn over any papers the deceased may have left in his keeping, anything that mentioned industrial processes and equipment. Emmett had pretended to think about it, and had then said it didn't sound like something he was interested in doing. Harper nodded. "I understand. I could, perhaps, go higher than five thousand, under the right circumstances." Emmett still wasn't interested, so Harper brought out Plan B: a stack of eight-by-ten glossy photos. Stasevik might have been an idiot, but the list of names his thug had sent in had proved useful. "I believe you know these people?" he had asked. Emmett kept a straight face as he looked at pictures of Arnold, Calvin, Evelyn, and some others, each with a set of drawn-in crosshairs centered on the face.

"Yeah, I know them," Emmett said. "So?"

"So," said Tom Harper, "you either play ball with us, or the crosshairs become real. That's how it is."

So you think we're playing ball, do you, Emmett thought. Well, we're not; we're playing poker, and you just showed me one of your hole cards. "Whatever you paid to find out who my friends are," Emmett said, "you paid too much. I'm a lawyer, Mr. Thomas. A lawyer has clients, a lawyer has colleagues; a lawyer does not have friends. Everybody dies, sooner or later, and those people are no different, so if you kill them before old age does, that's on your head, not mine. But since we're being candid, yeah, I know about Dawson's process, enough to know it's worth more than any five thousand dollars. Now, do you want to talk business, or do you want to play footsie a while longer?" In other words, Emmett thought, I'll see you, and raise you.

Harper had thought he knew how the lawyer would react when the photos came out. Either he would try to tough it out, claiming he didn't know anything, or else he would cave. It hadn't occurred to him that there might be a third option, so he stuck to his plan. "You think I'm joking?" he said, pointing to his stack of pictures. "You think we won't do it?"

Emmett showed him a serene smile. It was the same smile he used in court when he told a jury how thin of a case the DA had. "You might do it, you might not," he said. "I don't know, and frankly, I don't care."

Harper leaned forward. "How about if we put you in the crosshairs? Would you care then?"

So I'm your other hole card, Emmett thought; you don't

know about the kids. He leaned back in his chair. "Me? Yeah, I'd care, but you're not going to do it. A while back, I had some break-ins here at the office. Maybe you already know that? Yeah, I see you do. So anyway, I had some cameras put in. If anything happens to me, the cops may not know your real name, but they'll sure as hell know what you look like. Now do you want to do business or not?"

Eventually, they settled on a price. Emmett would give Harper the secret of making amorphous metal, and Harper would give Emmett a million dollars in gold. Harper didn't actually have a million dollars, in gold or anything else. Hal had talked a lot about salary and bonuses, but Hal was gone, and the people in Brussels had no record of any agreement, or they said they didn't, so Harper's plan was that, after Emmett had given him the process and he had made sure it worked, he would dispose of Emmett, then find where the security cameras sent their photos. If he couldn't find them, he would move to some country that doesn't extradite rich people and then put the secret up for bids.

Emmett didn't know Harper's plan in detail, but he didn't seriously expect to get paid. In the gothic language of contract law, the situation presented the issue known as the meeting of the minds, which has to exist for there to be a valid contract. The final exam in a Contracts class might put the problem this way:

A. If the parties agreed on the terms of an agreement, but one of them intends at the outset to violate the terms, was there a meeting of the minds?

B. Assume that, at the outset, the second party knew that the first party intended to violate the agreement, but agreed anyway. Would your answer to question A be the same?

C. Assume that, at the outset, both parties intended to breach the agreement, but only one of them knew of the other's said intent. Would your answers to part A and part B be the same?

D. Assume that, for whatever reason, the parties' agreement is not a binding contract. Assume further that the state's gambling statute bans wagers on games of chance, but not on games of skill. Can the agreement be defended, and enforced, as a form of wager?

Emmett had survived three years of exams like that. This, he told himself, was just another final, except that the course wasn't Contracts; it was Survival.

◇◇◇◇◇◇◇◇◇◇◇◇◇◇◇◇◇●◇◇◇◇◇◇◇◇◇◇◇◇◇◇◇◇◇

Years before, Emmett had brought up the idea of a bogus journal. "When would there ever be a need for something like that?" Wade had asked.

"I don't know," was Emmett's reply, "but I do know this: If we ever do need it, there won't be time to write it."

"And, it will say what?"

Emmett grinned. "It'll be kind of like your real journal, just spiced up a little."

"You think I can write something spicy?"

"No, are you kidding? I'll write it. That way it'll have just the flavor I want."

Emmett wrote fast, but it still took better part of two weeks, with constant editorial critiques from Wade, for him to finish it. Then he had to type it, which took another two weeks; Emmett was not a good typist, but he didn't want Evelyn involved in this. Now, after years in a lock box, the manuscript had the authentic yellowed look and musty smell that only time can give. *The Other Science, by Wade Dawson, PhD*, it said on its title page.

It was during the North African campaign that
I found it. Our unit had come under fire from
some Italians. We tried to tough it out, but
they had us outnumbered, so we fell back toward
higher ground. That was when the sandstorm hit
us, the kind of storm that gives you a bad
choice: either face it like a hero, or hide from
it like a rat. You see a lot of rats in the
desert, and not many heroes. I found a pile of
rocks and I hid.

When the storm was over, there was no one
else from of my unit around, but I did have a
companion, of a sort. The storm had uncovered a
man's hand, withered and crisp, sticking out of
a ragged khaki sleeve. An hour of digging
brought up the rest, but there wasn't much
there. I don't know if it was birds or jackals
or what, but my companion had made a meal for
something. Near his skull was a pith helmet, the
old, tall kind that nobody wears anymore. Based
on that, I would guess he had been there for a
long time.

"I'm intrigued," Wade commented when he read that part. "Who is your dried-up guy?"

Emmett shrugged. "I dunno. Explorer, archeologist, adventurer; take your pick. He could be British, or French, or German. This is a lie, after all, and liars get caught if they give too many details. The dead guy is whoever the reader wants to think he is."

I found his other hand not far away, with
something still clutched in it: a brass tube,
the sort of thing you might use to keep the sand
out of a telescope. Now it held a rolled-up
scroll, covered with odd-looking symbols. I
thought the writing was Egyptian, but when I got
it back to the States and had a chance to look
it up, it turned out to be Hittite. I don't know
where the dead man had found it, but I can
speculate. Every soldier I knew took some
souvenir of the war back home with him. Maybe it
was an SS dagger, maybe a helmet with a bullet

hole in it, but they all took some physical
object to remind them that the war had really
happened, that it hadn't been just a fever
dream. I think the scroll was somebody's war
souvenir. Maybe it got put in his tomb, and my
crisp companion had found it. For all I know, my
rockpile could have been that tomb, but I wasn't
about to dig down and find out. There are things
worse than rats that live in rockpiles, and I
didn't like my chances of surviving a snake bite
or a scorpion sting.

I had the scroll framed when I got back home,
and hung it on the wall in my office when I
joined the faculty. That was where, several
years later, one of the history professors
happened to see it. He recognized the writing,
but he couldn't read it. He mentioned it to a
colleague of his who could, which is where the
story really starts. The scroll, I found out,
described a religious rite, a sort of
purification ceremony. The translator asked if
he could publish it in an academic journal,
which I readily agreed he could, but he never
did. He got one of his students pregnant shortly
after that, and hanged himself rather than face
exposure.

One day, on a whim, I tried the first step in
the rite, which was described as cleansing the
mind of what is seen, and seeing instead what is
true. It took a while, but the first time I was
able to break through and do it, I knew I had
something special. I did not realize how
special, but now I do. I am now able to melt
anything made of metal without using heat, and I
can combine incompatible metals which, when
melted in this way, make alloys that are,
according to orthodox metallurgy, impossible.

"You're putting a lot of bait on one hook, don't you
think?" Wade asked."

"I have seen enough men ruined by greed," Emmett
replied, "that I have some idea of its power. I hope I never have to
use this thing, but if I do have to, I don't want it to fail for lack of
bait. I won't be fishing catch-and-release."

```
The scroll included a lot of mumbo-jumbo,
probably invented by the old priests to make
what is really quite a simple procedure seem
mysterious and grand. I have managed, by years
of trial and error, to simplify it down to its
two essential elements: the quantum form that
each metal has, and the unique tone that helps
focus the mind on that form. Visualizing the
form will require some study. I will begin with
iron, the easiest of the metals, but once the
technique is mastered, it will work with any of
them.
```

Wade read it again. "Quantum form? What in the hell is a quantum form?"

Emmett shrugged. "I have no idea. You remember how I said that liars get caught when they give too much detail? Quantum form is an anti-detail. It doesn't really mean anything, so it can mean literally anything."

"I see why you went into law," Wade said.

"I'm sure you mean that the good way."

"I mean that the truth doesn't seem to limit your creativity."

"You know, it sounds bad when you say it like that. Anyway, it isn't really a lie, except the part about the rockpile and the dead guy and the manuscript."

"And the part about working with any metal, and about iron being the easiest."

"Quibbles. The important part, how to do the iron melt, is pure, sweet, truth."

"You left out the part about needing a cat. That makes it a lie."

"No, that's just makes it an incomplete truth. There are any number of truths I might have put in; the thing with the cat is just one of them. Does omitting a detail make a truth into a lie? I would argue that it doesn't."

"I've always wondered: Did they teach you to think like that in law school, or were you born that way?"

"Don't be snide. It's called thinking like a lawyer. I don't think it's teachable, but yes, they do claim to teach it. I think what they really do is weed out the ones who can't do it."

"And so the madness continues. Sometimes I think it would be easier just to destroy the journal—the real one—and then we wouldn't have to worry about any of this."

Emmett shrugged. "I suppose you could do that."

"No, I couldn't. I made a promise to pass it along, and if I can't keep that promise, the journal will keep it for me. But his Rider Haggard journal of yours scares me. I hope we never need to use it."

"So do I, but I'll bet you we do."

"You're on. A dollar?"

"A dollar."

◊◊◊◊◊◊◊◊◊◊◊◊◊◊◊◊●◊◊◊◊◊◊◊◊◊◊◊◊◊◊◊◊

Mr. Thomas, as Harper was still calling himself, glanced down at what Emmett had just handed him, a three-ring binder holding perhaps a half inch of typewritten pages. He riffled through it. No blueprints, no formulas, no equations; just text, and a couple of sketches that looked like modern art. "This is a joke, right?"

Emmett rocked back in his chair. "What did you think it would be, stone tablets? No, wait, I know; you thought I'd hand you the whole thing, didn't you, and then trust you to pay me. I'm not a complete fool, Mr. Thomas."

Harper kept a straight face, but Emmett had pretty much nailed it. His men were waiting outside, ready to come in and clean up as soon as the goods were delivered. Once he had the process, he could let Carlisle Macrotech know that they had a new supplier for that special alloy they needed. And if they didn't want it, the Japanese would, or the Chinese, he really didn't care as long as they had money. "Hmph," he said. "Well, I'm not paying a million dollars for some kid's research paper, I can tell you that right now."

"What you have there," Emmett said, "is a show of good faith. As the table of contents will show you, the book is quite long. This is only the introduction. It gives the key to the process, the method, as Dr. Dawson called it, and the particulars for applying it to iron, the easiest metal. Take it with you, study it, try it out, and you'll know if it's what I claim it is. Then, once you know it's the real deal, come back with the money. I'll give you the rest of the manuscript, and we can do the exchange. Somewhere in public, I think. Like I said, I'm no fool."

That was twice Emmett had said he wasn't a fool. Twice ought to be enough, he thought. In Emmett's experience, people who insist too often that they aren't this or aren't that, usually are this or that, and he thought Mr. Thomas probably knew that too, at some level. He hoped so, anyway. Emmett had won a lot of cases against big-city lawyers by letting them to think he had just rolled off of the turnip truck.

"No, I know you're no fool," Harper said, "and I hope you know I don't plan to cheat you. If this is what you say it is, you don't need to worry about your money. You have my word on that." And that word, he thought, is 'sucker'.

After the man left, Evelyn came back to Emmett's office. "I don't think I like him," she said. "There's something creepy about him."

"Yeah, I agree," Emmett said. "Well, maybe we've seen the last of him. Oh, and while I'm thinking about it, isn't there still some money in the Dawson estate account?"

"Yeah, not much."

"Time to close it out, I guess, but before you do, cut me a check for one dollar. Make it to me personally, not to me as executor. Call it a gambling debt. He lost."

"Wade, or the man who just left?"

Emmett thought about that. "Both," he replied. "Yeah, I would have to say both."

Chapter Forty-Four

When Evelyn opened up the office there was a message on the answering machine from six o'clock the previous evening. Calls at dinner were usually a recorded message from a politician, alerting everyone to the other party's latest outrage, but this one wasn't. When Evelyn hit Play, a woman's voice said, "Hello. My name is Tara Mirza. I am trying to reach Evelyn Peetmon. If you are she, could you please call me back? This is about a lost cat."

Evelyn looked over at the white cat, which was taking its ease in a window sill. "I think your people have found you," she told the cat, which gave her a look that seemed to say, So? "I hope they're willing to drive here, because you're not getting on another airplane."

The cat was technically Tori's, and Tori did come and visit with it. The first time that Dee came with her, she had stared at the cat, open-mouthed. "The crate said she was a Persian?" she asked. "I don't think she is. I think she's an Angora. White Angoras are special; I have never seen one outside of Turkey." She petted the cat, which pretended not to notice until she stopped. Then it reached out, snagged her hand, and dragged it back for more.

"I don't know about special," Evelyn had said, "but I will have to admit, she is a good cat. She comes when I call, which is more than he does." She gestured to the back office, possibly meaning the orange cat. "I'm almost hoping her people don't find her."

Well, now they had. She dialed the number the woman had left, and someone answered, "Efendim."

Evelyn assumed that meant Hello. "Uh, yes, may I speak with Tara Mirza? My name is Evelyn..."

"You are Evelyn Peetmon!" the voice interrupted. "Oh thank you, thank you for calling back! I will be very fast, as I know this is a long call. I seek a white cat which was misdirected by an airline. Can you help me? It is very important!"

Evelyn looked over at the cat, which was apparently asleep.

"Does it have different color eyes?" she asked. There was another explosion of excitement from the phone, which Evelyn took as a 'yes'. She held the phone away from her face and made a tch-tch sound at the cat, which jumped to the floor, then up onto Evelyn's desk. To the phone, Evelyn said, "You want to speak to her? Here she is." She held the phone near the cat's ear.

"Minnosh," the phone said, followed by a flood of words with a lot of consonants and, it seemed to Evelyn, not nearly enough vowels.

The cat listened for a few seconds, said something like "Mawauii?" then jumped to the floor and headed for Emmett's office. "I don't know all that much about cats," Evelyn said into the phone, "but I think you just got dissed."

"I am sorry; dist? I have studied business English, but I do not know dist."

"It's short for disrespected," Evelyn explained. "The cat heard what you had to say, but she didn't seem to impressed by it."

"She is like that. Minnosh is a very...how should I say it? She sometimes has...opinions? Or perhaps it is attitudes. Which-ever it is, she is not easily persuaded to change them."

Evelyn understood. "I work for a man who is a lot like that. Probably that's why he and the cat—Minnosh, did you say?—get along so well. She'll curl up in his office and just watch him, for hours. Then he'll scratch her behind the ears and tell her what a pretty cat she is. He doesn't think I hear him."

"My employer does the same thing. He loves that cat, but not as much as his daughter does. We have not told Nisa—that is Mr. Shahin's daughter—that Minnosh was lost; it would have decimated—no, devastated—it would have devastated her. Why her father put the cat on an airplane is past me, but he did, and now Minnosh is not where she should be. May I tell Nisa she can come for her?"

"Of course," Evelyn said. Much as she liked the white cat, she didn't want to deprive a girl of her pet. "I can meet her here any time she can make it. Where would she be driving from?"

"She matriculates at Greensboro, in Northern Carolina. Is that very near to you?"

"Depends on what you mean by near." Evelyn tapped a few computer keys. "The trip here takes a little over four hours, if you don't stop along the way."

"Knowing Nisa, she will not stop. I will have her call you."

"But what if she's a really bad person?" Tori wailed to Dee. Evelyn had called to tell her the white cat's owner was coming for her on Saturday. "We have to be there. If she's awful, well, she just can't have Miss Kitty, that's all there is to it."

"What do you think we can we do?" Dee asked.

"I don't know. We'll think of something. And you two," she told Bart and Jamaal, who has just come in, "are coming with us. We may need backup."

"Yes ma'am," they said together. When Tori used that tone of voice, they had learned not to stand in the way. Bart risked a question: "When?"

"Saturday morning, bright and early."

"Okay. I need to check out the cabin anyway. Mr. Schroder says they've finished the repairs. Anybody up for a weekend?" He had worried that the business with Murad and the man with the gun might have soured the girls on the cabin. As it turned out, he needn't have worried. Dee summed it up this way: Bad things happened at the cabin, but also good things, and if bad things could put a place off limits, where on the face of the earth could anyone go?

Nisa had told Evelyn she would be leaving Greensboro at six in the morning. That should have gotten her to Emmett's office around ten or ten thirty, but when Evelyn went in at nine, there were two girls sitting on the front steps. Evelyn didn't have to ask how they had done it; the vanity plate on the red Miata in the parking lot was all the explanation she needed: UR 2 SLO . The shorter of the two girls stood up. "Mrs. Pitman? I am Nisa Shahin." She looked at the other girl. "This is Shelby." Shelby was bobbing her head, listening to music on some little in-the-ear headphones, and added a head-bod in Evelyn's direction. "Shelby is one of my housemates," Nisa explained. "She agreed to come with me if we came in her car."

"She drives too fast," Evelyn said, then realized how old it made her sound.

Nisa nodded. "I agree. It is clearly not my day to die, because the last three hours have been one continuous opportunity to do so. But please, may I see Minnosh? Except for fiery death I have thought of little else since we left Greensboro."

Evelyn had barely put the key in the door when Jamaal pulled the Jeep into the lot and parked it by the Miata. Shelby gave the Jeep a disapproving look, as though it was a mutt that might try to breed with her show dog, but all she said out loud was, "Eww." Then she sank back into whatever tune she was listening to.

The girls wanted to get there before the cat-stealer did, and that meant Jamaal had to drive. The front seat was the only place with enough knee room for Tori, so Bart and Dee rode in back and held on for dear life. As she got out, Tori heard Shelby's comment, and right then she made a decision. If this head-bobbing snob was the cat-taker, there wouldn't be any white cats leaving Larson today.

Either because Evelyn sensed the looming storm, or from simple good manners, she broke the silence with an introduction. "Nisa Shahin, meet Tori Lasker. Tori was the one who got the cat from the airport."

Nisa's face lit up with a smile, and before Tori knew what was happening the shorter girl had run over and wrapped her in a tight hug, which ended with a pecked kiss on the cheek. "Oh thank-you thank-you thank-you; you have saved my little Minnosh

from starving in some dark warehouse! You are surely an angel!"
Then she buried her face in Tori's chest and cried.

By the time Nisa let Tori go, Evelyn had already gone into
the office, so Tori took a stab at introductions. "Uh, this is my
roommate Dee, and these are my friends Bart and Jamaal."

Nisa's name had sounded perfectly normal to Dee. It was
only when the girl called the cat Minnosh that her ears pricked up.
She asked a question in Turkish, Nisa replied in the same
language, and the hugging and crying began all over again, except
this time there were two of them doing it.

Bart and Jamaal went inside, partly for lack of anything
useful to do outside and partly so they wouldn't be sucked into the
hug whirlpool. Bart went up the hall to visit Hrrlle, and found
both cats curled up together, asleep in the basket. He tiptoed back
to the waiting room where the others had finally assembled, all
except Shelby who was still in her own world out on the steps.
"Shh," he whispered. "You have to see this."

Nisa bent over the cats and whispered, "Minnosh, wake
up." The white cat raised its head, opened one eye—the green one—
tucked its head back into the crook of the orange cat's leg, and
apparently went back to sleep. "Minnosh!" Nisa didn't whisper
this time, and added something in Turkish that made Bart blush
and Dee giggle. The cat stood up and stretched, taking her time,
then jumped out of the basket and rubbed against Nisa's ankles.
Nisa scooped up the cat and hugged it, whispering to it for a full
minute. Even discounting the fact that she was obviously a hugger,
the girl clearly loved the white cat.

Since Emmett's office only had two chairs, and since Nisa
wasn't quite ready for another three-hour terror ride with Shelby,
they all went back to the waiting room and made themselves
comfortable. Tori told how she came to have the cat, Evelyn
explained about the shredded baggage label, and Nisa and Dee
talked about learning American customs.

Once it was clear to Bart and Jamaal that they weren't
going to be the muscle for some dubious scheme, they wandered
back outside to entertain Shelby. They didn't know that's what

they were doing, but when she found out they weren't in a fraternity, they became just a jock and a nerd, and entertainment value was all the value they had. Jamaal realized as much when she said the Clemson Tigers should really be the Clemson Clems, and have some toothless hick as their mascot. Bart thought it might be a good time to change the subject. "Sweet car," he said, glancing over at the Miata.

"Oh, that thing," she said dismissively. "Daddy got it for me, for my eighteenth birthday. I asked for a Porsche Boxter, but he said a Boxter was too fast, that I'd get too many tickets. As if I couldn't talk my way out of a ticket." She batted her eyes. "Ninety-five? I was going that fast? Really, officer, I had no idea."

Somewhere on Jamaal's mental control panel, the smart-ass light came on. "No danger of that in the Miata," he said. "Don't get me wrong, they're great little cars, just kind of, you know, underpowered." Bart wasn't sure where his roommate was going with that, but if Smart-Ass Jamaal wanted to take the wheel, that was fine with him. He had about had it with Shelby.

"Underpowered?" she said. "Maybe, compared to a Boxter, but she's faster than anything I've seen around here." She looked over at the Jeep. "Don't you agree?"

"I imagine it's better in the curves," Jamaal said offhandedly, "but in the straightaways, you just can't beat four-wheel drive." Shelby rolled her eyes and put her ear buds back in. Jamaal didn't care. He had planted the seed. Now it needed time to grow.

The boys went back inside, and whatever conversation the girls had been having, stopped. "Are we interrupting something?" Bart asked. Tori and Nisa both shook their heads no, but Dee murmured something about going to the ladies' room, and hurried down the hall. Nisa leaned toward Tori. "Is your friend seeing anyone?" she asked in a whisper. Bart was about to ask which friend she meant when Tori shooed him and Jamaal back outside.

"You mean Dee?" she asked back.

"Yes. Is she...involved...with anyone right now? You know, dating?"

"No. She's Muslim, you know—yeah, I guess you would—and there aren't many guys here that she can date. One of the Saudis asked her out, but he tried to get her drunk and when she wouldn't go along, he told her she could walk home. She did, too."

"He was a Believer?"

"Yeah, but he told her the rule about drinking doesn't apply when you're away from home. Anyway, no, Dee isn't dating anybody. She's, ah, straight, though. I mean, if you thought..."

Nisa looked puzzled for a moment. Then she laughed, a silvery, tinkly laugh. "Oh, good heavens no. I am asking for my brother. He is studying business at Emory, and he isn't seeing anyone either. If he is not lonely, he ought to be, so I thought that..." Tori listened to the rest of it, but she knew where it was going, and she was already there. Match-making was her specialty and yet, for her best friend in the world, she hadn't found anyone suitable. And now suddenly, out of the blue, here was a fellow conspirator. She made a suggestion. Nisa liked it, and suggested a modification. By the time Dee got back, they had the plan all mapped out.

"So how come we drove all this way to get some cat, and we don't have the cat?" Shelby asked as they drove through town.

"I would have had to carry the poor thing in my lap, and I realized all the wind and noise would not be good for her," Nisa said innocently. "I am going to have my brother come get her and bring her to me." There was a roaring noise from behind them, and Nisa turned to look. "Isn't that the same car that was at the lawyer's office?" she said.

Shelby looked in the rearview mirror. "I think it is. I wonder..." They were coming up on a straightaway, and sure enough, Jamaal pulled out to pass. "Not gonna happen, Jethro," Shelby muttered. She downshifted a gear and floored it. The Miata surged forward, but the Jeep caught up and was soon beside them.

From the driver's seat, Jamaal waved and grinned. Shelby grinned back. "I've got another gear left," she shouted. "Do you?" Then she sped up again.

In fact, Jamaal did have another gear, but he didn't use it. He watched as the Miata sped off into the distance, then slowed down to the speed limit. In a few minutes, they passed the Miata by the side of the road, with a state trooper standing beside it writing a ticket. "Text Evelyn and tell her thanks," Jamaal told Bart. The trooper was some relative of Evelyn's, maybe a cousin, maybe an in-law, she didn't say, but when Jamaal had asked her where he might find a speed trap, and why he wanted to know, she told him it could be anywhere he wanted it to be, she just had to make a call. About an hour later, when they were back in the dorm, Jamaal got a text. "Tori gave me your number. The drive back is much less scary, now that it is slower. Thank you for that. Nisa Shahin."

◇◇◇◇◇◇◇◇◇◇◇◇◇◇◇◇●◇◇◇◇◇◇◇◇◇◇◇◇◇◇◇◇◇

"Demir? Do you have a minute?"

"For my little sister? Always."

"I need for you to do me a big favor. You remember Minnosh?"

"The kitten? Certainly. What about her?"

"Father sent her to me. Yes, I know he could not, but he did. Or he tried to. Instead of coming to me, she has ended up in some village in the mountains of South Carolina. Tara found her, and I need to go there to get her. I am afraid to do it alone. Can you help me?"

"Help, how?"

"Just be there with me, in case the—what do they call them?—hillbillies try to make trouble. I would feel so much better if my big brother was there. Please?"

"When would it be?"

"Next Saturday. Can you do it then?"

"You may count on me."

"You are the best big brother ever! I am told there is a statue in the town square. I will meet you there, at noon. "

"Does this village have a name?"

"Oh, indeed. They call it Larson."

Chapter Forty-Five

The last time the four of them had ridden through town, they had passed under a banner stretched across the street: FOUNDERS DAY FESTIVAL, it said, and named the next weekend as the date. Tori thought the banner needed an apostrophe. She mentioned it to Evelyn, who said that everyone thought so, but that they couldn't agree where it ought to go. Some said that since the first settler, Ephraim Larson, had arrived alone, the apostrophe should go before the S. Others noted that old Ephraim hadn't been alone for long, as his nine children proved, making Mrs. Larson at least as much of a Founder as Ephraim was, and maybe more; apostrophe after the S, in other words. The committee had pondered the matter, and in the end had decided to please nobody.

Tori didn't take sides in the apostrophe debate, but the idea of the festival made her happy. She took match-making seriously, and like serious practitioners of any art, she had theories about how it should be done. A first meeting, she felt, should always be in public, with lots of people around. That way nobody feels cornered, and the casual atmosphere takes some of the pressure off of making a good first impression. Meeting at some nice restaurant, in her opinion, all but guaranteed trouble. The diners have to choose between serious conversation and meaningless small-talk, both of which are deadly, and they end up, all too often, making a third choice, or really a non-choice: silence. Two people, saying nothing across a white tablecloth, was Tori's definition of a match-making disaster, and the longer the silence, the worse the disaster. Soulful silence—gazing into each other's eyes while savoring the moment—that was fine, but that was for later, after the ice had been broken. So whether it was Founder's Day or Founders' Day, she just hoped the weather would be good, because a big crowd was exactly the background she wanted.

Tom Harper's phone made the little beeping noise that meant he had a text message. "I hope you'll excuse me," he told Evelyn, "I need to see this." She may have thought that was rude, but she didn't say so; the tape across her mouth saw to that.

The text was good news: "I see him. Front of line at sausage tent."

Harper tapped in a reply: "Good work. Bring him here." From the crowd, a man named Carl, part of Harper's old Army acquaintances, started walking casually toward Emmett.

Emmett's attention was on his hoagie, a length of kielbasa smothered in greasy fried peppers and onions. Evelyn would have told him it wasn't healthy, but since Evelyn wasn't around he could enjoy the hoagie in peace. He had just taken his first bite when he felt something poking him in the back. "If you make a sound," a voice said from behind him, "I will stick a knife in your kidney and twist it. I understand that hurts. Just act natural, like you know me, and walk."

"Walk where?" Emmett said after swallowing his mouthful of sandwich.

"To your office. Mr. Thomas would like a word with you."

◇◇◇◇◇◇◇◇◇◇◇◇◇◇◇◇◇●◇◇◇◇◇◇◇◇◇◇◇◇◇◇◇◇◇

Emmett wasn't happy to see the Jeep parked in front of his office, but he wasn't all that surprised, either. He had told the kids they could park there and walk to the festival, since there probably wouldn't be any parking places downtown. The surprise was seeing Evelyn's car there too. She had said she wasn't coming to the festival until later. Maybe, he hoped, she had done like the kids and walked to the square. Maybe, in other words, she would miss out on whatever Mr. Thomas had in mind.

Evelyn was not at the festival. She was in the waiting room, taped to a chair. "She give you any trouble?" Carl asked Harper when he saw the tape over her mouth.

"No, I just got tired of listening to her," Harper told him. "You would have thought I was going to rape her."

Carl gave Evelyn the once-over. "Kind of choosy, aren't you honey? I mean, at your age, how else you gonna get it?" Judging by how hard Evelyn tried to reply to that, the gag had been a good idea.

Harper leaned over and looked her in the eyes. "Your boss," he looked over at Emmett, "has something that I want, and for your sake, you'd better hope he gives it to me. There are worse things than rape." To Carl, he said, "Mr. Schroder and I will be back in his office for a while. See that we're not disturbed."

◇◇◇◇◇◇◇◇◇◇◇◇◇◇◇●◇◇◇◇◇◇◇◇◇◇◇◇◇◇◇

"Look, there she is," Tori said, pointing toward the Confederate statue. She had told Dee that Nisa would be coming back today to get the white cat. She hadn't said anything about a companion. "And it looks like somebody's with her."

"Handsome guy," Dee said. "They...they make a cute couple."

Tori heard the catch in her friend's voice. "Is anything the matter?"

Dee seemed puzzled. "I don't think so, but for just an instant there, I felt a pain, except it wasn't physical, it was more like fear, or regret, or...I don't know what. It was a very strange feeling, and now it's gone."

Tori hoped so. This was no time for problems. "I don't guess we can put it off any longer," she said. "Let's go to Mr. Schroder's office and get it over with." If Dee wanted to think that "it" was the departure of the white cat, that was fine with Tori. According to her flowchart, "it" was the introduction, the focus of all her plans. They would go to the office, Nisa and her brother would join them, Dee would find out that the handsome guy with Nisa was both suitable and available, and then everybody would go to the festival and have fun. It was a good plan, Tori thought, one of her best to date. She had sent Bart and Jamaal on to the office, "to make sure the cat is ready to go," she had told them. Despite that they were about the same age as Dee, the two boys seemed to think of Dee as their little sister, and the last thing Tori wanted right now was a pair of big brothers giving her candidate the third degree.

They were almost at the end of the block when Dee stopped walking. "I need to sit down for a minute," she said. They found a place on the low wall that ran around the courthouse lawn.

"Is something the matter?" Tori asked. "Did you get another one of those pains?"

"Yes. No. I mean no, not again, not now, but yes, once before, and I just realized what caused it that time. It was that girl, Nisa, except she didn't, not really. I mean, it wasn't her fault, either time." Dee was starting to cry. Tori could feel her plan falling apart, but at this point she honestly didn't care. Her friend was hurting, and she could make other plans. She put her arm around Dee's shoulder, and together they sat on the wall.

Abruptly, the crying stopped. "Oh wow," Dee said. "I think I see it. I think it's..."

"See what? What's the matter?"

"Shh, I need to hold onto this for another few..." Dee's voice trailed off, then she turned, wrapped her arms around Tori, and gave her a hug. "There," she said. "I had to get that out of my system or I was going to go crazy." Tori's look said she might have gone a little crazy already, and Dee grinned impishly. "That wasn't from me; that was from Bart. That's what I just figured out." Tori opened her mouth, but nothing came out. "No, really, that's what I saw: he wants to hug you like that, and he can't, and holding it in was starting to hurt too much."

Tori finally managed to speak. "Dilara Ziya, I need for you to start wherever it starts, and then explain what you just said. I really, really need that."

Dee's grin eased into a smile. "I remembered that other time when I felt the pain, and then everything fell into place. It was in Mr. Schroder's office, when you and I and Nisa were talking about boys. She asked if you and Bart were, you know, an item. Do you remember what you told her?"

"I probably said we were just friends. Then Bart came in and we changed the subject."

"Do you remember that I had to leave the room? I went to the bathroom and cried like a baby, and I had no idea why. Now I know. I cried because of you."

"Because of..."

"Because you lied. You should be ashamed of yourself."

"Now wait a minute..."

"No! And Bart would have said the same thing, and it would have been a lie too, the exact same lie. I think I know how you feel about Bart; I *know* how he feels about you. Do you hear me? I know! He loves you. He would walk through fire for you. He wants to hug you so much it hurts, it physically hurts."

"Wait a minute, wait a minute. You know how he feels? How could you? Has he told you...?"

"No, he hasn't told me anything. I don't think he could, but he doesn't have to. You remember that awful day at the cabin, the day my cousin Murad died? How Bart and I got smooshed together, and how after that he could understand Turkish? I admit, I felt a little bit cheated, like I should have gotten something too. Well, I did, but I didn't know it until now. He got my Turkish vocabulary, but I got his emotional one, or at least I got a look at it. I know how things feel to him, if they're things he feels strongly about. When you told Nisa you and he were just friends, it was like a knife went into my heart, because that's how it would have felt to him if he had heard it. Then when I saw, a few minutes ago, what a cute couple Nisa and her boyfriend made, I got a feeling of...something, I don't know. Loneliness, but something else, too, and so strong that it almost made me sick. I think he would give anything to be part of a cute couple with you, but he knows that he can't have it."

"But...but...that's not..."

"But-but-but! I tell you he knows it. He's wrong, but it's still what he knows, that if he tells you how much he loves you, you will laugh at him. And you're no better; you don't tell him the truth either. Do you!"

Tori looked at the ground. "No.

"And why not?"

"Because...I don't know, I guess I don't want to scare him off."

Dee stood up. "Come on. We're going to Mr. Schroder's office. There's a boy there I want you to meet. I think you're going to like him."

◇◇◇◇◇◇◇◇◇◇◇◇◇◇◇◇◇●◇◇◇◇◇◇◇◇◇◇◇◇◇◇◇◇◇

Emmett was not a mind-reader, but it didn't take a psychic to know Mr. Thomas was unhappy. One clue had been the armed escort to the office; another had been seeing Evelyn, taped to her chair in the waiting room. Then there was the little pistol the man kept tucked in his belt. He didn't take it out, but he patted it every now and then, to make sure Emmett knew it was there. Now he held up the book Emmett had given him. "Did you think I wouldn't read this?" he said. "Or did you think I wouldn't know bullshit when I smelled it?"

"Then I take it you didn't bring the money."

Harper slammed the book down on the desk. "A million dollars, for this...this New Age garbage?"

Emmett nodded thoughtfully. "You're an engineer, aren't you." He saw Harper's lips tighten, just a little bit, what poker players call a tell. Yeah, he thought, you're an engineer all right; I wish I'd figured that out earlier.

"No." Harper bit the word off. "I am a scientist."

Okay, Emmett thought, I'll play it that way if you like. "Then as a scientist, you remember that the world cares what you think. You know how electrons are waves if you look for waves, and particles if you look for particles. That's not crystals and pyramids, that's modern physics." He had almost no idea what any of that meant, but it was something Wade had told him once, and it sounded good.

Harper did remember hearing about wave-particle duality in college physics, but it hadn't really registered. His eyes narrowed. "How do you know about that kind of thing?"

Emmett leaned forward. "Because, you idiot, I've read the book, the whole thing, not just the introduction." He paused to let that sink in, then he added, "And unlike you, I've actually tried it. I followed the directions, and it worked. You can call it whatever you want, but if it works, it's worth what I'm charging."

For a few seconds, Harper couldn't think of anything to say. Then, "Does, ah, anyone else know how to do it?"

Emmett had thought that question might come up, and he had thought long and hard about the answer. "Of course not. Why would I give away a million dollar secret?" That would make perfect sense to a greedy man. The fewer the people who knew a secret, the more valuable the secret was. Unfortunately, that axiom has a corollary: A secret reaches its maximum value if only one person knows it. Emmett had thought about that, too.

Harper leaned toward him. "You say you've done it; make me a believer. Do it again, right here, right now."

Emmett had played too much poker to grin, but that was exactly what he had hoped would happen. A demonstration would buy time, maybe a lot of it, since Mr. Thomas would then want the rest of the book, and he would think that only Emmett knew where it was. "You bring any iron with you?"

"I have this." Harper took a pen knife out of his pocket.

Emmett made a little tch-tch noise. The white cat appeared from somewhere and bounded into his lap. "Cats are calming," he explained. "She helps me meditate." He pointed over to the coffee maker. "Heat up your knife and let's do this."

Harper put the knife on the warmer plate of the coffee maker, and after a couple of minutes, he tossed it on the desk in front of Emmett, and took out his phone. "This is the note the book said to use," he said, tapping a button on the phone's screen. The phone began to hum.

Emmett had never done iron, but he knew its matrix. He had looked at it for a long time, the night the cancer had finally taken his wife. He had meant to go in and have done with everything, but in the end he hadn't. Cowardice, maybe, or Hamlet's dilemma: What if you're trapped there forever, with the same black cloud hanging over you? In the end, with the help of some good friends, the black cloud had dissipated, more or less, but he remembered that matrix, oh yes he remembered it. He relaxed, stroked the cat, and entered the void. After years of helping Wade with alloy melts, that part was easy. It was what came next—meeting the ones that Wade called the others—that worried him. Oh well, he thought, it's like anything else: you do your best and you hope it works out.

◇◇◇◇◇◇◇◇◇◇◇◇◇◇◇◇●◇◇◇◇◇◇◇◇◇◇◇◇◇◇◇◇

"I still say she was trying to get rid of us," Jamaal muttered. "My sister used to do the same thing when she had a new boy-friend coming over. 'Go make sure the cat's ready'. That's thin; you know that's thin."

Bart agreed. "It's like she thought we were going to mess everything up and tell Dee it was a set-up. Or give the guy the third degree or something. We wouldn't have done that, would we?"

"No. Well, maybe a little. I mean, would it hurt to know something about him? No, it wouldn't."

Bart nodded. "They're coming here for the cat, so there'll still be time to ask him stuff." He wasn't sure what stuff he wanted to ask, but they would think of something. It wasn't like they were going to trust their Dee with a total stranger.

At Emmett's office, Carl heard the creak of the steps. The blinds were closed and the door was closed, but when he looked at the knob on the deadbolt, he realized he hadn't locked it. In three steps he was beside the door with his back to the wall, his pistol drawn and ready. The door opened. "It's unlocked," Bart was saying to Jamaal as he came in. Only when they were both inside did they see the man beside the door.

"Come in," Carl said very softly. He closed the door behind them, making sure to lock it this time, and gestured toward the couch with his pistol. "Sit still and keep your mouths shut. The boss doesn't want to be disturbed."

Emmett remembered what Bart and Dee had said about the shimmering colors, so that part weren't a surprise. But instead of visible music or flower jewels, what he saw reminded him more of a lava lamp he had in college, except with lots more colors. He had loved that lamp. "Very nice," he thought. "I like it."

"Some do, some do not. Perhaps you can explain why."

The voice wasn't a surprise; the implied question was. He had thought the others understood everything; apparently they didn't. So what was the question, again? Oh yes, why doesn't everyone see the same thing. "I don't know," he thought, "but it might be because we look for patterns, and if there isn't a pattern, we'll generally find one anyway. What pattern we see depends on us, and we're each different. All I know is, I see you my way, and I like what I see."

"But surely you know that we are not what you see. Why would you adopt a perception you know to be imperfect?"

"You don't play poker, do you? No, I guess you don't. Poker is a game, a contest, in which..."

"You need not explain; we saw the rules of the game when you thought of it. How is poker relevant to our question?"

"You have to ask? I thought you could read minds."

"Normally we can, to some extent, but your mind is not organized as others have been. Your friend Wade, for example, had thoughts which closely paralleled his words; your thoughts do not, nor are your thought processes as linear as his were."

"Yeah, he used to bring that up. Anyway, back to poker. In poker, when your turn comes around, you have to act—bet, fold, raise, whatever—even though you can't see all the cards. You try to make a pattern out of what you do see, and you base your play on that. If you can't do that, you shouldn't play poker. I play."

"Thank you. We do not, as you noted, play poker, but we under-

stand about having to act on incomplete information. In a small project which we are conducting in your world, we are necessarily doing exactly that."

"I thought you couldn't act in our world."

"To do so directly involves difficulties, but the guide creatures come to visit us when it suits them, and sometimes they are willing to perform small tasks for us."

"You use cats?" Wow, he thought, now there's a worldwide spy network for you. Then a suspicion hit him. The white cat had shown up exactly when it had to, for him and Tori to take it to Larson. Had that been a coincidence, or was she part of their small project?

Apparently they heard. "Yes, she was, and is, part of our project."

"You had her mess with the luggage tag?"

"We cannot compel, but when we asked, she was willing. Apparently her kind enjoys doing that sort of thing."

Emmett thought of all the drapes and upholstery that the orange cat had so cheerfully shredded. "Yeah, I don't imagine you had to twist her arm. But what sort of project needs a cat from halfway around the world?"

"Your world is perhaps not as large as you think. Hrrlle, the guide who came here with Knirra's far-daughter, was lonely. He is a friend, so we found him a companion."

"That's it? You did all that so a tomcat would have a girlfriend?"

"Is that not a sufficient reason? You assist your friends, do you not? Your presence here, for example; did you come just to visit?"

They had him there. "No, it's more of a gamble. The odds say I'm screwed, but if there's a lay of the cards that has any chance, I have to try it. Let's say I'm going all in on a Hail Mary."

There was a pause. "Could you say that in a different way? It was even less clear than what seems to be, for you, normal."

Emmett sighed. "Damn, I wish we had some cards. You say you know the rules of poker? Okay, now let me tell you how the game really works..."

◇◇◇◇◇◇◇◇◇◇◇◇◇◇◇◇●◇◇◇◇◇◇◇◇◇◇◇◇◇◇◇◇

Carl, Evelyn decided, was not just a thug; he was a slob. He was sitting on the edge of her desk, where he could keep an eye on the boys. There hadn't been room for him to sit on her desk, but that hadn't bothered him; he had simply swept her stack of files onto the floor and shoved everything else to one side. "You might as well relax," he told his prisoners. "This may take a while." He didn't bother to glance back at Evelyn when he said it. She wasn't a potential threat; the two on the couch were.

Bart started to wheeze, and when the man gave him a hard look, he gasped, "Asthma." Bart didn't have asthma, and Jamaal knew it, so something else was going on. He flicked his eyes around the room, spending no more time looking in Evelyn's direction than anywhere else, but it was enough to see what Bart had already seen. The white cat had crept up the hall, and was messing with the tape around Evelyn's ankles. Bart wheezed again, adding a gasp this time. Jamaal reached over and started whacking him on the back. He didn't think whacking would help a real asthma attack, but together with Bart's wheezing, it might help to cover the sound of tape being slit by a cat's claws.

The cat had gotten to Evelyn's left wrist when another noise got the guard's attention: the creaking of the front steps. He pointed his pistol at the boys on the couch, and motioned for them to be quiet. The knob rattled, but the man wasn't worried. The door was locked this time. Everybody relaxed. Then they heard the soft ticketa sound that a key makes, going into a lock, and the knob on the deadbolt started to turn.

"It doesn't look like they're here yet," Dee said as they came up the walkway toward Emmett's office. The blinds were drawn, and when she tried the door, it wouldn't open.

380

Tori reached into a pocket and pulled out a key. "Evelyn said if we got here early, to just come on in."

Carl was back on Evelyn's desk. He had had a problem when he only had two kids; now he had four, all crowded onto the couch. In the long run, it was going to pose a disposal problem, since the major wasn't going to want witnesses. But that was for later. In the short run, the major had said he didn't want to be disturbed, and four gunshots would probably count as a disturbance. Oh well, that could wait, unless somebody tried something. Then he would deal with it, disturbance or not. At least, for now, the skinny kid was over his asthma attack. That had been getting on his nerves.

Behind him, Evelyn was trying to decide what to do now that her wrists were free. She could jump on his back, but she didn't know what good that would do. There was a plaque on the wall, saying what a fine guest speaker Emmett had been at some long-forgotten Rotary Club meeting; maybe she could hit him with that. Was it heavy enough? The ashtray on her desk was heavy enough, but it was going to be a long reach to get to it. Maybe she could stab him with a pencil. That would make her feel better, but he would probably still shoot everybody.

Tori was thinking, too, about what she would do if she was Evelyn. Whatever it was, it probably had to happen soon. What the situation needed, she decided, was a little disorder. "Hey," she said to Carl, "I need to pee."

Anger, despair, pleading: he was prepared for all of that, but not for that simple declarative, and it took him a couple of seconds to digest it. "What? You need to pee? Listen, what you need to do is to not piss me off." That was almost a play on words, he thought: pee, piss; he would have to work on that, so it would sound good when he quoted himself someday.

"No, really, I need to pee real bad." She leaned forward on the couch. "Can I just...?"

"You can stay put," he said, sliding off the desk. "I'm not..."

Probably what he was not, was not kidding, but maybe he was not going to tell her again. Only he knew what he was not about to do, and he never got around to saying it. Evelyn had made her move. The plaque was too light, she had decided, and she didn't trust the pencil to finish the job. In one fluid motion she stood up, leaned across the desk, scooped up the big glass ashtray, and flung it like a Frisbee. The paperclips all slid out, making a rattling noise when they hit her desk. It wasn't a loud noise, but Carl heard it and started to turn toward her. She had intended to hit him in the back of the head, hard enough that his eyeballs would fall out. As it was, the hard-flung ashtray slammed into his left temple. If it hurt, he didn't say. He didn't say anything. The pistol fell to the floor, and he fell on top of it.

Harper stared in disbelief at the lumpy blob that used to be his pen knife. Whatever the lawyer had done, it had worked. This was big. This was more than big. And more to the point, it was all his. Hello, money. Hello, private island. And as soon as he got his hands on those other books, goodbye, lawyer

From up the hall he heard a dull thunk as Carl's gun hit the floor, then a louder one as the ashtray followed it. Probably nothing, he thought, but still, best to be sure. "Carl?" he called out. "Everything all right?" He got no answer. "Carl?" He stood up and drew his pistol. He would have said he chose it—a .32 PPK—because it was concealable. That it was also what the really cool spies used in the movies, hadn't hurt, either.

In the waiting room, no one moved until Carl hit the floor. "There's another one in back," Evelyn whispered. Jamaal nodded understanding. He bent down to roll the man over while Tori reached under him to retrieve the dropped pistol. That was how matters stood when Harper got to the end of the hall.

Harper had not been trained as a line officer, but even

engineering officers have to qualify with the standard Army sidearm, the Beretta M9. Like the PPK, the M9 has a fairly light trigger pull, except for the first shot. The first pull of the trigger is long and stiff, because it has to cock the hammer. A lot of soldiers will say that the first shot is the warning shot, since it may or may not hit the target. Tori, the one nearest Carl's gun, was Harper's target, but the hard trigger pull of the PPK warped his aim to the right, and he missed her.

Jamaal had been bent over, and now he sprang toward Harper, grabbing the man's right wrist with his left hand, and raising it toward the ceiling. "Let the gun go," he told Harper, who tried to twist away. Jamaal jammed his right hand into Harper's underarm, then pulled the captive wrist down like a pump handle. Everyone in the room—everyone except Carl—heard the shoulder joint dislocate. Harper let the gun go.

Evelyn was on her way to Emmett's office before Harper's scream of pain was completely over. She was back almost as fast. "Something's happened to Emmett," she said, loud enough to be heard over Harper. "He's passed out or something."

Bart was partway to the hall when he realized that his abdomen hurt, and that there was blood on his shirt, "Darn, not again," he said, and started back toward the couch. The only reason he made it was that the girls caught him before he collapsed.

◇◇◇◇◇◇◇◇◇◇◇◇◇◇◇◇●◇◇◇◇◇◇◇◇◇◇◇◇◇◇◇◇◇

Jamaal saw the iron blob in front of Emmett. "Go call 911," he told Evelyn. "And I'm going to need Bart's phone." He found the orange cat hiding behind the couch in the waiting room, and coaxed him out with some coffee creamer. Bart's phone had done the iron note at the cabin, so he knew it was tuned right. The only problem was going to be achieving the trance state after so much excitement, but he knew what to do: he got into the zone. All good athletes know about the zone. Get into the zone, and the world becomes just you and the ball, or the track, or the target.

The crowd, the noise, none of that exists if you're in the zone. From the zone to the void was a very short step, and when the iron lattice formed, he slipped through it like a guppy going through seaweed.

Why had they talked about music and jewels? It was the sky on a clear night in Missouri, with fireworks instead of stars, except they were everywhere and they didn't die away. He wished he could spend more time there, but he knew he couldn't. "Uh, hello?" he thought.

"*Hello*," came a voice."

Bart had told him about the voice—them, he had called it, or the others. "I've come to get Mr. Schroder," Jamaal thought. "I need to take him out, before...you know."

"*Yes, we know. Move forward.*"

Jamaal did, and sure enough, there was Emmett. "Everything go all right?" Emmett asked.

"You mean with those guys in your office? Yeah, they're squared away."

"Evelyn, is she okay?"

"She's fine."

"Good. I was worried about her."

"She's worried about you, too. You know, you two remind me of an old married couple. It's none of my business, but have you ever thought about...?" He didn't finish the thought, and for a moment, Emmett didn't reply.

"I've thought about it," Emmett said finally, and in his thought was something of sadness, or maybe of loss. "Evelyn was Mary—my late wife's—best friend; she was there with me at the bedside when she died. It wouldn't feel right, almost disloyal to Mary, if I, you know..."

"Oh. Yeah, I see." He didn't, but Jamaal knew when to drop a subject. "You, ah, you ready to go?"

"I suppose. Let me make my manners first. Hey Guys?

384

Sorry I have to go. There are some nuances of the game I'd love to discuss with you. Maybe next time." He paused. "Or should I not risk a next time? Wade always worried you might not like my motives."

"*Your motives, to the extent we understand them, are very much like ours. We each look after our friends.*"

"So you're saying I can come back?"

"*That is what we are saying.*"

"Great. I'd love to stay a while longer, but I made a promise, and I'm still working on it."

"*We completely understand about keeping promises. Now, the two of you must merge. Yes, like that. Hrrlle, mmrrau'sst.*"

◇◇◇◇◇◇◇◇◇◇◇◇◇◇◇◇◇●◇◇◇◇◇◇◇◇◇◇◇◇◇◇◇◇◇

The EMS people had been standing by at the festival in case somebody choked on a hotdog, so they were at the office almost before Evelyn hung up the phone. Bart was still conscious, but he was pale and his skin was getting cold and clammy. "Shock," one of the EMTs radioed ahead, "incident to internal bleeding caused by an abdominal gunshot wound." She looked at Tori, who was holding Carl's pistol. "What caliber is it?"

Tori examined the gun, then realized why the woman wanted to know. "Oh, this wasn't the one. Jamaal?"

Jamaal had taken charge of the PPK. "Let's see. It's a .32." He ejected the magazine. "With...jacketed round nose: hardballs."

The EMT made a note. "That's good. That's real good."

"Does that mean he'll be all right?" Tori asked.

"Hard to say, but almost anything else would have been worse." And with that, they connected an IV drip and started to wheel him out.

"Wait," Bart said weakly. "I have to tell Tori something...I..." Then he passed out, and they carried him down the steps and out to the ambulance.

"Hey, what about me?" Tom Harper said. He was sitting in Evelyn's chair, surrounded by three angry women. "I'm hurt too!"

The head EMT came back in and looked at him. "You the one who shot the boy?" He didn't say anything, but everybody else nodded yes. "And you've only got a dislocated shoulder." It wasn't a question, more of a comment. Evelyn had given 911 a pretty good description of what had happened. "I expect the jail nurse will have a look at it." A police car pulled up in the front lot. "And look; your taxi's here already."

The two cops who came in asked a few questions, then cuffed Carl, who was conscious by then, and took him out to the car. Just before they did the same to Harper, Jamaal asked if he could have a word with him. The cops said that wasn't procedure, but Evelyn said Jamaal was all right, and since she had taught them both in Sunday school, they decided they could vary procedure a little. Jamaal leaned in close to Harper's ear. "If my friend doesn't pull through," he said, "I will tear your arm all the way off, and then beat you to death with it. I just wanted you to know that."

"You all heard that." Harper shouted. "He threatened me, and you're witnesses!"

The cops looked at each other. "I didn't hear anything," one of the said. "Did you hear anything?" The other one shook his head. "Sorry, can't help you." He looked Jamaal over. "But if I were you, I'd pray that his friend pulls through. I'd pray real hard."

Chapter Forty-Six

After they gave blood, there wasn't much to do but wait. Tori pulled the little bandage partway off and looked at the place where the needle had gone in. It wasn't bleeding, so she peeled the bandage all the way off and threw it away. "You all right now?" she asked Jamaal.

"Yes I'm all right," he replied, his eyes still closed. "It's not like I passed out; it just, you know, surprised me when I saw the blood shooting up that tube, so I flinched a little, that's all."

"It took two nurses and an orderly to hold you up," Dee told him. "You should have told us you don't like needles."

"Any word yet?" Tori asked Evelyn, who was just back from the nurses' station. Everybody but Jamaal had made that trek twice already, and each time the nurses had told them there wasn't any news yet.

"They only just got started, apparently." Evelyn didn't sound happy.

"Started?" Tori couldn't believe it. "They brought him here almost two hours ago! Why didn't they start then? And how come they told you, when they wouldn't tell us?"

"Because you don't know their mothers, and I do," Evelyn said. "As for when they started, it's a small hospital; there's not a surgeon in residence, and the one on-call is off at a conference. The doctor who's covering for him had to come over from Clemson."

Jamaal's ears pricked up. "It not Dr. Hodge, is it?"

"They didn't say. Why, do you know him?"

"Her. She was the one who patched Bart up the last time."

That got Emmett's attention. "What last time? I hadn't heard about that."

"You're kidding. Dee's father shot him; shot him down like a dog."

"Hey," Dee piped up. "Papa did not shoot him like a dog. How does a dog shoot, anyway?"

Jamaal needed a second to figure out what she meant. "No. Not like a dog shoots, like Bart was a dog."

"Bart is nothing like a dog. You should be ashamed of yourself for saying that."

Tori realized Dee was messing with him, and decided to pile on. "Move to censure Jamaal for calling Bart a dog. Do I hear a second?"

"That does seem cold," Emmett grunted. "I'll second."

"All in favor?" Everybody except Jamaal said aye. "The motion carries. Be ashamed."

Jamaal finally understood he was being played. "Let the record note my exception," he said with mock dignity.

Tori gave him a quizzical look. "What did you just say?"

Before Jamaal could respond, Emmett's phone buzzed. He saw who it was and held up his hand for silence. "This may be important," he told them. There followed a series of uh-huhs and well-nows. "Thanks, Duane, I appreciate it." He folded the phone shut. "That was Duane, over at the jail. Our Mr. Thomas has had a spiritual awakening, I guess you might say. Duane says he's demanding books on meditation, says it's part of his religion. Do you suppose the book store would have an introduction to meditation?"

Tori did a quick search on her phone. "They should. I see one for idiots, and another one for dummies."

"Good. Evelyn, would you mind running over there and seeing if they've got anything like that? If they do, take it over to Duane at the jail. Tell him it's an anonymous donation to the jail library."

"Well, I guess it'll give me something to do besides sit around waiting," she said. "But why?"

"Because I'm a generous, big-hearted person," Emmett replied, straight-faced.

Evelyn let that hang in the air for about five seconds. "No, seriously; why?"

Emmett leaned forward and whispered, "It's a secret."

She snorted. "Is it something about that thing Wade used

to do? That whatever-it-is that made the money that Green Cove spends? About the only thing I *don't* know about that is how it's done, and judging by all this, I don't think I want to know."

"No, probably you don't. But Mr. Thomas did. He wanted it bad. That's what he was talking about when he said I had something he wanted. So I gave it to him."

Jamaal frowned. "You told him...?"

"Oh I did more than tell him. I gave it to him in writing, all of it: the emptiness..."

"We call it the void," Jamaal murmured.

"...the musical note, the matrix, everything. Well, almost everything. Somehow or other, I forgot to mention the part about the cat."

Jamaal digested that for a moment, then turned toward Evelyn. "You got enough to pay for those books? Cause if you don't..." He reached for his wallet.

She looked back and forth between them. "I've got enough. Just tell me one thing: if this scheme of yours..." she made a gesture that covered both Emmett and Jamaal, "...if it works, what happens to Mr. Thomas?"

Emmett looked at the ceiling, as though searching for exactly the right way of phrasing something. "If it works," he said, "I think he gets to see Hell. Up close and personal."

Evelyn thought about what Mr. Thomas had said, that there were things worse than rape in store for her if Emmett didn't cooperate. "Well all right, then," she said. "You need anything else while I'm out?"

◇◇◇◇◇◇◇◇◇◇◇◇◇◇◇◇●◇◇◇◇◇◇◇◇◇◇◇◇◇◇◇◇

"What did you mean, he gets to see Hell?" Jamaal asked when Evelyn was gone. "I'm a Presbyterian; I know what Hell's supposed to look like, and it's nothing like what's in there."

"Uh-huh," Emmett said. "Tell me what you saw." Jamaal did. Dee started to disagree, but Emmett stopped her. "More and more, I think what you see there depends on what you bring to the experience, and you each brought something different. Suppose you had gone in, suspicious and hostile, maybe even evil. What do you suppose you would see then?"

Tori was feeling like the odd one out since she'd never been in, but now she saw her chance to contribute. "But you couldn't do that, could you? I mean, you couldn't even call up the void if you felt like that."

"Are you sure?" Emmett said softly.

She frowned. "Well, it just seems like..." Her voice trailed off. "Wait a minute. You're saying you know somebody who did that?"

Emmett stared off into a distance only he could see. "Knew," he said. "I knew somebody, a long time ago. We've fallen out of touch since then."

Almost a minute passed before Tori spoke. "You don't think you're going to just stop there, do you? What happened? Tell us the story!"

"It isn't a happy story," he said. "Did you ever read *The Rime of the Ancient Mariner*?" Nobody said anything. "It's about a scary old man who buttonholes a stranger and makes him listen to a tale, a horror story, really. I re-read it every now and again; it has a couple of great lines that I can sometimes work into jury arguments, but I'm thinking now about the last two lines, about how the stranger felt when the story was over. He was, the poem says, a sadder and a wiser man. The two seem to go together."

Jamaal glanced down the hall toward the nurses' station to see if anything was going on. There wasn't. "So you're saying, 'Enter at your own risk'. Fair enough. I like horror stories, and it looks like we've got time. I want to hear it."

"Me too!" That was Tori and Dee together.

Emmett sighed. The ancient mariner, he remembered, felt better for having told his story. Maybe it really did work that way. He hoped so.

Wade and I had gotten to know each other when I drew up the Green Cove Trust. He found out I could keep a secret, and after a while he asked if I wanted to take part in a seminar he was going to teach, about a subject he said was both strange and wonderful. Well naturally I said yes. It was a very small seminar. The professor was Wade, and there were three students: me, Bill, and Laurie. You can guess what the subject was. Wade wanted to pass along what he had learned, and we were the ones who were supposed to take the baton.

We met on weekends. The first class was the introduction to the concept, which naturally we all thought was pure nonsense until Wade gave us a demonstration. I guess you could say that set the hook. After that, we were supposed to study one metal a week. We didn't actually finish one a week, in the sense of mastering it, but that was mainly because I held the others back. They had the knack, apparently—Bill, especially—but I had to work at it.

Finally, all of us managed to do copper, so the next week was to be the grand finale: iron. We were all looking forward to it. The other classes had been at Wade's apartment in Clemson, but this was to be a combination class and graduation party, a cookout, and I volunteered to have it at my house here in Larson. Our house, I should say; my wife was still alive then. She helped me study the material, but she was already too sick to try any of it herself.

I had everything ready: the charcoal was hot, and the beer was cold. Bill and Laurie got there, and then we waited. No Wade. I found out later there'd been a wreck on 28 and traffic was backed up behind it. I tried to call him, and he tried to call me, but there wasn't the cell coverage out there that there is now, and the upshot of it was that we grilled the burgers and drank the beer, and then Bill said he was going to do it, he was going to do an iron melt. We tried to talk him out of it, but no, he said he had worked on it all week, had even called up the iron matrix and studied it from the outside. He was ready, he said.

Bill was smart, and he was curious, and he wasn't afraid of anything. He should have been, and Wade should have told us why we mustn't do iron without him, but knowing what should have happened won't change a damned thing. Bill went in. The sample was an old differential gear I'd gotten from Bud. We got it good and hot over the charcoal, and it melted exactly the way the other metals had. Except that Bill didn't come back after it happened.

After maybe five minutes of waiting, I tried calling Wade again, and this time I got through. Traffic had moved a little, I guess. I told him what had happened, and he told me what we had to do. You already know: somebody had to go in and bring him out. Wade had his cat with him, but he didn't know when or even if he could get there.

I was willing to try it, but Laurie said no, Bill was her husband, so it was her wifely duty. That's what she said, wifely duty. The people next door had a cat, so I borrowed it. I guess borrow is the right word; they weren't home, and it was outside. Anyway, I acquired a cat.

It was a black cat, all except for a little bit of white on its chest. I've wondered ever since then whether that was the problem, you know, all the superstitions about black cats. Laurie once asked Wade if what we were doing was magic, and he tried to explain, again, about quantum uncertainty, and how particles seem to know what we want, and how it was really science. I thought that might have satisfied her, but then one day she kind of casually asked me why, if cold melting isn't witchcraft, it isn't mentioned in the Bible. I told her that television wasn't mentioned in the Bible either, and it certainly isn't witchcraft. I thought that was a pretty good answer.

Apparently, that wasn't; she still had misgivings. But misgivings or not, when Bill needed her she took the cat and went in. Not for long, though. In just a second, she came back out. She said she had seen the fires of Hell, and that I could go there if I wanted to, but that she had repented, and escaped, and wasn't ever going back. Then she ran out to her car and left. I would have gone in; I tell myself that, but by then, what with all the commotion, the cat had run off. Anyway, I haven't seen Laurie since then. Or wanted to.

Bill died about twenty minutes later.

It was Dee who broke the silence. "That poor man, that poor, poor man. She left him in Hell, when she could have brought him out."

Emmett smiled. It wasn't much of a smile, but it was his first since he had bought the hoagie at the festival. "No, she didn't," he said. "Wade asked the others about that, the next time he went in. They told him that Bill's reaction when he got there was, 'Wow!'. That doesn't sound to me like he saw Hell. Bill's only regret, they said, was that he wouldn't ever get to play catch with his son."

Tori wiped away a tear. "They had a child? That makes it even sadder. Whatever happened to...?" She stopped.

Emmett finished the question for her. "...to the boy?" He glanced down toward the nurses' station. "Still too soon to say."

Dee looked like someone had slapped her. "That woman, that horrible woman," she whispered. "That was Bart's mother?" Emmett nodded, his smile now gone. Dee stood up, clamped her hand over her mouth, and ran for the exit.

Tori was right behind her. "We may be a while," she called over her shoulder, and then they were gone.

The waiting room had a heap of magazines on a coffee table. Jamaal had been through the heap once already, but about all he had found was *Southern Living* ("No, I don't want to know how they decorate cakes in Savannah.") and *People* ("No. Just, no."), but as the afternoon wore on his standards were starting to slip, and now he was trying again. "Huh," he said. "Somebody who can't sing is dating somebody who can't act. Why do I need to know that?"

He gave up the hunt and was almost back to his chair when a woman in surgical scrubs came into the room. "You two here about the Phillips boy?"

Jamaal's mouth went dry, but he managed to mumble, "Mr. Schroder, meet Dr. Hodge."

"Emmett Schroder." He held out his hand, which she looked at suspiciously. "Don't worry," he said. "I know not to squeeze a doctor's hand."

"Then you and I are off to a good start," she said, giving his hand a light shake. She turned back toward Jamaal. "You, on the other hand, are on my list. I told you to take care of that boy, now didn't I? Yes, I did, and no, you didn't." Jamaal mumbled something about it not being his fault. "Well, you can tell him that. It looks like he's going to make it."

"He'll be all right?" Jamaal asked.

"You wouldn't call it all right if it was you. We had to unpack his small intestines—they're the twisty ones, in case you've forgotten—and then feel along every inch of them to find all the bullet holes. Then we had to sew the holes shut and tuck everything back in. That boy is going to be sore in places he didn't even know he had, and when I say sore, I mean real bad sore."

Emmett rubbed his chin. "So what I'm hearing is, between the anesthetic and the pain meds, he won't be up to seeing anybody today."

Dr. Hodge nodded. "Tomorrow morning, at the earliest." The PA system spoke her name. "Oh, keep your pants on," she told it, then turned back toward Emmett. "Your friend'll be all right, but I think I'd better leave you in charge, this time. You take good care of that boy."

"I promise," he told her.

"I'll hold you to that." The PA spoke again. "Okay, twice says they mean it. Nice meeting you," she said that to Emmett. She looked at Jamaal, shook her head, and left.

"I'd be careful making any promises to her," Jamaal said after she was gone. "She keeps track."

"Apparently so."

"That the same promise you told the others about?"

"Oh, you heard that."

"Yeah I did. You said you had a promise to keep."

"I did say that."

"But you're not going to say what it was."

"No, I'm not. Can't."

"Let me guess. Confidentiality?"

"Right the first time. Let's go find our ladies, shall we?"

Dee made it to the hospital's parking lot before the wave of nausea crested, but even then it didn't amount to much more than the dry heaves. She had planned to eat at the festival, but after seeing the tattoos on the food vendors, she had decided she could wait. "Ugh," she finally said after spitting out a mouthful of foam. "That was disgusting."

"You all right?" Tori asked anxiously.

"I think so. It caught me off guard, coming all at once like that, but I'm over it now."

"Was it another one of those...of Bart's...feelings?"

"Uh-huh."

"He really hates her that much?"

Dee opened her mouth to answer, then closed it again. "Let me think about that," she said after a few seconds. She walked over to a bush and spat again, then sat down on the curb and thought. "It didn't feel like hate," she finally said. "More like disappointment, or maybe resignation. It was feeling of hollowness, of—I don't know how else to describe it—of failure."

"As a mother, anyway." Jamaal had told Tori some of the stories Bart had told him.

Dee shook her head. "No, not her. He's the failure: he didn't try hard enough, he wasn't good enough. I think that's what he resigned himself to, that he was a disappointment, that she never loved him because he didn't deserve it."

"There they are," Jamaal said. Dee and Tori were sitting on the curb, looking glum. "I don't know if I want to get closer to that or not," he told Emmett, but Emmett wasn't listening. He had turned his phone back on after coming out of the hospital, and was returning a call he had missed. "He's going to make it," Jamaal told the girls. "No visitors today, but he's going to make it."

"Any of you know somebody named Nisa?" Emmett interrupted.

Tori's mouth fell open. She had completely forgotten her grand plan. "Oh, my, god," she moaned. "She'll kill me. Where is she?"

"At the office. Evelyn went there after she left the jail, just to make sure the place was locked up—we did leave kind of quick—and she found them there, waiting on the steps, Nisa and her brother."

Dee's eyebrows went up. "Her brother?"

"What Evelyn said. Anyway, they're coming here to meet us."

Tori jumped to her feet. "They're coming here?" This was bad; this was more than bad. A first meeting in an empty parking lot, with nobody around except Dee's friends? This was a disaster. "How much time do we have?"

Emmett did a quick calculation. "Let's see, it's about a five minute drive, so I'd say..." He noticed Evelyn's car turning into the hospital lot. "...right around ten seconds. Give or take."

Chapter Forty-Seven

"How's it going?" Jamaal asked.

"I want books," Bart said. "I don't care what they are: textbooks, crosswords, it doesn't matter. Anything but that." He pointed toward the hospital room's TV, grimacing a little as he did it. "My mother used to say TVs were tools of the Devil, and after seeing what's on in the morning, I'm starting to believe her."

"Books. Will do. How do you feel? Dr. Hodge said you might be kind of sore."

"Sore? Is that what she said? Sore, like I might have done too many sit-ups sore? I feel like I've been run over by a gravel truck."

Tori was looking at a device that was plumbed into his IV line. "What's this thing do?"

"If the pain gets too bad, I can push a button and it squirts some kind of painkiller into the IV drip."

"When was the last time you used it?" She had noticed the grimace.

"I haven't..." he grimaced again. "...haven't tried it yet."

That was the answer she had expected. "And why not? You're supposed to use it if you hurt, and I can tell: you hurt!"

Bart shook his head. "I don't know, I just haven't."

"Uh-huh." Jamaal had told her about the other time, when Dee's father had shot him. Dr. Hodge had given him some pain pills, and according to Jamaal the bottle was still full. "Tell me something. As a kid, did you ever get hurt?"

He thought back. "You mean cuts, scrapes, that kind of thing? Sure."

"Anything that really hurt?"

"I broke a finger one time, when I fell off my bike. That hurt a lot."

"You get anything for it?"

"No. It was my fault, so I just toughed it out."

Damn, Tori thought. Dee was right. She wondered: what one woman can do, can another woman undo? Only one way to find out. Behind her back she made a shooing motion. Jamaal gave no sign that he had seen it, but in the course of five seconds he had gotten his turned-off phone out of his pocket, looked at it, said "Uh, I probably should take this," and joined Dee in the hall. The hospital let Bart have only two visitors at a time, and Dee had drawn the short straw.

When they were alone, Tori took Bart's hand in hers, and for several seconds she just held it. Then, without letting go, she said, "Bart, I need to know something, and I need for you to think hard before you answer. Do you trust me?"

Tears welled up in his eyes, but he blinked them back. Real men, after all, don't cry. "Yes," he said in a hoarse whisper.

"Then listen to me, because this is important. There are no more tests you have to pass. There is nothing more you have to prove. I love you, Bart Phillips, and I love you for what you are. Nothing is ever going to change that. Do you understand?" His lips trembled, but suddenly the tears he had blinked back were flowing in earnest, and the best answer he could manage was a nod and a squeeze of the hand. Now, she thought, we find out if that witch's spell is really broken. She leaned over, kissed him on the forehead, and whispered, "It's okay to push the button. You don't have to hurt any more."

◇◇◇◇◇◇◇◇◇◇◇◇◇◇◇◇◇●◇◇◇◇◇◇◇◇◇◇◇◇◇◇◇◇◇

"Can we go in?" Dee asked when Tori came out.

Tori shook her head. "No, he's asleep. I think the pain was keeping him awake, and once the painkiller hit he faded fast."

Jamaal's eyes widened. "You pressed the button?"

"No. He did." She tried to keep a straight face, but a grin peeked through.

Jamaal gave her an appraising look, then nodded. "I'm thinking I need to start looking for a different roommate for next year."

She thought about that for a second or so. "Not for next year. After that...we'll see."

"Uh-huh, understood. Oh, and for the record, whatever you did in there, thank you. That was good work, soldier. Damn good work."

The bell on the front door dingled, and Evelyn looked up to see Tori. "How is our boy doing?" she asked.

"The nurses say he slept well last night," Tori said happily, "and he looks better. Jamaal had a class he couldn't cut, but he sent some books over, and that really brightened him up."

"You don't have classes?" Evelyn said, as casually as she could.

"I do, but I also have priorities," was Tori's answer. "I can take classes over, if I have to."

Evelyn nodded. "Good, as long as you share him; he's our boy too, you know."

Tori came around the desk, bent over, and gave Evelyn a hug. "You guys are family, and you'll always be family. Which is why I'm here. I need to ask Uncle Emmett something."

"Uncle Emmett. I've heard him called lots of things, but never that. I guess there's a first time for everything. Go on back."

Emmett had a yellow legal pad in front of him, and was scribbling vigorously on it. "Give me half a minute," he said, without looking up, then scribbled some more. "Jury argument," he said when he was finished. "Now all I have to do is memorize it so it looks off-the-cuff. What can I do for you?"

"I need to know what you think about a thing. It has to do with, you know, the others."

"Ah. All right, what can I tell you?"

"Do you think they have a sense of humor?"

"Hmph. Well now, let me think about that. If they do, Wade never mentioned it, and they didn't tell any jokes while I was there, although I might have caught just a whiff of sarcasm once. But humor? Not that I noticed. Why?"

"Something Bart said. You know how I was trying to get

Dee together with Nisa's brother?" Emmett nodded; Evelyn had told him. "Well, Bart and Jamaal wanted to meet him, but they never did because of, you know, all the stuff that happened. Anyway, this morning Bart asked if they had ever gotten together, and I told him they had, and that they seemed to really like one another. He said he was glad, but then I mentioned Demir's name, and he laughed. He wished he hadn't—I could tell it really hurt—but he did, and when I asked him why, he said he and Jamaal wouldn't have to interview Demir after all, that he had already been vetted by experts. I thought he was bombed on pain meds, but he said no, that in Turkish, demir means iron. I looked it up, and he's right, but it turns out out that Demir is also a fairly common Turkish name. So here's my question: Do you think it means anything?"

Emmett looked down, then up, then he closed his eyes and leaned back. Then he opened his eyes, nodded, and said, "I would say it's a coincidence. Like people named Brown, or Green, who aren't brown or green, or people named Smith, who aren't blacksmiths. Maybe their families used to be, a long time ago, but anymore a name is just a noise we use to keep track of who's who, and I expect it's like that in Turkey, too."

Tori mulled that over. "Yeah, okay, that makes sense. Thanks, Mr. Schroder!" She came around and gave him the same sitting hug she had given Evelyn. "I gotta go." And with that, she wafted out of the office.

Emmett came out to the waiting room. "She seems happy," he told Evelyn.

"I think she and Bart have found each other," Evelyn said.

"That's good," Emmett said, and made a checkmark on a mental list.

"She said she had a question for Uncle Emmett," Evelyn said. "Did Uncle Emmett have the answer?"

His face altered this way and that, as his tongue explored the inside of his cheek. "Uncle Emmett, huh? Well, Uncle Emmett had *an* answer, and it was a pretty good answer, if you're not a stickler for the truth."

That got a raised eyebrow. "Emmett Schroder, did you lie to that girl?"

"Would I lie to somebody who calls me Uncle Emmett?"

"Well no, I suppose not."

"Interesting. Did it sound to you like I was denying it?"

She gave him a hard look. "Yes, you denied it. You said..." She thought about what he had said. "No you didn't, did you. You asked a question, and it sounded like an answer, except it wasn't. You are a devious man, Emmett Schroder. What have you done?"

"Do you know the expression, 'Never kick a running dog'? I had an old lawyer tell me that when I was first starting out. It means, when things are going in a direction that suits you, don't interfere."

"What does that have to do with you lying to Tori?"

Emmett paced across the room, then back. "Do you remember how you said that you know all about what Wade used to do, everything except how to do it?" She nodded. "Do you know about them?"

She frowned. "I don't know who you mean by 'them'."

"Well, it's time I told you. I first heard about them from Wade. That was back, let's see..."

◇◇◇◇◇◇◇◇◇◇◇◇◇◇◇●◇◇◇◇◇◇◇◇◇◇◇◇◇◇◇

"But what are they?" Evelyn asked, when Emmett had finished. It had been a long story, involving Wade's death, Bart's mother, and finally Emmett's own visit.

"I honestly don't know. Wade said one time that if string theory was right, the extra dimensions might explain the where, but not the what."

"Hmph. So they hang around out there somewhere, and spy on us with cats."

"If the cats cooperate. I gather it's hit or miss, even for them."

Evelyn eyed the orange cat, which was curled up on the couch, apparently asleep. Nisa had taken his ladyfriend back to

Greensboro. "I still don't understand what all this has to do with some lie you told to Tori, and what that has to do with running dogs."

Emmett told her what Bart had said about Demir. That Bart understood Turkish had taken some explaining, but it hadn't been the strangest part of the story, and she had accepted it, even if she hadn't understood it. "So I told her it was just a coincidence, that it didn't mean anything."

"But you think it does?"

"I got to thinking about a question I had asked them. When they told me about the white cat mangling the shipping tag so she would end up here, I asked if they had done all that just so he"—he nodded at the orange cat—"would have a girlfriend. And they did the same thing I did a while ago. Instead of an answer, they came back with a question. And I let them get away with it! Those guys are slick, I mean to tell you."

"So you think...?"

"I think they sent the cat because they met Dee and decided she needed a boyfriend."

Evelyn got a look of awe on her face. "It's like what Tori tried to do, only a lot deeper. They're matchmakers!"

Emmett nodded. "Something like that. That's the running dog I don't want to kick. If Dee thinks it's that kind of set-up, she might get spooked, but if the others think it's a good match, my guess is, it's a good match."

"Did they say anything about it?"

"No, but think about it. They have access to pretty much anywhere in the world where there are cats. If there's an ideal match for somebody, anywhere in the world, I'll bet they can find it, except this time I don't think they found just one."

"You think there's more than one ideal match?"

"I'm starting to think so, yes. I think they found more than one for Dee, and when one of the good ones was named Iron, they used that as the tie-breaker. Or else I'm completely crazy. But if I'm right, that is too beautiful of a scheme for me to jinx, so when Tori asked me what I thought, I told her a lie. I'm not proud of it, but there it is."

Evelyn raised a finger as though she had a point to make, but she didn't say anything. The finger began to follow along as she thought about a document she had typed the year before. Then she nodded. "Uh-huh. They're female! Some of them, anyway. No male would have set up something this devious."

Emmett couldn't decide if that was a compliment or not. "You wouldn't have let me get away with saying that."

"No, but I'm a woman; I know our work when I see it. And you're right: it's beautiful, only I think it's at least a full layer deeper than what you thought. What's Bart's name?"

"Phillips."

"No, his first name."

Emmett thought for a second. "Victor. So?"

"So, Sherlock, what do you think 'Tori' is short for?"

"I don't know if it's short for anything."

"I'll bet you a dollar it's short for Victoria."

Emmett absorbed that, then smiled broadly. "Well I'll be damned. The tie-breaker. You're good; I hadn't made that connection. How far back does this thing go, do you suppose? Years? Decades?"

"Maybe they amend the plan as they go along. Like you do with cross-examinations."

"They'd about have to, I guess. Too many variables to plan real far ahead." He glanced at his watch. "Huh. Time for my walk." He went to his office and came back with an apple.

"You're doing that again?" Yesterday, out of the blue, Emmett had announced that he was going to skip lunch except for an apple, and spend an hour walking around town. Evelyn hadn't thought much about it, but twice in a row was looking like a pattern.

"Yeah, I decided I could be in better shape, so I'm going to try to start walking every day. Don't know why I haven't done it before now."

"Well good for you. What can I do to encourage you?"

"Get some better apples. These are kind of mealy."

"Apples. Will do." She thought for a few seconds. "It seems like just walking the streets would be boring. Would company help?"

Emmett took a long moment, then nodded. "You know, it just might."

Chapter Forty-Eight

The Wednesday night poker games always started out the same way. One of the players would shuffle the deck seven times, then pass it to his left for the cut. Wade had told them that seven times was what it took. He had also explained why—something involving hypercubes—which none of them had understood.

Emmett cleared his throat. "Before we start, there are some issues I want to bring before the board. Any objections for lack of notice?" His eyes swept the table, and one by one they each shook their heads. No objection.

Jim Perkins was this year's secretary. The office alternated from year to year between him and Arnold. Emmett was the permanent chairman because nobody else wanted the office, and Calvin, the retired banker, was the permanent treasurer. Jim reached into the briefcase he always brought with him, just in case, and pulled out a three-ring binder labeled Minutes. "Give me just a minute," he said. He found the first blank page, dated it, then gave Emmett a nod.

The other three were lifelong friends of his, but as if he had never met them Emmett intoned the opening formula: "I now call into session this meeting of the board of successor trustees of the Green Cove Trust."

"Good morning," the man said to the secretary at the front desk. "I'm Wade Dawson, and this is my sister Emily. We have an appointment to see Mr. Jenkins."

The secretary hoped the man wouldn't notice how nervous she was. She was starting her second week at the law firm of Jenkins & Schroder, and this was her first crisis. Mr. Jenkins, as it happened, wasn't in. After assuring her that he didn't have any appointments, he had left for a seminar at Myrtle Beach. "Oh dear," she said. "I'm, uh, I'm afraid Mr. Jenkins is, uh..."

"Billy got called down to Columbia on a death penalty

appeal he's doing," said a voice from the direction of the hallway. "I'm Emmett Schroder, his partner. Come on back; let's see if it's something I can help you with. Mrs. Pitman, could you bring us some coffee? How do you all take yours?" And with that, he ushered them back toward his office, a little room off to the side of the hall.

Evelyn Pitman hadn't had many dealings with the firm's junior partner, and she still wasn't sure what to make of him. As a Baptist, she knew it was wrong to tell a lie the way he had just done, but as a soon-to-be divorcee, whose husband had emptied their joint account before he left town, she had a guilty feeling of gratitude for the lifeline he had just tossed her. She really couldn't afford to lose this job.

About an hour later, Mr. Schroder and the two clients came back into the waiting room. "All right, I'll see you then," Mr. Schroder was saying. "Mrs. Pitman, would you block me out an hour for this time next week?" After they were gone, he came over to her desk. "Want some advice?" She nodded. "Every day, before Billy goes home, make him empty his shirt pocket onto your desk. He writes his appointments on little scraps of paper, then he crams them in his pocket. If they make it home with him, there's about an even chance you'll never see them."

She absorbed that. "So you're saying I should train my boss?"

"If that's what it takes to get your job done, then I figure it's implied in your job description. You're new; you'll learn. Oh, and that reminds me. When I told Mary that Billy had hired somebody new, she said we should have you over for dinner one evening."

"Mary?"

"Mrs. Schroder."

"Well, sure; I'd like that. And by the way, I'm not Mrs. Pitman; I'm Evelyn."

"Evelyn. Got it. I'll have Mary give you a call and the two of you can pick a day. Now, somewhere around here we have a copy of the Probate Code. You get a minute, see if you can find it for me. I've got some heavy-duty drafting to do."

One night the next week, Evelyn was driving through town and saw a light on in the office. That wouldn't do, she thought. She was supposed to turn out the lights when she locked up at the end of the day. She went in to turn it off, and then realized she wasn't the only one there. From down the hall came the distinctive sound of a poor typist: Chunk, chunk-chunk, chunk-chunk-chunk-chunk, zaack. It was Mr. Schroder. "You know," she said from the doorway of his office, "I actually can type."

He didn't even look up from what he was doing. "Uh-huh." Chunk-chunk-chunk.

"And I don't just work for Mr. Jenkins. If you've got something you need typed, I'll be happy to do it. Really, it's what you pay me for."

"Uh-huh." He typed another word or two, then hit the carriage return. Zaack, went the machine. "There, I think that does it. Yeah, I know you can type. You type a hell of a lot better than I do. But I also know you're doing an appeal for Billy, plus the paperwork on the Jones-Kelsey closing, and my arm ain't broke. Plus, this was something I told the clients I'd have ready tomorrow."

"That trust for the brother and sister?" He nodded. "You want me to proof it? I don't mind."

He pursed his lips. "Well, you see, I promised them nobody would know how the trust works and who the beneficiary is. Nobody but them and me and, if it comes to that, the successor trustees."

"But surely they didn't expect you to type it yourself."

"I don't know what they expected." Actually, that was only half true. They hadn't discussed who would be doing the typing, but they had made their other expectations very clear. "Bill is our only heir," Mr. Dawson had said, "and we want to leave the old family place at Viney Cove to him. But if anything happens to him, we want his son to have it, not his wife. Nothing against Laurie, we just want it kept in the family."

Emmett had thought about that. "A will may not be what you want, then. Have you thought about a trust?"

Emily Phillips didn't like the sound of that. A frail, older lady, she reminded Emmett of the face on an antique cameo pin. "You're not just trying to jack up the fee, are you?" she asked.

"Emily!" said her brother.

"Hush. I'm old; I get to say what I think." She looked at Emmett. "Well, what about it?"

Emmett shrugged. "The fee's the same for a will as it is for a trust. I'm just thinking that if your son dies while the boy is underage, his mother could ask the court for permission to sell the property. She'd have to say she needed the money to raise the boy, but it could happen."

"If she got it, she wouldn't spend it on him," the old lady said. "She'd just buy more of those damned collector plates she loves so much."

"Emily!" her brother said again. "That's a terrible thing to say. You know Laurie wouldn't do that. Still, Mr. Schroder may have a point. Can a trust be changed, if circumstances change?"

Emmett assured them that it could. "It can be amended as long as either of you is alive. Give me a week, but I'll have something for you to look at."

"Just don't drag your feet," said Emily. I've already had one stroke; I probably won't survive the next one."

"Yes Ma'am," Emmett told her. "I'll get it done. I promise."

◇◇◇◇◇◇◇◇◇◇◇◇◇◇◇◇●◇◇◇◇◇◇◇◇◇◇◇◇◇◇◇◇

"I now call into session this meeting of the board of successor trustees of the Green Cove Trust," Emmett said. "First, a report. The boy is out of the hospital. He's still in a wheelchair, but he's on the mend. Already taken a couple of his finals, and should be done with the rest of them by the end of the week."

"That's good," Calvin said. "I was afraid he might miss them and have to repeat a semester."

"No, he won't," Emmett said, "but that brings up my second item. He's says he's thinking about taking a semester off. After that, maybe he'd go back and finish, maybe not."

Jim frowned. "Most kids who do that don't ever go back, do they? That's not a good sign." He got nods of agreement from the others, all except Emmett.

"I think you're right about the first part," Emmett said, "but I'm not so sure about it's being a bad sign. He asked me an interesting question, one I hadn't ever really thought about. Let's see what you all think. Calvin, what courses did you take in college that have had a lasting impact on your life?"

Calvin leaned back and thought. "Early on in my career, I would have said economics. But now, as I understand it, everything I learned was wrong. Same thing with psychology. I honestly don't know. You asked what courses had an impact. I did learn some important stuff in college, but not in class. I learned, for example, that I don't like marijuana."

"You smoked weed?" Arnold snorted. "I'd have paid money to see that."

"Yeah, I'm told I was hilarious. What I remember is being stupid. I don't like being stupid. Never have tried it again."

Emmett turned to the fire chief. "Jim?"

Jim Perkins chewed his upper lip for a moment, then said, "I took French. I took a trip to Quebec once, but either my French wasn't any good or theirs wasn't. I took calculus, but I never use it, and I've forgotten all the chemistry. But like Calvin said, I learned some stuff outside of class. I remember this girl named Leslie. I learned a lot from her, and yeah, I still use some of it."

"Way too much information," Calvin muttered.

Arnold strummed his fingers on the table. "I think I see where you're going with this. I never went to college, and for a long time I wished I had. Then a couple of years ago a salesman came to the house and tried to sell me a set of books, encyclopedias or something. 'Think where you would be today,' he told me, 'if you had had these when you were in high school'. Well, I did think about that, and you know what? I'm there. I'm doing something I like to do, I've got good friends, and I live in God's country. I'll guarantee you there's plenty of college grads who wish they could say that."

"I always wanted to be a lawyer," Emmett said, "and you have to have an undergraduate degree to get into law school. That's pretty much what I got from college, a sort of a transfer ticket for the last leg of the bus ride."

"Okay," Calvin said, "let's say we agree that a college degree may just prove you've gotten so many hours of class credit. What does the boy plan to do with those hours if he's not sitting in a class?"

"Now that's where it gets interesting, at least I think it does. He told me he thought it was time he asked himself a question that Wade never would ask him: what did he want to be when he grew up? He said he wants to be useful—that's what he said: not rich, not famous; useful. And he wondered if a diploma would do anything but make him look better to people who judge by appearances."

"A valid point, but not much of a life plan," Calvin said with a slight frown.

Emmett agreed. "No, although I've heard worse. But whatever plan he does come up with, that's a good foundation for it, don't you think? He says he's going to study, but it'll be his own curriculum, not somebody else's. He plans to study metals, particularly alloys, and I don't guess I have to tell you what kind of alloys. He told me he wants to start paying the trust back for what it's spent on him."

"He still doesn't know it was made for him?" Jim asked.

"No. He thinks Wade just wanted to tear down old buildings, and maybe give out the occasional pity scholarship." That got some chuckles around the table.

"I hate to interrupt," Arnold said, "but speaking of old buildings reminds me: What did Fred put on Floyd's death certificate?" Fred, the elected county coroner, was not a medical man. A retired deputy sheriff, his chief qualification for the office was that everybody liked him.

Emmett smiled. "He said a shooting would just upset the tourists. I let him know the shooter had been taken care of, and he said that as far as he was concerned, Floyd died from alcoholism, complicated by malnutrition." That was one of the reasons everybody liked Fred; he understood that the true story didn't always have to stand in the way of a better story, if the outcome was going to be the same either way. There had been no suicides in Keowee County since Fred took office, although two or three people had died accidentally while cleaning their guns. That made the relatives feel better, and as far as Fred was concerned it didn't hurt anything.

"Let's get back to your report," Jim said. "You said he wanted to learn to do alloys and, obviously, sell them. Does he know anything about running a business?"

"Not a damn thing," Emmett said, "but he knows somebody who does. A, uh, friend of a friend is about to graduate from Emory with a business degree."

"Do we need to interview him?" Calvin asked.

Emmett shook his head. "I don't really think that'll be necessary." No, he thought, Demir has had his interview.

Arnold cocked his head sideways. "Why would an Emory grad move here? Don't get me wrong, I meant it when I said this is God's country, but I've heard a lot of tourists say we're a hick town."

"Demir—that's his name—has found the love of his life," Emmett said, "and she likes it here. So does he, what little he's seen of it." Plus, if the others had thought he would hate it here, they probably would have picked somebody else.

Calvin spoke up again. "But you'd be the company attorney, wouldn't you?"

"For a few more years, until my successor is out of law school. Have I ever told you about Bart's roommate? Big fellow, sharp as a tack. For some reason, he's decided on a pre-law major, starting next semester. Going to clerk with me next summer."

"And then you'd do what, retire?" Arnold scoffed. "I don't believe that for a minute."

"You don't know; I might want to travel."

"I took a cruise once," Jim said. "Up the coast of Alaska. You eat good, but it's kind of lonely if you're by yourself."

"I wouldn't necessarily be by myself." Nobody said anything; nobody had to. They knew what he meant. One by one they held their fists out over the table, thumbs up.

"So," Jim said, "are you saying the boy's ready?"

"Let me put it this way," Emmett said. "He told me the other day he was thinking about getting rid of Wade's old Jeep. Said he thought he needed something more family friendly."

"The girl with the hair?" Arnold asked. The regulars at the Diner had gotten used to Tori's hair-color whims, but she still got odd looks from tourists.

"Yeah, the girl with the hair." Arnold nodded, and gave another thumbs-up. Jim and Calvin hadn't met Tori, but if Arnold thought she was all right, that was good enough for them.

"Let's say he's ready, then," Calvin said. "That's the trust's first stipulation. What about the second one, that his mother not get—and I think I'm remembering this right—'a damned thing'. Isn't she still the boy's only heir?"

Emmett nodded. "Unless he makes a will, and I intend to see to that he does. I won't be able to talk about it, but if I call for a vote in the next couple of weeks, you'll know I've squared it away. That's it; that's what I've got."

"Move we adjourn," Calvin said. Everybody grunted yes. "So what are we waiting for? Ante up and deal the cards!"

◇◇◇◇◇◇◇◇◇◇◇◇◇◇◇●◇◇◇◇◇◇◇◇◇◇◇◇◇◇◇

"What do I need with a will? I don't have anything to leave to anybody." They were sitting on the front steps of Emmett's office. Bart had made it that far from the Jeep on his own, but he wasn't up to climbing steps yet.

"You never know," Emmett told him. "You could get run over by a rich playboy, and all of a sudden your estate is worth a million dollars." Close to that anyway, he thought, once we sell the Hutton lot. "And without a will, it would all go to your mother."

Bart made a face, then brightened. "But if I'm married, Tori would get it all, wouldn't she?"

Emmett had seen that coming. "Say she gets run over with you, and dies just before you do. Once again, everything goes to your next of kin. Make a will. All I need to know is who you want to have it if Tori's not around."

Bart thought about that. "Huh. Okay, Jamaal. And Dee. Half and half. And if they're both gone, half to the Larson public library."

"The library?"

"I owe a lot to a library. Someday I'll tell you about it."

"What about the other half?"

"The other half to the animal shelter."

"Animal shelter; got it. Come back in an hour, and we'll have ourselves a will signing."

"An hour? Gosh that's fast. I don't want to rush anybody."

Emmett smiled. "Don't you worry; if you're ready, we'll be ready. You can trust me on that."

Epilogue

"Have you heard back from Lolita?" Tori asked. She had decided that McIntyre was all right, but her earlier name for him had stuck.

Bart frowned. "No. He hasn't even gotten the message. When I called, Col. Menendez said something to the effect that he was 'out of pocket'. Apparently the whole bunch is out of pocket."

"I guess in their line of work, they're out of pocket a lot."

"Yeah, but the colonel sounded unhappy when she said it, like she didn't really know where they are."

"Seems like she would."

"Yeah, it does." Bart thought about that for a minute or so, then reached over and stroked the orange and white kitten Nisa had brought on her last visit. "I wonder..."

"Any luck with the radio?" Bragg's voice had gotten weaker since the last time he had asked. Blood loss will do that, and the tourniquet McIntyre had put on the captain's leg hadn't quite stopped the bleeding.

"No sir. I'll keep trying." The radio had caught a ricochet, and the only thing it was picking up was static. Whether it was putting out a signal, McIntyre didn't know, but he doubted it. A bullet smacked into a rock just above them. It was a message from whoever was out there, saying they knew where he was. The real attack, he knew, wouldn't come until the sun went down.

"You idiots, we're trying to help you!" McIntyre screamed, then he repeated a more polite version in Arabic. He was using a phrasebook, so he probably wasn't pronouncing it right, but he didn't think pronunciation was the problem. The shouted taunts from out in the desert hadn't sounded like Arabic. Whatever language it was, it didn't sound friendly. Oh well, McIntyre thought, maybe we can take some of them with us.

From somewhere out in the desert came a noise, faint at

first, then louder, as something with an engine got closer to them. McIntyre risked a quick look. "Pickup truck," he told Bragg.

"Any markings?"

"Just a flag. Red crescent moon in a white field. Tunisian military, maybe?"

"Is there a red star," Bragg was almost whispering. "inside the crescent?"

McIntyre did a quick head bob. "No star." A bullet smacked against a rock near where his head had just been.

"Not Tunisian, then. Just a red crescent... It's the Red Crescent! What are they doing out here?" The Red Crescent does what the Red Cross does, in places where a cross still reminds people of the Crusades.

An amplified voice echoed across the desert floor. Someone with a bullhorn was speaking the language of the attackers. The voice paused, and a shouted reply came from somewhere farther out. The conversation went on like that for a couple of minutes, then the bullhorn spoke in English. "You, in the rocks," it boomed. "May I ask why you are here."

McIntyre took a deep breath. "We are trying to deliver medicine to the clinic at Tanasa," he shouted. "There has been a cholera outbreak."

The bullhorn answered him. "We had heard of the cholera; we had not heard that medicine was available. The Bedouin think you are mercenaries, come to take their children. It has happened before. Let me explain this to them." Whoever it was switched languages again, and another few minutes of conversation ensued. "Gentlemen," the bullhorn finally boomed, "They say they are sorry they shot at you. You may come out now."

"Yeah, we'll certainly do that," Bragg muttered. "When pigs fly."

"Sir," McIntyre said, "What have we got to lose?" He stood up. Bragg motioned him to get back down, but instead he scrambled down toward the truck. "I'm unarmed" he called out, raising his hands.

A short, leathery-looking man stood beside the truck,

holding a bullhorn by his side. "I am unarmed as well. Are you the leader of the expedition?"

"I speak for him." He didn't want them to know how badly injured the captain was.

"I see. Would one of your men, by chance, be named McIntyre?"

McIntyre wondered if that last bullet really had missed him. Maybe this was all be a trick his dying brain was playing on him. Oh well, he thought, he might as well play it out; he had nothing better to do right now. He gave a slight bow. "J.B. McIntyre, at your service."

The shorter man smiled broadly. "Then you are the men we sought. I am Yazid, from the Red Crescent post at..." he gestured toward the north, naming a town McIntyre had seen on the map, but couldn't pronounce. "Sheikh Abdullah's son Ahmed called us from Wadi Qadr, to ask that we come here. He said you might be having a problem."

McIntyre tried to make sense of that. "He knew where we were?"

Yazid shook his head. "No, but he was able to describe a hill which one of our helpers recognized as Dead Man's Head." He nodded toward the rockpile. Reaching into a fold of his robe, he extracted a folded slip of paper. "Ahmed also asked me, if I should meet a man named McIntyre, to deliver a message. I wrote it down so that I would get it exactly right, as it seems to be in some sort of code."

McIntyre took the paper and unfolded it. For a few seconds, he stood speechless, then he faced the rockpile and shouted, "It's all right. They're friendly."

Yazid called out something in the other language, and a group of men ran out from behind a small hill. "They will carry the medicine to the clinic. We, for our part, will take your men back to our post, where we can attend to the injured." He said something, this time in Arabic, and several men got out of the back of the truck and started toward the rockpile.

McIntyre turned back toward Yazid. "Did the one you spoke with—Ahmed?—say how he knew we were at—what was it?—Dead Man's Head?"

Yazid shook his head. "He said only that someone he knew, a friend, had called to say that the caller's friends were in trouble, somewhere in the desert at a place that looked like this. The friend asked if Ahmed could help. Ahmed called us with the same request. The Sufis are good people, and a friend of theirs is a friend of ours. Friends, we believe, should look after each other."

Up in the rockpile, men from the squad were crawling out of their hiding places, and men from the truck were helping them bring down the wounded. As they carried Bragg past, McIntyre motioned them to pause. "Sir," he said, "I have a problem."

"State your problem," Bragg replied, weakly.

McIntyre gestured toward men from the truck. "I don't know how, but they were sent here by our friends in Larson. That's a serious security breach, and we have to report it, but you know the kind of inquiry that will set in motion. It seems like a poor way to repay a favor."

For a moment McIntyre thought the captain wasn't going to say anything, but then Bragg spoke, very softly. "Listen carefully," he whispered. "Our rescuers arrived by a happy co-incidence, nothing more. Do you understand me?"

McIntyre swallowed. "Yes, sir." He glanced at the note he held. "What I don't understand is..."

Bragg held up a hand, a movement that took all the strength he had left. "Think of it as if it were need-to-know, Mr. McIntyre. Some things you don't have to understand. Some things you just accept." The hand dropped back to his chest, and the men carried him on toward the truck.

McIntyre read the note one last time, then tore it into tiny fragments which he let the desert wind carry away. He supposed the captain was right: he really didn't have to understand how the note had found him. It was enough that he understood what it meant. It meant that somebody cared. And yet, all it said was, "Jeep for sale. "Make an offer."

◇◇◇◇◇◇◇◇◇◇◇◇◇◇◇◇◇◇◇◇◇◇◇◇◇◇◇◇◇◇◇◇◇◇

The tall two-legged ones finally went away, and the little gray desert cat whose rockpile it was came out of her crevice. The sparkly ones had never asked her to do anything for them before, but she hadn't minded; they were good company on cold nights, and letting them look around through her eyes hadn't been any trouble. Now, with the two-legs gone, she could get back to what was truly important: dinner, specifically a lizard that was sunning itself on one of the rocks nearby. She tensed for the pounce, all thoughts of the two-legs and their noisy ways forgotten. Life was back to normal, and as far as she was concerned, normal was good.

Made in the USA
San Bernardino, CA
16 March 2013